THE
CHILD
OF
UKRAINE

BOOKS BY TETYANA DENFORD

Conversation with Love
Conversation with Motherhood
Conversation with Grief

THE CHILD OF UKRAINE

Tetyana Denford

bookouture

Published by Bookouture in 2022

An imprint of Storyfire Ltd.
Carmelite House
50 Victoria Embankment
London EC4Y 0DZ

www.bookouture.com

ISBN: 978-1-80314-764-2
eBook ISBN: 978-1-80314-763-5

For Babchya—

You gave me the story of your life so that
I could change the course of my own.

And to the immigrants who are searching for a place on this
earth: may you always know that your stories are our music;
without you, our hearts would never learn how to dance.

During and after the Second World War, millions of Eastern Europeans migrated to New York, England, and Australia, to start new lives.

Many lost entire families along the way and never saw them again.

PROLOGUE
MELBOURNE, 1954

On a cool afternoon in April on a quiet street, Julia put her hands in the pockets of her brown threadbare coat and stared at the house. It sat politely at the end of a concrete path, set off from the road, with a sturdy white wooden porch that wrapped around the front like a smile. The lamplight in the windows glowed warmly against the darkening haze of the afternoon, and well-dressed people gathered inside.

She straightened her shoulders. In her fingers she held a folded piece of paper. Her heart beat in her ears, her breath as thin as the breeze that blew across her legs. She was there now; she couldn't turn back until she'd seen them—it would take her four and a half hours to get back home, and her bus would leave soon.

Love takes courage, her mother used to say to her.

She walked slowly to the door, happy conversations and the smells of a roast dinner hovering in the air as she approached. She knocked once. Then twice. She looked down at her shoes. On the pristine white porch, they looked even more battered than usual.

A woman, dressed in a green silk blouse and full skirt, opened the door. "Yes?" The pearls at her ears shone at the edges of her icy blonde hair.

Julia smoothed her dark hair and tucked it behind her ears, revealing a small scar on her jaw. "Hello. I—" She faltered, and then cleared her throat. "Are you Mrs. Douglas?"

"I'm Irene, yes, and you are...?"

"I'm..." She started and shook her head. Her name wouldn't matter. Julia reached into her pocket and retrieved the folded paper, showing it to the woman. "I wanted to give you this." Her hands were shaking.

Irene looked at it quizzically, then back at Julia. "What is this?"

"I'm sorry, I just... I want to..." Tears filled her eyes as she rose on her tiptoes to see over into the hallway, craning her neck forward and moving closer.

Irene suddenly understood and moved to block her view. "You can't be here," she said, coolly.

"I know."

"How did you find this address?"

Julia searched the woman's face. "Please," she whispered. "None of this was my fault. Please, just listen—"

"I don't know what you're trying to say—"

"I was..." Julia interrupted, and then she heard children's laughter echoing in the house. It was *their* laughter, as bright as the sun. Desperation flashed across her eyes.

"I can't have you do this." The woman's heels clicked as she moved back. "I don't want to have to call the police. Please leave."

Julia nodded, tears spilling. "I understand." And then, knowing it was her last chance, she suddenly lurched forward, grabbing Irene's soft hand in her own calloused one, crushing the paper into it. "Just," she pleaded, her eyes shining with sadness, "*please* give this to them. Keep it for them. Maybe one day—"

Irene extracted her hand, the paper inside it, and retreated into the hallway, gripping the door handle. She attempted a smile, but her mouth stiffened. "You have to leave," she said a final time, before closing the door.

The shadow of Julia's body against the inlaid glass dissipated, little by little, and vanished.

Irene turned the latch and walked down the hallway, slipping the paper into the pocket of her skirt, its rough texture in stark contrast to the smooth cotton. She passed the kitchen and found the dining room, the table filled with children wearing colorful masks, playing games.

One of them, a little boy with scarlet cheeks playfully elbowing his sister, smiled as a cake, alight with candles, was brought to the table. She placed a hand on his dark mop of hair and kissed his cheek as she watched both their faces lean toward the flames to blow them out.

"Happy birthday, my loves."

* * *

Later that evening, as the children slept deeply, the remaining sweet conversations bubbled out of the dining room, down the hallway, before fading quietly.

Gold hats littered the polished floor of the hallway, some with broken elastic straps, and the smell of candles and sugar wafted from the kitchen, mingling with the lilies of Irene's perfume. Voices grew louder as guests prepared to leave, shrugging into elegant coats and hats, offering handshakes and saying their goodbyes to Bill, politely commenting on the chill in the air, warning of the coming Australian winter.

Pale-colored balloons happily bumped against one another as people shifted their feet. Irene had tied each balloon herself with a long, thin gold ribbon, securing a note on the end of each: *Happy Birthday* said one. *You are 4 today!* said another. *Mummy and Daddy love you both.*

In the square, cream-walled sitting room where the fireplace popped and hissed underneath the mahogany mantle, a row of cards had been carefully erected on the antique sideboard beside it, next to the family photos, awards, and heirlooms. Across from the fireplace was a cream fleur-de-lis sofa with oak end-tables on either side.

Irene sat there, stockinged feet tucked under her, two unopened envelopes in her hand.

The first one was from Auntie Sylvia; the other was from Bill's brother, Joe. She placed them on her lap and then withdrew the paper from her pocket. It was yellowed, as if it had traveled in a storm.

She let the words unravel in front of her.

My babies—

How I miss you. I am sorry I can't be with you, but you must be so happy, with so many gifts to open. The other day, I found the two waxflowers that you gave me for my birthday so long ago, and it made me think of you. Do you remember that day? They have their color still—pale pink and white. They remind me of your faces.

I won't be able to write for a while again, but when I can, I will try, and tell you more. Just remember I love you very much.

Mama

Out in the hallway, the heavy sound of wood as the door closed, a crack in the silence.

Irene fed the letter back into her pocket.

"Well, that's the last of 'em." Bill looked at his reflection in the glass inlay. He was tired, all of his forty-eight years now gathered in the stoop of his shoulders and the hollow of his cheeks.

Approaching the sitting room, he saw his wife, motionless, staring down at her lap. The room was warm, but felt oddly hollow and expectant: like the pause before a piece of music.

He cleared his throat. "So, sweetheart, what'd you think? Was pretty nice, having a few people around. Nice to celebrate. You did really well."

"Yes."

"Yes, you liked being a hostess?" He leaned against the doorframe.

"Sure, that's part of it, I guess. It was a great evening." Irene nodded and looked up, her eyes focusing through him, distant. "Thank you, darling." She rested her hands on top of the cards on her lap.

"You okay?"

"Yes, of course. Just a bit emotional about the whole thing, I guess. I'd be grateful for a drink, though."

"Well, I have an idea. How about—"

"Now, please? Thank you." She smiled sweetly.

He winked, and bowed exaggeratedly, a sandy tuft of hair falling over his eyes. "Sure, sweetheart. Can do. Be right back."

As he disappeared past the doorframe, she stood up—a couple smoothly diverging—and delicately padded across the room, cards at her fingertips. She carefully placed Auntie Sylvia and Uncle Joe on the sideboard next to the other sentiments of birthday wishes.

Four years, she thought gratefully, despite being wary of old wounds.

She turned to look toward the hallway; the balloons were already deflating. She placed her hand in her pocket and withdrew the letter.

And then she walked toward the fire.

I'm kissing you now—across the gap of a thousand years.

—Marina Tsvetaeva

PART 1

UKRAINE TO GERMANY

1941–1947

CHAPTER ONE

UKRAINE, 1941

The wheels of the cart thrummed along the ground, a silhouette moving under slate skies, the figure of Julia's sister cut out in black, holding the reins.

They were now hours away from what they had left behind, the unknown ahead of them. The horse steadily followed the tracks of people who had gone before, and Julia watched, curled under a blanket, as the fading stars moved through the small opening in the canvas that covered her. Night was safest for this type of journey.

She held her coat to her body, the wool too thin for the raw spring cold. She still felt the lingering warmth of her mother's arms around her, and the rosary she had given her lay delicately around her neck.

"Maria?" She called to her sister softly as she clicked the horses onward. "Can't we just turn back?"

"Keep your voice down."

"But it's so early; no one will hear us."

"Russians have taken over the entire village, practically. They'll be looking for anyone they can get their hands on, now that they've killed our brothers," Maria hissed.

Julia sighed as she tried to block out the pain, but it swelled within her nevertheless. She wanted nothing more than to turn back, to go home and run into the house that still had memories of her childhood, of her brothers. She wanted her mother to tell her it was safe, and that they would be alright. But it seemed none of it existed anymore, so she did what her sister told her to.

"Okay," she whispered. "I understand."

Maria shrugged. "Listen. Maybe I just don't want to hear your doubts right now. I have enough of my own."

Julia surrendered to the dark, the memory of what she'd left behind leaving a hollow pain in her chest. They were children abandoning their childhoods, at the mercy of a world they had no control over.

Like a receding tide, it had all shifted suddenly under their feet: the humble farm that sat comfortably in the clean still air, beside the rows of pear and apple trees that stretched across to the river, gilded in the pink of an early morning sun and giving off a soft scent on the breeze; the cows and horses huddled in clouds of breath, standing in silhouette against the wheat fields beyond. This had been the hand on her back, and it was being taken away, and she faced her life without direction now. The ashes of burning cities would settle there soon, and the home where Julia had lived for eighteen years would be no longer.

The sisters had walked with a new uncertainty from school those final days, before it was closed and students were evacuated by the Russian police. Families were hunted, forced out onto the streets holding their belongings in their arms, children clinging to their siblings, frightened eyes bearing silent witness from shop windows and side streets. Homes were emptied and strange new tenants took possession, most of them soldiers. Curfews were installed. Some tried to run, and were shot in warning, cries haunting the streets. Neighbors began to distrust each other's alliances: it affected them all, like an illness, from one family to the next—hushed dinners and secret meetings spent behind closed doors, words of prayer and clasped hands, mourning dead sons and brothers who had not had proper funerals.

It was only a matter of time before it all reached Julia and her family, creeping toward the edges of the farmland that they used to call home. And the uniqueness in Julia was that she found a place in her heart for the beauty in the melancholy, like lullabies sung in minor keys.

It was self-preservation.

Julia propped her head onto her duffle bag, the chalk of her name leaving a dusting of white on her shoulder. Just yesterday morning, she had been singing a beautiful song, and she had been unafraid. Just yesterday afternoon, they had learned of their brothers' deaths.

Her eyes stung, and she hummed softly, the clattering of the wheels muffling the melody as she let a memory surround her. Just yesterday, she had been home, in a room where her voice echoed happily. It felt like a lifetime had passed since then.

* * *

The cold spring sun streamed through Julia's bedroom window that morning, casting shadow branches on the wooden floor. Her voice trilled and meandered in the maudlin tones of the song that her mother and grandmother had taught her, as her pale, delicate fingers eased buttons through the holes in the shirt that was now too small over her teenage body, and her skirts moved with her hips in awkward rhythm.

"Mama?" she called out, her dark hair trailing over her brow and down her shoulders in molasses waves. She pulled her tights over her bony knees. Her body was tall and strong, womanly, but also still coltish in the sharp angles of her elbows and knees.

"Yes, mouse?" Anna replied warmly from the kitchen.

"Are you making tea? Is Papa out already?" She looked out

through the window in her room for him, and thought she saw his silhouette in the distance. "He's out, I can see him," she murmured to herself, her breath moistening the glass as she plaited her thick hair.

Her father always disappeared early, before everyone else, and not entirely because he was still processing the arrest of his sons and fearing for their fate. It was because it was the calm he craved: getting out of bed as the sun was still rising, lacing his boots and walking outside into the thin light, hearing the animals in their pens shift and rustle and breathe in jittery bursts.

The farmhouse and the surrounding twenty acres of farmland had been given to him by his father shortly before his death, when Mikola was nineteen. The farmhouse was a large, white-walled house with worn wood-framed windows and a thatched roof thickly sheltering the six rooms within. It sat peacefully on acres of lush green, neatly folded within the valleys on the outskirts of western Ukraine, at the base of the Karpaty mountains. Mikola and Anna had married shortly thereafter, but their four children arrived later than they had anticipated, when Anna had assumed it wasn't in the cards for her to have any children.

In the spring, the smell of crocuses and mineral earth filled every breath. The rich, dark land—the chernozem—once so proud and large, now whittled away by a famine and war, spread down to the river, with a small orchard at the back of the house, and animals that constantly moved in it and around it like a familiar song: there were small families of cows, twenty sheep, a clutch of hens, a handful of shaggy stallions, a few mares, three dogs, and geese. The air smelled of wet hides and manure and grass.

The crops were meager now, though they had been plentiful long ago, but they had been stripped bare like so many families, during the great starvation, Stalin's Holodomor. Families like theirs watched as their grain silos were looted and crops were destroyed in an effort to cripple Ukraine's economy. People gave everything they had: vegetables covered in soil, fresh milk, wild blackberries, sweaty fat plums and sticky pears. Now, they lived on what they had stored, and any crumb of bread they found they would kiss gratefully before eating, knowing that it suddenly felt as though they might lose everything in a moment's notice. They cherished the few food cards they were allowed as part of the occupation. And it wasn't even a case of finding secretive ways to grow crops... police checked on them regularly, so they had to be careful.

Julia strode into the kitchen and ran her hands over the heavy wooden table beside her mother, her palms feeling the soft grain of it. The kitchen was warm, open windows decorated with red-embroidered curtains looking out to the fields. There was no food set out yet, and she was hungry. Her mouth watered for sugar, and preserves, and sausage. She could imagine it, taste it.

Julia reached for the oven, and her mother, without turning around, slapped her hand away.

"Chekai. Wait. It's not ready yet." Anna crouched in front of the stove, hovering in impatience, and then moving again, keeping busy. The flesh of her arms vibrated as she kneaded a small ball of dough for bread. Her wiry, graying hair was scraped back off her face to reveal a strong jaw, dark blue eyes and creased, milky skin. Her face had a weariness to it, but her eyes always shone like stars.

There was no butter, only some salo, salted pig fat, that they had stored. But Julia had grown accustomed to the taste now.

"Breakfast after your chores," she said, then groaned slightly. Her back suffered often. "Your sister will help later, but right now there is only you and your father and me, so we have to work harder." There was sadness in her voice, as there had been for months. She wiped the table in front of her, clearing a path in the flour there to make more dough.

"How is Maria?" Julia walked across the room to get her coat and glanced at the small, closed door across from her own bedroom. Maria had been ill of late, an occurrence in her life that had been common since she was little—a dry cough had become almost a pattern of her speech. She was slight. Pale. Her body was always fighting to remain strong. "Is she still asleep?"

"Yes. She needs her rest."

Julia held her coat in her hands. "It has always been this way. Seems as if she has been ill forever."

"I know." Her mother shrugged and pressed her palms together as if in prayer. "Bozshe miliy. Good Lord. For twenty years. Same as always. Tired."

"Will she ever get better? Isn't the older sister supposed to teach the younger one aboutlife? About boys?" Julia blushed coyly and laughed, her roman nose and sharp cheekbones jutting, but then stopped herself as she saw her mother's face. "Sorry, I just wanted to lighten the air."

"I know."

Julia turned, as if looking for an answer past the door, in the bed where her sister lay, imagining her heart beating feebly.

The kettle boiled with a squeal, and Anna was grateful for the interruption.

"Mama..." Julia, now by the door, slid her foot into a boot.

"Hmm?"

"I love you."

"Little Julia, moya dusha, you are young. Foolish."

Julia chuckled as she fastened her coat. Her mother still referred to her as her center. Her soul. "Fortune favors the foolish." She winked at her mother.

Anna wagged a finger. "You are impulsive. Be more wary."

Julia came over and kissed her mother's cheek, the soft skin flushing on impact, and then retreated with a smile.

Her mother waved her away with a cloth that sputtered flour off the ends and watched her move to the door. "Wait..."

"Yes, Mama?"

Anna wiped her hands on her apron and walked over to the heavy wooden dresser that hulked against the wall by the door.

On top of it sat a small brown-paper parcel, addressed to Kharkiv prison, and wrapped in twine. It smelled of sausage. "Take this to the post office. But be careful. Keep—"

"Yes, yes, I know," Julia interrupted, tying her scarf around her hair. "Keep my head down and don't draw attention to myself."

Anna nodded, ushering her off.

Julia walked into the crisp morning and knew that her mother longed to see the faces of her sons.

CHAPTER TWO

Uzhorod was in the distance. The sky had bloomed in grays and pinks as the sun rose, and now the corners of Hungary and Poland were at their sides and under their cart as they progressed. The edges of the woods teemed with families on similar journeys, all quiet, none exchanging looks with anyone as they kept their heads down, their belongings on their backs. The flat wood of the cart rumbled beneath Julia's hips, rattling her bones, her clothes not nearly enough to pad the space in between or keep her very warm. She missed her bed, she missed the smell of her mother's hair, she missed the sound of her mother's knife thudding the wood of the kitchen table as she sliced crisp vegetables, or the scratch of it as she scraped the skin off potatoes. She pulled her coat down further on her hands, covering her fingers.

"Maria?"

"Yes."

"I want to go home."

"Yes, I know you do." Maria's voice was weak, although still brave. The focus of the road ahead helped her overcome the fist that sat in her chest now, the icy cold feeling that reminded her she was not well. But she was older, she would keep them safe, like her brothers had promised they would. Now, in their absence, she felt it was her duty. "Think of it this way." She cleared her throat. "There's no home left for us, Julia." Her voice still faltered, even in its whisper. *Gather yourself, Maria,* she thought. "We had no choice."

"I'm hungry. I wonder where that parcel went," Julia murmured, absentmindedly. "We could have kept it. It smelled delicious."

"Oh. The one that Mama told you to send to—"

"Yes. The prison."

"I know. Well, we have enough, for now."

"We could have kept it," Julia repeated as if in a dream state of grief, suddenly feeling the loss of everything. "It's gone. They're gone. And now—"

Maria cut her off. "Stop. We didn't know, Julia. We didn't know then. We don't even know now how we will survive. but we have what we took; it is at our feet, and we cannot look back at what was once. Our brothers fought nobly until the end, that is what I choose to believe, and that is what we have to do."

The boys were both several years older than she was, Bohdan the eldest, Milo a year behind. They were protectors; they had been there for both of them anytime they needed to find a bit of mischief, a bit of strength. They taught them both to be strong.

Julia's eyes shone like tiny stars in the burgeoning light, and she held her hand flat against her coat.

The parcel. She had clutched it to her chest, denting the stiff paper with the shape of her hand. She had been tempted to open it, the smell of sausage oil and spices under her nose.

Her stomach grumbled as she remembered a moment at the kitchen table when she was ten, when Milo had come in from town with a satchel hung over his shoulder. He'd sat next to her and took out warm bread, and a small length of fresh *kobasa,* along with a small fist of cheese. *Had a meeting,* he winked at her, which always meant he'd met with his friends, planning more activist mischief. *These are little treasures for you.* Even now, in the dark, she felt his hand on her head as he left. The parcel had been a connection to him; it had felt like hope. She wanted him to feel her hand reaching out to wherever he was.

The path to the post office had been as familiar as if it were her own skin, and yet the shaded trees held secrets and fear, and the air was peppered with new sounds: unfamiliar trucks, new voices, horses and carts that had a wary urgency. Lviv was once beautiful, full of cafes with people seated at tables that spilled out into the streets, music wafting on the breeze through open windows, the smell of bread and honey and freshly fried sausage. Now, it was haggard and empty, like an old woman who had seen too much pain and given too much of herself. Russian soldiers didn't care. They took what they needed and left nothing behind.

The day of her brothers' arrest, the NKVD—the Soviet secret police—had splintered and scattered across the field late that summer, a broken wave of dark uniforms with silvery buttons glinting in the sunlight. Anna had covered Julia's mouth before she could shout and pushed her and her sister toward the cellar, her father whispering "Go, go!" behind them. Before she climbed down into the dark room, she saw her brothers appear, standing next to their mother as she pressed her back against the wall, her hands clasped in prayer. Milo, Julia's favorite—the one who had taught her to read, the one who had counted stars with her—stood in his pajamas with his arm through his mother's. He had smiled at Julia before she sank beneath the earth; she didn't know it would be the last time she saw his face.

The soldiers pounded on the door demanding Milo and Bohdan leave the house immediately, as their names had been found on a list of Ukrainians collaborating in anti-Russian propaganda. The brothers' "meetings" had been risking their own lives, like so many, and yet they cared not. Their fear was replaced by pride for the country where they stubbornly spoke Ukrainian, never Russian. They were a part of the young resistance, and they were to be sent to prison.

The sisters had huddled out of sight, underneath wooden planks that were covered by a wool rug, clinging to each other, barely breathing as they heard footsteps above them, voices growing louder. The glass and metal of family treasures crashed above them; the smell of cigarette smoke lingered as the men searched the rooms.

Julia would always remember her mother's voice, plaintive and raw. "Please," she had said. "Please, not my babies."

Soon after, the family began sending parcels to Kharkiv, the prison the brothers had been taken to—it was where most people were interned before they were released, or deported. They sent them what rations they had left—cheese, bread, and small pieces of sausage—weekly, without fail, and had done for a year, waiting for news of their release in the form of a list, or a letter; they were a kind of currency in war.

The parcel, in the end, had been useless. Julia had posted it, and had walked back home in the sunlight, her thoughts on the day of chores ahead, and her sister's health.

Those had been the innocent things she was doing when the letter arrived.

They had been with their mother, collecting eggs, when her father had called them inside. She had seen it, sitting delicately in the center of the long kitchen table, their address written in black block letters on the front:

MISHIK FAMILY
STRIY
LVIV OBLAST 82424

There had been no return address.

They all looked at it on the table as if deciding what to do with it. Worry settled like rain.

Her father had poured a glass of vodka and clenched his teeth around the stem of his pipe as the smoke wafted against his face. He didn't look at them as they walked up to him, his face lined and somber, his hair shining its silver strands in the daylight. He kept a vacant stare at the center of the table, sitting on his chair, slightly perched forward as if about to run.

Her mother had pointed at the glass. "Starting early?"

Julia and her sister had chuckled softly.

He moved the envelope on the table with his fingertips and inhaled sharply.

"Papa, what's that?" Julia looked at him, and then at her mother.

"I think he's about to tell us." Maria rasped. "Papa? What is it?"

Anna sat down and ran her fingers through her hair. The two girls pulled up a chair on either side and sat down. The air was heavy.

"So. What's this, then?" Her mother leaned forward on the table.

"I have a strange feeling," her father said.

"You always have strange feelings."

"I'm serious."

"Alright. What's happened, then?"

He gestured at the envelope, as if it was a bomb. "I don't know, but I know I don't want to open this."

"It's a letter."

"Yes, but from whom? There's no return."

Anna suspected now, and looked at the girls.

"Mama?" Julia's eyes drifted from her father to her mother. Maria took Julia's hand and squeezed hard.

"Oh, well, just open it then. It's a piece of paper." She spurred him onward with a hand waving it away and then set her teeth and watched as he ripped the thin edge of the envelope, taking care not to damage what was inside. "No use fearing a piece of paper."

"Anna." He stopped, his eyes skimming the words and then drifting to hers.

"Mmm?"

Before he went further, they both went quiet. The world, for a small second, was held in suspension.

Her father read the first line wearily: "*I have seen your boys —and I felt compelled to write to you...*"

It was at this point that there was a choice: he could read on and see where this would lead, or he could close the letter and hide it away and never know. He looked over at Anna, and then at Julia and Maria. Both girls had water in their eyes already.

"Go on." Anna laced her fingers together.

"*I had a son of my own. He died when he was a boy, and I never had a chance to see how his face would be, as a man. You may be wondering how I came to see your boys. You see, I have been working at Kharkiv for the past three years, and I have seen many men, all ages, pass through these doors in my time here, very few surviving. Your boys arrived together, and they were put in the same cell along with three other men. They were afraid and proud, as most have been, awaiting immediate deportation or release. They had hope and would not silence it. It was dangerous for them...*"

Mikola stopped, his throat thick and catching. Pipe smoke seeped out of his mouth and nose in slow rivulets.

"Keep going," Anna urged. "Truth is always a necessary pain."

"*... because struggling only makes the punishment come more quickly. And now how do I tell you this? Because this will be hard for a parent to hear. Your sons were brave Ukrainian boys. You should be proud.*"

"*Were?*" Mikola swallowed slowly. "I cannot do this. No, Anna." He folded the letter.

Julia stood up and embraced him, Maria following behind. "Oh, Papa," they whispered, over and over again.

"You must." It was then that Anna realized that, despite the death of her sons, she was still a mother, not a widow, but a mother with dead children, and that would never be repaired.

She opened the letter and continued.

"*I am sorry to tell you that your sons died shortly after they arrived*—No! Oh, God..." Julia put a hand over her mouth, the color slipping from her cheeks, and Maria held her.

"*They were gathered in a group of twenty-five men, and all were promised their release that morning. They were fed thin soup and bread, and as they walked out past the prison walls, they saw the sun; for though the frost had been thick on the ground, the sky was clear and bright. And they were told to stand against the wall in front of them, and a few men tried to run.*

"*I cannot even send you any of their belongings, as the NKVD took everything that was of use and that could be sold. I know that this is not the peace you seek, but as a father myself, I could not spend another day thinking of your hope for their return. May they, and you, find peace with God one day.*"

There was no signature at the end, no name on the small white death certificate they hadn't been expecting on a day that was sunlit and beautiful. It was the last page of the story of two children who had been loved and lost, their parents and their sisters now sitting staring at the walls of a small room that grew yet smaller in their sorrow.

That evening, the sisters fell into a heavy sleep, lulled by grief. Anna and Mikola were free to speak, and they sat at the kitchen table in the glow of a large kerosene lamp, the remnants of their day scattered on the surface: the bottle of vodka, glasses, a few plates and half a loaf of bread. No one had been hungry that evening.

"Anna." Mikola passed a glass back and forth between his hands meditatively.

"Kolya, please." She spoke through her hands, and then slowly dropped them from her face, looking at him. "I know what we have to do. Maybe just give me the time to grieve."

Mikola sat back and nodded, withdrawing his pipe from his shirt pocket, tamping it with his index finger. "I know," he said, sadly. "But we don't have time. Don't you see?" He nodded to the letter, still lying on the table. "What is happening to this family is happening to all families now. The chaos is beginning. We thought Russia and Germany were allies, but now Germany is in Poland and pushing east toward Russia. Our enemies are now seen as our friends

"Kolya, I don't understand."

"Russia is trying to clear out all Ukrainians before Germany recruits many of us to help them in their march to Stalingrad—these are not standard arrests. It's all political. They want to erase us." He raked a hand through his hair. "They have cleared the prisons, and they will clear the towns, and further. Russians cannot concede defeat." His eyes became dark. "Russia is full of soulless people ready to kill their own mother to gain victory. They will not stop until Ukraine does not exist."

"What can we do? Nothing."

"But there is." Mikola reached for Anna's hand. "We can adjust to a life where we fight for our survival in whatever way we can, no matter what. We fight to help our children survive."

She nodded, because she knew what he meant now. But instead of moving her hand to his, she moved her glass toward him, and nodded to the vodka bottle, now only half full.

He poured. "I know, Anushka. This is too much. It's anger and sadness in a dark cloud. It's hovering over all of us." He moved closer to Anna. "We're dealing with government, here.

It's pointless." Smoke veiled his face. "They'll come back for the girls in the next round of deportations. They'll check again. We're on the census. We don't have a choice—we have to save the girls."

"Choices are dangerous." She looked at her husband, and her heart ached. "Mikola—"

His voice was steady, to hide the pain. "Bohdan and Milo are dead, so who will be next? Us? We have a farm that is useful to them, so they will come back for it one day, and we will be left without any food. Or they will shoot us, for we are too old to leave now."

Anna nodded, and ran a palm on her forearm, her lined skin marked with age spots.

Mikola rested his tanned hand on hers. "Both Germany and Russia seek out the children, and they seek them out to put them to work, to work them to death. The girls can work, so Russia will happily send them both to the Gulag." He saw Anna's face settle into worry briefly. "Even Maria."

"I'm not sure I can imagine it."

"What?"

"Seeing them leave."

"But we cannot watch them die."

"I know." Anna took a deep breath and held it, releasing it slowly before she spoke again. "So. What do we do?"

"Right." Mikola felt the stubble on his chin and stared up at the ceiling. "West. West is obvious. I assume it's the safest option. I've heard the alliance is better there—" He shrugged, and Anna winced at how helpless he looked.

"Either has danger."

"We are in the middle of two wars, it seems." He rubbed his eyes and reached for the vodka and poured; the bottle was now almost empty. "To go east and join the Soviet army would be a short-lived existence. They would surely freeze at the edge of the world. Go west, and there would be work—there is a displaced persons camp in Austria, near Mauthausen. They can stay there, work, help Germany until it is all over, and then come back to us."

"But... these are Nazis."

"We have to choose survival now. Germany seek to be victorious over Russia, and the way I see it"—he clenched his fist knowing the words coming out of his mouth felt so wrong —"Germany is the only hope for our girls to survive."

Anna made the sign of the cross over her heart, understanding her husband's reasoning but feeling sick at the same time.

There was a creak in the hallway beyond them, and they paused and turned to look, but saw nothing but darkness. The quiet settled again.

Anna downed her vodka, her eyes searching Mikola's. "Many have gone to Germany already. I've heard that trains leave Kyiv and take people there."

"No, they don't." Mikola shook his head. "That's what they want you to believe."

Anna didn't question this. She trusted his instinct.

Mikola continued. "I'm not putting our daughters on a train. God knows where they'll end up; trains can be diverted. They are old enough; we can help prepare them."

"Aren't those trains to deport the Jews? We're not Jews," Anna offered, weakly. "At least we have that."

Mikola frowned. "You think God will save us? Nothing matters now. We have friends who are Jews. This is a war against humanity, nobody is safe."

Anna set her teeth and her chest tightened. She clasped his hand, their wedding rings clinking together as their hands met. Mikola saw the sadness in her face and his heart was heavy.

"Let's prepare a horse, a cart, supplies. Maria knows how to drive well, she is older and she will need the purpose so her body can be active despite her illness. And they can both sleep in the covered wagon if they need, or stay at a camp along the way."

"I worry for Maria." Anna's voice caught. "It's as if we are casting them aside." The thought was devastating. "But we have to hope that God will protect us."

Mikola's face darkened. "You think He listens when you pray? God has no part in this."

"Mikola. It is what we do when we hope and when we mourn. We bring God with us."

"Anna—" Mikola raised his index finger, shaking it at her words. "Sometimes I think God has betrayed us, Anna."

"Maybe so." She walked to him and took his face in her hands: it was so much older than the face of the man she had first seen so many years ago, as the slight, shy boy she had met through friends in a neighboring village. She had seen him surrounded by friends, his unshakeable laugh piercing the air with so much promise. She saw that boy now, in the tenderness as he looked at her, despite their age.

The metal of her wedding band, which had sunk deeper into her skin over time, now glinted as she looked at him.

"But still, we must pray."

Julia covered her face with her hands as she sat in her night-gown in the darkness. Her sister's thin coughs had punctuated the voices of her parents, but she had heard enough. She slowly tiptoed back to her bed, pinching her nose to prevent the tears. She would pray, as her mother had said. It was the only thing she could do.

CHAPTER THREE

They were now at the border of Austria, with little food left. They would need to stop soon.

"Why don't you rest?" Maria advised, turning around to see Julia, her eyes staring, hugging her knees and leaning her back against the shallow wagon. "Try and sleep instead of being curled up in a ball like that." Maria wondered where they could stop next, as her hands burned from clutching the reins. "That can't be comfortable."

It was early afternoon now, and Julia had unhooked the canvas to let her see the road, the skies, and the trees as they moved past. The sun was finally warming their heads but the autumn air chilled their bodies. Julia stretched out like a cat. For a second, she imagined she was in her bed, before she curled up again, drawing her knees to her chest.

So far, no one had asked for their papers, and no dark groups shadowed them. They had finished their scraps of food from the last farm that they had stopped at, where they had been lucky enough to get half a loaf of bread and fresh milk.

"I can't possibly sleep, because it *is* uncomfortable," Julia growled. "This is so ridiculous. Don't you think we can turn back?"

Maria fought away tears and was grateful that her back was to her sister. "Yes, Julia. I feel the same pain that you do; you can't imagine it. But we have no choice. We have to keep on."

Julia screwed up her face in annoyance. "It's entirely rotten, this plan." She scowled.

The other duffle bag rolled at her feet: the chalk had worn off a bit during the journey, and the surname was now missing an "IK," so it only said "MISH." *Mouse*, in Ukrainian, and the irony of such a sweet word in such circumstances wasn't lost on her. Her mother used to call her that. *Mishka*. Little mouse. Her stomach rumbled with hunger again. She groaned. "Can't we turn back?" In her heart, they were closer to home than they were to anywhere else; and she wasn't ready to leave that hope behind.

"You can switch with me soon. I'm getting tired." Maria tightened her scarf and clicked the horse onward. She'd lost weight in the last two weeks—her collarbones protruded delicately above her chest, and she couldn't get rid of a chill that had descended on her lungs, despite the warmth of the sun on her face.

Tall and preternaturally thin, Maria's hair shone with toffee-colored lights. It clung to her shoulders in two thick plaits, swinging as her lean body moved. Her green eyes seemed brighter than usual and were piercing above her flushed cheeks, but tinges of gray hinted at her temples and under her eyes. Over time, and many doctors offering tinctures and rest, she'd adjusted to her fragility and proceeded with caution. And then there were days like today, when, despite the thin bones underneath alabaster skin, and despite the cough that permanently took hold of her, her gaze was protective and wonderful, and there was a strength that comforted Julia immensely.

"Yes, okay, fine." Julia reached for the small tin flask of tea that had settled by her feet. Blessedly, it was still hot, though little was left. "You need to stop, I think. Your skin is as pale as a scared rabbit."

"I will be fine." Maria cleared her throat and it settled into a raspy cough that lingered. She tasted blood. "I'll tell you when I've had enough." She laced the reins through her fingers. They felt suddenly heavier than the day before. "We'll stop soon."

* * *

Julia had been guiding the horse and Maria had been asleep when they arrived the following morning in Salzburg, where there was a large displaced-persons camp. Recognizable from its rows and rows of what looked like elongated sheds with corrugated tin roofs, crowds of people milled about: tired, filthy, lost, wearing all their clothes on their backs.

After a stuttering explanation of needing somewhere to sleep and something to eat in the few German words they knew, they settled in the only space there was left: two small cot beds in the corner of an old barn at the back of the camp, a kerosene lamp beside them. The horse was tethered to the post outside.

That evening, the sisters had been given thin bone broth and stale bread, and they were now lying facing one another, fully clothed, under a rough woolen blanket, the lamp flickering weak gray shadows. They could barely make out each other's faces as they spoke. Maria's forehead was damp, and her eyes had a sheen to them. She shivered, and Julia covered her with her half of the blanket.

"Julia? What do you think it will be like?"

"What, exactly? Which part of this ridiculousness shall we try and understand?"

Maria laughed, progressing into another cough, reddish saliva settling on her lips. "I'm serious."

"So am I, Maria. And also, you need to rest. We can't understand any of this right now." Julia watched her sister's face. Something had changed in it, so she answered her original question. "Do you mean, our life? Is that what you wonder about?"

"Maybe."

"No one knows the future. But that's probably for the best."

"What will become of us?"

"You will be fat and have lots of babies, and I—"

Maria smiled. "No, no. Where we're going. Ending up."

"Germany?"

"Yes."

"I wonder about that too. But maybe we have to remember that we are safer in Germany for now. There is no possibility that Russia can beat Germany. The huns are fearless and wickedly clever, it seems."

"Does it scare you?"

"It does. I hate Nazis as much as I hate Russians. But I don't know what else we can do." Julia knew that the anger covered her fear. It was better that way.

Maria swallowed hard. "I'm afraid."

"I know you are." *So am I.* The tears threatened, because she knew her sister was weakening, so she willed herself to be still.

Maria searched for Julia's hand underneath the layers and Julia was startled at how cold she was.

"Maria, we have many hours to think about it tomorrow, on the way there. We're almost there and then at least we have somewhere to rest for a while." The horse nickered faintly outside.

"I wish you hadn't mentioned that. I don't think I can take getting in that wagon again."

"Well, we can't stay here."

"I know. I just..."

"What?"

"I miss home. Maybe this reminds me of home. The barn,

just us, this is nice." Maria's voice grew sparse and thin. She was tired.

"Home feels very far away now."

"I can barely remember when Mama stood there and packed our bags."

"You had an apple in your hand, with that knife. I have no idea why I remember that." Maria laughed feebly and squeezed Julia's fingers. "It's stuck in my memory, that stupid apple, and that knife. You turned it over and over in your hands like you were about to throw it—or throw the knife."

"Oh, yes. Can you imagine if I had?"

"It probably would have helped all of us, to be fair."

"In what way?"

"A bit of laughter in the sadness, I guess."

Julia lifted the corner of her mouth. "I should've kept that knife. It could be useful now."

* * *

Julia remembered that afternoon. She'd come home from school and heard her mother's voice in the bedroom and followed it, only to hover in the doorway and watch as she placed clothing and pieces of jewelry in worn leather cases, preparing to send her daughters away. "These have seen better days, but they'll serve their purpose," her mother had said, as she ran her palm across the top of an old suitcase.

She took a small piece of white chalk and wrote the words MISHIK in capitals on both sides. "Mark the suitcases," her husband had told her. She wiped her palms on her skirts and walked over to the dresser and proceeded to remove two gold brooches, a necklace, two rings and a fur stole that had belonged to her grandmother. This was currency, and the value was priceless: it meant freedom.

"Did you know that Germany offers food and shelter and work? And that you get paid a small wage?"

Julia had responded in silence; her eyes said it all.

"Here it is so unsafe; a better life for you is far away from here. You have your things from home"—she pointed to the cases—"and you and Maria can help, work, during the war. Russia is already pushing back and Germany is moving toward us, and they will want to recruit as many as possible to help with the effort. Would you rather go to Siberia and die? Or try and survive? If you go to Germany, one day you will come back home to me, alive. Do you understand?"

She had memorized her mother's face and listened to her words, but Julia's real feelings seem to be inaccessible suddenly, as if they lay beneath glass and she couldn't reach them.

A few pieces of jewelry lay sparkling in her mother's palm. "These were mine, but I have no use for them, which is why I am giving them to you."

"And what use do *I* have for a gold ring, an amethyst, a gold chain, and a fancy pin, exactly?" Julia had palmed an apple from one hand to the other, holding a knife, about to cut it. She wasn't hungry, suddenly.

"Little one—"

"Mama. No."

"Yes, okay, not so little. *Julia*, then." She rested her hand on the dresser. "We need to talk, you and I." She folded a blanket and placed it in a suitcase.

"About what, exactly? Am I going on holiday?"

She had been angry and scared. She knew what this would be about.

"Julia. Your father and I have watched our friends, and our children's friends, pass over to God, because of war and famine. We have seen families broken, and for what? For the sake of money and politics?" Anna's eyes were hard and shining. "This is the world we live in. I have lost my sons. I cannot lose my daughters." She paused. "It would kill us."

Julia speared the apple and set it on the dresser. She had watched quietly as her mother pulled things out of drawers: clean skirts, dresses, tights and an extra pair of shoes: all folded and fitted into the case with such care. A small gold byzantine cross on a necklace hidden in the very front of a shoe. A small gold signet ring with a square diamond in it: it had been her grandfather's. A black and white picture of her parents, taken at Christmas. They stared out solemnly at her, in their dark clothes.

"I know. You are sending us away."

The words, they reeked of abandon. They felt like daggers. "Oh, Julia."

"Mama."

Julia had walked over to the bed, and sat down. She remembered it even now, giving way under her slim body. She had looked at the room around her. The room had felt small and worn and ancient, as if she'd already left her childhood behind.

"I am *not* sending you away. One day, you will have children that you want to protect so much that the world becomes very small and decisions become very important."

"Will I? And what will I do?" Julia knew this conversation would have an ending that she would need to be brave for.

"You *will* have children, Julia. And you will do what is right for them. Just as we are." Her mother raised a scarf to her face and inhaled deeply. Clothes that smelled of Julia, of Maria, smelled of home and salt and earth and oil, memories unraveling and ending. "I know we can do this. I know we can be brave. But it seems so impossible, the thought of it."

Julia heard footsteps behind her and a warm hand settled on her shoulder. It was Maria. She suddenly seemed much older than her twenty years.

"We understand, Mama." Maria spoke evenly. "And we will be back, as soon as this is all over."

As if to finish the discussion, her mother had snapped the cases closed. Then, almost as an afterthought, she lifted the rosary from around her neck. She clutched it in her palm, her fingers marking from the facets of the pale blue stones digging into her flesh, and then placed it in both the girls' hands, covering them with her own. "Be brave. I will be with you always."

* * *

Julia looked over at Maria, small and fragile now, her face yellowed by the lamplight, and bit her cheek to stop from crying. *We will be brave, Marioshka.*

Silence. The horse moved outside.

"Maria?"

Maria's eyes opened slowly, carefully, as if the world was suddenly too bright. Julia watched her smile wanly, and then watched as she turned her body, pitched her head forward, and vomited all over the floor, the hay darkening under the bile. And then again.

Julia sat up. "Oh, bozshe, are you okay? What can I do? What's going on?"

Maria groaned and stayed curled over the edge of the mattress. "I don't know."

"Is there a doctor in this camp? There is, isn't there? They'll have them *somewhere*." They'd been in camps previously that had had a doctor, and she prayed that there was one here.

Julia rose and fled the barn, just as Maria rolled onto her other side, moaning and shaking, clutching her knees to her chest.

. . .

Julia ran carefully in the dark, her tights sagging and catching on brambles, her breath in clouds, her eyes adjusting to various shapes of sheds and houses and fences, and paths that led out too far, searching for help.

Julia had seen groups of German officers in the town square, in the cafes and the bars and the shops, and she knew enough to know the words for *medicine, doctor*, and *help*. She wiped her streaming eyes and scanned the sheds and the makeshift tents. Minutes felt like hours as she walked swiftly and impatiently until her lungs burned, knocking on doors and pleading for help for her sister, her voice rising in panic.

"Please! Hilf mir! Kranheit hier!" *Please, help me. Illness here.*

No one answered.

When she finally found a doctor who had escaped Kyiv with his own family, she explained to him in broken sentences what she needed, and he walked back with her to the barn where they found Maria, shaking and huddled, moaning.

Her breaths were shallow, as quiet as whispers, and Julia wondered how she had gotten so ill so quickly. Had she missed something important? Could they turn back? She so desperately wanted her mother.

"Maria?"

She wheezed in response.

"I found someone."

Maria turned her face toward Julia, and her face in the light looked as if the skin had been pulled tight across her skull. Her lips were wet from fresh vomit, as was her hair.

The doctor placed a mask around his face and approached her. "Miss? May I examine you?" He took her wrist in his hand and took her pulse. "Hmm. Very rapid." He frowned. "Your wrist!" He started, and pulled up her sleeve to reveal angry red spots. He leaned over her and spread open the collar of her dress. He found them there as well. "Is very bad, I see." He gestured to Julia in reference. "See here, this very common for many. Typhus. Is what it's called."

"What does that mean? I don't know what that means, this word you're saying." She spat her words out, indignant and infuriated at this man, who could come to a conclusion so quickly. Weren't there many, *many* illnesses that she could have? Surely it couldn't be this easy.

The doctor remained unreasonably calm. "Typhus is headache, fever, vomiting. It can last for weeks or it can only last days, miss."

"So, fix her."

"I cannot. These camps have disease, it is very common." His hands ran delicately through his hair, fingers uncomfortable in this interrogation.

"I don't understand!" Julia moved him with her arm—she needed to see Maria more clearly—and small bottles clinked in the bag at his feet. "You have medicine in there. Can't you *use* it, for God's sake?"

"Listen." He placed a hand on her arm to stop her from shaking. "Your sister is very ill."

Stupid man. She felt like taking his mask and shoving it down his throat. "Well. Yes, I *know* that. But how do I *help* her? She cannot be ill forever!"

The doctor took the mask off his mouth and sighed, chewing the dry skin of his lip. He seemed preoccupied. He'd seen too many of these cases, and there were many ways to convey a diagnosis, depending on the person he was speaking to.

"There is no way, you see."

"What do you *mean*? There are always ways."

"Well, I will be honest with you, it's a horrible disease.

"Yes. Diseases are common. We're in a goddamn *trench*, practically. We're all ill."

"No, I mean, we have no medicine for it. We have not been given vaccines for it."

"Well, why not?"

He shrugged his shoulders and said the only thing that made sense, but was incredibly cruel: "War."

Julia looked at her sister. She was listless on the bed, eyes closed and sleeping. Her hands were loose by her side and peaceful. She looked like a lost child.

She softened in that moment. "What do I do, then?" she pleaded, grabbing him by the arm, and then corrected herself, embarrassed by her behavior. "Help me. *Help me.* What do I do?"

The doctor was closing the bag that he'd carried with him. "You can only pray."

When he left, Julia sat down on the floor next to where Maria lay, tracing the lines of her sister's hand. As she was doing this, she imagined that they might be able to leave in the night and progress to Germany and then at least she could have proper medical care. She wondered if she could lift Maria and cover her with blankets in the back of the wagon and she thought she could. And maybe tomorrow morning she would be well enough to continue on the journey, and she would promise Maria that she would drive the wagon the entire way there, and she wouldn't have to do anything apart from rest. They would try and steal extra bread from somewhere, or someone, and Julia would explain that it was for her ill sister, and she would slowly get better. Fresh air might do her good.

It will be alright, she thought. Their mother would nod and tell them that that was a good plan and that Maria would recover quickly, because she always had.

Julia watched as Maria's face grew paler, more still, as the minutes passed.

"Maria." She stroked the hair that once shone so brightly, now dimmed. "*Marioshka.*"

Maria opened her eyes, though feebly, as if in a bright light.

"Do you remember the song?"

"Which...?"

Julia began to hum softly, the words whispered and pure:

Look at the sky, so clear and free,
Come out, come out, sweet darling
Though you're weary from work,
Come and spend a moment here with me.

Maria smiled. "I remember." And then she closed her eyes and tightened her hand around Julia's.

And then they were in the fields of their memories, plucking handfuls of old leaves and throwing them into the air like offerings as they laughed and played. Julia spoke of their brothers, and of their childhood together underneath banners of blue skies, and how they would whisper secrets to each other about the world and where its magic lay.

"You know, Mama used to always say that we were mother and daughter, not sisters, remember?" Julia was tired, but she kept on, staring at Maria to see the shallow rise and fall of her chest. And then she remembered. "Let me show you something."

Julia had a picture of them that she had always kept beside her bed, a picture from four years ago taken by a friend, and she'd placed it in her coat pocket the day she left. She found it there now and withdrew it to show to Maria, but she was already asleep, so she looked at the faces staring out: it was of the two of them sitting in the fields, hair in plaits, dresses with shortened sleeves for the heat, palms raised to shield their eyes from the bright sun.

She remembered that they had gone flower picking, and that they had made chains out of the wheat and the wildflowers and secured them in a kind of wreath, *vinok*, with blades of young grass. They had worn them as they walked slowly home, and when the wreaths dried and became stiff, they left them in their rooms as reminders of that one day. She thought of the warm air, and how the insects had hummed in the shade. Their life was nearly what they wanted it to be, then: they'd possessed a sense of wonder still.

Julia took the photo and placed it next to Maria, inside the blanket warming her suffering body. She looked at the woman who had promised to take care of her, the woman who was now small and childlike, and squeezed her alabaster hand as it lay limp, listening to her thin breath course through her lungs and gently out of her parted lips. "We'll be alright," Julia whispered, and it was to be one of many times she would utter words that she was dreadfully unsure of.

Maria's eyes flickered faintly as Julia rested her head on the edge of the mattress, and they both fell asleep in the buttery glow of the lamplight.

* * *

Julia woke to the sound of gunfire and tanks on the ground. Having seen and heard them before in her village, her entire body braced as the walls of the barn vibrated.

As she listened, the events of the previous night came flooding back to her and she turned to wake Maria. "Oh God, please," she murmured to herself as she saw that her sister's face was still, eyes closed, her mouth slack and lips thin.

Julia pressed her lips together and kept the cry in her throat, bringing her sister closer, feeling for any warmth that was still there. A part of her wondered if she would wake up, if this had all been a feeble, feverish dream. Julia's body curled toward her sister and stayed there, not caring about the world around her.

She stayed hidden in the far corner of that barn as the day brightened, her eyes pink and wide, her face red and swollen, listening as soldiers approached, bellowing: "Raus! Herauskommen!!"

She heard hurried footsteps and people shuffling outside, waiting to be counted, panic in their voices.

She stayed a moment longer, and then she finally rose and stood staring at her sister as if giving her the chance to wake up. *Just one more minute. Wake up. Be brave.*

Silence.

"Alles kommen raus, bevor ich schieße!" *All come out before I shoot.*

She looked at the barn door—and then back at some loose boards in the wall by where she now stood. She had two choices: she could risk making a run for it, breaking out of the barn's side, dragging her sister, hiding in the shadows, making a path through the woods, toward the Russians, toward certain death... or she could try and survive, and promise to stay alive to see her parents one day, to have children and a family of her own. Her sister would tell her to choose the latter.

Her hand reached for her scarf and turbaned it around her hair. As she did so, she wondered if within this decision there would be grief either way. If so, she would have to take that with her, to a place where she might not survive, and the weight of that choice now lay heavy on her slim shoulders as she felt a knot in her throat.

She did her buttons slowly, one by one, her hands trembling, smoothing the layers of her clothes. She remembered her father's voice as she put her gloves on.

"Papa. Will we see you again?"

"I don't know."

"Well, all this madness will be over soon, and we will turn back and you and Mama will be here, and it will all be like before, yes?"

"I need you to find your way, no matter what happens. Find

the use in the broken things, the courage in the frightening things, and the joy in the sadness. There will always be sadness."

The soldiers were at the door.

Steadying herself, Julia knelt by her sister, so small now. She saw that Maria had worn brown leather shoes; they were practically new. Julia looked down at her own, the battered lip of the sole undone at the front. They would slow her down. She whispered, "I'm sorry, *Marioshka*," and her tears wet the hay as she removed her sister's shoes swiftly and put them in her duffel. She brushed a lock of hair off Maria's forehead and told her softly that she loved her. Her eyes creased at the corners and the few tears that came again made her face shine as she steeled herself.

Julia covered her sister with the still-warm blanket that they had both shared, took both of their duffels, and slowly walked to the barn door.

"Jetzt! In die Autos!"

Into the cars. Her legs trembled as she opened the door and walked into the cold, hollow light, two duffels in her hands.

A black truck waited for her.

CHAPTER FOUR

GERMANY, 1941

Henry Rudnick liked the strange irony of where he was now, and wished that he could tell his father how it was, not that the old man would care. "A Ukrainian man from a wealthy family celebrates a birthday with a bunch of German soldiers," he mumbled to himself as he walked toward his barracks and flicked the end of his cigarette expertly behind him. *Old man, at least I'm doing more than you ever did with your life.* And this was how he would remember the afternoon of his twentieth birthday in the middle of a war he'd run head-first into, away from a life that offered him too much privilege and not enough adventure.

Henry stepped into his barracks on the far eastern corner of Neumarkt labor camp and emptied his pockets onto his bed. He had a tarnished lighter, cigarettes, a handful of coins, and the train ticket that he'd used to leave home. He was sure he'd made the right choice, despite the distance from everything he'd ever known. He shook his head. It was better this way. He had never remembered a birthday after his mother had died. He had been a stranger in his own home, just as he was here.

Henry had arrived in Germany earlier that year, once his

town became occupied. He had seen how everyone had welcomed Germans, and he knew that he couldn't stay and be subservient; he needed independence. He used his own money to buy the train ticket, the rest of his money hidden in the linings of his shoes and sewed into the pockets of his thin wool coat.

They'd had an argument the day before he'd left home, one that had stung Henry deeply, as his father grew more impatient with a son he didn't understand.

"You just wait!" Ivan's voice had been dark. "Just wait until you have to understand what direction your life will go, during a war, during hunger, during pain"—a fresh cigarette, sparks flying, punctuated his words—"trying to make decisions on life, decisions that no one will warn you about. You just wait until you have to pick up the pieces of a life that you never wanted but had to withstand. You have no idea who I am, son."

"But I don't *want* to," Henry had replied, and stopped, finding immense power in the moment. "You don't *make* me want to understand. You don't even try."

"Correct."

"But why?" And his voice had turned soft again. Young.

"Because men don't need to explain themselves to boys. Life is too complicated."

"So why did you become a father?"

"Stupidity, if you ask me. Love. Nonsense. Feeling as though it was my obligation to your mother. Also..."

Henry had hoped for something kind. "What?"

"Survival of the family name." Ivan had stamped out his cigarette. "That's what parents do, to continue the family. Survival has nothing to do with love, and everything to do with purpose. Your purpose is to continue my life, and the name I gave you."

"And what if that's not what I want?"

Ivan looked over at his son, and then away, scanning the

fields. He turned back to him, squinting. "So, what is your plan, then? What will you do?"

"The war is on our doorstep. Aren't you afraid?"

"I'm not afraid of anything."

"Well, I don't want to stay here. There are jobs, there is money, and there is work. Did you know that I could work in Germany? Not as a laborer but as an officer? I know German, as well as other languages, and my friends have all said—"

"Hironimus. You are so naive."

"Am I? I think it's smart to hope for something. And this isn't what I hope for, for my life, Papa."

His father had softened at the name his son had called him as a small child, but only briefly. "Hope is dangerous."

When his father turned his back to leave, Henry had first seen a fleeting glimpse—it had vanished almost immediately—of a man whose life had stripped him bare.

Henry now took off his uniform and laid it carefully on the bed, changing into a crisp, pale gray shirt and gray trousers, the only other clothes he now owned. There was a small mirror on the wall of his barracks, and as sunlight filtered through the room, Henry watched his reflection, how his cigarette was clamped firmly in the side of his mouth, his shirt unbuttoned at the very top showing an undershirt to keep warm. He had been deciding what to do. His ranking officer—having seen that Henry had a knack for languages and an eye to charm people to do what he needed them to do—had given him his daily field-work assignment to survey the camps on horseback and report any inconsistencies or items that needed repairing. Once finished, he was given his papers to leave the camp if he wanted. He was luckier than most, as he could walk into Neumarkt and eat and drink there with the other officers who didn't need to adhere to the strict rations that other workers had. But today, he decided to stay at the camp and meet a friend.

He examined his wavy dark brown hair that was long at the

crown and short on the sides, his brown eyes, and the way his long lashes shadowed his cheekbones. He ran his slender fingers through his fringe and swept it back, pausing to flatten his anemic mustache before placing his lighter in his pocket.

"My father's face," he mused. His flat lips lifted at the corners, but he felt nothing.

The autumn sun was sinking lower still, glinting on the metal tables in the outside common area as Henry strode over, clapping Yuri on the back forcefully and sitting down next to him, drawing a cigarette out of a creased packet.

"Well? What's new? What's work been like?" He found a match and sparked it on the edge of his metal chair. He looked at his friend: young man, old body, hair the color of straw, face lined, blue eyes shining under a worried brow.

Yuri lowered his head, shaking it. "Germans. I mean, doesn't it make you angry?"

"What, exactly?"

"Being..." Yuri paused and looked up, limp hair drooping in front of his left eye. He looked hopeless. "Here. *Here.* Cattle to the slaughter."

Henry felt a bead of sweat along his temple and wiped it with his arm, tapping the cigarette packet on the table, turning it over and over in his fingers. "What else is there? What other options do we have right now?"

He heard the trucks approach in that moment, and saw groups of men, women and some children piling out in groups, hovering far beyond where he now sat. He watched as they were herded and directed where to stand and when to stay silent. He had seen this before, but some groups were treated with more humanity, while some were sent farther to places like Belsen and Birkenau, and he knew already what that meant. This group was staying.

He turned back. "Yes, fine, you're right. But *dignity*, that's what I mean." Yuri wove his fingers together and undid them slowly, over and over. "Animals. We're not exactly living the life in here."

Henry turned back to his friend. "Status doesn't feed us."

"Since when did you get so philosophical?" Yuri wanted an answer. He was clinging to the future but it was like holding fistfuls of sand.

Henry pushed his cigarette into the table and then flicked it away. "Look. This won't last forever. Wars aren't forever, nothing is forever. We do what we can with what we have for now, and the only thing we can hope for is to survive."

"And who the hell left you the cock in charge of the hens?"

Henry laughed. His father used to use that phrase. "Well, I know how to manage a situation." He tapped his index finger to his temple. "Don't let it get to you."

"So, this is a"—Yuri stuck his hand in the air between them, cigarette aloft, and circled it as if he were conjuring—"situation, you say?"

"Mmm."

"Death is everywhere, Henry. Don't you think we could be next?"

"Do you really think wasting time worrying about our lives is a way to live? No. Surely Germany will win this war, and we will go back. Hell, maybe even start a new life somewhere else, who knows. But for now, play the game." Exhale of smoke. "Be smart."

"About...?"

"About how *you* can make yourself useful to *them*." Henry looked up and saw a pair of officers striding across the ground, and he nodded in deference. He leaned toward Yuri. "As soon as you look hopeless, weak, they have you." He made a fist with his hand and released it. He lit another cigarette and clamped it in the side of his mouth, his trimmed mustache grazing it lightly as he rested both his hands on his friend's forearm. "We survive."

"Sure." Yuri stood up to leave, still unsure of his friend's summary of things. "Well, I'll leave you to it."

"Wait. Just wait." He left his hands on Yuri's arm but his gaze was directed at something across the ground, past the fencing. It was then that he saw her.

He'd seen so many people come and go, so many languages pass through these strange fences, but now he became curious: the small girl with the faltering, elegant walk seemed familiar. Yes, he knew her. He had known her, and had seen her before, he realized, but couldn't place where. He'd seen her once before (*or was it twice?*), as she sat with someone (*her sister? a friend?*). Her hair was careless, thin wisps flying around her face getting caught in her eyelashes and lips. Today she was in her dark uniform with plain skirt that grazed her knees ever so gently, flat black shoes making it easier for her to manage the hours she was expected to be on her feet. Her head was covered in a scarf, and her nose was sharp on her face, softening slightly when she smiled timidly at the officers as she passed. *Most smile out of fear,* he thought to himself.

Looking at her felt sobering, like cold water in stifling heat. He wanted to see her hands: a ring would tell him more, though she could have hidden it, or sold it. She moved as if she had music at her feet, but her body looked painfully aware that it was in a crowd. He looked again. Wished he could place her from somewhere.

Yuri's head turned behind him and he understood as he followed Henry's gaze.

"Yeah, a good girl, that one. Bit plain." A cat slunk over to Yuri and he kicked it away, distractedly. He leaned in and studied Henry's face. "Surely you know her? Sister of that kid from school. Milo. Lived on the *selo*, not too far from Stryi."

Oh, right, Henry thought, and nodded, inhaling his cigarette smoke slowly, squinting as it passed through his lips and dissipated into the air. *Sure. A nobody. No one of status.*

He bristled as he heard the voice of his father in that moment. "Don't waste time with anyone you can't get anything out of," he would often tell him. He shook it off.

"Well, interesting anyway." He looked at Yuri and smiled. "We should go."

Yuri sighed. "Finally. Thought you'd never let me leave. I have a party to attend," he said with a comedic tone, and loped off, waving his hand in departure.

Henry watched his friend, watched the curve of his back tighten his shirt. The boy was a hard laborer. His hands were chapped, his shirt had dust in the creases, mirroring the lines that had gathered around his eyes as he spoke. He was tired, like all of them.

Henry sat staring at the road outside for a moment—a road separated by barbed wires and concrete blocks on either side—and wondered where he was.

He was hungry, but he was safe.

Yuri's voice suddenly bellowed out in front of him as he walked away. "Julia! Hey, Julia!" Yuri gestured across the filtering crowds. Henry looked to where he was waving to, and saw a face in the distance that smiled in recognition as she saw Yuri. She waved back briefly, and then followed Yuri's hand as he gestured to Henry. She stopped waving as their eyes met, and then the crowd closed back in around her like a dream, vanishing.

And then a memory descended on him: a mere four years ago he had seen Julia, when they had both gone to church on Christmas Eve. Their lives had intersected often in fact, as they lived only thirty minutes apart as the crow flew, and Lviv was small—certainly small enough so that people didn't forget faces. The crowds had stood silent and cold to listen to the sermon underneath the vacant stares of the gold icons surrounding them. And he had watched in a daze as she smiled the kind of broad smile that someone does in private, without awareness of others. Her hair had surrounded her face in a kind of dark halo, while beneath her headscarf her cheeks were flushed from the cold. Her young body was tall and lean and he had felt a kind of longing to walk over to her; it had caught in his throat and he kept it in his memory as he walked away that night, hoping to see her again.

Henry left the embers from the other cigarettes burning in the ashtray and walked back the way he had come, thinking about her, as he would do every moment until he saw her again.

* * *

Julia carried the grief of her sister's ghost with her, like a shadow, as she stood at the brick and iron gates of the labor camp with a few hundred others, two duffels in her hand.

Even though Julia knew she would be given food and shelter and was hired as a bookkeeper because of her schooling, she still felt like she had placed herself in the lion's mouth: rows of identical gray-hued wooden buildings, made to look like barns; long, narrow houses plain and square. They were squat and wide, and seemed to go in an endless line toward an empty distance. A metal fence wrapped around tall wooden posts—with what looked like sharp metal teeth adorning the wiry tops—bordered the perimeter as far as she could see, displaying flat, deserted earth. The place looked like it had risen up to be used, sucked dry, and eventually swallowed up by the very ground that had given birth to it.

The camp was far away from town, separated from it by bare forest, isolated and vanishing.

An afterthought, is what she felt her life suddenly was.

"Welcome to Neumarkt. One stop before Hell." A woman spoke as she drifted by, all yellowed teeth and sunken eyes.

Julia made fists of her hands to keep them warm and stop them shaking, and held them to her sides as the guards started separating one group from another, *for what?* She had no idea, but she hoped she would be safe.

She was shuffled into a group and then into a building to be disrobed, examined, standing in front of concrete walls that were bruised orange and brown from rust and paint. Their eyes were stretched open, and thumbs prised their lips open to check teeth and throats. Hair was inspected for lice and skin for disease, and then they were to bend forward, exposing their spines to further checks for stability and strength, their body cavities searched.

When she was allowed to dress again, Julia was given a dark uniform made of stiff cotton that hit at her calves, thick tights, a headscarf, and a blue armband marking her as an OST (Eastern Worker). They then all walked to a building where they would be given their work orders.

"Hey." A girl in front of her, slim, with thin yellow hair underneath her headscarf, whispered to her. "You see?" She pointed.

"What?" Julia whispered back.

"They are looking at us. Like a zoo."

Julia followed her gaze and saw a handful of officers standing and pointing, all with wide grins and powerful stances.

" Hey Mädels, was guckt ihr euch alle an?" *What are you girls looking at?* One of them spat on the ground and turned around.

The girls both turned back, flushed and embarrassed as the officers moved on. As they parted, Julia caught sight of a man she'd seen before. Tall. Dark hair. Broad shoulders that seemed too sharp for the clothes he wore. They locked eyes for a second, and then the crowd of women moved and gathered across her field of vision again, and she lost him.

* * *

A few months later, Julia and Henry were seated side by side in the late winter sun on the narrow step by the barracks door, the shadow of an SS officer pacing a few hundred feet away. The step wasn't wide enough for two people, and she'd moved closer to him, the worn material of her work dress almost brushing Henry's uniformed arm, her heart pounding. Had they been anywhere else, there would have been a lake nearby, or a field, and a group of friends with a variety of food on a wool blanket, the grass itching their bare legs. But it was in wartime, and they did what they could.

"We have to stop meeting like this, Julia." He watched her face, his eyes smiling.

"But I thought you'd asked me to come to see you?"

"It was a joke." He laughed, a wide smile, his eyebrows raised, and shook his head.

"Oh." She felt her cheeks redden.

Henry nodded to one of the officers as he passed by, eyeing the pair. This meeting would be short, today.

"Did you eat enough today?"

"The same, but not bad. Some canned mackerel and bread and one of the other bookkeepers had vodka!" she said almost too excitedly. She awkwardly crossed her arms, feeling their thinness.

He smiled. "Listen, I have some of my rations that I can give you. I managed to get a hold of a bit of cheese."

Her mouth watered at the thought. "Henry, I can't keep doing this. It'll get you into trouble."

"Don't worry about me. I have it easier than you do."

Julia shrugged. "They'll start wondering why I'm one of the healthier ones." She looked shyly at him. "All this special treatment."

He was a *Werkschutz,* an elite worker who oversaw production and maintained delivery routes.

Henry had chosen her, after seeing her daily. The first few weeks of innocence had turned into companionship: his hand on her shoulder as he passed by her workstation, their bodies brushing up against one another as they walked, first accidentally then with purpose. They navigated the invisible barriers that separated their stations in that camp, following narrow, overgrown paths at the perimeter of the camp's eastern corner, discreetly and at night, for that was all she was allowed in his company. There his dark eyes moved over her face, and she thought of the way her slight body would fit neatly into his.

He told her of his mother and how he had lost her as a child, and of his father's cold nature, and she felt relief as she unburdened the loss of her sister to him. They uncoiled their pasts and gave them to each other reverently, and slowly this trust became a kind of love.

They clung to it immediately, because it was all they had.

Henry paused, his eyes scanning the movement of the officers around him. "Meet me at your shift change," he whispered. "I'll have a few things for you. Not a lot, just what you can hide underneath your coat."

She looked up at him. "Thank you."

He looked over at her, his eyes letting the details of her seep into his memory: her hands were scarred, and her nails had been bitten to the quick. Her thin arms displayed a burn mark and a bruise was hidden amongst a smattering of freckles, like a constellation. Her uniform had a tear in the hem, the blue fabric displaying threads splayed through the dust that had collected on it. Her face was strong, sharp and proud, and he loved the way she looked at him: with a wary abandon.

She felt complete longing at the feeling of his tall, warm body inches from her slight one. She moved closer, keeping her head down. He offered her a cigarette, and her fingers brushed his as she cupped her hand over the flame, watching the end glow. She inhaled, a sputtering cough erupting as the smoke tickled her lungs. She finished half, then stubbed out the ember delicately, saving the other half for later. When it cooled, she placed it in her shoe, and Henry laughed at the strange behaviors of their small lives there. That was the simple way it began.

* * *

The winter of 1942 was bitter, and despite not being in a prison camp, Julia and the other workers still had to layer newspaper and hay within their clothes to stay warm most days; their bones felt as if they would break at every step. After her shift ended and the night workers replaced the bookkeepers and watched over the locked boxes of money, she quietly navigated the dark path to Henry's barracks, for it had heating, and though it was incredibly risky, it was worth it. Julia began to spend nights there with increasing regularity, always leaving for her building before the night skies faded into morning.

They belonged to, and protected, each other.

* * *

It was a few years later, just as the war had begun its slow, painful decline, that their lives would change forever.

In the winter of 1945, Henry was sent on delivery orders to a different camp for two months. When he returned, Julia told him of the pregnancy, as she had begun to show. Her work shifts had begun to take their toll too, as the population of the camp diminished—the Nazis had begun to evacuate the workers as the Allies approached, and Julia feared the worst.

They decided to marry swiftly, holding on to one piece of joy amongst the ruins. They gathered one evening in the back of a barrack block that smelled of wet hay and cold concrete, with witnesses that they didn't know, and a dying priest who had recently finished his metal-polishing shift. Henry wore a suit jacket that he'd stolen, his hair freshly wetted and finger-brushed, and Julia had nothing apart from her dark uniform, but she had removed her arm band before placing her arm through Henry's. Maria's shoes were on her feet, and her mother's rosary in her pocket.

Henry left, and the sirens announced the workday two hours later.

Their daughter was born soon after, in the spring of 1946, on a lonely bed in the medical barracks, next to a disused brick furnace, with the help of a kind midwife with whom Julia had shared a wooden bunk. Henry had been transferred to another camp again, so it was three months later, when the camp had been liquidated and he was no longer needed there, that he came back and finally met his daughter. He'd never thought of himself as someone's father and protector, and yet, here he was, looking at a tiny child with bright eyes and a doughy, round face. His child. His future, looking up at him with a purity he'd never seen before.

He asked Julia what she'd named her as he placed his broad hand on the baby's head, his eyes filling with tears at the soft, warm skin underneath his own.

"Meet your little Slava," she replied with a smile. *Glory,* in Ukrainian.

CHAPTER FIVE

As the liberations slowly tapered off in the summer of 1946, Julia and Henry, along with seven million prisoners and forced laborers, left Germany, mostly travelling slowly west, without families or homes to come back to, as the east threatened more oppression.

The new family had taken their belongings, wrapped Slava in a partially torn blanket that had been discarded in one of the barracks, and ventured into town, hoping to find a house to stay in temporarily with rent that they could afford from the little money Henry had saved from the jobs that he'd had at the camp. Deutschmarks were worth something—for a short time at least, before the economy collapsed again—and they had saved their rations to take with them.

Neumarkt looked partially deserted, but was coming to life in fits and starts, with shops opening their windows and roads empty of military vehicles. It would be dangerous for them to stay in an empty house that would most likely be occupied by the Russian military soon, so they wandered off the main street and wound their way toward a group of houses on the Caritasstraße until they finally found a tiny room to rent.

It was at the back of a small house with an orange, pyramid-shaped roof and a narrow door with one window beside it, owned by an old woman by the name of Helen Wasser—a seamstress with a small shop in the middle of town. The shop had not survived the war, and most of her stock had been looted, but her spirit remained. She was short; her gray hair was cut sharply to meet her jaw and was always worn pulled back with black hairpins; thin glasses perched on her small nose; and her wide face was welcoming and curious.

She was kind to them and gave them a small room, and encouraged them to use the kitchen as if it were their own. "Warm food is almost as important as kindness," she would say. "Nourishment within a heart comes in many ways." It made the family feel safer than they had in years and allowed them to have a semblance of a life for a little while.

* * *

It was late January 1947, and Henry was rubbing his cold, dry hands together, reaching for the kettle in the kitchen. Helen had gone out for the morning, and had left them eggs, bread, and a tin with coffee in it. He pulled his clothes to his body. Everyone was dressed in many thin layers, with heavy woolen socks.

"Julia." There was affection in his voice as Henry watched her feed Slava, who was dangling her legs off a highchair at the small kitchen table. He made a face at Slava, and she squealed her response, reaching for him.

"Ach." Julia had been peeling a freshly boiled egg, and winced as it burned the tips of her fingers. She rolled her eyes and smiled at the two of them. "Stop distracting her, she needs to eat." Henry became serious again, and Julia directed him: "Yes, go ahead. I'm listening," she said, as she broke the egg apart.

Henry sat down across from them. "I think we need to talk about what is going to happen to us. Germany is falling apart, and now the Russians will come back in. Reparations. A new Germany. It's going to be for us like it was ten years ago, back home." He folded his arms across his chest, waiting. "We cannot stay here, Julia."

Slava squealed again, wanting attention from the two adults who suddenly weren't looking at her. Henry stroked her head absentmindedly, as he watched Julia's face for a reaction.

Julia put her head in her hands, and then moved them to her lap. Her head moved slowly back and forth. She looked defeated. "Henry, I really wish you'd just left this morning, just done something else with the time you have, instead of hovering. Worrying." She looked up. "I can't think about another move. Can we please discuss this later?"

He folded his hands and leaned on the table. "Alright, but when, exactly? Because I'm the one who has to think ahead for the three of us." Sensing a barrier between them, he softened. He had known this would be difficult. "We can't live here forever, pretending to be a happy family."

"Why not?"

"Do you really think that Russia coming back here is a good thing for us?"

Julia shrugged. "Well—"

"Please don't be naive. I need you to think back. To the arrests. To the lists. To everything that we left behind. You and I will be on those lists still. We can't even write letters home yet, because they'll be tracking us, expecting us to return. And then, we keep looking over our shoulders. Do you want to relive that?" He looked over at Slava, and back at Julia. "We have to find somewhere where we can stay. Build a life."

Julia looked past him into the small room. The rust-colored paint had faded on the crumbling plaster walls, the wooden cot was pushed up against the unmade bed which was then pushed up against the wall, and the window was too small to let any decent amount of light in. It felt like a rabbit warren.

She looked back up at him, her voice even and calm. "We can't go back home."

"No, Julia." He leaned closer to her. "Listen, we've talked about this before. We can't go back to a country that is under Soviet rule. It's too restricted, violent, unsure." He reached into his pocket and withdrew a folded piece of newspaper from his pocket, which looked like it had been in there for weeks. He flattened it on the table and pointed at one of the articles. "Here," he said, boldly. "*Here* is where our new plan is."

The small print had strayed and smudged a bit, but Julia could make out the words where his index finger rested:

MIGRANTS NEEDED

and

WORK THE LAND AND RECEIVE YOUR OWN.

Julia knew what he spoke of—she had heard it on the small kitchen radio over the last month. News of countries accepting the overspill of refugees from war-torn countries. The United Nations had sanctioned it, and handfuls of countries had opened their doors.

Henry lit a cigarette. "It is money. Freedom from this." He gestured around excitedly, the smoke floating to the four walls surrounding them, then disappearing into the air. "It is a way for us to leave this collapsing Europe and start a new life for ourselves." He let out a stream of smoke. "Julia, there is nothing left for us here."

She hesitated and looked at Slava. She smoothed her palm

over her daughter's head and suddenly felt her own mother's hand on her cheek. "But what about me? What am I supposed to do?"

"What do you mean?"

"A new country? Again?" She leaned back and looked up at the ceiling. "I feel that if I move again, I might collapse."

"I know. But we can do this. I know we can. We have to." Henry reached out for Slava's warm little hands, and then reached out for Julia, his hand open, waiting for hers. An agreement.

Julia was torn, for where she belonged was with them—this was her family now—but her heart yearned for the miles beyond, still.

"I feel you're right but, also, I feel so *angry*." She frowned, and his hand retreated back to his lap. "It's not only about you and what you need. We only just survived one event in our lives; is it possible to survive yet another?"

He bristled. "So, you want to stay here, then? And do what? Constantly live with one eye on the shadows?" He sighed, stubbing out his cigarette and reaching for another.

"I don't know. Maybe Germany will get better over time."

Henry snapped his lighter closed. "Julia, did you even ask me where we can go? Where we could work and live and actually receive our own house and land?"

"I'm not sure I want to."

"Australia."

Julia's eyes widened. "Isn't that somewhere on the other side of the world?"

"Yes. But"—he counted on his fingers—"they're offering paid work, our own house, our own land to farm and, after three years, we become citizens there."

Julia smiled weakly at his eagerness. "Henry, it's a world away from what we know. I feel that I can't keep repacking our bags, hoping we stay somewhere long enough for it to feel like home." Her face was a mix of exhaustion and understanding as she looked at him, hoping she'd be heard, despite knowing that he was right.

He was done with being patient. "You're being selfish."

Julia wiped Slava's mouth and picked her up from the chair. She placed her down with a small stuffed rabbit, then stood up, her arms at her side, giving herself the space for an argument. "No. I'm telling you how I feel."

Henry's face darkened. "What about how *I* feel? I made a promise to take care of you, and now you're saying I'm *selfish*?"

"It takes two people to make a decision, Henry. Two people to make a child and create a life and a family."

"Which is exactly my point. We have to be together in this."

"I don't think I can move again. I don't know if I have it in me."

"Julia, please listen." He came to her and grabbed her by both arms, shaking a bit, his fingers digging into her flesh, making her wince. "We can't stay."

Julia wrenched out of his grip and sat back down in defeat, rubbing her arms. "What do you want me to say, then?"

Henry placed his hands in his pockets. "Maybe we need the space to let it settle. We have two months to make this decision, but the train leaves then, so we have to put ourselves on the list."

"Train?"

"Yes, from Munich station. Trucks are taking people there, and then from Munich, we go to Acerra, Italy."

Julia lifted her mouth in a smile. "As if we're traveling the earth."

Henry smiled, sensing that she would come around. "But then, from Italy, we make the trip to Australia on a boat." He put his hat on, ready to leave. "A boat, with food, and a view of the sea, and maybe even a cabin to sleep comfortably."

Julia nodded. "Alright. Let's give ourselves time to think."

Henry walked out, not saying where he was going, but he left without a glance back. He knew he'd been hard on her. But he couldn't face another day looking over his shoulder, wondering about an uncertain future that was out of his control. Plans. He needed plans.

Julia cleared the plates off the table and stood at the sink retying her apron. The floor beneath her feet felt unsteady. It was shifting undetectably at first, and then she felt as if she were falling through. Drifting. Needing an anchor when there was none. She looked through the small window next to the door and stared out onto the street. Rows of small houses huddled together, quietly; the streets were empty apart from a few Russian military jeeps. Maybe Henry was right.

That afternoon, Julia was outside, the laundry line heavy with sheets snapping in the wind. Slava was at her feet.

She heard a sound behind her, the footsteps slow, deliberate. Julia turned, expecting to see Henry as he hadn't yet come home. But it was Helen. Julia smiled and walked toward the older woman and kissed her papery cheek.

"Hallo, Madame Helen! Schön dich zu sehen!" *Nice to see you.* Helen reminded Julia of her mother, and her voice was plump with affection.

"Julia, it is nice to see you outside with the baby." Helen looked at Slava. "So German-looking—all that blonde hair and pale skin." She chuckled softly and looked at both the woman and the child. "What an odd pair you are, and yet so matched. Dark and light."

Helen's thick embroidered blouse erupted in waves on her arms, tucked into her full skirts, hands in pockets, with thick ankles stuffed into leather shoes. Her glasses were on top of her head, her skin soft and clear on her face, topped by a chaotic sparse white bun threatening to unravel in a shock down the nape of her neck.

"Your German is getting good, yes?" She glanced down and smiled at Slava looking up at her. "And your little one is very happy today, I see." She pointed up at the sky. "Gray clouds hiding the sun—maybe a good omen, with the sun coming out. Good things to come, no?"

Julia placed the clothes pegs in her pocket and looked up, squinting, the sky still bright despite the gray. "Well, yes, maybe. Who's to know."

Helen grabbed her arm affectionately and squeezed. Julia tensed, as the bruises on her arms were still tender from the recent argument. "You seem sad. And your arm is so thin. Come. Some tea." Helen gestured for her to follow.

Julia hoisted Slava onto her hip and went inside.

Helen moved around her house as if it were larger than it was, due to her full skirt and the way she gestured as she spoke, with life and color. It was the prerogative of the owner, it seemed, to know how to use the space, despite there being little. Julia would remember this always. She studied it, this kind of rooted energy.

Helen smoothed the front of her dress and reached into the cupboard for a tin of tea leaves, withdrew two cups and saucers, and placed the kettle on the stove.

"Now. What is it?" She sat down and nodded for Julia to join her.

"Oh, Helen, it's nothing."

"*Not* nothing, Julia. I know your face by now. You speak even without saying anything. Your eyes are sad."

Julia ached suddenly, for only a mother would say that. She fought the tightness in her throat. "Henry said he thinks we should leave. Leave here, find somewhere else to live, to work. Ridiculous." She looked down at Slava, happily rattling a few clothes pegs on the tiled floor. "I'm so tired, Helen."

"Yes, that I understand. We are all so tired." Her hands rested on the table, fingers mildly bowed and arthritic, blue veins running like rivers underneath milky skin. "But, Julia. Think to yourself. Why is it so foolish? Staying *here* would be foolish. Look at how much it is changing already. The rules are always changing for all of us. It is quiet now, but for how long?" Helen's eyes grew intent. "Why do you not trust him?"

"I do."

"Well, then." The kettle boiled, and Helen left the unanswered words to hover. Julia watched Slava gum the clothes pegs as Helen poured the tea delicately and brought the cups to the table.

"Oh, no. That won't do, little one." She withdrew a biscuit from a small metal box and took the clothes pegs from her chubby fingers. "Trust him, Julia."

Julia sipped the hot tea and placed her cup back on the table. "Well, yes, but I think—"

"He hopes for the best for you both, I imagine. You know, when Martyn was alive—"

Julia smiled. Helen spoke of Martyn often. They had never had children, though they had tried. They had lived a quiet life and then Martyn had been recruited to be a soldier in the German army during the First World War. He had been young when he left; they had only been married for two years.

"—he made the brave choices that I could not. He encouraged me to live in his absence. He guided us both when the world felt as if it were on the edge of insanity."

"I don't know, Helen. This is what I struggle with. How am I supposed to know? What about me?"

"But you are one and the same, now, Julia. You are a family. You are not alone anymore."

"What if something happens? What if I have nothing left, and all of this has been a struggle for nothing?"

Helen placed her hand on Julia's: cool, smooth skin atop her own warm skin. "Julia. There will always be tragedy and sadness. You cannot spend time thinking about what might happen. You must make choices and sacrifices for the ones you love. It is part of life. It is part of being a woman, and a mother."

The steam dissipated and the tea grew cold as their thoughts filled the room.

That evening, after Henry had returned, and when the house had finally settled into its quiet and Slava lay sleeping, the couple sat and listened to the faint strains of a radio broadcast filtering through the walls from Helen's room. On the center of the small wooden table were two very small glasses of sweet wine, poured from a dusty bottle that Helen had found earlier in a drawer in her room: "Take some. It would be sensible for you both to enjoy something."

There were two kerosene lamps in either corner of the room, flickering a ghostly orange light. Julia had undone the plaits in her hair, and it lay across her back and down her shoulders in a way that made Henry ache with a peculiar kind of sadness: a sadness that only existed when loving someone.

She didn't notice him watching her, for she was looking down at the newspaper clipping that had stayed in the same spot since that morning's argument. She smoothed it down with her long fingers and he noticed she'd been biting the skin by her nails. She spoke first.

"Australia. Are you certain?"

He paused briefly, for his answer would never be as clear out loud as he heard it in his head. "Well, we will finish the things we need to here, and then we have to try and build a life for ourselves in a place that is offering us work. At least try."

Julia stood up and moved toward him, stopping next to his chair. He looked up at her and noticed that the skin around her eyes was a faint red, swollen, as if the tears had long dried but the sadness remained. She bent down and turned his face to hers, and gently, quietly, kissed him, and then drew back, and then kissed him again, lingering long enough this time to make it mean something.

She turned and padded to their bed, Henry following behind.

CHAPTER SIX

MUNICH, 1948

Munich train station was teeming, vibrating with groups of people—so many more than they saw in Neumarkt—like ants on a piece of food. There were covered wagons, train cars, military vehicles, police officers, families, soldiers. The station itself had a grand main "hall": an impressive stone structure that stood in the middle of the forecourt, but as with other buildings after the Second World War, it was being reconstructed due to bomb damage. It stood proudly with parts crumbling and defaced, and yet still looked taller than it was: grandeur in the face of humility.

One hundred and fifty-three kilometers. Four hours of road. Julia looked out of the back of the truck, trying to see through the gaps between people's legs. It was early afternoon, and gray skies offered no indulgence of view. All she saw was a shrinking horizon, familiar landmarks that were moving out of her reach and changing into something new.

Eventually, the roads underneath their bodies started changing from grit to a smoother, more sympathetic terrain. The air felt brisk and efficient, as if its sole purpose was to push them faster toward their destination. *Keep looking up,* she told herself. She clutched Slava to her side, feeling a tightness in the center of her chest.

The trucks pulled up and stopped abruptly. Everyone was ordered off. Julia held Slava as she shuffled off the back onto the ground, and looked around, making sure Henry was there with their cases. Everyone stood in groups, looking left and right, listening intently.

A command. Pointing. Shouting. Henry and Julia deduced quickly that they were to form a queue and walk toward the six train carriages that were to take them to Naples. The trip would take eighteen hours.

"Henry, will there be food on the train? I'm so very hungry. I only have the bread that I took in my bag from Helen's earlier." Thinking about food just made it worse; she didn't want to think about it.

"I don't know, don't expect it. Just ration what you have."

"Okay." She thought the best thing was to save the bread for Slava. She felt her breasts instinctively and realized she could still feed her as long as she had enough water for herself, so they might be alright for a while. She looked over at Slava, happily clutching her battered gray rabbit, now missing an eye, its legs dangling comically.

No one spoke, though glances said more than enough about how similar they all were. Not speaking felt like the last shred of privacy that one could keep; they had their own secrets and musings and fantasies of elsewhere to rely on. Julia leaned on Henry's arm, clinging tightly to avoid being separated.

* * *

Acerra was a small town on the edge of western Italy and would be the final land under their feet before they boarded the boat to take them to Australia.

It was dark when they arrived at the station, finally rumbling to a steaming, squealing stop. The few lamps dotting the station building looked like small phosphorescent balloons. It was one o'clock in the morning, and Slava was asleep on Julia's shoulder. Henry was leaning out of an open window, smoking, the smoke clouds mixing with his icy breath in the air. He had been in this position for the last two hours, unable to sleep.

Julia braced herself for shouting, the panic, the worry. She had been used to it for so long. But none of it came. When the doors opened and kind Italian voices reminded everyone to stay together, Julia almost wept with relief.

Yawns mixed with the shuffling of tired feet, and bodies, spilling out onto the platform. The night makes years out of mere moments, and that night stretched like a dream with no end and no beginning. But, soon, everyone was organized into lines and directed with torches to walk a mile toward rows of small stone houses. Julia scanned the faces around her, and behind her: men carrying bags, sleepy children burying their faces into their mothers' necks, old men and women huddling in groups like children. She heard conversations peppered with "... where we go now?" and "... where do we sleep?" and "... is there food?"

Men were separated from the women and children, but not for any reason other than medical exams and modesty. There was no threat in it, and because Julia felt safe, she adjusted.

"Henry, where will I find you tomorrow?" She searched his face for answers as he separated with groups of other men, filtering from the crowd.

"The line for food? I'm not sure, but I am guessing that

during the day, we can be together, and at night, we sleep separately."

He nodded respectfully at one of the Italian volunteers, and the man walked over in response, overhearing the conversation.

He clapped a hand on Henry's back. "Name?"

Henry looked at Julia and back at the man standing in front of him. "Hironimus."

"Dio! That's a tough one!" He laughed, black curls falling on his tanned face. His teeth were stained from nicotine. "Tell me an easier name."

Henry smiled. "Henry."

"Much better, eh?" The man curved his body as he lit a cigarette and straightened again. "You all sleep in separate camps, eh?" He pointed to the rows of stone houses with flat roofs, divided by a long building in the center, to which he pointed. "Those are toilets." He looked down at Slava, clinging to Julia, and pinched his nose, grimacing. "Whew! Very smelly!"

Slava laughed shyly.

He took a drag on his cigarette. "Daytime, you can go and take the train to the beach. Takes a little over two hours, but the weather has been nice for it."

"And food?" Julia interrupted.

"Meh. Food is terrible. Not much." He shrugged. "War, eh? But. Not too long until the ship comes." He smiled and clamped the cigarette in the corner of his mouth, his hand outstretched. "My name is Angelo." Before he walked off, he leaned toward Slava and whispered: "Means 'angel'."

In the morning, Julia looked around at where she had slept: rows of cots with thin blankets, with cups and saucers next to the beds to use for food later. Cases and duffels were piled in a corner. The walls were cold and damp, but not unpleasantly so.

Bodies moved, slowly waking, and mothers hushed their children back to sleep in their embrace.

Julia walked outside of the barracks in the quiet morning, the sun peeking through the gray. The air was damp and mild, and the ground was thirsty.

There were rows of brick houses that had been designed to look intimidating in their hardness, but they were small and ugly in size, with small steel-barred windows and a square concrete slab as a step in front of the door. They had corrugated steel roofs, undulating and silver in the yellow light as the sun rose behind them. They looked recently abandoned by their previous inhabitants, and Julia wondered where they'd gone.

High metal fences surrounded the compound, though they weren't electrified, and they didn't have barbs at the top.

The air smelled different, not better or worse, but with more substance to the breaths, more humidity, more of a mouthful for the lungs, and it tasted faintly of the sea.

Julia knew Slava would be awake soon, so she walked slowly back to the barracks, stopping at the doorway to listen to the heavy breathing of so many tired souls. Slava wriggled, pushed her face into the bed, let out a yawn and stretched her arms toward Julia.

A figure in the door appeared. "Prima colazione!" *Breakfast.*

Lines of people streamed out of the barracks, faces curious, some even breaking into smiles. They all followed their guides to the main building where they would stand patiently, then receive their food with their bowls in outstretched arms. Julia wondered if she would see Henry there.

There were no tables, no chairs, just queues of hungry people and aromas of bread and broth mixing with the smell of soil, petrol, and chlorine hovering over it all. It was because of the toilets: they were in a separate building in the middle of the empty yard, and were doused occasionally with large buckets of disinfectant, the smell permeating the top layers of air with a sharp, acidic pong. It didn't matter. There was food. It was all anyone cared about.

Julia looked down at her bowl: two slices of bread sitting on top of thin porridge. A piece of ham. She took a cup of weak tea and both of them slowly shuffled a few feet away from the line and sat down on the ground.

"Mama?"

Slava pointed at the bowl.

Julia ripped off small pieces of bread and ham and watched as her daughter ate happily. And then, separating himself from the line, there was Henry. She saw his familiar walk, and watched as he approached them both, his shoulders softening with gratefulness.

* * *

Three weeks had passed.

Julia packed their last few things into the same worn duffle bag that had lived through too many battles. The chalk had faded, and the thick canvas was scarred with the paths she'd traveled.

As she balanced on her knees and folded Slava's pinafore, she remembered her mother, in their last moments together. The stitching of her daughter's dress had come undone on the hem and she wondered if she had time to fix it, and that detail led Julia to search for a needle and thread, looking through coat and dress pockets and finally a pocket that had a picture in it. It was a picture of her parents: one given to her by her mother, on her departure so many years ago. She turned it over and reread the message on the back; she had read it from time to time these last years, as a kind of reminder of where she had come from, and how strong she had become.

May this picture be a lasting memory of us,

forever in your heart.

Love, Mama

She pressed the photograph to her chest and then slipped it inside the duffle, with Slava's toy rabbit on top, followed by a blanket. She brought it up to her face and smelled the sweetness of Slava's skin that clung to it, and she realized that the pain and nostalgia she was feeling was that of motherhood: her mother had felt it, and so had her mother before her.

It had been raining all day, and Slava was napping on the mattress on the floor, a single sheet wrapped around her fat thighs. The doorway to the building was open, and the air felt heavy, while the tin of the corrugated roof added a metallic taste to the air as Julia inhaled deeply. Henry had arranged for them to have a space on the next ship out to Australia. March 31, 1948. Tomorrow.

As Julia stood up to reach for one of the other cases, her stomach suddenly cramped intensely, and the ground started to spin, her breath catching in her throat. She held onto the edge of the bed feebly and, just before she fell back, before the spinning became too much and before her head hit the floor, she looked over at Slava, still sleeping. And then, black.

Have I been asleep for long?

Her eyes fluttered but didn't open yet. It was pleasant, this feeling. It felt weightless, as if within a dream that lay heavy on her body. Then, a hardness underneath her hips.

Why am I on the floor?

She heard a cry. It was Slava.

She rolled over onto her other side and lay there for another minute. The heaviness was leaving her, and she was waking more, and then her eyes opened at the sound of another cry.

And then she felt her body stiffen, her stomach muscles tightening in a knotted nausea again. She grimaced, waiting for the pain to subside.

She noticed the unevenness of the floor: it had faded and bowed with footsteps over time and smelled of old varnish. There was no urgency to tend to Slava just yet; she was protected by pillows in a sort of cushioned fortress.

The pain subsided for a moment. Perhaps she'd not eaten enough, but she wasn't particularly hungry. Julia stretched out and felt her spine expand deliciously. And then her stomach contorted again, in a hot new burst of pain.

Nerves, probably. Anticipation. She waited for it to dissipate.

Slava peeked over her barrier, punching it with a doughy fist, exclaiming "Mama!" and then falling back onto the mattress in a flurry of legs and giggles.

Outside, the entire camp was buzzing with energy, bodies of families milling about with a focused urgency. The air had the faintest smell of salt again, and it wafted in so gently that it reminded her of a dream she'd had about the sea. Or maybe it was the chlorine from the toilet block again.

Julia moved slowly, her thoughts ahead of her, running rampant in last-minute questions about where they would live, what would they wear, where exactly they were headed, and more importantly, why she felt so ill.

In the last few days, the camp had reunited the families in preparation for the journey ahead, and it was now that Henry walked in, his energy abrupt, opening the door and surveying the barrack before approaching Julia. He had yellowed papers in his hand, and he was fluttering them with excitement and apprehension. In his focused state, he failed to notice that his wife was on the floor.

He dropped down to his knees and placed his hands underneath her, lifting her up, reading her face. "Oh, bozshe, what's going on with you?"

"I fainted."

He looked more intently at her. The blood had drained from her face.

"Are you alright?"

Julia pinched her cheeks to bring back the color. "I think so. Yes. Fine." She clasped her hands in front of her stomach and suddenly a new thought entered her mind as she looked at him, but it quickly vanished.

"Right. So, tomorrow. We're ready?" He looked over at Slava, and back at Julia. "Well?"

"Yes, but..." Julia started, wanting the questions in her head to tumble out like coins onto the ground. She wanted him to pick them up and answer them and give them to her and make her feel certain again.

She wanted him to make her feel safe.

"What?"

"No, nothing. Yes, we're ready."

He picked up Slava and brought her to his chest triumphantly: a father feeling like a man, having a conversation with his family about the life they would have. He cooed at her and his answers came rapidly as if shutting out the doubt that they all felt creeping forward: "It'll be fine. Australia is warm. They have plans for us—we'll have a house. You'll be able to find work when Slava starts school."

Henry began to walk away, but then turned back to Julia. "We will be fine, Julia." He then moved toward the door and out into the light with their daughter, leaving Julia standing there, their life quite literally at her feet.

"Fine, yes. Fine," she whispered, to no one in particular.

* * *

"Mama! Papa! Korabel!" Slava pointed. The ship that loomed at the harbor was bigger than anything Julia had ever seen in her entire life. The sound of hollow, creaking, cavernous metal settling in the dock rang in her ears and reverberated around her.

She looked up at it, tenting her hand over her eyes. The ship was bold and dark, in contrast to the bright sky behind it, the blue water sitting below it, the bulk of metal splitting the surface of the water like a knife. She looked around at everyone else, wondering if they'd had the same thoughts, and were also in awe of what was before them, and they seemed to be: groups of people standing and waiting with bags, with children, all looking up, hopeful.

Big white block letters branded the boat's flank: GENERAL STUART HEINTZELMAN 159. Julia wondered who he was, this German, who had been so important to have had something this big named after him. What had he done, and how many had sacrificed their lives, possibly, for the man? One hundred and fifty-nine, maybe? The irony of the fact that this ship would bring them away from war was not lost on her—an American ship that would take them to a kind of freedom. And she was finally ready to give herself over to it.

There were passengers already walking onto the boat; from where, she had no idea. Some looked to be dressed nicely, looking like they had money to spare. Julia held onto Slava's hand tightly.

"Hey!"

The family turned and saw Angelo loping across to them, his hands behind his back, his shirt with stains and sweat marking it. "I thought I would say arrivederci, eh?"

Slava stood by him. She had now grown comfortable around the "nice man with smoky face."

"Can you say it, little Slava? The word for 'goodbye'?"

Slava shook her head.

"Well, in that case, I cannot give you the present. Ah, well." He pretended to turn away.

"Aree-dechee."

Henry chuckled, watching the scene. Julia's face creased, grateful that a kind man would make Slava smile. Perhaps creating a memory for her amongst the chaos.

"Perfetto!" Angelo bellowed, and moved his hand from behind his back, revealing a bright, round orange, as bright as anything Slava had ever seen.

Slava gasped and looked up at Julia. "Mama, can I have it?"

Angelo straightened up to face Julia and Henry. "My nonna has an orchard, and the most beautiful orange tree that I remember as a child. It was a happy memory, having my first orange. I think it will be her first one, yes?"

Julia nodded.

"Well, then." He stuck out his hand and Henry shook it. "Good luck."

Before Henry could say anything, Angelo walked off with a smile and a wave. Slava clutched the orange like a jewel, holding it to her face and smelling it with utter joy.

"Cargo! Cargo section!" Directions in the chaos, shouting to create order.

People were segregated by class—first, second, third, and cargo. *Would have been nice to be in a little cabin with linens and a dresser, and a seat by a window,* Julia thought, as she passed by tables set with linens and lamps and china plates.

Walking through into the lower section of the ship, it was as if they were all being hidden away. The family was ushered into a small storage area, with a tiny port hole and mattresses on the floor for people to share. The ship creaked and moaned as more people loaded into its spaces.

Henry sat on the floor, his back against the metal of the ship, looking at Julia. "You feel strange?" He knew her face so well now.

She nodded. "Feel a bit tired."

"Aren't we all." He leaned his head back and closed his eyes. The smell of the orange was filling the room, Slava's hands sticky with it.

The door? Ramp? Gangplank? Whatever it was called— she'd heard too many words that day and couldn't remember— was being pulled up. The small hatch was closing.

Julia watched through the small, red-painted porthole, her tiny circle of a window like a changing portrait of a strange world. She watched as the sandy coast became more and more distant, until the harbor slowly became smaller as the blue of the sea met the pale horizon of the sky, it was a salve to mend her broken story and make it whole again.

Julia prodded Henry. "I need some air. Can you keep an eye on Slava?"

"You just need some rest." He reached up and took her hand, and she was grateful for the safety of his touch.

But she was restless. "Sure. Maybe I'm just hungry." She felt her stomach contract, and then a warmth between her legs. Her cheeks flushed.

Henry cocked his head to the side. "There's food: black bread, some soup made out of potatoes. Maybe even sausage."

The thought made her want to retch.

She shook her head. "No, no. I just need air." She started walking away, impatiently. It was starting again. She winced at the pain.

"Okay, I'll be here."

Julia made sure she remembered exactly where he was as she left, trying to push her way around and through groups of people as her stomach began to cramp again, this time in quick spasms.

When she finally, slowly, climbed the last flight of stairs and found the doorway to the long, flat walkway above, she walked out and carefully gripped the railing that traveled the perimeter of the ship. It was extraordinary how the world looked there—it was the first time she'd ever felt the expanse of the sea surrounding her.

She breathed deeply and gratefully and then prepared for another fresh burst of pain. And she looked out onto the vast emptiness of sea in front of her as blood from the failing pregnancy slowly traveled down her thighs, staining her legs underneath her skirts.

Afterwards, when Julia had found a toilet room and silently mourned what could not be, she used salt water from a filthy basin to dry the marks on her legs, tearing off a piece of the inside of her skirt to finish the process, and then a bit more to soak the tears off her cheeks—though they kept falling faster than she could catch them—and erase the story that had been, and was now no longer. And then, aching still, she carefully walked back to her husband and daughter. He placed his arm around her, and she pressed her face against his chest, watching Slava's breath become even as she fell asleep on the mattress, the orange peel in her slack hand.

They were once again a family of three.

* * *

The next six weeks they were all moving: the ship, the people on the ship, the sky and sea surrounding them. And yet, they were standing in one place, and able to unfurl themselves.

The first-class cabins were on the upper deck, the wide wood circling the entirety of the ship and secured with heavy steel poles and railings. There were lifeboats piled up and tied close to the bow of the ship, an American flag snapping its colors at the stern. There was a hall in the center of the ship that served food to everyone but first class (first class had linens and fine crystal and silk-backed mahogany chairs), and there was also a small pool of fresh water where everyone was allowed to swim at marked times (first class always went before everyone else). Julia and Henry occasionally walked the length of the ship, arm in arm and holding Slava's hand as other families would, talking as the sea air blew across their faces, people-watching, having polite conversations with other immigrants who were emigrating to Australia. They shared food with other families, and watched each other's children play games on the wooden decks. Some evenings there would be glasses filled with rum and card games in the lower-class cabins, which helped pass the time and made them feel as if they were on an adventure to discover new lands and live in long-awaited freedom.

Occasionally, Henry and Julia sat and looked at the stars, Henry teaching her the constellations that he had learned about in school, pointing his finger to the sky and outlining the shapes of Aries, or Orion. Julia would ask him how he had remembered all of these strange names and figures. He was a wonder to her, in those moments, and revealed much of the quiet man he had always been.

The ship worked its way peacefully along the length of the Suez, around the corners of India, on the edge of Singapore, and then down toward the southern coast of Australia, stopping at various ports. A few days before it arrived in Melbourne, where the Bonegilla Migrant Reception and Training Center would receive them all, Henry and Julia sat one evening on the middle deck, after a dinner of boiled potatoes, ham, and vegetable broth. Slava was sleeping in their room already. They were imagining what their life would be like; the newness of the idea was exhilarating.

"I think the house will be small, but sweet. Like a little version of my childhood home." Julia paused, confirming that

detail. "With a garden. And an apple tree, for Slava to climb."
Suddenly, Julia was young. Younger than her twenty-five years,
and her memories flooded her head. But they didn't make her
mourn her past—they made her want to recreate it, somehow.
Indulge in the celebration of it.

She continued. "Also, tsvity. Wildflowers. I love them. Or
anything pink and white."

"Orchids." Henry had read that orchids were a relatively
easy import, the seeds arriving from farms in Fiji that spanned
acres. But they were a rarity, and only afforded by the wealthy,
in Europe. They reminded him of his childhood, and his
mother; it was one of the only things that had remained in her
room after she had died.

"Why orchids?" Julia had never heard Henry feeling
nostalgia about something so delicate. Or anything much, really.

The warm air moved strands of his hair across his forehead as he spoke. "My mother loved orchids. She would have
them in her room, and I remember they were the darkest,
blackest purple color... Maybe we can have orchids,
somehow."

"Oh, a greenhouse, you mean." Julia nodded. "That's a
lovely idea."

Henry stood up and leaned on the railing. "Listen, I think
it'll be small, but we will make it as we want it to be, this new
life."

"Yes, probably. I think you're right."

Henry turned slowly to her in comical shock. "Yulia
Rudnick." Julia smiled as the Ukrainian sounds rolled off his
lips and he said her full name. "Did I hear that right?" He had
heard the contentment in her voice, and he saw the way her
arms rested on the arms of the wooden chair, as if she had
opened herself up to the night air. "I never thought I would hear
you say that."

Julia laughed. "Don't get used to it." She slipped her feet

out of her shoes and sighed at how good it felt. "I think we will have chickens. And cows."

"My little farm girl." Henry turned back to the black of the sea, the moonlight in small shards on the surface of the water. He smiled at the thought of Julia on a farm, Slava growing taller, stronger, under the gaze of a sibling or two. He thought of stability, and security, and not once did he long for where he had come from.

Julia interrupted his thoughts with another question. "What do you think cane cutting will be like?"

Henry gritted his teeth. "Hard labor." He reached into his pocket and felt for a cigarette. "I've spoken to some of the men on the ship. They've told me it will be hard; I really don't know." He struck a match and the flame ignited the tip, the red glow adding to the starlight. "Hard work doesn't scare me." He squinted as the smoke curled by his eyes.

"Nothing scares you." Julia's face shone in the moonlight as she tapped his leg gently with her bare foot. "You seem to be made of granite."

He turned to face her and leaned back against the railing. "Ahh, and maybe you are made of dreams. Always dreaming. Imagining. Believing."

"That's very true. But dreams vanish. Granite stays."

Henry smiled and shook his head. "Both are strong." He inhaled on his cigarette and let the smoke fade and curl out of his mouth lazily. "But both have a breaking point." He walked over and sat down next to her.

Julia leaned over and kissed his cheek and sat back in her chair, looking up at the stars. "I don't think I could imagine us breaking."

Henry reached for her hand. "I don't think I would want to."

Julia remembered her mother telling her once that "secrets are like promises: both are thin, both fragile." Julia and Henry's promises to each other felt quiet, and understood, and heavy on their shoulders. There was an unknown that they would be stepping into, and their promises took valuable space in their hearts.

But sometimes, promises can break, despite the care we take to keep them.

What is true, belongs only to me.

—Seneca

PART 2

AUSTRALIA

1947–1952

CHAPTER SEVEN

STRATFORD, 1948

They had arrived, the vastness of the land before them. Houses littered the dust like lifeless animals. Their faces were wide and open, children taking in a new world. They had no idea what they were about to do, or see, clutching their possessions to their bodies.

"Oh, Henry. My God. We're in the middle of nowhere."

Twenty miles outside of Stratford, Julia stood, wide-eyed, staring at the small white house that sat serenely on thirty acres of alternately green and arid land; land that was mostly flat and nondescript save for rows of farmhouses dotted in a line on uneven grassy parcels, bundles of tall trees and thrusts of grass decorating their sides. They all had screened windows and two wooden steps leading up to the front doors, and they seemed friendly and small, if a bit lonely in the vastness of the landscape.

When the family first arrived in Australia, they were among thousands of immigrants from war-torn countries who had come to look for work and make a better life for themselves on the country's wide open shores. It was at least a two-year indentured service, which culminated with a small parcel of land and automatic Australian citizenship. This was the new life that awaited them, 2,758 kilometers from the detention center in Bonegilla and a world away from the countries they had once called home.

POPULATE OR PERISH!

The slogan greeted them everywhere: on propaganda posters plastering shop windows and streetlamps, painted on wagons and printed on milk cartons, and it shouted out at them as they drove past in the truck that would transport them from the train station to the house that would shelter their life there. It seemed to be a noble act almost—come here and cultivate our land, and we will offer you the world. Try your hardest, and you shall be rewarded. It was a sermon of hope.

It took them over two days to get to Stratford, pitched neatly into the north-easternmost part of Australia. Tucked away amongst barren plains and borderless outskirts, it was quaint, and had quaint people.

There was a sheen to the landscape, most likely because of the arid air hovering over the dusty landscape. In the distance, cane fields dominated, standing twice as tall as the tallest man Julia had ever seen. It was more land than she could imagine having, and yet she immediately thought of her father standing next to her, his strong arms crossed over his chest and a capable glint in his eye. "You can do this," he'd say, and she would smile and lean her head on his shoulder and smell the tobacco on his clothes and the sweat on his brow.

After being in the detention center for a few months, they had learned that the Avon River snaked through Stratford, and nestled on the outskirts of the suburb of Victoria. In Victoria were the things that afforded them the convenience of a structured life: a post office, food stores, quaint little cafes, a hospital, a school, and a reliable bus service. But from where Julia stood, she may as well have been on the moon. Not much was visible—most things being farther than a ten-minute walk, westward, which would require taking the bus from the stop that lay at the end of the long path to the farmhouses.

Henry stood next to her now, and she didn't lean on him. Instead, Julia covered her mouth in shock, her feet rooted to the ground in front of this house.

"We are living *here*?" She squinted at the houses in view, and then at the one they would live in, and then her eyes widened. "Who, what... I mean... *how*?"

She turned around on herself slowly, taking in the vastness of where they were, and then back to the house.

It was timber-framed with a soft A-shaped sloping roof and shingled sides. It stood on wooden stilts (apparently protection from flooding and insects) that Slava found terribly funny ("Legs! *It has legs, Mama!*") with an outhouse to the back of it. There was nothing else; it was as basic as could be. It was very apparent that this was theirs to make into something bigger than it was.

The couple stood next to each other in silence.

"Come on," Henry encouraged. "It's our own, at least."

"Well. *Not* what I imagined." Julia's right hand made the sign of the cross in front of her chest, and then copied what Slava had said, her hands splayed out: "It has *legs!*" She pointed at the stilts underneath, that held the house a few feet off the ground. "A house on legs, Henry." She watched as he broke into a low laugh.

"I understand. But, remember how we imagined it?" He pointed at the far-right corner of the field, toward a sagging wooden fence with two chicken coops and a stable. "You could make a fine garden, I imagine. There's also space in the back as well. You'd probably have to clear it."

Julia cocked her eyebrow at him.

"*We* would clear it."

"Henry, it's a lot of work—"

"Come on. It can be good."

"You're very positive about all this."

Henry placed his hands up as if he were admiring a work of art, or gesturing at a palace that didn't exist yet, and spoke of things that he had only briefly learned in his childhood, with his father. *We can build a greenhouse there, in that far corner, and then maybe we can have a small farm, and then a garden out toward the back.*

Henry put his hand on her shoulder and felt it soften under his touch. "We have to be patient. Also, now that we're here..." and he looked down at her stomach and looked back at her, raising an eyebrow.

Julia laughed and pushed his hand off. "Oh, so *now* you see that as a good idea, do you? With everything else we have to undertake?"

He kissed her cheek, and she felt the sharpness of his cheekbones.

"Mama! Mama, Papa!" Slava was behind the house and they followed her voice. A discovery: a dark blue, rusted bicycle, as if someone was inviting them to explore.

Henry inspected the sad two-wheeled thing. The metal was still solid, but the paint had worn, and orange rust had settled on it. "Guess that's mine, for now. But we'll save some money and get a car somehow. Maybe tomorrow we can take the bus to the city and find food. See where we are, and how we do things in this new world."

Julia nodded. "We will take the bus and explore." Then she walked ahead, following Slava. "Wait for me. I'll help you up the stairs. Let's go see our new house."

That evening, Henry was gentle and attentive over dinner, however sparse it was. They were finishing the last of their rations that they had brought with them from the camp (small pieces of sausage, a half pint of milk, bread and weak tea in a tin flask) at the small wooden table in the sitting room next to the kitchen.

There were shelves behind them, and windows above the sink. There was also a kettle that boiled suspended over a wood burner, a few kerosene lamps, a few chairs, and two beds. Beyond the kitchen there were two square rooms; the footprint of the house was a tidy rectangle split into habitable parts. They ate, and sipped their tea, and Henry touched Julia's hand across the table as they spoke.

After she'd put Slava to bed, and Henry had gone to sit on the step to smoke, she went into their bedroom and sat down on the bed, their two cases at her feet. It took her a few moments to realize that the mirror leaning up against the wall was in a broken frame and had a crack right through the center, and she thought of the luxury of owning a beautiful mirror one day, one to reflect her lips in a cherry lipstick, or for her to fix her hair before she went out to see her friends. She craved staring at the familiarity of her own face and proceeded to trace it with a fingertip: the long slight arch of her forehead, the soft indentation of her temple and down to the cheekbones that had been so prominent ever since she was a child. She traced the aquiline profile of her nose, across the soft skin of her cheeks, down to her lips that had grown dry, the skin flaking. She went down the curve of her chin and then down her neck, the lines there creasing as she bent her head to the side and let her thick plait of hair fall. She began to unplait it one wave at a time, the dust from travel released from each bend, and ran her fingers through the length, finally shuddering it to life again.

* * *

The next few weeks, Julia woke early, her familiar restlessness a result of sleeping somewhere new. She would walk into the small kitchen, trying to remember where everything was: cold box, oven, plates and bowls on a narrow counter in front of a window; the steel kettle; a water flask propped up against the cupboard. It was starting to get light out, and Henry would be up soon after her. These long, strange days were a new rhythm: it seemed as if she wore a path into the floorboards of the house, but her gait was the same.

She lit the fire and put the kettle above it, fumbling in the cupboards for the tin of coffee she had bought in Stratford the day before. The bread was in the cupboard where things now lived temporarily until they found their permanent home: bags of rice, flour, barley, a jar of oatmeal, a jar of sugar, and six fresh eggs. Milk and butter, apples, bacon bones, and sausages were in the cool box by the window, and a large bowl of pea shoots, carrots, potatoes, beets, and lettuce were on the kitchen table waiting to be used for soup.

Julia moved to the cool box and took out two slices of ham from dinner a few days ago. She took them to the counter and placed them between two fresh slices of bread, wrapping the sandwich in wax paper for Henry's lunch that day. She would fill his flask with coffee and another one with water and place it all in the canvas bag by the door.

Sugar cane cutters were brutal, determined and hardy, generally working in "gangs" of six to eight, roughly fifty hours a week; days beginning at dawn and ending fourteen hours later. Gritty, unpleasant and occasionally deadly work, out in the open in all weathers, existing with snakes, rats, and other vermin that carried the risk of disease. It was hot, back-breaking work and only attractive because of the kind of money earned. Blood and sweat money. *Stoop, chop, straighten, top. Stoop, chop, straighten, top.* It was a rhythm that developed over the course of the day; hunched over in fields of green, stopping only every few hours to pause, drink from the flask of water at their hip, have a cigarette. Repeat.

And then there was the smoke: thick black sticky smoke that clung to clothes and skin like hot molasses. To get rid of snakes, rats, and trash, cane was burnt before harvesting. The sugar syrup, disintegrating from the flames, would start to ooze and bubble, making it sticky to handle; the cutters more often than not would end up being covered head to toe in soot and sweat. Some cutters wore a bracelet of flannel around their wrists to stop the sweat running down their arms into their hands. It was quite literally back-breaking work, bent in half for twelve hours a day, hacking away at the sturdy stalks of cane with heavy, hook-ended flat blades.

The more cane, the more money, and more money meant a sense of freedom that ultimately was priceless to all of them.

The kettle boiled, and she heard Henry move in the room beyond. Julia watched as plumes of smoke rose from small fires in the fields, ushering in the dawn; the horizon of cane would slowly diminish over the course of the day.

Julia's role mirrored all the other immigrant settlers that had a farm to work and a family to look after: she had tasks that were familiar to her, since she grew up on a farm. She had cows to tend to, and clothing to sew for Slava. She would cook with what they could use from the farm and from their government rations, and without the threat of war on their doorstep, she hoped that her future would be calm and without pain.

She turned and saw her husband's square frame looming in the doorway, as it would do at seven o'clock that evening, or later still, only his teeth showing through the soot on his face.

"Tea?"

He nodded. "Please." He laced his boots and prepared for the morning, a canvas bag at the door, his thin jacket on the chair. She watched him as he checked his chest pockets for cigarettes, two taps with his palm on the left, and then his hands would run through his hair briefly. She observed him as if memorizing the words of a song. Marriage felt like that.

"Henry."

"Yes?"

"Do you think we have time to...?" She strode up to him and put her hands around him, clasping them at his back, looking up at him with a smile.

And just then Slava cried out, and it broke the thought, and Julia blushed at her boldness and knew it wasn't the right time. She began to walk away. "Never mind."

He strode up to her, the steam of the kettle like a halo surrounding her, and slipped his arm around her waist, bringing her back into his embrace. She closed her eyes and smelled the warm, sweet scent of burnt sugar on his skin as she kissed him.

CHAPTER EIGHT

"Hello? What's all the fuss about? What's the noise for?" A rough voice bellowed as the door creaked open.

Julia had passed this particular house before, the one with the flowers outside the door and the large garden out the back. But she had never seen anyone, and now the voice jarred her. She couldn't judge if it was upset or teasing.

Minutes earlier, Julia had been standing at the kitchen window when she saw Slava vanish, her gray cotton shorts moving in rhythm with her white-blonde shock of hair, and then a faint giggle as she flew out of sight. Julia had been clearing lunch and, all of a sudden, she was gone. She would have to go after her, and it made her nervous: so many people worked the fields and lived in the modest houses beside her, and now, walking out by herself, shouting her daughter's name, had made her feel exposed.

She had walked out the door into the sun and muttered to herself: "Goddamn, this child will be the end of me." It felt like a sentence, having a two-year-old. She struggled knowing when to let her run free and when to snatch her by the wrist and relay her disapproval. And it had only been her acting as both parents, recently, for Henry had been absent ever since he'd started work—coming home in an absolute state, nothing left of him, his face gaunt, his hands displaying new blisters that had layered over his old, calloused ones. He had no sense of place or identity or loyalty to anything other than the fact that he was shackled to this life temporarily, and he had a bed to lay his head on. There were no conversations, no fleeting sense of contentment, no laughter or stolen moments looking up at the sky, just a few (more) cigarettes after dinner and then again before bed, and then he would sleep like a tired child, before the next morning when his whole narrative would repeat.

"Slava? Slava!" She couldn't see her. She couldn't hear her. She wiped her hands on her apron and called for her daughter again, and then suddenly she saw her appear like a sprite, with a naked chest, shining hair long around her shoulders and her shorts now filthy with dirt from the back garden of a dilapidated farmhouse down the road.

"Look at the *state* of you, you ridiculous thing!" Julia lifted up her hands in protest, and crouched down to grab her, lifting her up in her arms. "You must not run away like that. There are spiders under these houses," and she buried her face in the child's neck, blowing raspberries.

It was then that he had called out to her, as Julia stood up, her hair wild around her face, her face shining from sweat, her shirt open at the neck, exposing freckled skin. "Eh? Who's creating all this chaos?"

Julia turned around and recognized the muscular build and square features of Iliya. She smiled politely. She'd seen him before, but then again, she'd seen many of the same people in this strange cross-section of space, and she'd always kept herself to herself. She often saw him with Henry: they bantered—they worked together—and she saw both men standing together occasionally, talking about something that she didn't care to ask about.

She walked out from behind the house and stood on the dirt road that ran perpendicular, looking up at him standing in the doorway. He had light brown hair that was lighter still at the sides of his head, by his temples, and the skin on his face had browned a dark olive on his cheeks, nose, and forehead. He was leaning against the frame, holding what looked like a cane knife. She squinted up at him, not because of any brightness, but because she didn't particularly know him well and wanted to do something to effect confusion.

"Oh, hello. Iliya, yes?"

"Yes, and you're...?"

"Julia."

"Yes. Henry's wife."

"Yes. Julia," she smiled. She liked doing that, it gave her strength.

"Yes, yes. I know you, I think. You live down there." He waved his hand toward the house, ten down along the path.

"Yes. How do you—?"

"I know your husband. Everyone knows everything and everyone here, after a while." When he spoke, his mouth moved languidly, as if he wasn't in a hurry. He folded his arms.

"Ah. Yes. And you... live...?"

He moved his head, gesturing to the door. "Here. My wife is called Elina. She works at the small bookshop in Stratford."

"Oh, yes, I know her. Or, I have seen her before." Elina was tall like a reed, quiet, and held herself proudly and coolly. Beautiful gold hair like burnt honey.

Iliya turned around as if reminding himself where he was. "We have just recently arrived here, six months ago, though sometimes I think life here isn't all that better than living—" He pointed with his knife, and Julia's eyes followed the gesture, across the fields to where a faint line of sugar cane divided the sky. "—over there."

"Oh?"

"Poland. Ukraine. Still too many Russians there for my liking." He dropped his shoulders in a kind of resignation. "We all have the same stories."

"Well, that's true, yes." Her smile came quickly, and surprised her. "Anyway, sorry about the shouting. That's my daughter, Slava. She's a bit"—she didn't know why she was apologizing for her, but there it was—"too much."

"Well, we don't have children."

"Oh."

"Probably for the best." He leaned against the frame again and hooked his thumbs into his belt loops.

Julia blushed. "Ah. Well, they *are* a challenge."

"I'll take your word for it." He waved at Slava, and she stuck her tongue out. "She's quite sweet. Precocious."

Julia sensed the natural end of their banter, and used the space to gather herself, taking Slava by the hand. "Okay, well, nice to talk to you."

He nodded back to her, and moved as if to walk back into the house, and she turned to walk away. She knew he was watching her because she didn't hear the door close, and she was only mildly uncomfortable about it.

She spent the walk back to the house letting her mind wander a bit, thinking about how he had ended up there, and what he and his wife were like, behind closed doors.

"Let's go. We have to cook dinner for Papa, yes?" Her pace quickened.

That evening, after dinner, Henry was sitting with Slava on the bed, and Julia watched as he read to her, her blonde hair splayed out on his chest as she leaned against him and watched his index finger follow along the words. It was the only book she had, and it was about a mitten that had gotten lost in a forest, and each of the animals that found it tried to find shelter in the fur-lining within, until there were so many that wanted it for themselves, and the glove became too strained to contain them all, and it burst, leaving all of them to try and find homes for themselves in the cold winter.

"Papa?"

"Yes, love."

"Where they go?"

"They will find a home, Rabbit." This name for her had grown out of her habit as a baby to gum a carrot when she was teething. "Besides, they have each other to keep warm."

She buried her head into his chest, and he kissed her softly.

Julia walked off back into the kitchen and sat down, retrieving a pencil and a piece of white paper from the shelf behind her. Recently, she'd begun to forge a comfortable habit in a sort of diary written to herself, and letters that she would never send, all kept aside once they were done, maybe as a comfort to her. Tonight, she wanted to write to Maria.

My Marioshka,

I still see your face. It has never left me. Oh, how I imagined my life so differently, and without you, sometimes it doesn't make any sense. Henry is working many hours now, in the cane fields, and it is hard on him, he seems like a different man. Tired. Impatient. He smokes heavily, and his body is thin. He has started saying that he wants to build a greenhouse—a glass one—in the small square of garden out at the front of the house. And maybe that would be good for him; maybe the quiet hours doing something he loves would help him find life here. I have started a small garden in the back of the house, and we now have a small collection of chickens, as well as a few cows that we've inherited from an elderly neighbor. As for little Slava—I wish you could see her—she is two and a half now, and my love for her is deeper than anything I have ever felt. Truthfully, though, I have such sadness sometimes, and Henry finds it difficult to understand, because these are things that men cannot have time for—the luxury of feeling, I think. And yet I wish I could tell him how to help me, and maybe that would help us feel closer in some way. And maybe part of it lies in the fact that we keep trying for children and nothing seems to happen. I do hope it will, one day. The noise of children would make this life a little bit brighter, maybe. Anyway, I wanted to tell you how much I love you, and I wish so much that you were with me.

Love, Yulia

Slava padded out of the room and came over to Julia, burying her face into her skirts.

"Tired, Rabbit?"

Julia folded the letter in half, and then into a quarter, then left it resting under a cup as she brought Slava up into her arms. As she carried her into the other room, Henry walked past them to go outside. Julia placed Slava into her bed, tucked the thin sheet around her small body, and then sat down, the edge of the mattress softening under her.

"Shall we sing a lullaby?"

Slava nodded sleepily.

Julia turned the lamp down to a flicker and began to sing the notes to a song that she knew instinctively: a minor-toned, beautiful song that her mother used to sing to her, about love and beauty and death and sweetness.

> *The moon has gone,*
> *The sun is in its keep,*
> *Slava wants to sleep.*
> *Sleep my dear, sleep,*
> *Close your eyes, sweet,*

And I'll tell you a story deep.

In the bedroom there was a window, a little square one divided into four panes that looked out onto the small back garden, and though it was dark, Julia stared into the night as she sang:

> *And once there was*
> *An extraordinary war,*
> *And it lasted for many years;*
> *A cat ate the Prince*
> *A hound ate the Knight*
> *And a mouse left the Princess in*
> *   tears.*

Slava slowly fell asleep to the comforting rhythm of her mother's voice, her tones drifting with softness and care, landing delicately on the words of the song:

> *And in the end,*
> *The prince was made of chocolate,*
> *The princess was made of sugar,*
> *And the knight was made of sweet biscuit,*
> *So, none of them suffered.*

She'd just closed the door to the bedroom when she saw Henry sit down at the kitchen table and pick up the letter. "What's this?" He turned it over in his hand, a cigarette burning in the other. He started to open it.

"No, please, don't." Julia walked toward him, after leaving the dark of Slava's room, and took it out of his hands. "It's just for me."

"Oh. Why are you embarrassed by it?" He watched as her eyes revealed more than she cared to.

"It's just nothing. I wrote a letter."

"For whom?"

"For my sister. For me."

"Could you write to your parents instead? Would it make you feel better?"

"I should. But there is so much to say. Old wounds, I guess."

Henry leaned toward her, resting his face on his palm. "I have them too, you know." And then he leaned back in his chair, having laid the gift of honesty at her feet. "To this day, I wonder what would have happened to me had she still been alive." And another cigarette passed through his fingers as the old one dimmed, the metal tray full of dying embers. "Do you fear for them? What if you sent it?" he prodded.

"Yes. I fear that if I write, it would be a trail of some sort. As if, it would lead the Russians straight to their door, to their deaths." Her honesty felt like a hole in her chest that would never heal.

Henry's questions were necessary—two people should reveal their pain to the other—but it revealed her scars. She looked up at him and realized that he'd placed his hand in the middle of the table, to reach for hers, but had stopped and waited for her; he understood her pain.

Julia suddenly felt uneasy, so she stood up, shaking off the maudlin feelings as if an uncomfortable coat, and immediately started telling Henry about that day, about Slava being over-bearing and riotous, and how she had been outside most of the day, her shock of golden hair, thin as gossamer, disappearing in and amongst the wild grass and brush, like some indigenous, pale-eyed animal.

She'd told Henry that she'd been down the path and seen the other houses, after she and Slava had gone for a walk, and that she'd seen Iliya come out and say a polite hello. She asked what he knew about him.

"Ah, yes, Iliya. Good man. Keep to themselves, he and his

wife, mostly. He works with me, he's in my cutting group. Why do you ask?" Henry leaned back in his chair.

"Just curious, I guess. I see him sometimes, when I'm out with Slava. He's from Poland?"

"Yes. Lublin. They had a tough time during the deportations."

"I can imagine. We probably have such similar pasts."

"Don't know much about him, really." Henry exhaled and leaned forward to inspect a burn on his hand and a cut on his arm, both of which were difficult to see through the soot. "He's out with us most days; he does contract work on other things, I think. Contract work pays better, but you get moved all over the place." Henry laughed. "You feel sorry for him. You like stray animals."

"What? No, no. Just curious, that's all." Julia waved her hands as if brushing off the comment.

"Well, maybe we can invite them round for dinner one evening?" Henry looked over at her, a wan look crossing his face. "What do you think?" He saw that she was off in a thought. "Julia?"

"Yes?"

"Dinner? You didn't say anything."

"Oh, sorry, yes, sure. That would be nice. If you want to."

The night drew in and began the orchestra sounds of cricket-song and a child's steady breathing.

She walked softly into the bedroom, still deep in thought, and fell asleep listening to him lighting another cigarette.

CHAPTER NINE

"Why?" It was Slava's favorite word lately. *Why,* along with, *Mama.*

"We're having dinner, sertseh." *Sweetheart.*

"Why?"

Slava peered out from under a clean bedsheet in the other room, having fashioned it into a sort of limp tent hanging between the dresser drawers and the bed. Now, she proceeded to pull it off and onto her shoulders, wrapping it around her and dragging it behind her like a train. She pointed at the kitchen counter. "Chicken."

"Yes. For dinner." Julia massaged the skin with a small cube of butter, her fingers shining from it.

Slava pointed at the broom in the corner and the glasses set out on the table. "Why?" Her blue eyes were the color of the sea and they glittered mischievously.

Julia plunged her hands into a bowl of soap and water. "A nice man and a young lady are coming for dinner. A friend of Papa's."

She started peeling fresh potatoes and carrots, having rinsed off the soil from their garden. Her thoughts ran nervously over menial tasks: *Sweep the floor. Pluck the chicken. Wash the kitchen table. Tidy the rooms. Curl my hair.*

"Why?"

"Because it is nice to have people for dinner." Julia's voice grew firm to prevent any further questions, and she kept talking. "And sometimes, having people to come and visit makes me feel less lonely." She scraped the edge of the knife along the carrot and stopped. She hadn't expected to say that, but there it was.

"Mama, sad?" Slava held the sheet and walked regally, her dusty gray rabbit in her hands.

"Listen, *please* just let me do what I need to, okay?" Julia's voice was stern.

She saw Slava's face scowl at the reprimand, and she softened. "Oh, you're such a lovely nuisance, though," she said, and ran over to her daughter to grab her face and plant a kiss on her forehead. She still had a carrot in her hand and gave it to Slava. "Here, Rabbit. Now, Mama has to get busy with the dinner."

That evening, the sky turned a bitter orange, touching the flatlands farther than the eye could reach. It looked a bit like the sky Julia used to see seeping through her bedroom window. And the memories crept in as she leaned against the kitchen table and inhaled the smell of the meat crisping in the oven and the onions simmering in salty oil. The smells were *home* to her. Nothing else managed to affect her in the way that this did.

"Mama, hungry!"

She opened her eyes and started cutting the carrots into chunks. "Slava, just wait. Soon, dinner is soon." She pushed a few bits of paper and pencils across the table—a little too forcefully, to make a point—to Slava. "There. Draw. A nice picture, please."

It was evening and the sunset had passed, and the sky was black, and neither of the men had come back yet. The food was settling, warm in the oven, and the table was set with simple plates and cutlery, nothing pretty because no one could afford anything expensive and delicate.

Slava was perched on her chair, drawing circles with jagged lines all through them, talking to herself. "No! No more room in the mitten, it will break! It will break and then…"

The door squealed open. *Must oil that, what a horrible sound*, Julia thought.

And then there were three smiling figures in the doorway. Slava squealed "Papa!" and dropped her pencil and ran to the door.

"Julia, this is Iliya. Is dinner ready? Smells like you've actually gone to some effort."

Julia looked at Henry, her eyes sharp at the unnecessary comment. He smiled in response and winked. She smoothed her skirt and stood up, walked over with her thin pale hand outstretched. Now that Iliya was closer to her, she could see him more clearly: he was tall and straight, almost as tall as Henry. His face was narrow and his hair slightly wild in its curl, and his eyes were bright blue and almond-shaped, his smile genuine yet inaccessible. There were small creases by his temples and the corners of his mouth, which meant that he was older than thirty—thirty-five, maybe? His shirt hung on him disinterestedly, like crisp paper.

"Hello, Julia." He smiled and took her hand lazily, hers disappearing in his weighted grip. His eyes looked at her intensely from underneath his careless hair.

"Nice to see you again." She withdrew swiftly, cheeks flushing already.

He gestured to the woman standing beside him, very thin, with bright eyes, her honeyed hair cascading in waves onto her shoulders, the freckles on her nose moving as she smiled.

"This is my wife, Elina."

She produced a slim hand. "Hello, Julia. Thank you for having us."

"Yes, of course," Julia returned, feeling suddenly conscious of her nerves. "We don't do this often, and it's nice to meet new people." And then she excused herself, mumbling something about the dinner, and walked back toward the oven.

Henry and Iliya took their jackets off and laid them on the backs of the chairs, wiping their sooty hands on them in the process, whilst Elina took a seat and spoke to Slava animatedly.

"Are you hungry, little one?"

"Yes!"

"How old are you, then?"

Slava looked slightly confused and splayed both chubby hands out to her. "Four."

"That's a *very* grown-up lady, I think." Elina placed her head in her palm, resting her elbow on the table. "Or are you a princess?"

"I am a princess," Slava said, matter-of-factly.

Julia turned and saw Elina's face as she spoke to Slava. Was she the only one in that room that could sense her longing?

"I think you are a beautiful princess," Elina said, smiling. "Your Mama is lucky." Elina stood up, breaking herself off from the conversation. "Well, something smells delicious." She turned to Julia. "Do you need help? Because"—she gestured to the front door and the men outside with their cigarettes, chatting about their day as they waited to be served: thin arms expressive and agitated—"obviously the men are preoccupied with righting the world's wrongs."

Julia was grateful for her kind tone. "Well, isn't that always the case? Men will fix things? We all know that isn't true."

Elina laughed, and it sounded like clear water. "Yes, agreed. I think you and I understand each other."

Julia asked. "Do you have children?"

"No. Not yet, anyway." She looked over at Slava. "Maybe one day." She smiled and took the plates to the table.

"Well, in time. God has funny plans." Julia brought the knives and forks to the table.

"Iliya has other plans, maybe. War has been hard on him." Elina shrugged.

Just then, the door opened. "Right." Henry clapped his hands together. "Let's sit."

As Julia began to spoon the potatoes and carrots onto plates, Iliya spoke up: "Just a minute, I brought something," and he removed a small flask of vodka from the bag that he'd brought with him and set it on the table triumphantly. "In thanks."

"Oh, goodness." Elina groaned and put her fork down. "You and your vodka." She winked at Julia.

"And you and your controlling. Let me be."

"So serious, husband." Elina laughed. "Always very serious about the vodka." She placed a hand on his shoulder, and he bristled, but smiled regardless, and Henry interrupted.

"This is much appreciated. Let's pray that we always have such good fortune."

They all prayed in a cursory way, all hungry and impatient and discarding the "Amen" quickly so that they could keep serving themselves.

Julia reached for the vodka and sighed happily. She turned to Iliya, the glasses clinking as she moved the vodka to the center of the table. "So, what is your story, then, you two?"

She spooned out the potatoes for Slava, and then passed them to Elina, everyone's hands reaching and mingling, the food glistening on chipped plates. *Someday it would be nice to have good plates,* she thought.

"She's a curious one, Henry!" Iliya clapped his hand on Henry's shoulder like a brother.

Julia was embarrassed and instantly silenced, focusing on chicken legs and boiled carrots and carefully cutting up Slava's food. The warmth of the alcohol radiated through her.

Elina leaned over to Julia. "Don't mind him. He likes to tease." She smiled.

In between mouthfuls, Iliya and Elina provided information.

"No, we have no family anymore. I came out here from Poland, and Elina was in a school in Krakow when I met her, seems that we have similar meeting stories," he looked over at Henry. "I heard from him about how you two met."

"... Iliya was looking for work. My family made it to New York..."

"... more potatoes, please? Thank you... Yes, I had a sister, she was a twin. The other twin, a boy, died from illness when he was two... No, I don't know what he died of... Well, my sister..." Iliya hesitated and placed his fork down. "My sister and my parents were deported to the gulag. I hid in the attic of my parents' bakery. They never found me."

Henry grunted in a kind of sympathy, poured Iliya a small vodka, and looked at Julia, watching her reaction. He lit a cigarette.

"We were some of the first Polish Jews to be rounded up." Elina rested her hand on Iliya's arm. "I was in school and when it was closed down, I was enlisted to work in the ghetto, embroidering linen napkins and tablecloths for the Nazis."

"And how did you find each other?" Julia asked.

"He and I knew each other through school friends, and when I saw him one night trying to find his way to the shop for food, I took care of him for a time, before—"

"—before I was thrown into a passenger train and shipped to a sub-camp."

"Which one?"

"Plaszow."

"Plaszow wasn't one of the death camps, right?"

"No. But it may as well have been. Even on the train ride there, I saw starving bodies collapsing at my feet. It was torture."

Julia turned to Elina. "And you? Were you ever sent out of the ghetto?"

"Well, yes, of course. I thought I could hide, but they would do roll calls, and if they found me, I would have been shot on sight." She sighed heavily. "I was shipped to Soldau. And you, Julia?"

"We were at Neumarkt."

Elina nodded. "I had two school friends that ended up there. They died just before liberation."

"Mama? Mama finished. Finished!" Slava proclaimed, jarring the quiet.

"Okay, Slava, you may leave." She wiped dried potato off her daughter's cheek. And then: "If you will excuse me." Julia suddenly shot up and followed her into the bedroom, steadying herself on the dresser. Her reflection in the mirror was white, probably more so against her dark dress.

She gripped the edge of the dresser.

"Mama?"

"What's happening?" Henry called after her, exasperated.

"Nothing. I'm fine."

After Slava was asleep, Julia took her place back at the table, sitting quietly, smiling when the conversation required it. She played the good wife, piled the dishes in the sink and afterwards served *medivnik*—honeyed bread—for dessert, with bitter coffee.

"Julia?" Iliya leaned forward on his elbow, his eyes sleepy from alcohol, and yet still like a man who knew exactly where he was and what he was doing. "What's your story? How did you end up here?"

"Ah, well. Not that interesting, really."

"Iliya, stop, maybe she—"

He put up his hand. "No, I'm interested. Everyone has a story to tell." He leaned back in his chair. "And I'd like to hear this quiet creature with the dark hair."

Julia blushed and flattened her lips. Henry looked over at Iliya, and then at Julia.

Before she could speak, Henry intervened. "It's all the same, we all have the same story, Iliya: we're born into war, we live our way out of it, we have children, then we die, and hope God forgives us for our trespasses."

"Child," Julia corrected, in monotone.

"Eh?" Henry poured another vodka.

Julia smiled and shook her head, a sign for him to ignore her.

And in that silence, he may have understood, but she wasn't sure.

Julia continued: "Well, Iliya, I lived on a big farm with my family, and then my brothers were arrested..."

"They were activists," Henry interrupted, nodding.

"Weren't we all, at the time." Iliya smiled, sadly.

"Yes, well..." She continued, her eyes pricking with tears. "They were arrested, and I never saw them again, and then I left home with my sister, Maria, and then..."

"And where is she?"

"Too fragile for this earth. She became very ill."

"Ah. I'm sorry."

"The German soldiers came and rounded me up at the migrant camp. All of us that were there were put into trucks. Only the strong ones. They left the old, and the children, behind." She sighed. "And then, there I was, in Germany."

"You must have been so lost," Elina said, her voice

sounding wounded.

"I don't remember anymore. I wasn't allowed to feel anything, just survive, just get by, day to day. And then I meet Henry." Julia smiled and turned to her husband. "We had known each other back in Ukraine..."

"Never in the same circles," he interrupted, turning to Iliya, using his hands to measure the degree of difference. He immediately regretted his tone when he saw Julia wilt. "Well, we knew of each other, anyway."

Iliya nodded. Julia waited for her turn to speak, but it was Henry who continued the story for her.

"We had Slava, and then we knew that Neumarkt wasn't the place for us to raise a family, so we—well, I—decided to leave for Australia. So, here we are." He stubbed out his cigarette, the bitterness of the coffee smell mixing with the burning embers.

Iliya stared unflinchingly at Julia, his eyes bright in the glow of the lamplight, and she caught his eye, connecting only for a second, then turned back to examine a gouge in the wooden table underneath her fingers. She kept picking at the wound in the wood, scraping her nail into it, grateful for the distraction.

Elina cleared her throat awkwardly.

"Hmm." Iliya drummed his fingers lightly on the table. "What a story." He turned to Henry. "And you a traitor, eh?"

Henry flinched. "That better be a joke. I earned my way out of that hell. I didn't kill anyone."

Iliya waved a hand dismissively. "Hey, hey, calm down. I was just teasing. We all had to do what we needed to survive."

He turned to Julia again, observing her as if he were examining her, trying to figure out what to do with her, or what to say, or what she was thinking about the evening in its entirety. She wasn't sure if it was out of pity or curiosity but, either way, it made the side of her face burn without even lifting her head up. "A toast!" he suddenly said.

Henry raised his glass. "Again? What more could we celebrate?"

Julia and Elina lifted their glasses.

"To new friends." Iliya smiled broadly, looking around the table and finishing on Julia before downing his drink.

The end of the evening descended into simmering laughter and, as the glasses emptied and when the plates were cleared, Henry stood up, his chair scraping the floor.

"Well, that was plenty of food and drink, and I think this should be a ritual, maybe. Dinners like this." He looked around the table. Julia looked at Elina and smiled. "We have discovered a friendship here, in this bowl of dust." He laughed lazily and put his hands in his pockets. "We are lucky."

Iliya took his lead, and stood up, walking over to Julia. His fingers lightly touched her shoulder. "Thank you. Dinner was lovely. Chicken slightly overcooked but..." He shrugged and laughed. Julia shot him a look at the cheek of it, eyes flashing and mildly amused. Iliya laughed. "Just a joke. It was delicious, of course. As was the company."

Elina straightened in her chair and stood to pick up her coat. Iliya turned to Henry, clapping him on the shoulder. "Good to meet your family. You're a lucky man."

Henry flinched at the comment, but let it go. "I am. Yes," he responded.

Iliya reached over to the table, grabbed a remaining glass that had two fingers of vodka left in it and swallowed it all. He smelled of stale sweat, and soap, and cigarettes.

Elina walked over to Julia, her coat in her hands. "It was so lovely to meet you—can we do this again? Maybe just you and I?"

Julia touched her arm delicately. "I would like that."

· · ·

"Well, that wasn't too bad, was it?" Henry had changed into a cotton shirt and soft trousers for bed, and washed his face, and his hair was damp after he ran his hands through it.

He walked over to Julia, still dressed, sitting at the table in a daze.

"Hey." He moved her chair back with a bit of force, so that it faced him, and stood in front of her, his knees moving her legs slightly apart.

Julia looked up at him. "It was. I'm just tired."

"You look like you're thinking."

"You know me well."

"Is it because the chicken was burnt?"

"It wasn't burnt!" Julia laughed. "It was perfectly fine."

"Yes, apparently it was *delicious, of course.*" Henry mocked Iliya's tone.

"Oh, stop it." Julia smirked. Henry acted protectively when he was drunk. Some would call it jealous. "He was being nice."

"Sure he was."

"Don't be like this."

He was careless, too, when he drank.

He reached over and touched her shoulder, his hand running down the front of her shirt. "Like what?"

Julia moved his legs aside and placed hers back together sharply, annoyed. "Henry, you *know* I don't know anyone here, I am trying my best, and it was good to meet new people." Her head dropped to the side, still looking at him.

His eyes were dark. Heavy. His languid body moved confidently around her.

He leaned in toward her, his hands gripping the arms of her chair. With one hand, he fed a few buttons out of their holes, at the top of her dress. Her distractedness didn't register on his face; and how could it, as he wasn't looking at her. "Hey. I'm just protective of you." He was breathing heavily. "What's wrong with that?" He searched her eyes.

Julia knew he longed for her, but she felt like a possession in that moment. She felt uncomfortable when he acted this way, as she felt powerless. "Nothing is wrong with that. Protecting me is good. But sometimes"—Julia shrugged—"I don't need it."

He hung his head down, and then buried his face into her neck. "Come on."

He took her by the wrist, gently at first, and then firmly pulling her up from the chair, and with that momentum, guided her into the dark beyond them as she wrapped her arms around his waist, stumbling into him.

CHAPTER TEN

It was a few months later that Julia saw Iliya again, and the meeting piqued more of her curiosity.

She had taken Slava to Stratford, to the butchers, then to the park to get some ice cream, and had stopped off at the bookshop to say hello to Elina. When they'd gotten off at the stop, Slava ran off down the path ahead, her little legs carrying her farther than Julia could chase her since she was carrying two shopping bags. She saw a figure approaching her from a distance, and then recognized the voice.

"That way!" Iliya shouted, hooking his thumb to the road behind him, wagging his finger in mock admonishment, his smile bright.

"I *know*! I see her!"

Iliya was walking toward the bus stop, and as they neared each other their voices changed to a normal tone. Julia shook her head. "Why is it that you always catch me when my child is out of my control?"

He stopped a few feet away from her. "I seem to attract the wildness."

Julia rolled her eyes, then looked down the path. She saw

the flurry of blonde hair, playing, so she turned back to Iliya, who continued: "Where does she get it from, I wonder? I bet that is from you, but you choose not to reveal it to people." Iliya rolled up his sleeves. His thin blue shirt billowed in the breeze and his hair flopped to one side, revealing the side of his neck. It felt somehow provocative, that bit of skin.

Julia felt her cheeks grow warm. "You should talk."

Iliya's eyes darkened ever so slightly. "Eh? Has my wild reputation been in the wives' gossip circles?"

"That wife of yours is a saint." Julia knew more about Iliya than he realized, and maybe she had spoken out of turn just now. Elina had confided in her about how his moods would change like flipping a light switch, and how she was wary of him, yet making excuses for him as she loved him. It intrigued Julia.

"Oh, you think so, do you?" he teased with a sharpness.

It was a simple comment, but it made Julia feel for her friend. Women were taught to endure their husbands; it bothered her. She noticed now that he was carrying a rucksack, and he was close enough to her that she smelled soap, as if he'd just had a shower. "Where are you off to? How do you get to take the day off?"

Iliya paused and adjusted his bag, as if he was looking for an answer that would satisfy her. "My back, you see—it has too much pain. Today is not a day for being out there." He pointed at the hot fields beyond them. "I take the time when I need to."

Julia squinted. She'd never seen or heard him complain before. "You seem perfectly fine now."

"Oh, it's better." He adjusted the strap of his bag. "Comes and goes, really."

"Well, isn't that convenient." Julia raised an eyebrow.

"Skeptical?" Iliya snapped, and then recovered quickly.

Julia ignored it. "Well, who am I to judge? But it's not as if you're an old man. You're the same age as I am."

"Listen, I do what I want. I get by. Lucky me." He shifted his feet, marking his place confidently.

Julia turned and called to Slava, cupping her hands around her mouth, and saw her in the distance coming toward her. She put her hands on her hips and focused her attention on Iliya.

"Well, Henry doesn't get that same luxury. But we are happy. All my time is spent here, and his is spent"—she looked at the cane fields—"there. And it's enough for me."

Julia smiled, because at first, she had said this just to defend herself. But then she felt it: she meant it, and was pleased that she felt warm at the admission.

"You're a curious one." He was watching her again with that intensity, like she was under a microscope.

"In what way?"

"Dark, but light. A contradiction. Like a secret that's out in the open, meant to be discovered."

Julia laughed. "Iliya, I think the heat has gotten to your brain." Slava arrived and pulled on Julia's skirts. "Off to your business then, or wherever it is you're going. I'm to mine."

"He's a good man, your Henry." Iliya struck a match and put it to a cigarette then exhaled, walking away, dirt forming clouds at his heels.

Julia nodded. Iliya and Elina encouraged a normal and familiar energy. Playful. Open. Teasing. She felt maternal around him, but also electrified. Wary.

The following afternoon, Slava was in Marta's garden. Marta was a neighboring widow who had arrived at the settlement a year before Julia and Henry had, and had helped with Slava occasionally. She offered normalcy, and most importantly, a kitten for Slava to play with.

Julia had met Marta during a moment that divided a day into two parts: happiness and grief. Marta was an older woman, childless, who had recently become a widow. She kept to her house and sewed intricate embroidery to sell at the weekly market in Stratford. She was generous and kind, and had been beautiful once, but grief had mapped her face in soft lines. Peter, her husband, had been working in the cane fields and had suffered a devastating heart attack that killed him instantly. Henry had delivered the news to her as he'd arrived home that evening, walking over to see her. "It's Peter, Marta. I'm so sorry," he'd said, his face implying exactly what she understood to be true, and he had caught her as she collapsed in her grief. They all seemed connected now, in a kind of thin understanding of sorrow.

Julia was folding laundry, occasionally looking in the mirror, gently prodding a yellow bruise that was almost healed.

It was on her upper arm, where Henry had grabbed her one day, shoving her out of the way because he had to leave for work. He had apologized immediately after, but it had been cursory. *He is a good man, your Henry.* She winced. It had been the morning after an argument. It was fine. She was fine. Slava hadn't seen much of it, so that was a silver lining.

Julia felt swollen and tearful. So what if he took his anger and frustration out on her? It was normal. It was *normal*, she repeated to herself, stroking the yellow bruise, outlining with her finger the faint edges that had faded into new skin.

She walked into the kitchen. The burners were off, the small radio that they owned was off. The house was beautifully quiet. She opened the front door slowly and closed it behind her. She walked absentmindedly down the front steps, not entirely sure where she would walk to. She just needed some kind of escape.

She finally sat down on the bottom step, looking past the houses down the road to the end.

Was it odd to want to see Iliya? Was he even there? Probably not. She smiled at the thought of his mischievous face.

She stood up, walked farther down the road, but felt and heard silence and open sky. She felt stuck and restless. She looked back at her house, walked past it back to Marta's house, called out to Slava and watched as she ran to her, then scooped her up and attached her to her hips before walking back down the path. *Oh, just keep going. Stop being pathetic, it's not like you're doing anything wrong*, she reassured herself.

She walked to the very last house, up the one creaking step. Three knocks. Silence. She turned around. *Bad idea.* She turned back to face the door and knocked again. Nothing save for the wind through the trees beside her.

She looked to the right, and then to the left, and then rationalized that this was a friend, and she was visiting a friend, and wouldn't it be nice if she waited for that friend? Or at least brought something with her for that friend? She looked down at her empty hands and disregarded that one detail. She turned the small handle of the door and wondered if it would open for her. It did.

"Mama?" Slava asked curiously.

"Shhh," Julia replied. "We've come to see a friend."

And then she was inside, and the door quietly closed behind her, and she had walked into someone else's life that was displayed in pictures on the walls, a tattered yellow sofa that had a small woolen blanket on it, and a tin coffee pot with wildflowers in it. There was a cream wool rug on the floor, a *kilim*, with red, green, and black patterns woven into it, and there was a small, cracked mirror on the wall beside where Julia stood. She sensed a female presence in this house, for it felt known to her. Familiar. Soft.

The door swung open abruptly, and she spun around.

"Hey! What are you doing here?" Elina stood with her hand still on the door handle, a fistful of flowers in her hand, the light behind her amplifying her hair. "I thought I heard the door open—" She placed the flowers down by the door and came up to Julia, her hands dark with fresh soil. "I didn't realize it would be you." She looked at Slava standing next to Julia's legs. "Hello, little miss. Nice to see you."

Julia backed away, embarrassed. "I am so sorry; I was just looking for—"

"Me, I should hope."

"Yes, of course! I just wanted to see if there was anyone around. There are only so many loaves of bread I can bake and eggs to collect."

Elina smiled. "Of course. Tea? Come, let's sit outside." Slava ran ahead of them.

"Yes, please." Julia suddenly felt awkward, like she'd interrupted a couple's conversation. "I went for a walk and thought I would check in on you, and..." Her cheeks and neck turned scarlet as she fumbled for an excuse. "... and I thought I would look, and the door was open and, sorry! Sorry, it's an odd day, I just had no one to talk to."

"No, no, don't be silly, I understand. Do you want to come in?" And then Elina laughed as she realized what she'd said. "And, well, here you are! Well. Never mind. You're here now."

"Thank you. I'll stay for a minute."

Elina closed the door behind herself and walked past Julia to a basin of water to wash her hands. Julia sat on a wooden chair. It squeaked and settled under her. She watched as Elina walked into the house and returned with a silver kettle and two little teacups.

"Freshly boiled, with fennel leaves, if that's alright?"

Julia nodded. "Where's Iliya?"

Elina laughed. "Why would you want to know? Isn't he enough of a bore at dinner?" She turned and dried her hands. "We keep company with people who have similar stories, don't we?" She narrowed her eyes, observing. "So, what's happening. You look like a dog without its owner."

Both laughed at the sadness of that comment. Julia's back relaxed into the chair.

Elina walked over to her and sat down on the chair across from her, placing the tea on the table between them.

"I must keep an eye on the time," Julia warned, watching Slava happily wrap blades of long grass around her fingers. "Slava will be wanting her supper soon."

"Yes, of course. So. How are you, Julia?"

"Happy. Just a bit lonely sometimes, I guess."

"Ahhh, welcome to life here." Elina laughed. "We all survive the best way we can."

"The space, however, the quiet, is wonderful compared to—"

"—compared to what we've all been through?"

Julia nodded. Elina cocked her head to the side. "Well, what a God-awful comparison *that* is." They both burst out laughing again, and Elina gestured to the back of the house. "Come."

The garden was a large postage stamp of green, with two metal chairs and a rusty metal-latticed table, a wooden bench in one corner and rows of green leaves poking through the soil on one side. On the other, a little woven fence with rows of yellow and orange flowers climbing up to the top. Next to it was a tomato plant, its bright green vines and dark red globes secured to wooden posts, and across from that, a washing line with a few sheets snapping in the breeze. Julia took a deep breath and closed her eyes. It smelled of mineral and bright green and hot perfume and soap. She heard the rustle of leaves and distant brushing of long grass. It smelled of her childhood.

"Here." Elina brought the teapot and cups and sat down across from her. "It's lovely out here, isn't it?"

Julia sipped her tea. The aniseed of the fennel made her remember home. "Elina, this is wonderful. Thank you."

"For what? Tea isn't that difficult, Julia."

"No." Julia chuckled. "For being a friend without complications."

Elina rolled her eyes. "Don't be silly. We all need a friend sometimes. Isn't that how we find our strength? Leaning on others?"

Julia folded her hands in her lap, covering the bruise that she suddenly realized was exposed, her face reddening.

Elina noticed. "Don't worry." She turned away to look across at the fields, and the trees to the left of them, and not at Julia.

"Worry about what?"

She turned back. "The things you try to hide, and the things that you can't."

Julia nodded and looked away. "Life can be confusing sometimes."

"That's to be expected. Are you happy?"

"Yes. But sometimes, I want more."

"Don't we all." The sheets snapped crisply. "Children?"

Julia shifted in her seat and placed her hands in her lap. "Well, yes. Maybe a bit of everything."

Elina nodded. "Not a little too much, then."

Julia laughed. "Well, maybe I *am* asking for a lot."

Elina took a fistful of her hair and brought it up off her neck, fanning her neck with the other hand, looking at the garden. "I know that feeling. I understand it."

"Are you happy?"

"Yes. For the most part. But it's not without a certain amount of ignoring things."

"Like what?"

"Oh, it's not even something to discuss in detail, but let's just say that Iliya is tricky, has an itchy eye." Julia frowned, and Elina clarified. "He wanders."

Julia understood. "His charm."

"Quite." Elina took a spoon and dipped it in a pot of raw

honey that sat on the table, spun it around itself, and then brought it over her tea, watching as the glistening strands worked their way down into the cup.

"They are all confused in some way, I suspect. Just like us."

"Probably worse." She stirred the spoon and let it rest. "Women are incredibly strong. But we reveal our weakness to each other, not to them."

"They don't reveal a damn thing." Julia took a sip of tea and brought the cup back to the saucer. "We bring it out in them. So, it is up to us—"

"—to be strong," Elina finished for her. "Absolutely. It is one of the best things about being a woman. Perseverance and sacrifice."

She reached over and placed her hand on Julia's. "Which is why you should never feel sorry for needing friends, yes? We need one another." She removed her hand and curled it around her teacup.

A cluster of birds flew out of a tree, beating their wings against the leaves. When Elina began to speak, there was a wildness in her eyes that matched the thoughts that suddenly unraveled into the space between the two women. "I found him those many years ago, when he was lost. I saved him, and took him in, and gave him what I could. I became his mother, his sister, his lover. I was the only person he had. And yet, instead of being open with one another because of our past, it's as if we hide from each other in plain sight." She looked into Julia's eyes, her own eyes calm and even, as if she'd thought about these things her entire life and knew how to understand them. "Sometimes I feel as though I'll burst, and yet I have trained myself to let it go."

Julia felt a peculiar strength blossom in her story. "I imagine it must be difficult."

Elina leaned on her elbow, her head delicately perched in

her fingers, with a crooked smile. "It is. But we persevere. And look how strong we are."

Not long after, the women met again as it was the morning of Slava's birthday and the occasion felt like one for a coffee and something sweet, even if they could only afford corn bread.

"My goodness, she's very tall for three." Elina watched as Slava clutched a pencil, her tongue out in concentration as she drew on a piece of paper, her little body perched sweetly on the edge of the chair.

"Yes." Julia nodded, placing her hands on her lap and smoothing her skirts over her stomach, still tender. She ached for the recent loss, but when she looked over at Slava, she reminded herself to be patient. "She is tall, like Henry."

Elina wore a simple cotton dress the color of butter, and flat shoes. She always looked beautiful, despite limited options. Her hair shone, and her cheeks looked flushed and coy under her freckles. Julia envied that.

"How are you both?" It was uncommon for even close friends to ask such questions, but for them, it felt normal.

Julia explained her frustration with Henry but apologized for revealing such intimate details of their marriage. She had no one that she could trust, and over the last few months, Elina had become a confidante, friend, and advisor. The friendship had centered Julia.

Elina's thin arm reached across. "Oh, sweet Julia. I do think they are all like this, these stupid, arrogant men. Or maybe we picked the best of them. Lucky us, eh?" She smiled, but it looked more like a wince. "Listen, our men have been through so much. They have a temper. It's absolutely normal. Nothing to get upset about."

"But he has never been that way with me, at least not when

we met, *that* I'm certain of." Julia straightened in her chair. "And he can be very sweet, and he works so hard."

Elina withdrew her hand and placed it on her lap. "Well, yes, I can sense that. But war changes people. Look at Iliya."

"Can you tell me?" Julia had begun to learn more about him and was curious.

"Too much pain, in here." Elina pointed to her temple. "He gets angry often. He wants to control his life, and me, I imagine, and likes things to be a certain way. His temper is explosive. Impulsive." She shrugged. "But, like all the others, I imagine, he loves strongly."

"The past is strong in his memory then. It's a hard battle."

"Yes."

Julia nodded. "I know how he feels."

Elina cocked her head in sympathy. "Oh, Julia. We *all* have such strange beginnings. Stringing together our lives with little bits of hope."

Julia glanced at Slava, happily occupied. "Elina, can I tell you something?"

"Of course."

Julia trod carefully. She was about to reveal a weakness, and she felt somehow that it would risk something in herself.

She would remember this, in the future. She would remember how she laid herself bare, and that this could give someone power over her. But at the time, it felt right.

"I lost one."

"I don't understand."

"I... was pregnant, and then..."

Elina covered her mouth with her hand. "Oh, God, Julia. How far along?"

"Two months, I think." Julia smiled through her tears, reaching for strength. "I'm alright now."

Elina reached for her hand and squeezed it. "Does Henry know?"

"He does. *This* one."

Elina knew exactly what Julia meant, and her expression withered. "Oh, Julia. I'm so sorry. Were there many?"

"Two. He was kind when it happened. Understanding."

"You're lucky."

"Sometimes." Julia sighed. "It's never perfect, is it?" She sipped her coffee. "What about you? Have you ever—?"

Elina shook her head, looking down at her wedding band and fingering the smooth metal. "No, it's never happened. Never even stuck, so to speak. Not meant to be." She looked up. "And I had thought it would, standing in your kitchen that evening when we met. That it might."

"I remember that." Julia put her hand on top of Elina's, smiling at the memory. "But it *could,* no? Life happens in strange ways."

Elina smiled sadly. "No, I don't think it will. We've been to the doctors, and I am not sure how they can detect these kinds of things, but the doctor said it is common for the woman not to be able to carry. I suspect it's me."

The waitress came by to clear their coffees, and the women nodded a silent thank-you. She was about to speak and then thought better of it, seeing their faces.

When the waitress had gone, Elina continued, lowering her voice. "When Iliya is drunk, he reminds me as much. Says I am like a lame horse—pretty to look at, but useless." She pushed a lock of hair off her forehead and looked at Julia. "Funny, right?"

"No, Elina. That's not. That's terrible."

Elina threw up her hands. "Well, such is life. We must abide and be happy with what we've been given. Make the best of it." She winked at Julia, her standard way of protecting herself. But her eyes showed a kind of defeat.

"Maybe one day, Elina. You are young. You have plenty of time."

"I am not. Twenty-five is not young." She smoothed her hair

and brushed a lock of it behind her ear. "Anyway. You are very lucky."

"In what way?"

"It's happened once. It can easily happen again, despite the losses." Elina looked up, straight into Julia's eyes. "It *will* happen again. You will be a mother. I just know it." She looked over at Slava, her hair done in two shining braids resting on her shoulders.

"Slava, can you tell Elina what you're drawing?" Julia rested her hand on her small head.

"Heart." Slava looked up at Julia, and then Elina. "For you." She handed over the small piece of paper, a muted pink heart scrawled on it in messy, bold strokes.

"Thank you." Elina smiled, her eyes watering, and looked over at Julia. "Maybe one day."

When they parted, Julia's hands felt heavy, despite the light grip of Slava's fingers. She and Elina had secrets, *hiding in plain sight.* It emboldened her and also undid her, knowing that such strength existed in these kinds of revelations. Elina had given up her life to save someone, and she compromised who she was to create a stable life. Was that enough for her? Was any of it enough for them all? It posed a few questions for Julia that she couldn't answer.

That evening, Julia sat with Slava, her arms around her sweat-sticky, sleepy body, reading a story but not really listening to the words, her thoughts on the things that had been stirred up from the afternoon, like silt in the sea.

When Henry came home, she threaded her arms around his waist, and reached her face up to his, hoping her thoughts would settle.

CHAPTER ELEVEN

It was a month later, and Julia's knees stung from the gravel and dry grass digging into her flesh, so she slid onto her backside, finishing what she had started. She was tending to the past, positioning a small row of white stones into the shape of a cross. "I'm sorry," she whispered, as the soft ground collected under her nails.

The loss had happened early, and had been brief this time, and the pain hadn't been too great. This time Henry knew what was happening to her, though she still didn't tell him about the ones before. "Maybe we should stop trying," he had said to her, when he found her standing by the outhouse in the semi-darkness, waiting for him, leaning against the corroded wooden side.

"Maybe we should just persevere. Keep trying," she had replied, and he held her, confused as to what he could have done, or even what he could do then.

Today, in the full, hot sun of the afternoon, she needed to remember; she needed to remember in order to someday forget.

As she sat and watched Slava dart in and out of her periphery, Julia was slowly realizing that it was Slava who was teaching her—the impact of her physical and emotional presence, and her daughter's love for her was a gift that Julia was grateful for, and wanted more of. This childhood was an anchor for all of them now, and for Julia especially, and she craved to be surrounded by children, at a table full of voices, as though transporting herself back to Lviv. The way her mother's skin would smell of salt and spices and oil, the air thick with the scent of onions and mushrooms and dough and flour rising; these were the things that mothers created for their children: sensory memories that were permanently etched. And within that lay the foundation of love.

Henry came home early enough for the light to still be settling on the fields, and to have dinner with Slava, which pleased them all. They craved the smell of him, the stale sweetness of smoke like he'd been forged in a fire. That was their security.

"Papa! Papa...!" Slava tapped him incessantly on the arm, her voice almost at shouting level.

He kissed her and waved her away. "Slava, stop being so loud. What? What do you want to say that's so important, hmmm?"

"I climbed a tree!"

He splayed his hands exaggeratedly. "The whole thing?"

"The bottom!"

"Keep practicing, that's not terribly high," he teased, tousling her hair.

"Henry, don't be mean." Julia looked over at Slava now nibbling on her peas, one by one, pinching them between her fingers.

Henry looked at Julia, scowling. "What's with you today?"

Julia glared. She had two choices: she could either reply or stay silent. Her reply would be met with a withering comment, the conversation would be a cyclical battle that she would inevitably lose, and that was the dynamic that he often favored.

So, she stayed silent, as she had done lately. She didn't know what to expect when he came home, and there was no point in battling with him.

Dinner finished in silence. Julia thumbed the broken edge of a glass and Henry finished a second helping of potatoes, scraping the plate. He stepped outside for a cigarette.

"Shall I put her to bed, then?" Julia threw over her shoulder as she tidied the plates away.

Silence.

Later, she read to Slava. She made bedtime long and protracted, and she invented a story about an evil queen who put a curse on a village, and the curse was that anytime someone was unkind, they would turn into a toad. It felt good to smile.

"And then"—she wrinkled her nose and put her face in front of Slava's—"there was a village full of horrible, smelly toads!"

Slava grimaced. "Eww, Mama! How could the curse be broken?"

Julia gripped her tightly, her hands moving her silky hair off her face. "Oh, love. True love can break any curse. And true love is always the best kind." She kissed her.

Henry appeared in the doorway, his hands in his pockets. "Hit a nerve, did I?" And he disappeared again.

In half an hour, Slava was asleep, and Julia walked out of the bedroom.

"What exactly is your problem tonight?" Henry immediately challenged when he saw her. He was sitting on the couch skimming a newspaper, holding a cup of tea, milky white.

Julia placed her hands on her hips. "Well, your words hurt me sometimes."

"What? Since when did you stop having a sense of humor?"

"That's not fair. You only see the things you want to see; hear the things you want to hear." Julia sat down heavily on a chair opposite. "It's as if you only see *some* of us and I feel invisible. I imagine that you're overworked..."

Henry interrupted, raising his hand to stop her. "This makes absolutely no sense; you sound crazy."

"Well, you asked me what was wrong—"

"And I was hoping you'd say something a little bit more constructive than pointing at the ways that I'm failing you."

Julia stood up, and he motioned her to sit back down. "Please."

She remained standing.

He lit a cigarette. "You think I'm overworked."

Julia nodded.

He exhaled a plume of smoke. "Yes, how about that, then? I'm trying my best and some days are better than others, do you ever notice that? I love you, but what do you want from me?" He brought his open palms out, cigarette bobbing in the corner of his mouth. "What exactly do I have? I find pleasure in drink, in smoking, and occasionally, only *occasionally*, mind you"—he pinched the cigarette between his fingers and pointed it at her —"lying with you. And even *that* leaves something to be desired."

He delivered the words in such a measured way, it made them sting so much more. It was vicious.

Her body tensed as she stood in her spot, silent.

He continued. "You think I wanted any of this? But I'm doing the right thing, aren't I? Why can't you understand that?"

She raised her hand. She'd had enough. "I *do* understand. But as much as you need me to listen to you, I need you to listen to me, and what I want and who I am. I am equally found and lost here." Her voice was removed, as if a light had gone out of her. "How do you think I feel, being the quiet little wife married to a self-important man, sitting at home taking care of the child that he barely sees? I'm doing the right thing, aren't I?"

He stood up and walked over to her, grabbing both of her

shoulders and willing himself not to shake her. "Yes, we are both struggling, but we have it better than most. We left Germany with a promise"—he set his teeth at that word—"a *promise*, to each other, to try and build a life together, which is what we are doing. You cannot run back to the broken walls and empty rooms of your memories. This is what marriage is. *This.* It's a promise to stay."

She nodded. There was something to be said for perseverance. Elina had said that to her. It couldn't just be about love.

They went to bed that night in a separate stony silence, but eventually reached for each other and found a quiet acceptance. Of course Julia loved him, because he was her husband, but she understood that the desire she had was not for him, but for her own happiness.

The next morning, Julia got up before dawn, packing Henry's lunch and boiling two eggs and cutting fresh bread for breakfast. The smell of bitter coffee filled the room. It was up to her, she thought. Her own strength would grow in her head and be turned over and over again like dough.

His shirt crackled under the stiff cotton of his jacket as he threw it on his shoulders.

"I'm not coming home tonight." His voice had a finality in it that made her ache with apologies.

"Why?" *I've failed*, was her instant thought. And then she reprimanded herself silently. She couldn't keep doing that, it diminished her.

"The cutters' camp is easier for me to sleep in after finishing work. Plus, I may get extra time in so that I can get more money." He set about putting a small sandwich in his bag, not looking at her.

"Okay, I understand."

Slava started to rustle in the other room, murmuring half-asleep noises.

He straightened up, looking at her. "Julia, I may stay a couple days. I don't know. I just..."

"What?"

His face looked as if he would soften to her, and make amends, and tell her they should try again and forget about what had happened, and she wished he would. But he didn't. "It feels confusing right now, this"—he gestured to the space between them—"*this*, whatever it is."

She grabbed his arm and came closer. "Running away isn't the solution, Henry. Sometimes we have to try harder to see it through." He shook his head. "Is it because we haven't been able to have more children?"

"No. But maybe space is something where you and I can figure out a new way of doing things. Everyone has tricky moments."

"Sure." She stared at him.

"Besides, the more shifts I work, the more money for us."

"Gold in the dirt." It was an expression that her father had used.

He smiled weakly. "That's one way of thinking about it."

He turned on his heel and walked out of the house, his steps fading, increasing the distance between them for now. Slava woke finally, and Julia knew she would have to get on with her day. But she couldn't move. Her feet clung to the floor by the door. She was looking out toward the pink sky, watching it turn to blue, starting the book of her day. Turning the page.

"Breakfast?" Slava pulled on her wrist, delicate hands with a strong grip.

"Yes, yes."

* * *

A week had passed, and they hadn't spoken in what seemed like years. Henry stayed in the cutters' camp, the single men's refuge. It was food, and a bed, and peace, and that's all he wanted, to be removed from a home where he felt like a stranger.

When he'd arrived, the current shift of cutters was crouched in front of a row of freshly cut cane, the line of their bare chests covered in sweat and grit, dark against the bright green behind them.

He leaned his bicycle against the barrack block, its metal scraping against the wall.

"Jesus, you look like someone dragged you off the cross, ha!" An older cutter who had come from Italy was sitting on a metal chair across the large room, chain smoking. He had a scar on his tanned, thin cheek and his black hair was matted from sweat and pushed back off his forehead.

Henry bent his tall body under the doorframe as he walked in and dropped a small canvas bag on a cot. "Wife and kids driving me to drink."

The wind blew through the door, bringing with it the familiar smell of sugar smoke, mingling with the sweat and stale body odor of the men who had been living there for days, some for weeks and months. The thin wood echoed with their grumbling.

Another man, lying in the corner on a cot picking dried sugar from his nails, groaned. "Who'd have them anyway, honestly? Though, I wouldn't mind a few here and there. Your wife, the dark one, right? Very nice."

Henry's eyes flashed in response as a few other cutters walked in, laughed at hearing the tail-end of the conversation as they dropped their belongings and lit cigarettes.

"Who's this?"

"Women."

"Which one?"

"All of them." They all laughed and nodded their heads.

"Henry's one." A blond Polish man, broad and short, pointed, cigarette in hand. "She's a good one."

Henry sat down heavily. "Alright, that's enough. Do we really need to do this?" He emptied his pack onto his cot. Bread, water in a dented hipflask, some sausage, a clean shirt, cigarettes, and a deck of cards wrapped in twine. "They're exhausting."

A tall, lean Russian laughed, exposing a gold tooth at the side of his mouth. "Ah! I agree! Can't be bothered. Who has the energy? We're all barely alive here." He flexed his arms, the wiry muscle wrapped around the bone. He had a dog's body, ribs protruding. "Look! How handsome I used to be, and now I look like a stalk of wheat!"

Henry leaned back on the bed, propping himself up on his elbow. "Alive. Just."

The Italian threw an empty cigarette pack at him, teasing. "Fool, don't be so down. They're great to look at, though, not like those fat old *babushkas* that make—and eat—pies all day."

"You could always see what's on display in town, you know." The Russian winked.

The Polish man groaned. "Who has the time? We are here for long days and short nights, and every day the same."

"Listen." Henry sighed. "It's not helpful, any of this." He needed a drink. He needed to feel something more than duty, though his father's voice rang again in his head, and he would probably shake his head in disgust at the son he had raised to be what—a farmer? He was a disappointment to the man who raised him and the woman he had loved once (and did, still, he knew it). "I need to rest."

Henry closed his eyes. Another day settled and the humid night closed in, and he was sleeping next to men who were lost.

As his breath became shallow, he realized he was one of them.

* * *

One of the things, the very few things, Julia enjoyed about life there, was not being overlooked. She appreciated the beauty in the space finally: it was the space beyond the farmhouses, beyond the cane fields and flat skies where she could reach a world where her parents still were, thinking about her; being outside in the small garden, hearing the shushhh of the trees and the grass as they swayed in the cool breeze before the coming rains soaked the earth and left a sweet residue on their skin.

Julia felt that she would finally write to her parents because she'd dreamt of the day she could and forsaking all else, she needed to tell them she was okay and to know that they were somehow alright and the farm was protected. The thought of this attempt made her heart swell with the love that she hadn't let herself feel for nine years. She had so much to tell them, and much that she could not, and she wondered how long it would take for her words to reach them.

That evening, after dinner, Julia sat with Slava on her lap, her arms around her, reading her a story, but impatiently waiting for her to fall asleep so she could sit in peaceful silence and write.

"Mama, sing please?" Slava traced the freckles on Julia's arm absentmindedly, the dark hairs standing up as she went against them with her fingers.

"Yes, love." And she sang softly as she rolled her daughter's sleepy body softly into bed:

> *Dream passes by the window,*
> *And Sleep, by the light.*
> *Then Dream asks Sleep:*
> *"Where should we rest tonight?"*
> *Where the cottage is warm,*

Where the child is small,
There we will go,
And rock the child and all,
And there we will sleep,
and will sing to the child:
"Sleep, sleep, my little dove,
Gentle and mild."

"Slava? Slava..." Julia whispered softly, her voice still raspy with the remnants of the melody. Slava's eyes were closed, a halo of soft hair on her pillow.

She tiptoed toward the door, turned off the light and stood in shadow, listening to the faint, shallow breaths. She walked to the kitchen, by the small window that looked out onto the rain soaking the sugar cane, and sat down to write a letter that she would finally send.

Mama, Papa—

In the absence of you seeing my face and judging for your-
selves, I will tell you that I am the same, for the most part: I am
healthy, and I am living in Australia with my husband, Hiron-
imus Rudnick. You may remember him, as he lived in Stryi.
Papa may have known his father, Ivan.

After we left, Maria and I struggled to continue on, after
stopping in a migrant camp in Austria

Julia put the pen down. She decided, resolutely, that she would not tell them. It would be too great a burden to bear, and sometimes a lie is better.

but we made it eventually to Neumarkt. Winters were cold,
and there was not much food. It was incredibly hard. I worked
as a bookkeeper. Others were metal polishers. I didn't think I

would survive the long days. I slept three across, on the hard ground in one of the buildings. We had a woman in our group, Lina, who would pray every night, and I prayed with her.

When I met Henry, I was happy again. I did not hope to find anything like love, but it was there, and I am so grateful that we survived.

We left there after the war ended, and we are now in Australia with our daughter, Slava. You would love her immediately.

I am happy with my life, I do not want you to worry, but I do often wonder what could have been.

With love to you and Papa,

Yulia

Julia folded the finished letter but before she could find an envelope, she heard footsteps at the door, followed by a knock.

CHAPTER TWELVE

She turned around and saw Iliya. Behind him, the sky was so dark that the edges of the trees were barely visible.

She walked up to the door, held onto the doorframe and welcomed him in. "What on earth are you doing here?"

He leaned forward and caught his stance, faltering a bit. "Where's Slava?"

"What? Sleeping. It's late." She shifted on her feet.

"Hmm. Where's Henry?"

"Camp."

Iliya raised his eyebrows.

"Long story," Julia replied. She looked down at her bare feet and suddenly felt a chill.

"Argument?"

"Usual things."

Iliya nodded, running his hand through his black hair, revealing his sun-mottled forehead. Julia's smile was wide, suddenly. She appreciated the company.

"How is Elina?"

"Yes, yes, all good. She was with some girlfriends at dinner, I suspect she'll be home soon." He shrugged. "I was supposed to

meet a few of my friends as well, but I didn't, in the end. Told
her I might see Henry." He cracked his knuckles. "Much better
idea."

"Ah, well." She ran her fingertips over the edge of the door.
"Can I help you, then?"

Iliya stood tall suddenly, remembering himself. "Oh, um, I
needed something from Henry." He waited, his hands in his
pockets, filling the doorway with his height. Julia wondered if
she was supposed to invite him in.

"Ah. Well..." Julia shrugged at her husband's absence.

"No, how awkward. Sorry. I just thought that he'd be here."
And then Iliya moved a foot back off the step as if presenting an
exit, and Julia felt suddenly apologetic, so she extended the
conversation.

"Actually—"

"Yes?" He leaned forward.

"A cup of tea?"

"That'd be nice." Iliya's tanned face softened into a boyish
grin.

Julia pushed her forearm into the door and gestured for him
to come in. She smelled the alcohol on his body as he passed
by her.

"I don't suppose you have anything to eat?" He strode in
comfortably, shedding his coat onto a chair and relaxing into the
sofa. "Elina is terrible at stocking the cupboards." He finally
noticed where he was sitting and patted the cushion under him.
"This new?"

Julia struck a match and put the kettle to boil. "Henry
bought it from a small charity shop in Stratford. The one on
King Road, not far from the—"

"Shop that sells ice cream. Hmm. And he brought it home
in the...?"

"We actually managed to get a hold of a car, which was
lucky. He met a man who fixes old ones that are practically

crumbling, and he had one that constantly squeaks and leaks occasionally, and..." *Why was she justifying this to him? Nerves?* "Anyway, he had to leave the back open completely." She laughed.

When the kettle had boiled, she poured the water into the teapot and let the leaves steep, drowning them with a spoon repeatedly if they bobbed back up. She felt him staring at her.

"Car. That's nice." He lit a cigarette and she noticed that he swayed a little, despite the fact that he was sitting down. "We don't have a car. Elina prefers to spend money at the hairdresser."

Julia smiled and pictured Elina's shining hair being manipulated into waves of gold, framing her freckled face. She thought her beautiful, the light to her dark.

"The car is very useful—though the color is, well, 'muddy' is the best way to describe it." She laughed.

Three months ago, she had discovered that Henry had saved up enough money to buy them a car, and when he rattled home in it (she heard him on the road before she saw him), she'd wondered then if she had made a mistake. Not because of the car, or the color of it, but because it was a sort of an ordinary thing, a car, or maybe even a bit bourgeois, she felt. But he was proud and happy as he stepped around it and gestured for her to come out and have a look, as his arm swept across the length of it, long and wide with low seats and a profile reminiscent of a boat. "It serves its purpose, that rusty old thing."

She brought over his cup, and then sat down on the chair across from the couch, her arms folded across her chest as she let her own tea darken. There seemed to be no urgency with Iliya tonight, and the energy felt neither electric nor still.

She would later recall that nothing felt wrong about it: it was a friend whom she could talk to, and he to her; they were friends with similar pasts.

"So. Julia. What is this business with the husband?"

"Did you know that male geese hover over their nest whilst female geese sit on their eggs?"

"Eh?"

Julia threw her head back, giggling at the impulse to share this piece of useless information. "Oh, Iliya. I don't want to talk about Henry, I want to talk about useless things."

"No idea how to respond to that kind of diversion except to drink my tea and look at you strangely." Iliya winked. "You're a strange creature."

"Strange. Yes. For me it has been a strange couple of weeks, if I'm honest."

"We all have strange days here." He cocked his head toward the fields. "Some days you can go mad from the day-after-day of it all."

"But I don't mind that. My life has been *too* full of days where things have been too heavy to bear. Here, I feel calm. Silent. I just want to *be*." She sipped her hot tea and placed it back on the table. "Thing is, I love having someone to talk to." She focused on a pane of glass across the room that had a crack in it. "My burdens feel lighter when someone else listens. I'm sure you feel the same...?" Iliya was lighting a cigarette and she felt embarrassed suddenly. "Ah, I've said too much. Never mind."

She was fidgeting at the admission, her legs crossed firmly, her back pressed into the corner chair.

"No! This is of course excellent. You"—he pointed a finger at her—"need someone to talk to. And I"—he pointed to his chest—"do as well." He lit the cigarette and watched the smoke tendrils rise.

"But you have Elina."

"Elina, yes." He nodded. "She's... well." He exhaled smoke. "Everyone has their stories, no? The connection." Iliya leaned forward off the edge of his seat, toward Julia. His eyes looked heavy. "Do you understand? You, strange creature, have a story that I understand. A good connection." He leaned back again, his head resting on the back of the sofa.

He didn't apologize for the way he threw his arrogance around, and it was very much a young man's prerogative. It was so different to Henry. Henry was caring, of course, but he held his cards close, and in many ways, despite the differences in their marriage, it did influence how Julia operated as a result: she always felt aware of herself around him.

Julia stood up and walked to the window by the kitchen. "Do you think of your family often? Do you wonder about them?"

"No, not really."

"Why?" She knew why, before she asked the question.

"Because I can't do it—I can't think of them without being angry."

"I can understand that. What were they like?"

"Kind. Hard-working. Patient. My sister was deliciously funny. Silly. Long hair, the color of hay. Always messy. Big green eyes. She hated being wrong. Always liked to win. She took care of me." His voice trailed off.

"Do you remember the last time you saw her? What she looked like?"

There was silence at first, and then the sharpness of a match striking the side of its box. He lit another cigarette and inhaled deeply.

"Yes. We'd had a fight. We were children. Playing and then fighting. And then I saw fear. The last thing I saw in her face was fear. I thought she'd hide, just like me, but she didn't follow. I think I remember her telling me that she would find me." His eyes closed, as if exorcising the memory. "That was the last time I saw her."

Julia never asked Henry too much about his family. Partly because he didn't like talking about it very much in general, but mostly because she'd suspected a hidden anger that was too easily accessible if he talked about his father. He had left his father to find a better life, and now he was a father who never saw his family, despite his efforts. He didn't talk. He drank. He read. He smoked. He was rough. But he loved her, and she loved him despite knowing the darkness. She understood why he was this way, as much as she was frustrated by it, and so she kept a fair distance from those kinds of questions.

She walked back to her chair and sat down, folding her hands on her knees. "Life doesn't feel real, sometimes, I think. It feels like a collection of memories and photographs and tears. But it won't always be this way, I'm sure of it."

"Yes." He nodded. "You're probably right." And when he opened his eyes to look at her, something had changed. His face was set and his eyes rigid and focused, as if he had made a decision that Julia knew nothing about.

"Listen, it's late," Julia started, standing up. "Another day tomorrow, and may we live to see it, and the next after that."

"Hope for another day—a very good outlook, sweet Julia."

Julia blushed at the word *sweet*.

He walked toward the door. Julia didn't notice that he had left his jacket because she was peering around the corner to see if Slava's door was closed. It was ajar, and the sounds from her room were of deep, contented breathing.

When she turned around again, Iliya was leaning against the closed front door, watching her. Arms folded. "Or, maybe I could stay a bit longer." He moved comfortably, as if he were settling in. "You know, the conversation has been nice."

"Ha... oh, I suspect that we've nothing left to talk about." Julia's hands were moist, and she placed them in her pockets. "Besides, Elina will think you've gotten lost out there—" Julia gestured to the dark fields beyond them.

"I told Elina earlier that I was going to speak to Henry. She doesn't mind."

"Ah, well. I can tell him—"

"She already has one eye on you."

"What?"

"Oh, that is typical Elina. Always wary of the world around her." He pressed his palm behind him to make sure the door was shut and moved toward Julia. "She spends too much time thinking."

The room suddenly felt electric. Julia stood in the quiet, wondering if she should move, or stay still—if he would move toward her if she did. If he could hear how shallow her breathing was, and how loud her heart.

"Listen, Julia..." He walked to her slowly, as if he knew exactly what he was doing.

She folded her arms across her chest, moving away from him slightly. "Please, Iliya."

"Please what?" He stopped and smiled.

But he is beautiful, she thought, completely contradicting herself. *Is it so wrong to think that?* She couldn't catch her breath. "You're making me uncomfortable."

And then he moved to her again, echoing her, circling her, and she moved away, an awkward dance, her backing toward the wall. His palm found the wall behind her and he leaned in, his shoulder blocking her, his other hand gently on her arm, his palm warm on her skin. She was caught between fear and longing, and she wasn't sure which would win out, and she closed her eyes.

"Don't you think..." His face was inches from her own, his nose on her cheek, and he spoke to her quietly, looking down, as if sharing a secret. "... that we both share loneliness? Isn't this what it has all been about?"

"But you're my friend, Iliya." Her body suddenly felt cold, as if it weren't hers. Her voice wavered, her trust suddenly thin. She couldn't place her finger on what was happening but she felt... *guilt? Fear? Or was it attraction?* No, she knew what it was like to want a man, and this was not it.

She opened her eyes and looked at him: his eyes creased at the corners as he smiled, his face purposeful as he looked at her, examined her, his grip firmer on her arm now. She felt nervous. "Please." It felt wrong, but she started convincing herself that he was just being a silly man, taking advantage that she invited him in. *My fault.* So in her confusion, she couldn't find the words despite feeling them all rattling inside her head all at once. All she could say was *please.* And she also wanted to say *stop.*

"Friends give each other what the other needs, surely." His breath smelled of sweet alcohol and the bitter burn of stale cigarettes.

When Julia tried to turn her head and finally said *no*, he held her jaw in place with a wide, calloused hand, thumbs like a vice, and covered her open mouth with his own, the hard metal *clink* of his belt buckle the only sound in the room. She closed her eyes tightly, and a tear fell. *No, no* echoed in her head.

CHAPTER THIRTEEN

STRATFORD, 1949

It was the next evening that Henry finally came home.

The day had felt like a month as she remembered every detail of what had happened twenty-four hours earlier.

She had thought of Henry immediately after Iliya had left, she thought of Henry as she pulled her dress on while choking back tears, and she thought of him as she barely slept that night tucking her legs into her chest like a child, and as the sun rose the next morning and shed its milky light on the house and the quiet garden, she thought of him still.

She had made Slava breakfast, had taken her to play in the park by the river and later that afternoon back at the house, she placed the dirt-stained clothes in a tub of soap and water to soak and heated some water for the bath, so that she could clean her little body as she was covered in sand and crumbs and sticky stains of ice cream. She'd made dinner, scraping the skin and earth off some freshly collected potatoes, read a story—all with a kind of distant banality, as she thought of Henry.

All she wished was to see his face, to remember who she was.

Slava was finally asleep. The house was quiet. Julia looked

down at her hands: they were thin. Pale. Her nails were worn to the quick and had dirt under them, her skin was dry. Her dinner sat, untouched, and she stared at the door.

There was no feeling of sadness, or happiness, just a stillness.

She waited for, and feared, Henry's shadow to fill the space. She imagined his body gliding off his bicycle in the semi-darkness, walking up the path toward the door. The door that she never had fixed, in the end. The sound of its squeal rattled her now; it felt like a scar. She touched her face. It was still there, she realized, and she stood up, walking to the bedroom to peer at her reflection in the small round mirror on the dresser. Her face was pale, and her hair had lost its wave and sat lifeless at her back. Her lip was swollen and there was a red, angry cut on her jaw. She moved in the lamplight and pinched her cheeks and bit her lips to bring the color back. She opened the drawer at her fingertips and found a powder compact, hardly used, and dabbed on a bit of powder, camouflaging the red mark. She practiced a smile. *Hello, Henry,* she imagined saying when he came back eventually. *Things have been as they should be.*

And then she heard it. The gravel shifted and crunched outside. She walked back to the kitchen and stood in the middle of the room, waiting.

His slow footsteps passed by the door, to the side of the house. She turned her head slightly as she listened to the familiar sound as he walked into the garden to clean his hands in the washbasin there. She heard the water slosh delicately, heard him clear his throat. She heard the scrape of the match and smelled the cigarette smoke. She sat down at the table.

He opened the door and her chest felt suddenly tight, as if she were underwater. She breathed slowly, methodically; her eyes suddenly wet. She wiped them quickly with her palm before he could notice.

He dried his hands on his shirt, removed his jacket, and left it on the couch as he walked over to the table, sitting down in front of the plate of food. He prodded it; it was cold. He looked at Julia.

"Thank you." He rolled up his sleeves. "It's nice to be back. We needed the time, I think."

Julia nodded and smiled.

He looked at the plate. "Oh, wait. Is this yours? Have you eaten?"

She stared at his face, searching his eyes. She smiled, stiffly. *No need to tell him.* "No."

"Why not?"

It's okay not to tell him. "Not hungry."

Henry frowned. "Oh. Why not?"

He will be happier not knowing. "Because I wasn't hungry," she snapped back, instantly regretting it. "Sorry, I'm just tired. I missed you."

"It's okay. I'm only asking. You seem bothered."

"I know. I just... it's hard, sometimes."

"What's hard?" Henry was tired, hungry, and now confused.

"I don't know." Julia shook her head as if to wake herself. "Never mind."

He picked up the fork and started to eat. "I can still eat this, though. Is that alright? Is there any more?"

"Yes."

"Okay. Thank you." He narrowed his eyes. "Are you sure you're okay?"

Julia sighed. "Yes. Yes, I'm fine." Each word was a lie. Each word felt painful as it drifted out of her mouth.

She looked down at the table as he ate, every once in a while looking up, and his glance would meet hers, and he would offer a smile, and she in return, and that was their communication. She preferred it to too many words.

When he finished and walked outside to check on the

progress of the greenhouse and the new orchids that he had planted she followed him, hovering a few feet away until he noticed her. He turned around.

"Julia?"

"Henry, I..." She clasped her hands together in front of her skirt, squeezing tightly. She squeezed harder, the blood draining from her fingertips. She just needed the strength to tell him, to tell him everything that sat in a ball at the base of her throat. "I just... I wanted to tell you that..."

He waited, the quiet of the dark behind him, the ember of his cigarette glowing like a star.

"... that I was sorry," she continued.

It was only part of the truth. It was all she would say for now.

He stamped out his cigarette and walked over to her, confused, but assumed it was an admission of her mood. Henry knew her to be like this occasionally: lost in her thoughts, prone to too much thinking, finding her own stillness and strength.

"Hey, hey." He put his arms around her, his warm body enveloping hers. She smelled the smoke clinging to his clothes. She began to cry silently, the girl with skin so soft and bones so delicate, folded into the arms of a man who loved her. "Don't worry. I know things are difficult right now. We'll be alright." He leaned back to look at her closely, pushing her hair back off her face.

That's when he saw it.

"Hey, what's this?" He ran a fingertip over her jaw.

Julia covered it with her hand. "Oh, that's Slava being a tornado again." She smiled painfully. "Ran straight into me. Fell headfirst into me as I sat with her in the garden."

"Hmm." Henry let her hair fall back over her hand that still rested on her face. "Love can be a bit violent." He smiled and laughed softly.

Julia leaned back into his arms and closed her eyes, her heart tightening like a fist.

CHAPTER FOURTEEN

When she remembered that night, the memories rushed at her like knives, scattered and sharp and searching for weakness. She fought to forget, but the more she fought the more they pressed into her: she felt and saw him everywhere. And that was her prolonged punishment, though the physical effects had worn off.

Already a month had passed in painful, crawling minutes. The unfortunate result of harboring a secret is that it forces you to pay attention to the details; you are forced to remember how you were *before*, and then how you were *after*, and these two worlds had entirely different colors and shapes, and even tastes. The way Henry touched her felt different, the food she ate was tasteless and, occasionally, she didn't eat at all.

Julia floated in a kind of wan acceptance of her life in these two states of being, but then a silent irrational anger wishing that her husband had never existed would suddenly erupt in absolute clarity. *None of this is Henry's fault,* she had to remind herself.

She tried to seek solace in the mundane. At the very end of the road they lived on, past all the houses, there was a small, winding path that rose up to a main dirt road that cars and buses would use to get into the main town of Stratford. She walked with Slava to the bus stop and took her into town—seven stops, like always, and seven stops back. She would visit the butcher and distantly ask for a five-inch square of meat that bled onto the parchment. She took Slava to the park to feel the breezes off the river on their faces. She would smile coolly at women who had bright red lips and delicate hats and dresses, and she would adjust her skirts and pat down her shirt, glancing at Slava to see if she'd tied her hair back properly, for beautiful hair displayed a certain kind of status (of which they had none). She watched, removed, as the days passed on their parcel of land, hours and minutes marked by mealtimes, sleep, sunrises, and sunsets, and she healed ever so slowly, and reached for a strength that she had been gifted by her own mother. It was getting warmer, and she was desperate for a change in season that marked more distance from a day in July that had brought her so much shame.

* * *

"Hey, is that mine?" As Henry packed his bag for work, he glanced up and saw her as she stood watching him, as if behind glass, her hands gripping a cup of coffee. "You look tired. Dazed."

They'd slept together a few times since he'd arrived back, and he noticed a sadness in the way she kissed him, or a confusion, almost. But she'd not been sleeping well, and he assumed she was also still annoyed about the fact that he'd been away so long.

She blinked and forced herself to focus. "I was thinking of taking Slava to the river today. For a picnic. Sit on the banks and relax for a bit."

"Sounds good." He zipped up his rucksack and looked up.

"Are you sure you want to do that?" He squinted. "It'll be warm out today."

"Just tired. I feel fine otherwise." She sipped his coffee absentmindedly.

He grabbed the coffee out of her hands. "If *that*'s 'fine', I'd hate to see what 'ill' looks like." He gulped a mouthful. "Thanks for drinking my coffee, by the way."

He handed it back, then left quickly, jumping on his bicycle for the long ride into work.

"Mama." Slava padded out into the kitchen in her thin nightdress, soft hair matted by sleep.

"Hey!" Julia crouched down to her daughter's height. "We need to pack some things with us because we're taking the bus to the river for an adventure today."

"Mama, will we see ducks? Can we feed them?"

"Sure, love."

After breakfast, Julia picked a few of Henry's shirts and trousers off the washboard and wrung them out in the sunlight, pinning them to the line stretching horizontally across the garden, and attached to two wooden posts. Then she dressed Slava in a light cotton dress that she had sewed a little while ago, a thick pinafore that always survived play, a hat, shoes, and enough bits of food in the straw bag for the journey.

At the bus stop they waited expectantly, pleased at how soon the bus arrived. It was a beige-painted vehicle, with convenient pram hooks for mothers with children to board without issue.

All sorted, they settled into the generous leather seats— Slava by the window, Julia beside. Slava liked to play a game called "What Is That?" and "Who Are Those People?", the result of a curious education of sorts: travelling so much and so often, her young mind was now conditioned to make an adventure of it all, a game.

As soon as the bus jerked and rumbled to a start and the dust rose around them, Julia felt herself go cold and her forehead dampen in mild panic. *I forgot something.* She looked around her, patting the pockets of her dress. She looked in her bag. *Tissues, money, sweets, lipstick, food. That's it, yes?* She looked at Slava, who was now kneeling, clinging to the seat and peering over at the gentleman behind her. She scanned her little body. *Her hair is tied back, she has the clothes that she needs.* Yet Julia still had a knot, a subtle dread, like she'd left something behind, though maybe it was exhaustion. Distraction. It unnerved her.

"Sit down, Slava. Seats are for bottoms, not for feet." Distracted, she held Slava's arm too tightly, her sudden frustration making her react to everything.

The bus lurched over rough patches of gravel, making everyone on the bus grab their stomachs. "Oh, honestly this is very unpleasant. My breakfast feels like it's swimming."

Slava erupted in giggles. And then: "Oh, Mama. I'm hungry, Mama. Do you have anything to eat?"

Julia rummaged through her bag and found some water crackers. She took one for herself and gave a few to Slava. Her stomach ached.

After what felt like a year-long trip (it was forty-five minutes, but, oh, how they dragged on), the wheels squealed to a stop, and everyone stood up, grabbing various coats and cardigans and bags.

Slava raced ahead and stood at the front excitedly. "Mama! We're here! Let's go, let's go! Mama!" The sun was bright in the sky and the air smelled sweet. Julia smiled. She needed this.

And then she felt a strange lurch in her stomach again, only this time it wasn't from the bus ride, and suddenly her food was rising in an uncontrollable tide. The vomit came embarrassingly quickly, right between her feet. She bowed her head partly in shame and partly to make sure her dress wouldn't stain.

Slava looked on, mouth agape. "Oh, no..."

Julia felt a hand on her shoulder; it felt like a man's. "You alright, madam?"

"Oh, sorry. I'm so sorry." She didn't dare look up and see the faces watching her in disgust. She stared at the ground, the glistening, vulgar patch in front of her framed by pale red dust. Wiping her hand across her lips, and then on her skirt, she walked around the mess and pulled Slava's entire body up and over it, making no eye contact, and walking ahead.

I've forgotten something.

It lingered, that thought.

They saw the river glistening through the slender trees that were planted along its length. The road they walked on was busy with people and cars, but manageable. It was an easy walk —ten minutes, with clearly marked signs saying where the park was. The banks were lined not only with trees, but also flat grassy patches dotted with benches all along the way: it was the perfect spot for the two of them to burn away the hours of the day.

"Here!" Slava picked a spot next to another family: a husband and wife and a small baby. They looked wealthy, in the sense that their clothes were pressed and cut in a clean and modern way, the jewelry tasteful and the baby looking immaculate.

Julia nodded a quiet hello and then looked down at her own dress, which she had sewn for herself from a pattern she had found in something called *Australian Home Journal*. The magazine displayed drawings of slim women with carefully coiffed hair and long eyelashes, wearing perfectly acceptable dresses that every woman should have. Julia's was in a light blue cotton with a pattern of small red rosebuds, tied at the waist, with cuffed sleeves leading up to a v-shaped neckline. In comparison to the other woman, it was plain, and Julia paused, thinking to continue to another spot.

When the couple nodded back but turned away mumbling something about "another immigrant," her mind was made up, and she pulled on Slava's hand, urging her daughter away.

The grass stretched along the length of the river like a green ribbon, people dotted on and around it on days similar to theirs, she imagined. They placed their belongings on another spot that Slava picked, and settled for the day.

Julia took her shoes off, watching Slava run up ahead to the playground. She leaned back on her elbows, looked up at the sky, and let herself heal. And, slowly, her need to remember dissipated, and her breath languished in a stillness.

* * *

"Oh God, not again."

It was two days later, and Julia was walking past the pavilion in the park, watching Slava eat ice cream, when the nausea hit her. She doubled over, clutching her stomach, hoping no one would notice. People walked by, and it was busy, which hopefully meant that she could be inconspicuous as she ran over to a tree, the vomit spilling from her mouth and hitting its base.

Slava was watching, distractedly.

"Wait a minute, Slava. Just wait there, I'm not feeling well." She gestured weakly with a hand, the other one propping herself up.

She looked up at the sky. It was blue. Irritatingly blue and perfect and serene. *What the hell is going on?* she thought, distractedly watching as Slava stood knock-kneed, ice cream dripping down her fingers. Julia felt her forehead: it was cold and hot at the same time. She hadn't eaten anything that morning, so she couldn't understand why her stomach had tried to empty itself.

She looked over and saw a woman walking past the pavilion. She had on a straw hat and sunglasses, white gloves, and a dress that looked expensive, the silky floral-patterned fabric resting importantly over her pregnant belly. She was beautiful and walked ever so lightly in her ladylike navy heels. A silk dress would feel lovely on her skin, and Julia imagined it would be cool to the touch and catch the breeze easily.

And then a curious thing happened: that understanding and admission when something that had been forgotten is suddenly remembered, when breath becomes fast and shallow. Julia knew exactly what it was, because it had happened to her too many times before.

She had been too distracted recently to notice, but now was feverishly recounting the times that she'd slept with Henry, and then the time with Iliya, and oh God, it all became too much for her to keep her balance.

She sat down on a clean patch of grass and spent the next hour watching Slava only casually, as she tried to understand what it was that was happening to her.

"I'm so sorry." She looked down, her eyes focusing on the dark blue cotton of the dress resting on the part of her that held the truth.

Slava sat down next to her and put her head on her shoulder.

Julia blotted her swollen eyes, the redness increasingly fading. "Oh, Slava, I really don't feel well. My head hurts, my stomach is funny, my heart"—she stopped short of saying *my heart hurts*, as Slava would have picked up on that as a bit more serious—"my heart is filled with happiness that you had your ice cream and now it's all over your dress and your face!" She distracted her daughter with disproportionate joy and laughter through the tears. Slava erupted into giggles. In a daze, Julia reached for her and placed her on her lap. She looked at her ruddy cheeks, leaner than they were when she was a baby, her blue eyes shining, expectant, for something magical.

Maybe there is a reason for all this. And who's to say it will survive, anyway. But maybe it will.

"Right." She wobbled her legs underneath Slava and she pitched to the side, rolling over in a squeal. "I think we should probably go home." She started to walk, slowly, waiting for Slava to catch up. She felt like walking for miles. She didn't want to go home—not out of fear, but out of a pure desire to make something unknown more solid, more understandable. She watched people pass her by as she held onto her daughter, and as she saw them she thought that everyone had their own thoughts in their head that others would never know, and she thought that it might be for the best that certain truths are left unspoken for a time. And immediately after she resolved that *that* was the way to think, she asked Slava what her favorite flavor of ice cream was, and what she would like for dinner, and then she told her she loved her as they boarded the bus home.

What had been then was a lifetime ago, Julia thought as she briskly pulled up fistfuls of weeds by the front door as she left the house that evening. When she looked down, she smiled with a sadness that had never entirely dissipated, even after all these years: she was wearing Maria's shoes that day. A memory of love, of sisterhood. Julia kissed the tips of her fingers and patted the faded leather. "You would like it here, Marioshka," she whispered, and turned toward the open sky, her cheeks reddening in the thin sunlight.

The smoke from burning cane sugar billowed in thick gusts that blew across the horizon whilst Julia walked, her thin shirt rising gently with the breeze. In the pocket of her skirts, her mother's rosary rattled softly. She felt comfort in knowing that as soon as the black clouds turned to gray and then white, Henry would be home shortly thereafter, and his lips would taste of burnt sugar and his handsome, lean face would have a dusting of soot.

Slava had been napping when Julia left, her small, hot body tangled in the bedsheets in the room where she'd now lived for the last two years.

The starlings were murmuring in the sky above the green and yellow fields as she proceeded toward the wooden fence at the perimeter of the house, a basket by her side, the small front garden shrinking in the distance behind her. In the past, there would have been four of them—she and her siblings—all in fields like these, crisp wheat crushed flat under their bodies as they lay and observed the sky. Now, only Julia remained with the memory.

She was soon passing Iliya and Elina's house. She knew Iliya was working in the fields with Henry, and Elina was finishing her day at the bookshop. Julia reminded herself that she would need to see her soon.

Julia walked to the pens, the cows like curious children, waiting on the pasture right in front of her. *Ck ck*—her tongue rolled at the back of her mouth and clicked against her back teeth. Fresh milk was a comfort that she'd had as a child: it was warm and sweet and thick, and she still craved it daily. *Ck ck ck* and, one by one, they looked up, shivering and swatting tails, lowing their greeting. "Eh, eh, eyyy," Julia murmured to a brown heifer with white socks and a white star on her forehead. She patted its flank. "My beauty," she whispered, burying her head into its neck.

"Look at the way they listen to you." Henry spoke from behind her, his voice gravelly, as he watched Julia, the cows moving toward his wife as she stood by them.

Julia looked around, surprised. Her husband was standing

on the dusty road behind her, his bicycle with its quiet tires balanced by his side.

"Hey! Wasn't expecting you." Julia smiled, standing up to greet him, her feet nervously knocking into the empty milk pail by her side. His presence had always unsettled her, and now, it was because she so needed to speak to him.

"A welcome surprise?" Henry lit a cigarette, his lean body curved as the flame sputtered, then straightening as he looked across at her. He was dashing, she thought, the afternoon light settling around him, his hair dark, his thick lips parting in a wide smile. *I owe you the truth,* she thought. But at his smile, the impulse vanished.

"Of course, it is." Her cheeks rose as she smiled. "Better than a kick in the knee, my Baba used to say." They both laughed.

"I see you're busy with company."

"My friends, all of them!" Julia replied, a smile lighting her face as she spread out her arms. "They keep me very entertained." She wiped an arm across her brow.

Henry laughed, and then a sooty cough caught his throat. "I think you're the one that keeps them entertained."

Julia sat down carefully on a bale of hay, gathering her skirts, watching as Henry hovered around the animals. He patted the brown flank of one of the cows. "Slava alright?" He looked back at the house in the distance.

"She needed a little rest. She ran me ragged today." She wondered if he was scanning her face.

She wondered if he knew already.

"Ah, well. Takes after her father." He walked over to her and sat down next to her, the hay bale sagging under his weight.

"Strange, isn't it." The smoke curled around him and hovered as he spoke.

"What?"

"Us. Here."

"Oh, I don't know." She looked at him. "Feels familiar."

"What does?"

She gestured at their bodies, sitting so close. "This."

He smiled and exhaled smoke, placing a hand on her leg. "We've only been here a short while." He straightened his shoulders. "But maybe it's because we no longer have fear in our shadow."

"Yes, no more looking over our shoulders." Julia sighed. "No more pain."

Henry coughed and looked down at his scarred hands. "I feel very old for my years. And we may always be looking over our shoulders, I have a feeling." He ran his fingers through his hair and left his hand resting on his head. "I just want this feeling to leave me."

Julia glanced at him and her breath caught. "What feeling?"

"Like there will always be yet another thing. Another worry." He looked squarely at Julia. "Unsettling."

"Maybe you will always feel that way, in one way or another." Julia looked at his profile. He was noble, his face sharp and contemplative, but the shadows under his eyes had defined him for as long as she'd known him. "Your father?" she whispered.

Henry nodded, looking down. "It's the past. It should stay in the past."

"Ah, well. That's the shame, Hironimus. Ghosts don't pay attention to time."

Henry stretched his head back, breathing deeply, releasing the spirit of his father. The skies were darkening, and the smoke had cleared into a thin veil, exposing a thin line of muted orange as the sun set.

"I feel safe here." Julia folded her arms across her chest and nodded, looking across and seeing the quiet houses lit with a faint glow, just like theirs, small and insignificant in the distance, underneath the blanket of the Australian sky. "Maybe the ground won't move under my feet again." She took off Maria's shoes and dug her toes into the dirt. "It feels good."

She was trying to convince herself; she was trying to hide a secret, and it was imperceptible even to her own husband.

"We are too small for it." Henry nodded. "Our little lives."

"This big, what they call 'dust bowl'." She leaned against him, her small body fitting into the crook of his side, a puzzle piece. "But I think I understand it now."

"Understand what, exactly? The dust on our faces?"

"Yes. The dust. The reason. Why we are here." Julia pointed at their house. "I mean, we have Slava, and we have time now. And, hopefully, well"—she pushed her elbow into his arm gently—"we can still create a life here."

"Ah. I see where this is going." Henry looked at the sky with a wry smile and felt for Julia's hand. "Do you still want more?"

Julia hung her head, placing her palm on her stomach and running it across gently.

Henry's eyes rested on her face. "What if it doesn't work again?"

Julia placed a hand on his arm and looked at him resolutely. "But what if it *does* work? And then we'll look back and realize that some broken things just need a bit more time to fix." She shrugged, smiling. She felt hurt, and confused, and yet here was a man who loved her, who stood by her.

Now. I will tell him now.

She stood up and moved in front of him, putting her hands on his shoulders. "Henry..." She paused, holding her breath. And then told him the truth. The truth about where she was now, and not about what the past had done to her. "I'm pregnant."

The words came out quickly and unceremoniously, and she looked over his shoulder at the fields behind him. Sometimes not seeing someone's face softened the news; made it less traumatic, more manageable. She turned her face back to look at him.

"Okay." He stood up and put his hands in his pockets, his cigarette firmly in the corner of his mouth. He scanned her face hesitantly for confirmation. "You're sure."

"Well, I've been really ill the past week." She sighed. "And then today I realized that I hadn't bled for a month or so..." She drifted off, hating that she couldn't give him any more of an explanation. Men liked a reason. A solution. She had neither.

"Well, then." He ran his fingers through his hair tentatively. His voice was charged. "What about a doctor? Why don't you just confirm it with a doctor before you worry? Or celebrate. We have lost before, so..."

"Yes, but what if? What if I really am?" She scratched her head absentmindedly and shrugged.

He leaned forward and brought his large square hand to the side of her face, stroking it quietly. "It means we have to have more chickens. And more celebratory dinners with friends, to share the good news." He put his arm around her and stamped out his cigarette. "You act as if this is terrible. We are not broken. You are not broken." He squeezed her to his side.

"*You* look broken, though." Julia laughed. "Broken and thin, like a scarecrow."

"Well, then. That's probably because I am desperate for some food."

"Honestly, Henry, I have no idea how we keep surviving this life."

"I don't think it's a good idea to count our blessings yet. It feels like only last week that we were in Germany, praying for miracles." Henry sighed. "And yet, here we are. With a miracle."

Julia nodded. "Come, let's go back. Our memories are the making of us, it seems. Besides, it's time to wake up Slava."

They walked back together, and Julia felt for his hand,

lacing her fingers through his. The last hint of sun left the sky, and the animals slowly settled their warm bodies close to one another, quiet secrets between them.

* * *

When the house was quiet that evening and everyone slept, Julia watched from the small window by their bed, as the dull orange glow of the fires in the fields that day died out. It reminded her of the gold icons of Ukrainian churches: glistening gilt portraits, melancholy and silent, glowing as if lit from within. A mile's walk from the farm in Lviv, there was a church full of them. The church was wooden, held together without a single nail, like a puzzle of architecture. It had three carved, tall wooden pillars that to her, as a little girl, felt like they could possibly be the gates to heaven. She felt small in that church, yet never lonely. She remembered the heaviness of the incense surrounding her; clouds of it emanating from hidden corners. The icons would wink through the smoke, watching her, smiling benevolently at her. The murmurs and chants of solemn prayers would fill the small space and vibrate through her body as she prayed.

She heard Henry's footsteps come up behind her. He positioned himself beside her and put his hand on her stomach tenderly.

"Listen. It won't be easy."

"I know." She nodded, wishing she could say more.

CHAPTER FIFTEEN

Julia spent the better part of the morning doubled over in the outhouse, her face flushed, expelling bile as she hadn't eaten yet. She'd deposited Slava clutching a battered toy at Marta's and then slipped away quickly, walking back to the house willing herself to keep the contents of her stomach inside her. *You look absolutely awful,* Marta had said to her as she waved her thanks and left her holding Slava's hand.

Julia took the bus into Stratford. Her handbag contained her identity card, some money, an apple, and tissues. The bus clattered ungracefully along the road as she looked out the window, not having any inkling as to what she would do when she arrived at the hospital.

The bus slowed its approach and positioned itself outside the main doors of an imposingly tall brick building, with a white wooden porch wrapped around it. There were a few nurses standing outside smoking, their crisp white uniforms like paper cutouts against the red of the facade.

Julia walked in, clutching her handbag too tightly, her heels too loud against the floor.

"Hello, can I help you, madam?" The woman at the desk

had a friendly round face, glasses slightly too big, making her appearance entirely more approachable than her tone.

"Yes, I would like to see a doctor, please."

"Why, exactly? What's the problem?"

"Oh, well, I think I may be pregnant."

"Alright, please have a seat." The woman handed her a piece of paper and a pen. "Fill this out, will you? And give it back to me."

When her name was eventually called, she walked in, was handed a cup with a lid on it, went to the bathroom, came back out and handed the nurse the yellow liquid. And then she walked back out in the dust, waiting for someone to confirm or deny what she knew almost positively to be true.

"Oh, look, nice to see you here," Julia heard him say. She immediately recognized the voice and her heart sank as if into ice water.

She was standing, waiting for the bus and checking her watch, steadying herself by staring at a point on the ground. When he spoke, she looked up and there they were: he and Elina, her arm through his, walking toward her. Her instinct was to run, but to where? Her face lost its color. She needed to go home, and it would look highly odd for her to leave suddenly as they approached. Besides, the people waiting alongside her had already heard Iliya address her, so she kept up the facade and parted her lips into a welcoming smile.

They stopped next to her, and Elina leaned forward to place a kiss on both cheeks. "Julia, how lovely to see you here. Where are you off to?"

Julia smiled, her insides in knots. "Oh, just home. Needed to do a bit of shopping."

Iliya leaned in. "What, no hello for me?" He kissed her on the cheek, offering a wide smile and a wink. He pulled out a packet of cigarettes. They were fresh. There was a black line of dirt under the tips of his nails.

Elina's eyes searched her husband's face, and then glanced at the bag near Julia's feet.

"Didn't come away with much, then?"

Julia's cheeks reddened. "Oh, no, I needed... well, it was just..." She watched as Elina studied her, and Julia panicked. "I was at the doctor."

"Oh, dear, I hope nothing serious." Elina's eyes widened. Iliya smoked and listened calmly.

"No, of course not. Just a cold." Julia moved the wave of her hair closer to her jaw, covering the fresh pink scar.

"Well, let me know if you need anything, of course." Elina placed a hand on her shoulder.

"Yes, anything at all." Iliya nodded, another smile appearing behind the veil of smoke. To everyone else he looked charming, rakish and handsome.

Julia nodded uncomfortably. And Elina looked at him, and then at Julia, her lips pursed.

"Haven't seen Henry in a while, since I moved to another group. Shame. More money for me, though." As he inhaled, he looked at her as if examining a statue, and then slowly let the smoke dissipate in her direction. "Maybe I should invite myself to dinner soon." He smiled, and she felt her stomach turn.

"I thought you went to see Henry just the other night." Elina looked at him, adjusting the handbag on her arm.

"Oh, well, yes, but such a short meeting," he replied, directly at Elina, and then looked over at Julia. "We should all do dinner soon." They both looked at Julia, and it took every ounce of her frayed energy to respond with, "Yes, of course, that would be nice." Her stomach lurched again and she swallowed hard.

A woman tapped her on the shoulder suddenly, and Julia

very nearly jumped out of her skin. "The bus just pulled up, ma'am."

Julia turned back to Iliya and Elina, waved goodbye, and boarded. She saw that the smile was still on his lips as he turned with Elina and walked on. Julia wondered if she feared him, or for her friendship with Elina, or the revelation of the truth. Or all three.

* * *

Seven days passed, and then ten, and then sixteen. And in that period, everything felt as if nothing had changed, apart from the fact that Julia began smoking her husband's cigarettes, the tobacco fibers constantly on the tip of her tongue.

That morning, she held one in her hand, the ash falling like confetti at her feet. She watched, sitting on the steps, as Slava played in the fields to the front of them, her feet dirty and her green dress hidden in the tall grass. It was Saturday, and the afternoon light was soft and yellow. She could see the hills rise far beyond, before they dropped toward the sea in the distance.

In her other hand was a letter.

Henry had gone into town, to meet someone who was interested in contracting him out in a cutting group for extra money. It was common for cutting gangs—despite the long hours and hard conditions—to want to earn more money with private companies. It was more than they could've made anywhere else.

She inhaled deeply, her fingertips hot from the ever-shrinking cigarette. Then she saw him down the road, approaching her, his body growing taller as he walked. His lean shoulders belied his exhaustion. They sloped and softened and shifted with each step.

He stopped at the bottom of the steps and saw what she held in her hand.

She waved the letter like a flag. "Well, here we are."

"Okay, okay... well?"

"Here."

He opened it. *Pregnant.* Big, black lettering. *Ten weeks.*

And then he was back in Germany, watching as the girl he barely knew tearfully told him how scared she was that they would bring a child into a war. And he had felt fearful, though he didn't tell her, which was why he had walked away. He feared that he would resent that decision, and that he would grow distant like his father, and raise a child who didn't love him, and yet, here he was, with a golden-haired child who slept in his embrace, and a woman he loved. And now he stood before the same scared girl, and they'd been given another chance to try again. And maybe they could. And now there was no war—but he still felt fearful, though he didn't tell her that.

"Let's see what happens." He shrugged, and smiled at her.

Julia's neck and face flushed, and she immediately felt the compulsion, the ache, to tell him finally; to tell him everything, about why this had happened, and how. But the reality was that he wanted this child as badly as she did, and the truth would forever extinguish the hope that arose from his words.

She blinked, and a tear fell quietly. "Yes, let's see."

CHAPTER SIXTEEN

APRIL 1950

The line of blood started it all.

Julia lifted her skirt up and, like a scarlet thread, it slowly progressed down her thigh, and though it scared her because of her prior miscarriages, she knew it was different because her waters followed after.

She had been trying to clear the table after breakfast, but a familiar ache had been distracting her: her back radiated with a consistent tightness, the lower part of her stomach muscles pushed in a kind of familiar rhythm, back and forth and down. She had done this once before now, and knew it would happen today.

She clung to anything to steady herself: chairs, the sink, the kitchen table with breakfast plates clattering as she pitched herself forward with a coming contraction.

She breathed. It was suddenly quiet. She turned to walk toward her husband, and it was then that she felt it: a burning, like a rope being pulled through her back, dividing every tissue of her abdomen on its way through to the other side. She doubled over and gripped a chair, its back shaking from her effort. "Hironimus." Her voice was insistent and flat. "This is wrong."

As she called for him, his name catching in her throat, she heard him in the other room with Slava. She had been in their lives for four years now, and they had hoped and tried for more children, but their luck had run out until nine months ago.

"Papa! Look at that!" Slava's joyful twittering mixed with his low laughter, and their voices echoed in the small house as if it were just another day: books and toys and pencils strewn across the floor, drawings of giant eyes and round faces atop spindly legs on sheets of paper that would eventually be torn and discarded. A life in one room as it was; a life that would begin in another.

But when the bright burst of new pain came again, she became uneasy and unsure, and nauseated.

"Henry. Can you ask Marta to look after Slava? It's... just..." The words drowned in a fresh burst of pain in her stomach and back. Her face went white.

It will end up a failure, like all the others before it.

Her husband finally walked in, hands in his pockets, as if he were waiting for the train. Henry was the calm one. Some might say cold, others would say controlled. She searched his face for strength. She looked down and, just before another surge of pain, she noticed that one of his socks had a hole in the toe, and she would remember that detail more than anything else in that moment, for some reason—probably because it was a little thing. A little thing that could unravel over time.

"Hey, hey..." he said softly, and came closer. His hands reached out and rested on her shoulders as he saw that she was pale and staring and though he was prepared for her to ask him something, he wasn't sure what, and he felt immediately unsure of how to respond. She looked different than she had the other time, with Slava.

"Tell Marta. And then take me to the hospital. I need a doctor."

"Why not Elina? I'm sure she'd—"

Julia shot him a look. "No. Not Elina. Just... because..." She searched her thoughts. "It would be better to have someone older, maybe. Or she's probably working." She stiffened and groaned softly. "Just please ask Marta."

She clutched her belly and took slow, steady breaths. In the pause between the pains she shuffled slowly to the bedroom, stopping occasionally to use the wall as support. She reached the dressing table—the dressing table he'd bought for her shortly after they'd arrived in Australia—and sat, leaning forward on her elbows and folding her hands behind her head, legs spread onto the chair and belly comfortably in between.

When she was alone, it felt better. Important things are sometimes better accomplished alone, her mother used to say.

The room was quiet, and the smell of soap and coffee hung in the air. She noticed the bed hadn't been made, and Henry's shirt—the one that he'd slept in—lay on the floor beside her, discarded from his body as if he'd vanished abruptly, leaving a soft shell. She picked it up and held it to her cheek and buried her face in it: it was still faintly warm to the touch.

She still found joy in these small things, and these things were important in a marriage.

Henry strode urgently down the path that cut through the tall, dry grass to the house three doors down. The earth hugged his shoes as his lanky body loped along.

Henry was surprised at how protective he felt over her, this woman he'd grown to love. Marriage was never what he'd wanted or even thought he'd deserved, let alone love. Love was not an economical use of a man's time, his father had always said. And yet he knew, as if he'd known it always, that their path had taken them to the right place: here, in Stratford, with their beautiful Slava, and another life on the brink of arrival. They hadn't thought, or planned, how to survive in the barren fields, surrounded by wind and rain, in a mill town that had a constant layer of dust on its doorstep, but they had given it a go.

This, he thought, was what he'd done for them, and more recently, after Julia had announced the pregnancy, he had worked harder than ever before. Working with a private group of cutters had led to thoughts of eventually moving the family to Sydney, once their time had been served there. His felt a warm sense of duty, and love, as he imagined his young family in a solid house sitting within view of the ocean.

He put his hands in his pockets and his face broke into a smile.

Henry took a breath, and then knocked. "Marta." His voice was hoarse but certain. "I need help. Julia needs help. Marta? Can you hear me?"

There was a shuffling and what sounded like something being dropped on the floor and then a drawer opening, and then a groan, footsteps coming closer still, and then she appeared, in a black dressing gown with faded red poppies on it, her dark eyes heavy, as if a light had been shut off.

"Henry. What can I do for you?" She rustled for a pack of cigarettes in her pocket, pulling one out and holding it, apparently confused as to what she needed to do next. She was missing something.

It was still early, and Henry was embarrassed that he had intruded.

"Marta, do you mind if I bring Slava to your house this morning? Julia is starting to feel contractions and she's"—he paused, letting fear escape his facade—"she's worried. She needs to get to the hospital."

Her eyes widened a bit, and then composed themselves again. She fingered the other pocket of her gown: "Yes, fine, bring her." He could always rely on Marta for taking any emotion out of things, but he knew she did so with kindness. It helped.

"Okay, thank you very much. She'll be over shortly. Thank you, Marta."

"Fine." With Marta, things were always "fine." She withdrew her husband's Zippo from her pocket and sparked it as she closed the door.

"Henry?" Julia called from the bedroom as he came back in.

"Yes, yes, Marta is fine to take her."

"All right, well, can you get her ready? I'm just here." She gripped the dressing table and sat immobile.

Slava's voice rang out like bells. "Mama! Mama!" She bounded across the floor, the untreated floorboards creaking beneath her feet.

"Oh, Rabbit," Julia murmured, as the child flapped at her legs. "Papa will get you dressed." She turned the little body away from her. "Henry, can you please...?" Her mind had already wandered to the things she had to do that morning, the things that would be forgotten shortly.

"Mama, but I'm hungry!"

"Marta has milk and bread," Julia answered, her breath hissing in focused energy as she watched Henry coax Slava's legs into tights and then a green cotton dress.

"Mama?"

"Mmm?"

"Mama, love you." She covered Julia's cheek with a wet kiss and patted her belly. "Sweet baby, in there."

"Yes, yes, okay, go. Go with Papa."

. . .

Julia dug her fingernails into her palm inside her closed fist as she heard Henry speaking to Slava. Their voices faded, and she felt again the sharpness of betrayal. She felt ashamed that she was keeping a secret that would change both of their lives. She'd heard him as he assured Slava that yes, they'd go to Marta's, and that yes, they could take a few buns with them and that Mama would be fine—she just needed to see a doctor because she felt unwell and the baby was coming.

Another contraction came and tasted metallic on her tongue, and then an acidic tightness radiated throughout her abdomen, sending her forward in a dry retch, saliva glistening at the corners of her mouth.

Suddenly, she felt a hand on her back, and she silently realized how much she needed her husband. She had spent so many days and months and moments brooding on her guilt, her complicity, but now she felt helpless. How good he was, despite it all, and how foolish she had been. She winced in regret; she winced in apology. They were connected, yet neither realized it.

"Julia, come. Are you able to make it to the car?"

Another wave of pain: her jaw tightened, and she grabbed his hand.

"Help me, Henry." Her voice broke, and she cleared her throat. "Would be a shame to have the baby in a car."

"I'm sure worse has happened."

So much worse.

"Just get me there. I will be okay." And she felt his arm circle her waist, the weight of him pushing her forward.

* * *

The pale gray walls and oval windows of the old hospital dwarfed her swollen frame, and his lean one, as she bent over her knees in a wooden chair and he paced the room. From the

outside, the hospital was attractive; the inside, however, smelled
of antiseptic and fresh cotton, and the floors were hard, so every
footstep echoed like a tiny explosion in the room.

Julia winced and groaned, looking down at her stomach, her
hands circling its largeness, feeling like the only person there,
despite there being roughly twenty women in the room all with
the same look of concern, wringing their hands and biting their
lips. She wanted her mother. And then another contraction, the
gold of her wedding band glinting in the dusty light of the room.

"Mrs. Julia Rudnick?" She and Henry looked up and saw
them: a man, tall, with glasses that were too small for his round,
pale face, and a nurse with mousy, graying hair standing beside
him, plain and quiet, both dressed in crisp white and blue
uniforms. "Let's have you come with us now."

Julia saw that they noticed the dried blood on her leg as she
stood up and she hesitated, looking around the room. She was
unsure. Her instinct was to run, without knowing where. Her
legs stayed rooted to the floor, her fists clenched. *Protect Your
Child,* a yellowed poster shouted from its place on the wall.
Lithiated Soda! and *Smart Mums Smoke Camels.* None of this
made sense to her.

"Madam?" *But the room smelled of bleach.*

"Julia." *Her dress had a hole in it.*

"JULIA!"

Henry's eyes were dark behind the thin curtain of cigarette
smoke separating them both. He had been pacing the floor and
then leaning against the wall, pausing only to light a cigarette
and now snap her back into the room where she sat, confused.

A faint smile flitted across her face. "Happy birthday, also.
Fate has been kind."

The corner of Henry's mouth lifted in a wry smile. "Thank
you for my present. You really know how to surprise me," he
said, and nodded for her to turn around and get going.

Julia stood and walked toward the hall, meekly sandwiched

between her two guides in white coats that would possibly soon be stained with her blood, her breath coming in short bursts to mitigate the pain.

They walked down a long stretch of polished, hardwood floor that seemed to split off into thousands of little doors, all hiding private stories narrated by soft voices that weren't for her to understand. Hers was the second to last one, with a white bed with starched pillows at the head, and a metal frame that creaked as she sat on it. Nothing felt comfortable, and then the contractions came again, and she gripped the frame and kneaded the mattress. They held her but she shifted constantly: she crouched and squatted, sat and rocked forward and moaned; bent over the edge of the bed; she climbed on all fours and begged the pain to stop. There were hands gripping her arms to stop her from moving and then she felt them shift her to the bed to lie still with her knees bent; it made her anxious. Something felt too urgent, too heavy. There seemed to be many more figures appearing through the doorway and spreading into the room; hushed voices and heads leaning toward one another in confidence and urgency, and then a hand holding her still as she felt a needle in her arm and saw a mask hovering to be placed over her mouth. And then a wonderful lightness lifted her away and loosened her jaw and even the skin on her eyelids settled as she listened to pieces of conversation.

"... breech. They could move more but the heartbeats have slowed..."

"... a section, possibly avoided, however..."

"... manual manipulation...?"

"... no, need her awake during..."

"... both heartbeats have stabilized..."

"Madam, I'm going to go ahead and put my hands inside to reposition the babies, alright?"

Julia nodded, her mind disconnected from their words, and her body disconnected from her. Their mouths and motions became softer and more distant as a medicine seeped into her body and her mind slowed its pace. She felt a vague sense of release in her chest—as if it were cracking open—with a pulling sensation further down, as if her body were split neatly in half. The lights were soft, and the faces seemed friendly, and she wanted in that moment to float above it all for a little while, gently brushing against the ceiling and watching the scene below as they moved her limbs and placed their gloved hands inside her. She imagined very vividly that she could then slip through the cracks and lines of broken plaster and float even higher and meet the damp branches of the trees embracing the late summer sky, and the vapor of the clouds. She would see the dust roads of Stratford, and the roar of Barron Falls, then the bustle of Cairns glittering like a jewel on the edge of the Coral Sea, and then the horizon would appear and she would drift farther away until both the sea and sky met in the blackness of night and her world would evaporate entirely and she, like gossamer, would disintegrate, piece by piece.

"Madam, we need you to push now." Their voices were urgent, their hands on her belly and her legs. Julia stiffened her arms, clasped the sides of her bed as if floating on a raft at sea, and closed her eyes. The remnants of nothingness were still there as she held her breath and

pushed through her chest and back and belly and legs. Her eyes felt wet underneath her lashes. She rested against the pillow. And now again, another push, another two. A breath. And then another, and yet another, and then her body felt suddenly empty of air and deflated, and a nurse held a small, doughy, white-covered baby smeared in blood. She sighed and her back and arms collapsed in exhaustion, back onto the bed.

"Madam, wait. You'll need to push again in a second. Here comes the other one. You're doing very well."

The other one. "Sorry? I'm not sure what you mean." Her blue eyes flashed. She was confused. "I'm sorry, I don't under-

stand." Her voice rose, breathless in alarm, as she'd not anticipated anything but a child, one child, inside her. She looked
across to the nurse, the doctor, their faces covered by cotton
masks beneath smiling eyes.

The nurse chuckled and placed a hand on Julia's thigh.
"Madam, you're having twins. Two babies—how incredibly
blessed you are! But now we need you to help the other one out.
Push *now*."

She held her breath. *Twins.*

A whimper caught in her throat, and she closed her eyes,
her body aching. Three, two, one, breathe. And again. Her
heartbeat was in her ears. And again. *Gently*, they reminded
her. With each space of breath in between, her mind looped
from one thought to the next: she wondered what Henry was
doing, and if their daughter had gone to bed peacefully, and
whether the air smelled of rain and if the orchids had pushed
through the soil; she wondered what the world was doing right
at that very minute, because it would instantly change in the
moments after; the present and past intertwining and colliding
in chaos.

The cries sounded the same: like an echo of each other, ripples
on water. Julia lay back on the pillow as one of the nurses wiped
the blood off her legs and the other held two small bundles.
Through the halo of her medicine, she saw two round faces,
both the same, and her first worry was that she wouldn't be able
to tell them apart. Their skin was like folded dough, like the
babka her mother used to make for Easter.

Twins. She had made two of the same, and although she
had been one of four siblings, while Henry was the only one,
there had been no twins in either family. This should feel like a
blessing, surely? What moments are these, that test the heart.

Julia smiled softly and felt a kind of ache overtaking her as they took them away, snuffling and snorting in the nurse's arms. Her body lay flat. Dehydrated. Wanting.

And who told you to do this? her mother would say, gripping her face with dry, thick hands. *Who told you?*

"I chose this," she whispered. "This is my redemption."

Darkness settled on the room, with only the distant rattle of metal trays and soft voices and curtains being opened and closed on the stories held within the halls. Footsteps moved upon the floors, louder with each step toward her room, as white figures stood in her doorway and filtered away as she drifted off to sleep.

* * *

The next day, Henry stopped in to see Julia: he hadn't been allowed to the night before, as Julia was in recovery and asleep.

"Madam, your husband is here to see you." A nurse opened the door carrying two bundles in each arm and handed them to Julia as Henry approached. The room felt instantly warmer.

"They told me. I can't believe it. Twins. A boy and a girl." He walked over softly, smiling, his eyes creasing as he approached the bed to look down at the little faces scrunched under tiny, knitted hats. "Oh, Julia. I honestly don't know what to say. It's a little bit terrifying, and wonderful."

"I know." She watched as he reached for them and she placed each delicately in his arms. "But you have a son." Her heart beat swiftly at the thought of a child in the image of Henry.

"What a life, eh?" He leaned his head back with a throaty laugh, his eyes wet and shining.

"Well, God has blessed us with a large family. Maybe a bit larger than we expected."

He chuckled softly. "God has a strange sense of humor, that's for sure. For years nothing, and now *this*." He swayed back and forth as the babies gurgled in his arms, their mouths searching. "What do you think about names?"

"What about Lesia? And Maksim?"

Henry squinted, pausing to think. "Lesia, *from God.* And Maksim. A leader. A strong son of mine." He nodded and smiled, kissing the pudgy faces. "Yes."

"Henry, we have three healthy children now. *Three.* And look at the heartache that we'd had for so long." A surge of positivity and adrenaline coursed through her.

Henry placed them back in her arms and watched as she settled them and began to feed.

"Julia, I need to get back to work." He kissed her softly on the forehead and walked a few steps, and then turned, looking at her for a moment. He tapped his chest pocket and retrieved a cigarette, a sigh escaping his lips.

Julia wondered, then, if she could ever tell him, but he looked happy, and she realized that he could be happy. *They* could be.

CHAPTER SEVENTEEN

AUGUST 1953

Three years rolled on without consequence as the family adjusted to the newness. The minutes, days, and months passed in a delicious headiness of childhood. Henry would come home and read to the twins nightly, as they curled up against his body in the small bed, their tiny hands and feet exploring his shirt, listening to his voice resonate. It was all a heady mix that Julia loved and felt consumed by, and it diminished much of her guilt.

Their lives had changed and stayed the same, equally, though Julia's relationship with Elina was now colored with a cool distance. Julia buried her secret in the deepest recesses of her mind, but every time she saw Elina, or Iliya, and pretended that life was as it should be, as they all moved around each other at polite dinners and smiled greetings, she grieved the loss of that friendship. Elina, for her part, graciously stepped back, assuming that Julia was overwhelmed with the twins. But she suspected something was amiss, and she observed from a distance.

Lesia's hair had grown thick and fast: it was a shade darker than Slava's, like a dimmed sunbeam, and it was soft, clinging in short, shining wisps to her neck, not long enough to be blown too wild by the wind. She had a small, round birthmark next to her lip, as dark as her eyes: an almost black-brown that contrasted beautifully with her light hair. Maksim's hair was dark and thick and the color of milky chocolate; Julia would run her fingers through it as she fed him, looking as his eyes slowly changed from the blue at birth. Julia wondered if they'd be hazel, like her sister's had been. Whilst Lesia was lean, Maksim was wide, and his head was large. Lesia needed constant affection, where her brother eschewed it: Lesia cried out to be held most of the day, whilst Maksim was observant and still.

Julia had started taking Slava to a small school in Stratford a few times a week, now that she was older, which left the days for her to spend with the twins.

They played constantly and their laughter had become her music. Julia covered them constantly with affection, peppering their faces and their hands with kisses. Their life together simmered with abandon and hope, and Julia fully claimed them as her own and felt that nothing had, or would, come between them; her heart swelled as the marks of her pain faded and she held their warm bodies to her own.

She healed in her love for them.

Henry was working more than usual, and he had told Julia of his thoughts on Sydney, but in her focused bliss and exhaustion as a new mother, she had put the discussion out of her mind. The air between them, the four walls that surrounded them, felt safe; the burdens that had weighed Henry down were released from his shoulders and he carried the love of his children as the grateful father he was. It felt like the patterns in their behavior had found a happy rhythm, and so Julia indulged the new life that had been thrust upon them.

* * *

That morning, Julia had been at the park with them, after dropping off Slava at the local school. The day was clear, and it bled its peacefulness into the afternoon. She took out a thin little pamphlet that she had found at home and brought with her: it was her accountancy and mathematics book. With its pale blue cover, it had survived the years-long journey from her school days, then through her work in Neumarkt camp; she had kept it as a kind of reminder of the days before her life changed so drastically. These were two classes that Julia had excelled in. She remembered the classroom with white, bare walls; shining wooden floors; and windows with limited views that were caked with snow in the winter. She remembered sitting across from her best friend, Sofia, and remembered her hair: always in a sharp bun, a white ribbon tied around it.

She thumbed a cracked, yellowed page: the ink had faded almost completely, scrawled in a hurried hand:

Started business—capital 100,000

Capital (100,000) + Liabilities (0) = Assets (cash = 100,000)

Bought furniture 25,000

Solution?

Capital (100,000) + Liabilities (0) = Assets (Cash = 75,000 + Furniture = 25,000)

Bought goods for cash 20,000

Capital (100,000) + Liabilities (0) = Assets (Cash = 55,000 + Furniture = 25,000 + Goods = 20,000)

Bought goods from Mr. Nelson on credit 5,000

Solution???

Capital ($100, 000$) + *Liabilities* (*Nelson* = $5,000$) = *Assets*
(*Cash* = $55,000$ + *Furniture* = $25,000$ + *Goods* = $25,000$)

She remembered she had once seen an accounting machine; the teacher had brought it in to show the class. It fascinated her: it was like a strange, heavy, stony-gray beast sitting atop the main desk, spattered with seemingly hundreds of pale-colored keys, uniformly spaced apart. It had purpose. She liked that it had purpose. It made her want to have purpose.

She smiled, closing the book. It felt good to see the parts of her that had been hidden for so long.

* * *

Along the river there was a small gazebo that had been built before the war: it was a cream-colored hexagonal structure with lattice-work sides, all converging into a pointed roof. There were small benches on each of the six sides within and it was big enough to hold groups of people relaxing by the river and taking in the view. Occasionally, there was a wedding party that took pictures there. Julia always liked seeing a gathering like that, for the dresses alone.

It was there, on one of the benches, that she saw him, though she wasn't sure at first and then wondered if it actually was, or if it was her imagination that was reeling. And then she looked again, and confirmed that it *was*, and saw him smoking with a few friends, sitting in the same languid pose that she remembered, arm draped on the back of someone's shoulders. There were two women with him, dressed nicely, and three other men.

They had probably been out to lunch, or perhaps were just setting off somewhere. Julia looked away, aware that she'd been staring, and turned her attention back to the twins. She watched them distractedly, only half paying attention as they sat at her feet.

She turned again to look, and regretted it instantly, for Iliya saw her, trapped her gaze, and waved. She watched as he turned back to his group, motioned that he would be right back to them and started walking over.

Julia cursed that she'd even looked, and wondered how quickly she could leave without creating any drama.

"Well! Look who it is..." He smiled as he approached—nothing remarkable about his face, it was just incredibly familiar. "Can I sit down? Is it just you?" The strength in the knowledge of what he had done, and that she would never admit to what had happened to her, emanated in a kind of smugness that could have easily been mistaken as confidence. He had that power, and they both knew it.

"No. Please go away." She stumbled over her words and tried to stifle the urge to scream or run—she couldn't decide which.

He crouched down next to her and rested his arms on his thighs. "I'm about to go off to lunch with a few friends, but I thought I'd say hello." He looked over to the group. They were casually watching them. He waved. "Henry probably knows them, some of the men worked with him. We're waiting for Elina to join us. How's the family?"

She wasn't looking at him, so he had a few indulgent moments to scan the side of her face: her hair was plaited loosely and hung down her neck; the buttons of her dress were silvery and neat, all done up and containing her modesty. Her wool coat that had always been too big now perched on her shoulders delicately, like a cape.

She turned to him, breaking his gaze. "Please leave me alone." Her cheeks were crimson, and he leaned into her. From afar, someone would say that they looked extremely comfortable in each other's presence.

Lesia walked up, found Julia's leg and clung to it, her cheek soft on her knee. Maksim was sitting next to her and reached to her for a hug.

"Time changes things, doesn't it?" He rocked back on his heels, staring at her a bit too long, and then reached for Maksim's head, attempting to stroke his soft hair. His eyes drifted over the faces of the children in front of him, and his face changed. It would've been undetectable to anyone but Julia.

Julia picked him up and moved him to the other side, hissing, "Don't touch him" only loud enough for the two of them to hear. "Many things change."

"Yes. Shame, all that." He waved his hand glibly in her direction.

"Don't." Julia's face burned with anger. "Have you no shame for what you did?"

The side of his mouth lifted. "Do *you*? For opening your legs to another man?"

Julia's face burned and her eyes raged. "How dare you?" She kept Maksim on her lap in direct contrast to the subject matter, to entertain him so he couldn't sense the tension, but also to avoid feeding him in front of a man who had seen her breast before.

"Life happens, sometimes. Desperate times, where we are." He stroked the side of her face with his index finger.

"Get the hell away from me," she hissed.

He laughed. "Don't worry. We're leaving anyway." He looked down at his hands. "Or maybe just me. I can't bear to stay in this shithole any longer." He looked at Julia and winked. "Shame, really. I'd begun to like it here." He leaned forward and kissed the side of her face briefly. "Pity they don't look more like me," he whispered.

Before she could recoil, the moment was witnessed by another person who had walked over to the group by the pavilion and had watched the scene play out, and whose suspicions had now been confirmed.

Julia rolled her body away finally and looked up at him.

"Either way"—he stood up, and then stopped—"nice to see you again." He smiled, and she remembered that smile, because it had been familiar, and now it destroyed her in so many miniscule ways. An anger erupted inside her as he walked away, seamlessly inserting himself back into his group, and they all moved off together, their laughter dissipating down the road.

She knew that that moment would keep hanging over her: the weight of panic looming on her chest, knowing that she had a part of her past that was indefinable. It existed, he existed, that night had broken her and pieced her back together; she was unable to erase it.

She started packing up the pieces of the day into her bag, in a daze, not really aware of what she was doing, unaware that her world would soon be scattered again, like leaves on the wind that she now felt on her skin.

CHAPTER EIGHTEEN

"Julia, come inside, please."

She heard Henry's voice call her from inside the house, and there was something in the tone of it that made the hairs on her arm stand up. The air felt quiet. It waited for something.

It was Saturday. Slava had been outside that morning, helping her mother weed the small garden at the back of the house, her hands caked in dirt, fistfuls of dandelions at her side. The twins were playing in one corner, on a flattened patch of brown grass, with some brightly colored toys that had been brought over by one of the neighbors. They were happily engrossed and the laundry had been hung up and was fluttering in the breeze like the sail of a heeling boat. The sky was gray.

She looked up, the wind making her eyes stream. "Wait just a minute, I have to finish."

She saw his face appear in the window and scan the perimeter of the garden. "No, you don't. They will be fine."

She turned back to Slava. "Wait here, I have to speak to your father. Look after Lesia and Maks."

Slava watched her leave; she watched her all the time, and listened always, and Julia knew it.

Julia didn't turn back, and walked toward the front of the house, praying for a swift end to whatever mood was approaching.

When she walked in, Henry was leaning against the table in the kitchen, staring past her, and then at her. He was silent. His eyes were knowing. She looked back at the garden. The children would be alright.

"Yes, what?" Her hands were on her hips, trying to gauge his mood. She felt a bit exposed, standing that way. She waited.

"You know what I heard?" he asked her, and she knew he didn't want her to finish.

She took the bait. "No. What?"

"I heard that I married a whore." He carefully lit a cigarette, letting *whore* hang in the air between them. He inhaled slowly, and then exhaled. "Apparently."

And, all of a sudden, Julia felt like she was choking.

"Oh, right, sure." Julia snapped herself out of her daze, though her thoughts were already a few steps ahead, searching. "And where, exactly, is this from?"

"A friend."

"Well. Some friend."

"I trust them."

"Obviously."

"Well?"

The staccato of the words stopped abruptly, and Julia felt anger approach her chest, in fiery defense.

"Wait, wait." Julia threw her hands up and closed her eyes as if to stop an army's approach. "You have no idea what you're talking about. This 'friend' of yours is terribly mistaken."

"Mmm, right." He leaned forward, his palms on the table. "So, how should we talk about this, then? Are you going to tell me, and will it be a lie? Or should I tell you what I heard, and you can respond? Either way, it's going to be damn painful for the both of us."

She crossed her arms. "Go ahead. Go ahead and tell me this ridiculousness."

He paused. He gathered his words. "I was told that you were with someone once. Were you?"

"What? When? Who?" She chose her words carefully.

"You didn't answer my question. Were. You. With. Someone."

"Well, it's a bit vague, isn't it? I've seen people, yes."

"Julia." Henry gritted his teeth. "The thing that makes me sad here is that I'm opening a door for you. I'm giving you the option to tell me what's going on—"

"No, actually," Julia interrupted, placing her hands on her hips, "you're not. If you remember, you just called me a whore."

He kept talking. "—and you're not being honest with me. So, fine. I'll tell you what I know. I know that someone told me they saw you in the park last week. Very comfortable, apparently, with you and the children. And that you apparently like to have a little meeting with that person, if I'm not around."

"STOP saying 'someone'! *Someone, someone, someone.* You know you're just trying to make me angry—is that it?! What do you want me to tell you to make you happy?" Her heart felt like it belonged to someone else in that moment; it felt foreign and pale and cold, like the center of her chest had a hole in it and she was about to crumble to the floor.

"Go ahead. Lie to me." Henry looked at her with a distant sympathy, as if he didn't understand who she was, but felt incredibly sorry for her. "Who, then?" He was almost irritatingly calm in his demeanor.

"Who? What do you mean?"

"That night, the one where I wasn't here, the fight when I obviously wasn't here, and then in the park. What's going on?"

She looked down. She'd forgotten to sweep the floor earlier. Specks of flour gathered around her toes. "That's not what happened," she whispered, almost inaudibly and in a daze.

"Excuse me?"

Her face was ashen as the memories of that night came flooding back. "You're talking about Iliya, aren't you?"

"Well, then. You're having an affair."

"No, no. That's not true."

"What was he doing with you in the park?"

The park. How would Henry know about the park? And then it dawned on her. *Elina.* "He came over to me. I didn't want to talk to him. He was trying to tell me—"

"—that he's upset that he can't have you? He can take you, for all I care."

"Henry, stop. Let me explain, none of this is what you think—"

"Obviously you slept with him."

She hesitated, and he saw it as an admission. "No."

"When did it happen?"

"I said *no*, Henry please, let me explain what happened to me."

"You're lying."

Julia let herself feel angry. "You've already made up your mind, Henry, and it leaves no room for me to tell the truth. The truth was that he forced himself on me."

Silence.

Julia pleaded. "Did you hear what I said? Do you understand what happened to me?"

"*When* did you start with that man?" Henry hissed, pointing at her face. "Tell me."

Julia realized then that he was choosing to hear something else. He was choosing to ignore her. She covered her ears with her hands, pleading. "Stop. Please stop."

He was standing a foot away from her, not letting her back away. He grabbed her and shook her violently.

She wrenched herself away and reached for the door, launching herself outside and into the light, the empty fields around her. She stopped, knowing he'd follow her, and she didn't know what to say. The less she said now, the easier it would be, she realized. It's a funny thing, truth. It can be more destructive than a lie.

And then she panicked as she looked back at all the times she had lied to him, and she felt her stomach lurch and a nausea erupt in the center of her.

She heard his footsteps behind her, and she turned around. "Henry, please." Her voice was withered, raspy. "I can't fix it; I can't undo what happened."

"You still haven't told me when it happened."

"Why do you have to know?"

"Fresh pain, Julia." He spat. "For both of us. So I can see you humiliated."

Her thoughts spun. *Do you remember when I told you that Slava had bashed into me? Do you remember? And when I told you I was pregnant? Do you understand now?*

"July."

"It's October. *This* past July?"

"Last... July." Her stare was unflinching, a tear caught in the corner of her eye. "Last year. It was one time."

He moved toward her, and then stopped. She thought it might be because he could forgive her.

One time.

She walked to him. The leaves battled each other in the wind above their heads.

"That was over a year ago."

"Yes."

He looked back at the house, heard the children in the garden, and then turned back to her and she knew he'd counted. He'd calculated.

She couldn't stop herself: she had been released from her guilt, and shame, and the anger that had been bottled inside for far too long, and she began to set fire to the air around them.

"Yes, after that, I found out I was pregnant. And it didn't make me want them any less. I wanted them because we couldn't have any of our own and my *God* you wanted them too, and you loved them just as much as I did, so what does it matter, please, what does it matter now... There is nothing to forgive, Henry."

Henry's face lost its color. The realization that his children were most likely not his own was devastating. *Catastrophic. Incendiary. Heartbreaking.* The words set off a chain of anger and disappointment in him that he had only once felt before: for his father.

In the hours that followed the revelation, Henry chose—because it was the easier option—not to believe his wife and, instead, began to convince himself that he had been betrayed by the one person he trusted. The arguing possessed both of them in a kind of bottomless mire: Henry needing to believe that she had been unfaithful, and Julia needing him to accept that she had been assaulted, and to release the past of its pain.

"No, are *you* hearing me at all?" They were standing in front of the house, the argument spilling out by the road, as Henry had started to leave to be anywhere but there. His world had been spun too far out of his reach and he was flailing. She had asked him if he was listening to her, and he had turned around to face her, walking toward her, a shaking index finger pointed at her face. "Are *you* understanding *me*? You slept with someone over two years ago, and now you're saying that he raped you. And, guess what: those two sleeping children in that house, *my* house, those two children that I have loved, and wanted and held in my arms"—his voice broke at each admission—"are they yours? Yes. Are they mine? I don't know. I don't *know. I don't know.* Do you have *any* idea what that feels like for me?" Tears threatened.

"But..."

"I don't know whether to be angry, or sad, or shout, or break apart everything I own, or take Slava—*my* child, I'll have you know—out of this house and leave you to your misery."

She grew cold, staring at Henry, not really seeing him, hearing words coming and yet feeling numbness between them.

"So what if they are Iliya's?"

Henry reached his arms to the heavens, dropping them down again in exhaustion. "Stop saying his *name!*"

"Why can't they be ours? They're here now. We've made a home for them."

"You're asking me to love children that are not my own!"

"But you *do* love them!"

"There are plenty of others who would love these children. I can't fathom raising children who are not my own blood." He looked across at the house where they now were, the boy and the girl who were strangers to him, and yet his heart broke and yearned for them.

"But *we* do. We have, and we wanted them. They are innocent in all of this, why would you punish them? Or me, for that matter? *He forced me.*"

Henry was shaking as he walked over to the car and punched the metal with the meat of his fist, his arms tightening as he pressed down on the hood. "Are you mad?" He stared at her. "You're asking me a question when, after *two years* with the belief that they were mine, the truth is that they're most likely not, and you tell me he raped you, and how am I to believe you when you have said nothing, *nothing*, for so long. Why? *Why* did you not trust me enough to tell me? I loved you and love you still, and you had no faith in me."

"But I was scared, and I'm telling you now," she pleaded, wondering if he would back down; if she could actually get him to believe her. "You have to believe that it's the truth."

"I don't think *you* even know the truth anymore, Julia."

"Please just listen to me—"

"Honestly, I can't. This is madness. You're actually asking me to take care of another man's children? Absolutely not."

He wouldn't change course, and his voice had become cold and still, so she pointed at the very weakest spot to see if she could break him open again. "Well, then, you didn't love them really, did you."

And oh, God, his anger flooded the space between them when she'd said those words. She meant them, and he knew it, and it broke his heart with more power than his father ever had and so when his palm came across her cheek, she'd expected it.

She knew to brace herself when she saw his eyes widen and his hand lift. She clenched her jaw, her lips soft and closed, as his hand connected to her skin; the sting and fire erupted like an explosion, repeated in burning waves, her eyes closed and tearing underneath.

He had been rough but had never overtly hit her, and now he felt sick at what he had done. He bent his head, shoulders dropping.

Her eyes remained closed, and she became the center of where she was, pretended that it was all revolving around her. As long as she stood still everything could happen: planets could revolve, the sun could rise and set, the children could play, and the world could go on perfectly without her.

"You have a choice, Julia."

She stayed quiet, unprepared as to what he would say.

He looked up at her. "Give them away, or I'm leaving."

"What?" Her eyes widened.

His jaw pulsed as he set his teeth. "That's right. Give them up. Or I'm taking Slava with me. Out of here."

Julia shook her head. "Give them *away*? That's impossible."

"There are plenty of families that are childless. They can have these... children." He stopped himself from saying *bastards*. His heart felt as if it were splintering into shards; there was too much for him to process.

Julia felt her skin grow cold, her heart falling to her feet, breaking at each corner inside her body.

Impossible.

"No. *No, no, no, no!* You cannot make me do that." Her voice strained through her throat as she spoke, she wanted to wail. "No. You're just saying that out of anger. You have to stay calm; you have to believe..."

"What choice do you give me, Julia? *WHAT. CHOICE?*" Henry's voice cut through the air around them.

"... that you can love them still."

Henry clenched his fists and his entire body shook. "I *did* love them. I still *do* love them. And yet you tell me they aren't mine. Can't you even understand what that *feels* like? Can you see how my entire world has burned in front of my eyes? What truth can I believe now? What am I supposed to do?"

"You cannot make me give away my children, the ones that we have loved, no, no..." Her voice began to rise, her lungs bursting as her breathing became erratic. "*Our* children. Please, please," she pleaded, and dropped her head into her palms, still speaking softly. "Oh God, Henry. Please, oh God, what have I done to us..." She began to sob uncontrollably, an animal-like sound coming from her; a keening from her exquisite, unhinged pain.

He was torn: the woman standing in front of him was the woman he loved, but the betrayal, the secret, the unknown story that his children now were a part of—it was all too much for him to take, and so he turned away, though he wanted to hold her. But the pain was too severe, the cut too deep. He felt powerless.

Suddenly the door opened, and Slava ran out, gold hair shining in the sunlight, dress billowing in the wind. "Mama! Papa! Stop shouting!" She began to cry, running toward them. "Why are you fighting?"

Julia held her breath to stop from crying, and was grateful

for Slava's body running toward her, pushing into the side of hers as she clung to her.

Henry looked over at Julia sharply, in admonishment, gesturing with a hand. "You see? This is what you've created."

"Oh, my love. I'm so sorry." Julia ignored his comment and spoke with an unwavering voice, though she was wounded beyond repair now. She knelt down, wiping the tears from Slava's cheeks. "Don't worry, everything is alright."

"Slava," Henry interrupted, "why don't you come with me"—Julia's heart went cold and she stood up, clutching the child's small hand—"for some ice cream. Would you like that? We can pretend it's your birthday again."

Julia released her breath slowly, grateful. Everything suddenly felt unpredictable.

"Yes, Papa! Yes!" Her eyes shone, and she smiled brightly. "Can we go now?"

"Yes, now." He held out his hand, and Slava grabbed it excitedly.

"Will Mama come with us? And Lesia and Maks?"

His eyes moved from Slava's face to Julia's, and back to Slava's. "Mama needs to stay here."

"Okay." Slava skipped as they started to walk. "Papa?"

"Yes, Rabbit."

"I love you."

He couldn't reply, the tears streaming down his cheeks. The pain of his choices would be his alone to bear—his father had warned him of it.

Julia raced back to the house, her feet raising dust as she hit the ground. She ran to the garden, picking up Lesia and placing her on one hip, and then Maksim on the other, sobbing. She knew she had one last option, and she walked quickly down the path, her body small against the backdrop of the sugar smoke and pale fields and blue sky, to a house that had become familiar to her.

When she arrived, she pounded on the door, breathless. "Iliya? *Iliya!*" Her voice was strident. "Open the door."

Silence. She knew he would be home, so she waited, the twins gurgling at her side. She held them to her suddenly, desperately, and each time she felt their skin or heard their voice, tears threatened to weaken her anger. She felt fire in her chest.

"God damn it, open the door!" She used the ball of her foot to hit the bottom of the wooden frame.

He appeared in the doorway and opened it. "Well, come in. This is a nice—"

Julia flew past him into the center of the front room, placing the twins on the floor by her feet. She put her hands up. "Spare me the welcome." Her face burned with anger. "I need your help."

* * *

By the time he and Slava reached Stratford, Henry's breathing had become more even. He tapped his chest pocket and withdrew a cigarette as they walked, clamping it in the corner of his mouth and wiping the sweat off his brow. Once lit, he sighed and looked down at his daughter. He was grateful that she was at the age where she held his hand often; he needed to feel her cool hand in his, especially today.

When they got to the ice cream shop on Griffin Street, Slava chose a sugar cone of sweet vanilla with a cherry on top. After Henry paid, he took her to sit on a bench facing the river. The ice cream glistened as she licked it, her legs swinging happily a few inches off the ground. He watched as families wandered together in the crisp afternoon sun and heard children's laughter in the playground just beyond.

"Papa, why didn't you get one?" Slava frowned, moving her hair off her cheek with a sticky finger.

Henry took a drag on his cigarette and looked at the water, the sunlight scattering on the ripples like diamonds. "I wasn't hungry."

"Because of the fight? Because of you and Mama?" She licked her fingers as the ice cream melted onto them.

"No, not really."

"Why were you shouting?" Slava squinted at the view and looked over her shoulder to the park where a few children played. She turned back, disinterested, and bit the edge of the ice cream. "I don't like it when you shout."

"I know, Rabbit." Henry's eyes filled with tears, and he looked away as he wiped them off quickly. Then he turned back to her and smiled. "Life can be tricky, I guess." He shrugged and looked down at Slava studying his face.

"Is Mama okay? She was crying. And you were angry."

"Yes." He cleared his throat. "We are okay."

"Because you love each other."

In that moment, Henry saw memories that would lose their meaning, like tarnished keepsakes: Maksim sitting for hours on the kitchen floor with Lesia, pencils in hand, drawing in bold strokes, and pointing, his giggles as Julia sat behind him, clapping at his progress; Maksim reaching for Henry; Slava with her sister, helping brush her hair after a bath; their soft skin and nightdresses in his arms as he embraced them before bed; Maksim on his lap, pointing at drawings in a fairytale, saying "Papa" when he saw a prince, and "Mama" when he saw a princess; Lesia asleep next to him, the moonlight in her blonde hair and across her round cheeks.

Henry watched Slava eat the last of her ice cream and didn't reply. He stroked her soft hair and remained silent, a storm of images swirling around him.

* * *

Iliya closed the door behind him and turned to Julia. "What help do you need, exactly?"

"Henry knows. He *knows*." Her lips quivered as she spoke, and she clenched her teeth.

Iliya dragged a chair over to sit down in, the metal scraping the floor. "Well, then."

"But he doesn't understand what happened, and now—"

"What do you mean, what *happened*?"

"He doesn't know the truth, Iliya, and he's going to leave me and take Slava—"

Iliya leaned back in his chair. "What truth?"

Julia stamped her foot. "LISTEN, will you? I am going to lose my entire family, my life"—she gestured to the twins—"if you don't tell him what happened. Otherwise, I have to admit adultery to him, and lose the two children that you see in front of you. I can't let him do that—you *have* to tell him the truth. Please let me keep my children, *all* of them." Her face creased in her anguish. "Please, Iliya."

Iliya looked down at the twins, crawling happily on the floor. He looked up at Julia and laughed cruelly, stubbing out his cigarette. "Listen, this is not my mess to clean up. Your truth is what you believe it to be. And besides, I'm not interested in ruining my marriage and my work—and for what? To solve your unhappy marriage that is in crisis?" He walked over and stood in front of her, her face now contorted in her helplessness. He wiped her cheek, and felt the scar on her jaw, now dark pink as she cried. "Besides," he whispered softly as he leaned forward, breath hot on her cheek, "who would believe you?"

Julia clung to his arms, disgusted at what she touched, yet pleading for what could be saved. "*Please, please,* Iliya. Please...." She hung her head and kept repeating the word *please.*

The door swung open, and Julia and Iliya turned to face Elina, her face stony with anger.

"What the hell is going on? What is *she* doing here?" Elina dropped her handbag on the floor, her eyes wide, surveying everything. She looked down at the twins sitting on her floor. "What in Christ is happening?"

Iliya smiled, and patted Julia on the shoulder. "Poor woman has lost it a bit. Very unhappy with her husband." Julia was too tired to deal with him and, instead, looked at the woman she'd once loved as a friend.

"I don't care what she's lost, I want her out of here." She shrugged off her coat. "And *you* can take your hands off her."

Iliya raised his hands and backed away. Julia wiped her eyes with her arm. She nodded, knowing now that it *had* been Elina."Please, Elina, just listen."

Elina walked over to Julia and stood in front of her, her full length towering a head above Julia. Iliya watched the scene, arms folded. "No, *you* listen. I don't care for your games." Her voice needled and pierced as she spoke. "You *poor* thing, your husband makes you unhappy, you're a lonely, pathetic orphan"—she grabbed Julia's shoulders and stared down at her —"and you look to my husband to save you. To give you comfort. Did you enjoy it? Did you?"

Julia grabbed the hands that held her. "Elina, stop, that's not what—"

"And now, you've ruined a marriage—"

Iliya shook his head. "Elina, that's enough. She's apparently going to lose these twins..." Elina shot him a withering look, and he raised his hands. "Alright, alright. I'm just..."

Elina turned to Julia and her eyes narrowed. "I knew it."

Julia spoke quickly while she had the chance. "Elina, Henry is forcing me to give them away..." She looked over at Iliya, who wasn't showing the least bit of concern about anything that she would say. She was powerless. No one would believe her. "He thinks that Iliya and I..."

Elina raised her hand to Julia, and everyone went quiet. The quiet settled as the three of them looked at one another. Elina looked down at the twins, and then at her husband, and covered her mouth, her eyes widening and cheeks trembling. Her hands started to shake as she pointed at Julia. "I cannot bear the sight of you. The both of you." Her head shook from side to side, slowly, and she walked up to Julia again, her face and neck erupting in bright red flashes of anger, her eyes full of hurt. "Congratulations. You have ruined a friendship, and now a family. Your very own family. You have destroyed it completely. And now you have to live with it all, for the rest of your days. And for what, exactly? A moment of misunderstood kindness? Pity?"

"It wasn't that," Julia whispered.

Elina cocked her head to the side. "What did you say?"

Julia looked directly at Elina, suddenly angry, her voice clear. "It wasn't kindness or pity, Elina. Your husband isn't capable of any of that." Julia's body tensed at her own words: they undid whatever pieces had healed so long ago, and obliterated them fully.

Elina walked close to Julia and reached for her collar and pulled it toward her, a dark fire flashing across her eyes. When she let go, she kneeled in front of the twins, touching their soft, warm heads. "Well done, my friend, what an example of a mother you are." She stood up again and looked at Julia. "Those poor babies, it breaks my heart." Her face softened for a second, and then snapped back into place as she pointed to the door. "You can get out."

Julia swallowed her sobs and crouched next to her babies, her arms shaking as she lifted Lesia first, and then Maksim, their happy faces searching hers. She turned, Elina and Iliya's faces watching her, the wall of their bodies standing firm.

"The truth, Elina," Julia said, softly. "If only you could see the truth. Maybe you will allow me that one day."

Elina walked past her and opened the door, gesturing to the outside with an open palm.

Julia walked home quietly, her grief unbearable, her sobs uninhibited.

She had lost.

CHAPTER NINETEEN

Julia hadn't slept, and barely ate. Henry disengaged from her, and from the twins—as they reached for him, they didn't understand why he would peel their fingers off his legs, and wouldn't pick them up when they needed him. Julia watched her family as if a voyeur, with a grief that had descended over her entire life, like a sticky film on a forgotten painting, or a glass that was slowly cracking, its fissures about to break and explode and disintegrate.

A part of her had died once already with one man, and now she would die a slow death with another, as he forced her hand. Would she survive this? Would her children? Would her marriage? In the darkest of nights, she wished for nothing else but an end, but her saving grace was their daughter. There was now a reason why they called her "Glory," and Julia reminded herself of the fact that she would, in fact, have to carry on with this life. Without them.

* * *

The morning was warm and quiet, the twins still asleep. Henry had left early to go for a walk, crept out without a word, which she was grateful for. She padded into her room and stood in the doorway, staring at the small bed in the corner with the two sleeping children. Lesia's hair was dark with sweat. Maksim's cheeks were lined from his blanket clutched so firmly to his face. Their breaths were slow and even.

These were the things she would remember, though they would fade over time. A childhood only captured in memories and stories, existing ever so briefly.

Julia's fingers curled around a cup of lukewarm tea, thinking about what she had, in the last weeks, decided. In her other hand she was holding a thin, small spoon, stirring the liquid in circles, around and again, the rhythm comforting, as if she was tracing the line of her thoughts and reaching the same conclusion, over and over again. She had not put milk in the tea, and she saw the lines of her face reflected in the liquid briefly, before disappearing again and again.

The trip to the courthouse was silent. They'd taken the train into Stratford, sitting side by side in resentment and heartbreak. Julia had taken Slava down the road to Marta's, and then asked another neighbor, Olya, to look after Lesia and Maksim. She felt completely bereft at what would happen soon but, ultimately, the choice was made.

In order to save her marriage and keep her family intact, she had to make the ultimate sacrifice.

The courthouse was small and white, formal and plain, set on a patch of grass with two benches out front. As they strode in through the door, Julia felt the heaviness of her footsteps as they clacked loudly on the floor.

"Yes? Do you have an appointment?" The secretary was pale and blonde, her straight shining hair pulled back in a bun at her neck, her cheeks flushed as if she had just run back into the room.

"Yes, we're here to sign a declaration, the consent to adoption order. We called a week ago." Henry tapped his fingers on the counter; Julia stood with her arms in front of her, holding her bag. Numb.

"Name?"

"Rudnick."

"Yes, I see you here. Have a seat, and Mr. Bennett will be with you in a few minutes."

Julia was confronted with panic. *I don't know English very well; how do I know what to say? What do I do?* She looked over at Henry: he was standing at the window, looking past the town, toward the sky, toward the fields that had turned gold in the dense summer heat.

Joseph Bennett was a man with graying hair and limited knowledge in how a suit should fit a man's body properly. His long face was accentuated with jowls on either side, and his tawny hair was thinning and almost entirely absent at the crown. His career in family law had seen him though twenty years of adoptions, and this case didn't seem at all unique, as the family were migrants, and he expected as much with people who lacked the intelligence to know when to stop having children. He was the sort of man to declare: *It's not like they have any other entertainment for themselves, dear Lord. Leave the thinking to the rest of us*, over dinner with friends, holding his crystal glass of wine in his fine little hands. And so today, he would meet his new clients, and go through the extremely tedious process of rehoming their children.

Julia saw him walk through the door, holding a folder of documents, and she searched his face, wondering if he would listen to her.

"Nice to meet you both. I'm Joseph Bennett, I'll be helping you with your declaration." He held out his hand. Henry shook it and followed him as he ushered them both into his office.

Henry started talking as Bennett shut the door. "We don't speak English very well, sorry, so you need to explain to us where we put our names. My wife"—he pointed at Julia with vague interest—"she's worse. Tell her what to do, please."

"Mr. Rudnick, I understand your concerns, but not to worry. I'll help guide you toward the best solution for you and your wife. Now, do you understand what you're here to do?"

"Yes, we have two children we need adopted."

Bennett nodded, turned to Julia. "Madam, do you understand, is this why you're here?"

"Yes."

"Okay, well, the first thing we have to do"—he shuffled the papers around on his desk and found a white form, and fed it into his typewriter—"is fill out this declaration. It's a statement that you need to sign, telling me the details that led you to decide to adopt your children out to a new family. This won't take long." Bennett leaned forward, folded his hands on the desk. "So. What is the reason, for my records?"

"My wife got pregnant with children that are someone else's. These are not my children, I'm not their father." Every word felt labored, but Henry steeled himself at each one.

Bennett swallowed abruptly at the admission, and then looked over at Julia. He nodded, soberly, as if he'd heard it too many times before. "Is this a fact?"

"Would you believe me if I told you the truth? That he forced himself on me?"

The men looked at each other, and the power of the truth and the freedom of the words that she'd wanted to say for what seemed like most of her life—even if they didn't believe her—crashed through the room and created a deafening silence.

Julia's eyes glistened. "Would you listen?"

"Madam, I hardly—"

"What about understanding what happened to me? Can I tell you what happened?"

"Madam. Is there a police report?"

"No."

"Well, if this man assaulted you, as you say"—Bennett looked over at Henry and saw nothing but a stony face, so he looked back at Julia—"then surely you would have reported it?"

Henry spoke first. "No."

Bennett stayed silent.

The keys clicked, spelling out black letters: "Julia," and then, "wife of Henry Rudnick."

"So. When did you commit adultery?"

And there it was. Despite her freedom in that moment, she was trapped again.

"July. 1949."

"And who was he?"

Iliya.

Henry answered for her. "Iliya Dalevich. He worked with me; he was a cane cutter."

"Is he aware?"

"No."

"And where is he now?"

Julia spoke this time. "I don't know."

"Okay, that's fine. And what happened?" *Click-clack*, the keys swept along with the dialogue.

Julia held her breath and then slowly let it out. She could answer one of two ways: the truth, which was entirely useless there, or go along with the story that her husband told. She pressed her fists onto her thighs and reopened the scar.

"He... well." *Slowly. Wrong story. Try again.* "We slept together." *Keep with the lie. The truth won't help you now.* She looked down. "Then, I found out I was pregnant. I told my husband the truth in October this year." *That's it. Well done.*

"So, let me be sure this is correct." Bennett stopped typing, resting his fingers on the black keys. "You committed adultery with a man, became pregnant and then had the twins, telling your husband that they were his?" He cleared his throat and looked at her. His face resembled a man who was watching a very dull movie. "Am I correct?"

"Yes. I didn't know if they were or not."

He began typing again. "Well, were you having, ahem, relations with your husband at the time as well?"

Henry interrupted and shifted in his chair. "Is that necessary?"

"Yes, sir, I'm afraid it is, to see the possibility of there being a different alternative to this case."

Henry lit a cigarette and looked at Julia and then back at Bennett. "No."

She was shocked. He was punishing her and it felt as if he had dug a cold knife slowly into her heart. He was lying. She looked at Bennett, imploringly. "But we *were*."

"Hmm. See, I do think, madam, that a man would remember these things quite well." He smirked. "And to be fair, your memory is a bit sullied with, let's say"—he motioned to the paperwork, and then to her—"what you were *preoccupied* with." He continued typing. "Regardless, it's safe to say that your adultery is a scandalous offense to your marriage, regardless." Bennett shook his head, and whether it was in admonishment or disbelief, Julia wasn't sure. She felt invisible.

"You told your husband, and you and your husband decided that the only choice was to put your two, possibly illegitimate, children up for adoption. Yes?"

They both nodded.

"Have you considered the possibility of raising these children as your own?"

"I already told you, no." Henry's heart had changed. It had built a layer of distrust around it, and it firmly stood in self-preservation, unwavering. If he didn't utter the words calmly and detachedly, he would break. "This is our decision."

Bennett turned to Julia. "Is this correct?"

Julia felt her chest grow cold and tight. "Yes. What my husband says is correct."

Two sheets of paper spooled out of the typewriter, heavy with words and dates and spaces to sign. Bennett handed them pens. He pointed at a final declaration that Julia and Henry had to sign, a simple confirmation of the decision made:

QUEENSLAND

STATE CHILDREN'S DEPARTMENT

I, THE UNDERSIGNED , OF STRATFORD NEAR CAIRNS, BEING THE MOTHER OF THE INFANT, HEREBY STATE THAT I UNDERSTAND THE NATURE AND THE EFFECT OF THE ADOPTION ORDER FOR WHICH THIS APPLICATION IS MADE; AND THAT IN PARTICULAR I UNDERSTAND THAT THE EFFECT OF THE ORDER WILL DEPRIVE ME OF MY PARENTAL RIGHTS; AND I HEREBY CONSENT TO THE MAKING OF AN ADOPTION ORDER IN FAVOR OF ANY APPLICANT APPROVED BY THE DIRECTOR, STATE CHILDREN'S DEPARTMENT. IN WITNESS WHEREOF I HAVE SIGNED THIS CONSENT ON THE 15TH DAY OF NOVEMBER, 1953.

Henry signed his without issue. She waited, her fingers hot as she clutched the pen. "I, ah, what does this mean?" Her eyes looked up from the paper, searching Bennett's. One possible moment of understanding. One possible explanation, reason or purpose that could help her find the clarity that she desperately wanted. Her hand hovered.

"Mrs. Rudnick, you are agreeing to an adoption, because as you have declared, you have committed adultery and your husband said he would forgive you if you gave up the children that he, and you, suspect aren't his. In signing this, you are agreeing that you will leave this in the hands of the state, and the state will decide for you who will have your children. You are agreeing that you will not have any rights as a parent to the children you are giving up." He clarified further: "You can't go back through this door once it's closed, do you understand?"

She looked down at the paper, a thin black line waiting for her pen to rest, and then looked over at Henry; he was looking toward the middle of the room, at no one, casually staring past her, cold and indifferent.

And then the slow destruction of her world finally began as she touched the pen to the paper, her fingers shaking as she carved her name with solid dark lines. She was being told the worst thing a mother could ever hear, a pain that wasn't even remotely imaginable by even the wildest scope of thought: that she was unworthy of the children that she had wanted and loved.

They left the courthouse as they had arrived: in silence.

* * *

In time they had left all together, Julia and Henry played the placid family game. Moments revolved and grew around the suppurating silence of a broken marriage; the trust was irretrievable, and as much as Julia reached, Henry drew back, walked away. She would catch him staring at the family, wondering if he'd still leave. Silences were only interrupted by young voices, a sometimes painful reminder that what was true now, would soon be so different.

Julia tried to ignore the inevitability that there was probably a couple, young and married, who were at that moment signing white pieces of paper in front of someone like Mr. Bennett. They would be smiling at each other. She would be dressed in a pale blue jacket and skirt, her hair done nicely but not too primly. Her husband would be leaning toward her, talking to her about the decision that they would be making. *Are you okay with this? Should we go through with it? Yes,* she would say. *I love you, and this will be a blessing for us,* is what she would say. This would all be happening at the same time Julia would be dressing Lesia in a dress that she made for her; Maksim would be in his shirt and trousers, his light brown hair swept to the side, blue eyes searching. It would all be happening as if in a slower, parallel life: this woman in her blue suit would be clutching her handbag, happily in conversation with someone official, watching her husband shake another man's hand, an agreement in place for their future.

Sometimes Julia would sit next to Maksim and Lesia, as if memorizing their faces.

"Slava, I need to tell you something." Julia was sitting on the bed folding laundry distractedly. Folding, refolding, forgetting what she was doing.

"Yes?" Slava responded, looking up from her drawing, then back down. She was drawing a woman with yellow hair and a big red smile, holding a baby. "What, Mama?"

"Slava, you know how Lesia and Maksim are here with us?"

"Yes."

"Well, they will be going on a trip soon."

"Can I come?"

"No, it's just for Maksim and Lesia. They'll be going on a trip with a man and a lady. They are nice people and they'll look after them for a while."

"Why?"

"Because..." She ran her fingers through her hair, words

failing her. And here is where she could be honest, here is where she could describe how complicated the world was, to her daughter who would one day become a woman and would have to fight herself. Oh how she wished she could tell her that these babies weren't her husband's, that these beautiful creations were the result of a terrible violation. That she was doing this to save her marriage because she was scared that otherwise she'd be branded an adulterer and have everything taken from her, including Slava. She wished she could tell her that the world is unfair, and designed for women to be obedient to bad men. She wished she could scream and cry and take all of her babies far away from this mess, from this world that felt too hard. If only, if only she could.

Julia swallowed hard and set her teeth.

"Because it will help us," she chose to say. "Papa and I decided it would be for the best." She got up from the bed, walked out of the room because if she didn't, she would break apart. "For the best," she murmured quietly through her teeth, to no one in particular.

"Mama?"

"Yes, Slava."

"Will it be okay?"

"Of course."

"Will they have a good time?"

"Yes."

"Will the people be kind?"

Oh, she hoped. "Yes."

She walked out to see the twins on the floor of the main room, with books, laughing and teasing, their hands mimicking each other's like shadows.

It was a scene that was too painful to watch, too beautiful to walk away from.

* * *

And then one day, a letter arrived in the post, stamped with the insignia of *The Office of Joseph Bennett*, addressed to *Mr. and Mrs. Henry Rudnick*. She ripped it open, and there in black ink was an appointment for them:

Dear Sir and Madam:

This letter is to advise you that there has been an appointed day for you both to come to the Townsville Receiving Depot to sign the adoption declaration, and for your children, Maksim and Lesia, to be placed in welfare before they are assigned to their adoptive family.

Please bring both children to the courthouse at 1 p.m., as well as any medical records, a few items of clothing and any personal possessions that they may require.

Sincerely,

Joseph Bennett

Solicitor

She was holding the letter delicately, as if it were a rare jewel, or a bomb. Her insides felt as if they had been scraped out. Hollow and lifeless. There were no tears, for it felt too great a flood to pick at. She had, in fact, destroyed her family, and she had ten days to fill her time without being tempted to take her own life, though wouldn't that be selfish? Evenings would be the worst, she knew. Every day the minutes would count down to her sentence; every minute lost was one less of seeing her children clutch at their well-worn blankets; every day was one less of smelling their skin when she held them.

This was irreversible, causing the most extraordinary,

consuming pain she had ever felt in her life; so much so that she had almost entirely gone numb to it.

Ten days crawled at a slow pace; some moments felt too protracted, and yet others felt like agony in their brevity. Ten days spent wondering how she would cope without them, ten days spent wondering whether she had done the right thing and whether she could eventually cope with Henry leaving her, because it was still possible.

This love, this guilt, tore at her like a fresh wound, over and over again, until there was no blood left.

CHAPTER TWENTY

Julia had run out of time, and the first thing she wanted to do that final morning was the mundane. It was as if she was discovering old memories, memorizing them, and then erasing them resolutely, preparing for a new version of the future: clearing the sink of empty cups, rubbing out the stains left from breakfast, and the clothes that needed hanging on the line. She was still a mother, after all, and would always be one, and this to her was a kind of comfort.

She checked every room and folded the sheets tightly on the bed and ran her fingers over the dust that had collected on the dresser.

She went outside into the fog that was lifting from the warm rains that morning, and walked to the back of the house, and shook out the clothes that had been left there the night before, the ones that she'd forgotten about.

She swept the steps and walked over to the chickens, throwing their feed in sandy bursts at them.

She scanned the garden to see if there were any vegetables ready to pick. A few soft ruby-colored tomatoes were ready, so she thumbed them off their stalks and carried them in her skirts back to the house.

After breakfast, Maksim and Lesia came running toward her as she sat outside, careering their bodies around the edge of a chair, narrowly missing the table, and falling into Julia's side. Slava came out after them.

Julia was folding clothes into a bag, putting favorite books on top. She felt Maksim's warm little arms around her own, and she looked into his searching eyes. "Where's your sister, mmm?" She looked across the garden as Lesia placed a ring of daisies around her head.

"Mama, look!" Slava shouted, as she stood behind Lesia. She whispered in her ear and then the two of them began to sing. Maksim giggled and ran over to be with them.

Julia watched as their arms stretched wide, a song on their lips that she had taught them, the Ukrainian words and melody surrounding the air around them, the sunlight on their faces. She murmured, "Yes, well done," and smiled, as her shaking hands placed the children's last few toys into a canvas bag. They were still playing, their hands linked together, when Julia stood. She watched as Slava brushed the hair from Lesia's face, and she knew it was an ordinary moment that was now burned into her memory.

"We must leave soon, yes?" Julia announced to them.

"Mama?" Maksim pointed. "Sad?"

Slava followed his gaze. She was almost six now, and she observed her world keenly. The children padded over to her.

Julia crouched down and stroked Maksim's face. "No, sweetheart. Not sad tears." Julia cleared her throat. "Happy ones. Too much love." She smiled weakly.

Slava placed her hand on Julia's shoulder. "Mama, what's wrong?"

Julia wiped her face with the back of her hand and moved forward to Maksim and Lesia. "It's time to go on your little trip, sweethearts."

"Oh, a picnic?" Lesia clapped excitedly.

Maksim looked up at Slava and back at Julia. "A picnic? Mama, with you?"

"No, not with me."

"What do you mean, Mama?" Slava frowned.

"Remember, I was saying that Papa and I have lovely people we know who will take you two on a little trip and you will stay with them, like you sometimes did with Marta—"

"For how long?" Slava interrupted.

Julia couldn't answer. Lesia reached out for her arm and Maksim stood there, distracted by the bag that Julia held next to her. "I have your toys in here." Julia patted the bag. "And you will have lots of fun because these are good people." Her heart felt like a stone as she said it, because the truth was she could only hope they were.

Julia held out her hand, and the twins placed their hands in her own. "Come, let's make you a little lunch and then we'll go, yes?"

Slava looked back at the garden and ran back to grab the daisy crown and followed them inside. "Mama?"

Julia turned around, letting go of the twins. "Yes, Rabbit."

"Where are Lesia and Maksim going?"

"They'll stay with a nice family for a while."

"But..."

"Can you put a dress on, please? You're going to Marta's."

Slava paused, frowning, waiting for more of an explanation.

"Please do as I say." Julia bit her lip: her curt tone wasn't for Slava, it was for the guilt. "Thank you," she called out to her when she walked off.

.   .   .

After lunch, Henry took Slava to Marta's house. Marta would surely know what had happened, and that knowledge leveled Julia with fresh pain and humiliation.

Julia brought the canvas bag to the front door. She looked back at the two children walking toward her, walking toward the open door that would lead away from the house, toward the car, toward the courthouse and through an entirely different door. One by one, they all walked down the steps, the children first, followed by Henry holding the bag, followed by Julia, after she had shut the door behind her.

* * *

The writing on the sign said, 'Townsville State Department of Child Welfare.' The building was as wide as it was tall, white boarded, with the roof extending in three separate points. The path curved gently toward the door, surrounded by green grass on either side and fences at the border of the property. It was expansive and appeared friendly and warm, despite circumstance. She wondered what the house was like on the inside, what the other children were like, and what ages they were, what languages they spoke.

Walking toward it, Julia felt a sick panic in the center of her chest. She looked behind her quickly and searched for somewhere to run, a path leading somewhere, anywhere, else. It was lunacy—she knew she'd make a spectacle of herself and Henry would probably have her arrested or, worse, taken away from the family entirely. She watched him walk ahead, bags in hand, saw his footsteps; they were purposeful, unlike hers. He had a reason to be there, but did she? She wasn't sure anymore. Maybe her life was not made to have them in it—the extra food and money needed for them. Maybe giving them up to someone else was the ultimate selfless act, for them to be safe, to be looked after.

Julia stood between the twins, their hair tickling her hands as they clung to her. She smiled. "Come. Let's go in."

At the door, the now-familiar Australian lilt echoed in the rooms within. Henry went in first; she followed after.

Two people stood up from their chairs: a woman dressed in a simple green linen jacket and skirt, her dark blonde hair cascading in waves down to her shoulders, and shoes that were polished leather. A man stood next to her, a few inches taller, dark hair that had been doused with a pomade, combed to the side. Dark trousers, white shirt, tie. Bennett stood behind his desk.

"Hello, I'm Gordon, from Welfare..."

"... and my name is Sarah. We work for the state and will be taking the children to their temporary home before they are formally adopted." The woman stretched her hand out. Her skin felt soft, cold; thinly stretched around her delicate fingers, like a doll.

They looked at Julia and the twins.

Julia nodded, clutching the children to her legs. As if feeling her hesitation, they responded by grabbing her skirt nervously, peering from behind it. "Mama, carry." Arms outstretched, waiting. Julia's instinct battled with what was expected of her. She felt an entire room watching her. She bent down and picked up Lesia, her body melting so perfectly into hers, like a thumbprint into dough. Maksim held onto her other leg.

"Here." Julia shifted Lesia off her hip and slid her down to the floor, holding her small hand. She watched as this Sarah woman knelt down and touched Lesia on the arm. She bristled.

"Hi there, sweet girl. Are you excited to come and stay here, and play for a while?"

Lesia, confused, looked up at Julia and reached for her. "Mama? Going?"

"No." The word rode the crest of her sigh. "No, Lesia, you

and Maksim are going with these nice people." She took her hand and gently guided it toward Sarah's.

Henry stood back and watched.

"Yes, your mummy is right, little one." Sarah stood up and uttered every word as if it would break. "You and your brother are coming to stay here. It'll be great fun, and you'll meet so many other children. Is that okay?"

Gordon spoke next, hurrying it along. "Thanks, Sarah, but it's a bit tricky, with the whole"—he spoke out of the side of his mouth—"English language thing." His palms made helpless shapes in the air. "You know, it's a bit hard on all of them."

Julia looked at him and he forced a smile as she scowled. She knew enough English to know when someone was being distasteful.

"Ahh, yes, sure, this is all new to me." Sarah folded her arms, and then dropped them quickly. Apologetically.

Bennett came forward. "Mr. and Mrs. Rudnick, you've signed and dated the required forms... the children will be brought to a temporary housing facility for children their age, where there will be a settling-in period, and the official adoption will be more than likely some point in the future. At that time, we will send you a new birth certificate as a record of the children's new birth names. Does that all sound acceptable to you?"

Julia and Henry both nodded in agreement. Julia sensed the end of the meeting looming, so she reached out to Sarah, despite every cell of herself not wanting to.

"Miss." She touched her arm, and then gestured toward the twins behind her. "It's okay, I will get them ready." She stepped back and crouched down, holding the twins on each side of her, wrapping both arms around their tiny waists, her head in between theirs as she smelled their sugary skin.

She looked at their faces and hungrily memorized them: the new freckles that had recently scattered on the bridge of Maksim's nose; the dark blonde hairs that changed to white at

Lesia's temples and the long eyelashes that had shone through suspended tears in the moments where she'd needed her. Julia raised her hand and placed her son's palm in hers. It was a fraction of the size, so small and fat and unlined.

Lesia's arm snaked around Julia's neck, and it felt so thin, like cold porcelain. In that moment, she saw them as they would be, without her: she saw them at five, as their legs lengthened, and their cheeks hollowed slowly. And then at ten, as their hair thickened and lengthened, and they discovered newfound strength in their small limbs. At fifteen, when they would heal from broken hearts, and find joy in burgeoning love stories. And even at twenty, when their bodies would find their grace and discover a world of their own.

She saw their entire, changing, vivid lives in that moment, and she indulged it and was broken by it: it took every ounce of whatever strength she had left in the very bones of her not to collapse in absolute grief.

She would do that later, alone.

"Be kind," she whispered, and then, "I love you," as she backed away, but they both began to cry and fell into her arms.

It was the hardest thing she had ever done in her life, letting go of them. She couldn't imagine that it would be the last time she would see their faces or say the words that comforted them. The thought was incomprehensible to her.

Sarah appeared by her side, and then a door opened to a different room, one that was behind Bennett's desk that she hadn't noticed before. As Gordon held it open, Sarah took both twins by the hands and led them away.

"Mam*aaa nooo!*" Lesia let out a protracted cry as she turned and saw that her mother wasn't walking with them.

"Please don't take my babies," she mouthed silently, her tears collecting on her lips as she spoke, her body shaking in anguish as she stood, rooted to the spot, Lesia's eyes connecting to hers for the last time as the door closed.

. . .

Julia was unaware that she'd been standing there for five solid minutes, her face and neck slick with tears. She had sobbed silently, her hands in fists at her side, the sounds catching in her throat as her body tensed. She finally became aware that once Sarah and Gordon left, Henry had left the room too, so the only person with her was a young secretary tidying up files and gathering paperwork.

Julia had been deconstructed in her shame, and left to gather herself, alone. She picked up her handbag and tried to find her coat, then realized that she hadn't taken one. She stood there, not understanding what to do with herself, or where to go. And then the only words she could muster were the ones that meant she might preserve some hope. She spoke, her voice fragile. "Hello, miss?"

The girl turned, not a hair out of place, her glasses perched on her nose.

"I... I am the..." Julia stammered, not sure how to begin.

"I know who you are, I logged the appointment," the girl replied, her eyes quizzical. "Can I help you?"

"Can I write to them?"

"To whom?"

"My children."

"I'm not sure that's allowed, because, firstly, they don't have a permanent home yet, and won't for a while, and, secondly, the adoption is closed, and only after a certain age would they be allowed to look for you, and even then, only if their adoptive parents allow it."

It was a list of hurdles that she presented, and Julia hung her head.

"Ah. Okay." She shuddered as she caught her breath and the tears gathered in her eyes again.

The woman approached, and Julia saw she was young. Her

eyes were kind, and her hair was more careless seen up close, wild wisps of it touching her thin neck and delicate shoulders. She reminded Julia of her sister.

"Listen, give it some time." She then paused, looked past Julia through the doorway, and then back at her. "Wait a moment." She walked over to Bennett's desk, opening a drawer and taking out a pen and paper and scrawling down letters and numbers. "I'm probably not supposed to do this, but here." She pressed the bit of paper into Julia's hand and looked intently at her. "This is the address of where they'll be going, as there is an older couple that has been waiting for two children for over a year now. You could write, but I would wait for a while. And maybe one day…" The woman shrugged delicately, letting the small hope linger.

Without looking down, Julia placed it in her handbag and closed it. "I'm so sorry," she murmured. "So sorry… my babies—"

"No, I understand," the woman interrupted, and paused as if to say something else; as if she too had had a broken heart that had been left to heal somehow.

And then she changed, her face stiffening, and she walked out of the office, her stride with a purpose, holding files that proved to anyone who'd possibly seen her that she'd been so busy with her work that she had spent a little while longer making sure it was all done properly.

Julia nodded. Turning on her heel, she slowly walked toward the door. As she did so, she noticed that her handbag had nail marks pressed into the worn cream leather. And in that handbag, she remembered that she'd brought the twins' original birth certificates with her, not knowing whether Bennett needed them or not. They were still there, folded into two small squares, next to an address, invisible to everyone but her.

PART 3

AUSTRALIA

1952–1953

CHAPTER TWENTY-ONE

MELBOURNE

The radio in the kitchen crackled briefly with a weather bulletin, something about *Cairns* and *flood warning* as Irene turned the knob and found a station with classical music, before sliding the lamb roast into the oven and heading upstairs to the bathroom.

She washed her hands, drying them on a towel that was folded neatly in the corner of the bathroom and, pin by pin, took down her hair from its nested bun, watching as it unfolded and dropped past her shoulders. She put each pin carefully in a glass box, and ran her fingers from temple to nape, her scalp aching from the past few days' happenings. She looked at her face—her eyes were tired, but the black of her lashes and the powder on her cheeks were all still in place; there had been no tears. She wondered if there would be, one day, but for now, all she felt was grateful.

She undid the clasp on her watch and set it down, walking down the hallway, and saw Bill standing in the doorway of the small bedroom opposite their own.

"Hey." She joined him and folded her arms across her chest. She watched, contentedly, as the two children in front of them explored their space, little arms out, wandering curiously as they reached for things they had never seen before: the unfamiliar beds; the soft, cool pillows; squealing at the beautifully painted toys. They touched these new objects to see how they lived in this world, and what their place was.

Their beds were separate, both solid wood frames, the sheets and pillows decorated in whites and pale yellows, embroidered with ducklings. There was a noble wooden rocking horse in the corner, positioned as if it had waited its whole life to be ridden. There was a small wardrobe up against the wall full of lovely clothes, and books laid out on the dresser that sat underneath the window, with two stuffed rabbits on either side of the pile.

"Mama?" said the girl as she stood by the rocking horse, her fingers entwined in its yarn mane. Her eyes were searching Irene's—she wasn't calling for her but another. "Mama."

"Yes, Roslyn? What do you need, Ed?"

Confused at the name, the girl wandered over to her brother who was standing unsteadily at the window, pointing. She grabbed his body to steady herself and then placed a little hand on the window, the fields beyond winking in the sunlight.

"Mama, Mama" she murmured softly, eyes searching.

Irene turned to Bill and saw water in his eyes, soft regret etched in his face.

She smiled and grabbed his forearm, squeezing it gently. "Bill. Listen. We'll be alright, sweetheart. They'll understand that their life started when we found them, and that's all they'll ever have to know."

"I realize that, honey. But God, what a crazy thing, this." He ran a hand through his hair and looked over at Irene. "We have kids now. A boy and a girl. They were someone's and now they're *ours*." He looked over at her. "Will they be alright?"

Irene smiled stiffly, a deep breath lodged in her chest. "Why wouldn't they be?"

"Well, there's a mother out there. We don't know her story. Will we? Will they, ever?" He nodded to the twins, seated on the floor, playing with a few wooden blocks. "I mean, am I right to even bring it up?"

"Why do they need to know her story?"

Bill shrugged. "Because they might want to know where they came from, one day."

Irene frowned. "Are you regretting this?"

"No, of course not, honey. We're so lucky. I'm just thinking out loud, that's all."

Irene patted him on the back and linked her arm through his. "I know. I guess we'll have to play it by ear, really. They didn't come from the best of backgrounds, really."

"How do you know?"

"An immigrant family—sugarcane farmers. Not exactly the most stable environment."

"Sure, I guess." Bill smiled as Roslyn looked up at him, showing him a book that she'd found. "Do you think they were happy?"

"I don't know. I assume so. But we could drive ourselves crazy second-guessing this. The most important thing is that we can love them, and take care of them, and tell them that we wanted them so much, that God granted our wish."

Bill leaned his head toward Irene and kissed her on the cheek. "You're right. They'll be happy."

She looked up at him, her eyes resolute. "Of course they will be, we'll always make sure of it. There won't be a reason to look back. Only forward." She smoothed her hair, a thin gold bracelet gleaming on her wrist.

"Right. Let's get the table set for dinner, yes?"

And before he could respond, she walked away, the hallway echoing with her footsteps, the children's laughter behind her.

CHAPTER TWENTY-TWO

STRATFORD, MARCH 1953

"Hey, Hank, would ya help us out with these here boards?"

The clang of bells erupted in the distance, but it didn't announce a celebration, for no one was at the church for joy—or for mourning. It was empty, and the peal was to warn of the weather to arrive.

Everyone who was able had left their houses that afternoon to prepare, to shield and make secure from winds and rain. Henry was in town that morning and the warning bells had pealed just as he was approached by the butcher.

Henry cringed. "Yeah, righto, Al. Give me a minute." No amount of reminding people would help, not even after years of living in Stratford: the iteration of his given name had taken many forms, and it was a useless cause—no one had ever bothered to learn to say his name correctly. There had always been a "Do you have a shorter name, mate?" thrown around since their arrival. Almost immediately, he'd been christened with a new, easier name, which had helped him fit with the group of laborers in the cane fields. He considered them all a boring, provincial collection of busybodies, but he reluctantly accepted it, for this was a lesson in humility, though the gossip would travel that it quite curious that a loving mother would punish her child with a name as ridiculous as "Hironimus," and "Henry" was so formal, so "Hank" it was.

He raised a few thin planks of wood upright, a hammer and nails jangling in the leather pouch that hung over his cotton trousers. It was almost useless, this preparation, because the farmhouses were sparse in material to begin with: thin pieces of driftwood reinforcing door frames, thick tape across windows. Moving crockery and furniture to recessed corners of their homes was all they could do, really, and pray that the destruction would be minimal.

The last years had seen Henry successfully earning enough money to buy more land around their house, and they'd developed it into a farm: it reminded them of home. A few more cows, and goats, and feral cats that lingered and languished on the porch. The expanse of it all had connected Henry and Julia with a thin thread, but it was enough, and now they'd met enough people that they would have the help if they needed it, and a bit of the burden was lifted. They'd arrived there so naive and hopeful, off a steamship from war, like artifacts from a building that was destroyed, and now it was a life that made sense to them, finally, despite the pain at the edges.

That morning, leaving the house, he had seen Julia holding Slava's hand in one hand and a basket in the other, Slava filling it with eggs that she had collected, and his heart felt a little less of the anguish that he had privately endured.

"I have never asked you, actually"—Henry embraced a pile of thick brown-parcel paper that had just been shoved into his arms—"about your name."

"Mine?" Al's eyes were perpetually half-lidded, as if he'd just woken up, or the sun had always been too bright for him. He stared at Henry as if a strange smell had been put in front of him, and ran his palms across his shirt, marking it with dirt.

"Yes. Is it short for anything?"

"Well." The man scratched his head and paused, as if no one had ever asked him this before, and he was sure no one would again. "Albert. But only my mum called me that, and only when I was bein' a right old pain." He smiled at another memory. "My dad always called me Al, come to think of it."

"It was my mother who called me by a shorter name. She'd always liked *Henry*. My father called me Hironimus."

"I thought your name was Henry."

"That's my shorter name."

"Oh, that's right. You told me you had a big, long name but God, that's a hard one to say. Do ya mind that I say *Hank*?"

Maybe I don't mind after all, Henry thought. Maybe Al had asked Henry for help because he knew he was good for something, and although he probably thought of him as the immigrant with the pretty, sad wife and the tearaway blonde girl, maybe this was a way that they fit him onto the page of their lives, in faint pencil script; this could be the way he would be understood, if only for a short while.

Henry smiled. "Albert, I don't mind."

Al caught the joke and laughed, clapping him on the back. "Let's get a beer." And the two men walked off, the oval shape of sweat soaking through the backs of their shirts.

The house was quiet because Henry had left, as he usually did after dinner. The sky that night had turned dark unusually early, and Julia was busy sitting with Slava, whispering the flourishing ending of a fairy tale.

Henry's solitary ritual began the same way each night: around nine o'clock he'd check his shirt pocket, feeling for the soft packet of cigarettes, and then roll up his sleeves as he walked out the screen door to the small square of land out front.

The wooden and glass structure was only as high as he was tall, and it had been one of the first things he'd put in when they arrived at the house. He had begun a small collection of orchids that he received from a florist in Stratford, who in turn had traveled to Fiji to procure them from an orchid farm.

Tonight, his hands hovered, tender and large, over their thin skeletons; lips and spurs never attaching to the soot on his fingertips, his eyes worshipful over each curve. A chipped tumbler held the dregs of some vodka, and balanced timidly on the edge of a short wooden stool beside him. He'd thrown that stool across the room in a fit of anger a few months before and had tried to repair the legs, but he hadn't done it very well, so it wobbled.

"You have yet to fix that," Julia pointed out, leaning against the frame. She had been watching him for a while now, and he hadn't noticed.

"Yes, I'm aware."

"Okay, well." She stopped, wanting to say something else of purpose. "What's the use in a broken thing?"

His jaw went rigid. He looked at Julia and plucked the back of his shirt, moon shapes of sweat marking his armpits. "I'll fix it. I'm aware." He prodded it with his hand. "It's still useful."

She watched as a tin-framed lamp cast a tall silhouette of his bent frame against the glass panels of the greenhouse.

"How long will you be?"

"Does it matter?" The corner of his mouth flattened into his cheek. "To you, I mean. Does it matter?" He leaned on his knee and waited, examining her face. It was plain and drawn, and he thought of what she had accomplished that evening: he imagined that she had quietly swept the floor after dinner; he imagined that she had wiped the back of her wet hands on the front panel of her skirt, and smoothed her hair back off the neck that he had touched so often. He imagined her to be the girl he'd seen, that day when he'd projected a future memory of her, as all men and women do. He looked at her now and felt a sour taste at the back of his throat. So much had changed, though he loved her still, but his anger hovered faintly above him like a moving cloud, following him, setting the rains on him when he thought of the past. He lit another cigarette and turned away.

Julia rubbed her palm with the opposite thumb, watching the shadows battle the creamy yellow lamplight. "Things matter, yes." She shrugged her shoulders. "Maybe, only to me."

They both kept a polite distance from the other. Politeness was survival.

He stood up, misting a petal—it was the darkest red, the color of clotted blood—watching as the water settled and veiled.

Julia pursed her lips at his silence.

"I'm going to bed." She looked up and felt the heaviness of the air. The farmlands were peaceful and deserted. She turned on her heel, her skirts kicking at the back of her knee as she walked into the night.

Not long after, as Henry closed the glass door behind him and the lamplight had flickered its end, he drew on the last of his cigarette. He stood in the dark, feeling the air change direction; beneath the layers of his skin, underneath his clothes, he felt it. He speculated, as he sometimes did, that he wasn't sure he could have been anything in particular in his life, but he could survive it, survive all of it, and wasn't that the point? Love wasn't the thing that he could understand. Perseverance was. And maybe within perseverance is a commitment to loving someone.

He stepped forward, taking a quick look back at the orchids, protected in their small, dark space, and walked toward the house, his footsteps heavy in his battered and torn boots. He finished the last of his cigarette, the embers dying in the ground as he crushed out the final spark. The winds picked up momentum, and he only vaguely noticed the glass shudder in response to the gathering storm.

· · ·

She thought she was dreaming when the howling started. It wasn't even dawn yet, and Julia sat bolt upright in bed, quickly realizing that she was definitely not dreaming. The wind was whipping around the house, slamming against the shutters, forcing the trees to bend and huddle and beg. The family had weathered wet season successfully before, but this was different. It was angry and inhospitable and relentless in its pursuit to destroy. She ran into the kitchen and tried to switch on a radio. Static. She checked the phone line. Dead. Henry was still asleep. She debated waking him as it was so early. Instead, she went back to bed and prayed for it to stop.

It didn't.

An hour or so later, and something hit the house. It sounded like a piece of wood. Then from the other side, a cracking sound. More wind, higher pitched sounds and moaning, like an animal dying. She got out of bed again, and this time Henry started to stir. She padded to the kitchen and looked out the window. Sheets and sheets of gray, horizontal rain, the sky threateningly dark and furious.

"Henry!" she hissed as she ran back into their room. "HENRY!"

"What, what is it? Why are you panicking?"

"There's a storm out there, it's bad. I don't know what's happening."

He ran out with her to the window. "Ahh, God damn it, the fields will be flooded soon." He ran back to get dressed in anything he could find. "Check the animals!" he shouted back.

Julia threw on a coat and boots and opened the door carefully, forcing her way outside. The winds were extraordinary; she felt like she could be lifted so easily, her arms and legs tethered to nothing and everything all at once. She made it outside, clutching the side of the house as the winds howled, running against the rains and into the pens to check on the cows and chickens.

She cupped her hands around her mouth and called, shrieked, shouted, and waited for sounds of reply. She kept walking, each footstep lifting off before she could plant it. And then she found them all, the cows huddled together, matted chocolate and white hides, lying in a corner of the pen, lamenting. The goats in the next pen, bleating their distress, a strange dog howling underneath the house, cats mewing their discontent.

She didn't know what to do, and she watched them helplessly. She needed Henry to guide her.

She ran back to see him surveying the damage on the outside of the house. He was soaked through, and there was a vulnerability in his face that she recognized from long ago. "I'm going in. The animals seem to be fine, but even if they weren't, there's nothing we could do."

"Okay, go in. Make sure Slava's room is secure."

"How?"

"Just... I don't know! Take things off shelves, get her on the ground, just *go!*" Henry ran to herd the animals to somewhere safe, and disappeared from view.

Slava had got out of bed. The wind was coming through the rooms with unrelenting force. "Mama! Papa!" She was sitting in the middle of her room, by the door, shaking, huddling under blankets as Julia ran in. "What's happening?!"

"Wet season... just more wet than usual, I guess," Julia joked feebly as she walked toward her. Just then, a loud cracking sound interrupted her, and she veered to the window to see a tree split in half as if by an otherworldly force and fall to the ground. *Henry.* She ran back outside, shouting for him, her voice suffocated by the winds, every breath drawn out of her.

She finally heard him faintly, and saw him in the driving rain, a small body moving across the grass, eerily bright. She stood resolutely, gripping the side of the door, letting the wind whip her hair, the weight of her dress increasing as the hem absorbed millions of drops of warm rain.

"Mama? What's happening?" Slava sat huddled under her blankets still.

"It's fine, Papa is sorting it out. It's fine." She turned back into the house, and then heard him clattering up the steps.

He pushed through the door, breathless. "Jesus Christ, it's bad out there. It's as if the world has been stamped flat." A sudden crack silenced them all, louder this time: it came from the left side of the house, as if the sky had imploded. Then a howl against the window, pushing in. She looked over at him and saw him reach for her. "Julia, down. Get down!"

Not a moment after he reached her and she crouched over Slava and he embraced them both, the window cracked in half and shattered completely, sending shards of wet glass and pouring rain into the middle of the room.

They waited. Slava was crying.

"Shhhh... shhhhh," Julia whispered. "Stay quiet." Just then, another aggressive gust of wind bellowed through the other window, crossing through the center of the house and lifting it up, an invisible hand unlatching the entire house and setting it back down like a toy onto the earth.

"Uuhm," Slava whimpered, her nails digging into Julia's arm.

"It'll pass, Slava. Be patient."

It took until late that afternoon for the winds to stop and the rains to slow, and it was only then, when people were safe to venture carefully out of their houses, that the devastation began to reveal itself. It was oddly peaceful. Julia and Henry stood outside the house, speechless at how much flooding there was. The first two steps leading up to their house were submerged.

The sugar cane drooped inches from the ground. There was no electricity for miles. It was a wasteland.

"How am I supposed to fix this?" Henry sat down on the top step, lighting a cigarette. "How the *hell* am I supposed to see past this? *This?*" He waved his hand at the scene in front of him. Restless, he stood up again and walked down the steps, stopping at the second one, his toes hitting the water. He looked down, trapped for the time being by his own country. He understood the feeling.

He looked across, to his left. He'd hoped against hope that the greenhouse would be intact. Julia joined him, placing her arm through his as they scanned the front garden: it was a mess of floating debris and broken things, the mixture of soil and the perfume of the crushed flowers on the flat earth combined to create a metallic, iron-rich fragrance, a watery grave of sorts; if it had been a funeral, Henry would have wept.

CHAPTER TWENTY-THREE

APRIL 1954

The greenhouse hadn't been rebuilt even a year later, and they were still finding bits of glass and gnarled pieces of steel that had been carried by the winds as far as the trees at the perimeter of the farm. They had gathered much of the carcasses of wood and metal from various parts of the farm and had given it to the town to use for scraps. The town itself was still healing, and shops were slowly, delicately, coming to life as if recovering from an illness. The houses had been flattened and emptied, the sugarcane fields partially destroyed. People stayed, promising to rebuild, honoring their commitment to what they promised as immigrants. They didn't feel they could go anywhere else.

None of the animals had survived, so they had used what very little they could from the flesh and buried the rest.

Julia wore trousers and a short-sleeved shirt as she dug in the garden, planting new seeds. Slava was sitting in her underwear next to her, the heat of the day on their backs. In the days leading up to the storm, Julia's one small source of hope was that her parents managed to finally write to her. The letter was simple and sweet, saying how much they wished to be with her and Slava, and that the farm was further weakened by Russian occupation, though they still somehow felt safe. Her parents, once devoutly religious, now could not attend church and had to worship in their own house with their own talismans and items that they had saved during the war. Julia was happy that they were still alive, and free of illness, but she ached to see them.

"Mama." Slava sank her small hand into the dirt and removed a worm. "Do you think Papa is sad?"

"About what, sweetheart?" Julia couldn't face a question about the twins, and she set her teeth in anticipation.

"The little ones."

It is still a wound, Julia thought, and winced."What little ones?"

"The flowers."

The greenhouse. "Oh, you mean the purple flowers?"

"Yes. Those. He was always in that little house with the 'little ones,' the little flowers."

Julia sat back on her heels, her knees folded underneath her. "Those were his orchids, yes." She looked across at the land that was empty now. "He worked hard protecting them."

"He loved them."

Julia smiled at her daughter. "He did. He loved them very much."

"Will he get more?"

Julia began to dig again, her tears wetting the soil. "No, sweetheart. We won't be getting any more." She looked over at Slava. "Hey," she whispered conspiratorially.

Slava squinted in the sun. "Yes, Mama?"

Julia hooked a finger and Slava leaned closer to her. Julia suddenly wrapped her in her arms and nuzzled her neck. Slava erupted into giggles as the soil sprinkled off Julia's hands onto her sunlit hair.

.   .   .

That evening the family celebrated Henry's birthday, the day of the twins' birth, and Julia would never forget what that day meant as long as she lived. Her heart freshly ached, as if the twins had been gone only minutes, and it was then, after the sticky sweetness of cake had faded and the coffee had been poured and Slava was asleep, that she knew she couldn't do this anymore. Not here. Not anywhere, really, but having the constant reminder of ghosts that never returned—it was too much for her now.

The cyclone had been an ending and a new beginning, but the emptiness was still there. Old memories living in the walls that surrounded her.

Julia leaned over the table and watched Henry as he sipped his coffee. She knew him well enough by now to know that his thoughts were wheeling in his head. "Henry. What are you thinking about?"

He put his cup down and it rattled into the saucer. He spun it slowly with a finger. "We spent a year rebuilding this farm."

"I know. It's getting better, slowly." She wondered where this would go.

Henry stood up. The room where they'd been through so much, the house where they never seemed to stray far from the pain and the arguments and the memories of love lost and gained; it suddenly occurred to him that he'd grown accustomed to it. He tapped his chest pocket and slowly reached for a cigarette. They had grown accustomed to life as it was, there, reinventing the story in the same spot.

"I have an idea." He snapped his lighter shut, and flicked it open again.

Julia held her breath. All of a sudden she wasn't sure what he would say, and she braced herself as if she would fall into the sea.

"I don't think the journey for us ends here."

Julia slowly let out her breath. "You're talking as if we're dying."

He placed his hands in his pockets and walked slowly around the room, a skeptical laugh in his throat. "Granite."

"What?"

He stopped pacing and faced Julia. "You told me once I was made of granite. And you are made of dreams. Rebirth."

Julia warmed at the memory, but it saddened her. So much had happened since then, and she wasn't sure she believed it now. "Yes, I remember. But what does that mean?"

"It means that we have to keep going. I don't think we're meant to be here."

"Why?"

"Well, most importantly, because there's not much left here, let's be honest. It'll take a slow time to rebuild the industry, despite the many willing to do so. My work has been rebuilding this farm, and not earning as much money as I could be. We are living off what we saved, and there won't be much left unless we change course."

Julia folded her arms. "What are you suggesting?"

"We move."

Julia dropped her hands to the table. "Our entire life has been about moving! Where?"

"I've been thinking for a while about Sydney. I've been planning. Meeting with people. Seeing where the opportunities lie. We need to earn money, and we can't do it here. Sydney has jobs for people like us. I don't necessarily care what it is, but it will be a sight better than cutting cane for fourteen hours a day. It's a city, so we can rent a small place like we did in Germany."

Julia shot him a skeptical look.

Henry walked over and sat down. "It will be temporary. But cities are where the opportunities are. We have to move with the tide."

Julia groaned and reached for his cigarette, which both

shocked Henry and connected him to her briefly. She inhaled on it and gave it back to him. "And isn't that the way, for us, Henry?" The smoke rippled out of her mouth. "Isn't that how we survive? The leopard that changes his spots for his world."

Henry lit a fresh cigarette, searching her face. "God knows we've made a meal out of the misfortune of the years past."

Julia stood up and walked over to the window by the door. She saw so little of what had been. "When will we come back to ourselves, I wonder."

"When the time is right for us to." Henry tapped fresh ashes into the saucer beside him. "But we can never get back to who we were. Life doesn't work that way. We learn more about who we are when we look ahead."

Later that night, after Henry had retired to bed, Julia remembered again that it was his birthday—their birthday. Soon, this house would be empty, deserted of the lives that they had created, and she would be gone.

And so she decided that she would write.

She would write to them finally, and she would see them, if only for a second.

She scanned the shelf behind her for a piece of paper and then saw it: the faded book that she had read to Slava so many times, about the lost mitten and the animals that had burst it at the seams. She opened it and wistfully shuffled the pages with her fingertips, stopping on something inside: two pressed wildflowers that they'd given her, and that she'd casually promised to keep but then actually did. She'd forgotten about this, and it flooded her memory with their faces and their voices and their laughter. She ran her fingers over the small, dried husks and flat petals and was grateful for the discovery, as she placed it back on the shelf and began to write, her tears staining the paper.

* * *

It was a week later when Julia walked down a quiet street in Melbourne, her throat tight, her hands trembling. She had been so close. She had almost seen their faces.

She had heard their laughter; she had seen the house. She knew they were happy without her, and it was a small comfort. But it would be the last time her footsteps would take her anywhere near them. The tide was receding under her feet again, but this time she would be different; this time, she would lock away a part of herself. And with each mile that took her back to Stratford, each road that she walked, each frame of landscape that passed by her window seat on the bus, she would grow stronger still, until this memory healed into a faded scar, like the one on her face.

Just before she arrived at the bus stop, she passed by a stone building with heavy, red-painted wooden doors. Worshippers were filing in slowly for service. She looked at the engraved plaque: *St. Maria Goretti Catholic Church.* She said a silent prayer that someday she would find them, and kept walking.

* * *

In 1955, the family resettled in Sydney. They found space in a hostel in the center of town, and Henry began to work for a wealthy property developer, collecting rent from tenement buildings down by the docks. Though the work was menial and occasionally hostile, he was the only one in the group of migrant workers who insisted on wearing a suit, as if he could see more for himself than this. It was a pleasing arrogance that caught the eye of the developer and he kept a watchful eye on the tall, dark-eyed man who kept to himself and didn't talk much.

Over the course of his work, he developed a liking for Henry, and would call him into his office for a quick chat, finding out more about who he was and where he had come from, and what family he had. It was on one of those occasions that he told Henry about his cousin in New York.

"You haven't ever been, I assume." The man lit up a fat cigar and unbuttoned his jacket, revealing a silk waistcoat. He had a paunch that matched the roughness of his face, and fat fingers that splayed out when his thumb hooked into his pocket.

"No, sir, I have not." Henry sat uneasily.

The man cleared his throat. "I sometimes forget that you're a Uke, a spillover from the war."

Henry was used to these kinds of conversations. They didn't matter to him anymore.

"Reason is, I think there's something about you." He chewed on the end of the cigar. "Something that I think I could use you for."

"And what would that be?"

"Work. You and a load of other immigrants that have gusto. Fire. Mettle."

"I'm not sure what you mean."

The man leaned forward. "New York. I have a cousin who has a few buildings in the city. A part of the city, anyway, called Brooklyn. He'll need people like you." He lit the end of his cigar again, took a few puffs, and leaned back.

Henry was interested. "What kind of work?"

"Oh, very wonderful and amazing. Job of a lifetime." The man smiled, knowingly overselling it, his bald head glistening as he sat behind his oak desk. "Beautiful buildings that need work and managing. He needs me to ship over a whole load of you to him, and he'll sponsor it. God knows both of us are rich enough, and there are too many of you here, crawling around, as it is. Australia needs a bit of a clean out." He stared at Henry. "Well?"

Henry flattened his mustache with his fingers, his breath even. "Where would we live?"

"Tenement housing. There are people dropping off boats over there, like little ants, getting work. It's the American Dream, son." The man was only ten years older than Henry but looked and acted as if he'd stumbled into money and grabbed it all voraciously. Greedily. "What do you say?"

Henry closed his eyes and wondered if this decision would finally be the one to destabilize him. Or maybe it would be the one that would build him back up again.

CHAPTER TWENTY-FOUR

Julia stood at the side of a white steel ship painted with huge black letters: **ORSOVA**. Sydney harbor surrounded her and countless others waiting to board. Black smoke poured out of the top of the ship like a boiling kettle, simmering, waiting for its owner to claim it. Spires of metal protruding into the sky, life rafts secured at the top, tugboats tethered to its side. Though it was so large, the ship projected a kind of submissiveness: it was tied to the docks, on both sides, with giant ropes the width of her legs, if not wider.

It all felt too familiar. Office buildings stood tall and watchful, rooted in their places, an unchanging landscape to her constantly changing one.

She held Slava's hand, gripping it tightly as if reassuring herself that this was all real, all right, all supposed to happen. Slava stood still, her recently bobbed hair glossy and thick underneath a hat. Her dress was thick, layered with a sweater and coat in preparation for the unknown weather changes. They were ready to board: Henry had already given over all of their possessions, and they'd signed the passenger list.

There was talk of fresh food and music and rooms that had

quaint portholes to watch the world go by. She didn't know what Henry had paid for, or what they could afford, and she was careful in her expectations. But in comparison, it sounded a more comfortable journey than the passage to Australia. *Leaving is nicer, it seems*, she thought, romantically.

"Three weeks or so, they say." A woman leaned toward Julia, clutching a pamphlet and fanning her face. Julia assessed her, as women do, quickly and surreptitiously: she had tight red curls gathered underneath a small cream-colored pillbox hat with lace edges, and wore a dress that cinched at her waist and was the buttery color of late-autumn sunflowers. She smelled extraordinary, like musty roses and lilies, and hanging off her thin wrist was an impractically small beige handbag. "Three infernal weeks stuck on this thing! Well, at least there's decent food."

"Mmm. Yes, three weeks." Julia nodded, immediately chastising herself for speaking to this woman.

The woman smiled, her claret-red lips revealing clean white perfect teeth; rich women always looked so immaculate. "So. America as well, then?"

Julia was taken aback by the small talk, and she smoothed her hair. "Sorry?"

"America. You are *going* there, yes?" Her words were deliberately slow, but that was imperceptible to Julia.

"Ah. America. Yes." She nodded a few too many times, but once she said it out loud, it felt real, as if a missing brick in a wall had been found.

Julia was too conscious of her own thoughts to hear that the woman had whispered something about "infernal immigrants" before she moved away.

One of the first things Julia noticed when they boarded was that there were soft lounge chairs. And tables with smooth wooden corners. And oddly shaped glass ashtrays. And crisp white napkins on tablecloth-draped tables in the main dining area. It was as if someone had poured the contents of a wealthy man's house straight into the belly of a ship. She was staring, amazed that such a thing existed.

"Madam, please keep going. Tourist class is down below," a steward said with a sneer, interrupting her thoughts. He didn't realize she'd knowingly been holding up the line.

"This, it's all so wonderful." She gestured. She'd never seen anything so grand that made her feel so insignificant.

"First class, madam," he responded, staring at her as if he'd smelled something awful.

"Mmm. Yes. Yes, of course," and deliberately, slowly, she walked in the direction he'd pointed in.

She had learned to stand tall in the face of ignorance.

"You did that on purpose," Henry admonished, laughter in his eyes.

"Of course, I did."

The family finally reached the lower level, and then it was onward to find their cabin: past the toilet room, past the hall with the hot machinery spitting steam, past many other cabins crowded with families and couples, and around the corner from another set of rooms, this time used for the storage of medical equipment. And then a small oval door, and they saw what their space for the next weeks would be: a small room decorated in green and yellow plaid cotton fabric and brown tones. There was a small wooden dresser that was secured to the wall, a sink and cabinet, and two beds, one on top of the other, in bunk fashion.

There was one toilet and one shower, and they were down the hall, and were communal.

They dropped their bags in a heap and tried to remember where the dining hall was, which now, looking back, seemed a gargantuan journey.

"Christ. Davai, Slava, come with me." Julia grabbed her hand. "Let's have a look around." As she left the cabin, she turned to see Henry leaning against the tiniest porthole, half the size of his head.

"Do you want to come with us?"

"No. You go. I can meet you later."

The ship felt like a small city, teeming with people dressed in immaculate silks and hats with grosgrain ribbons, men in suits carrying leather briefcases; it all felt as if she were in a dream, or part of a large theater, and background players were the ones that looked like Julia: plain cotton dresses and sensible shoes, hair tied back and faces slightly reddened from exercise or fresh air. Slava was in awe of it all, walking the decks with her mother, their hair whipping across their faces, listening to stories about this big city called New York that they would arrive in, and the new lives that would unfold for them.

In the weeks ahead, Julia would find time for reflection, and search for quiet moments where she was alone. The pages of her life had been scattered, but she felt that someday she would find the missing ones and stitch the story back together again—there was still hope. It wasn't just because she had kept the birth certificates: Henry had reminded her that she was made of dreams. And when the breezes combined with the water to cool the air surrounding her face, she looked at the sea and sky as they pursed the horizons together. And she finally almost felt whole again.

*Like billowing clouds, like the incessant gurgle of the brook,
the longing of the spirit can never be stilled.*

—Hildegard von Bingen

PART 4

NEW YORK

1955–1981

CHAPTER TWENTY-FIVE

NEW YORK, 1978

It was April, and Henry had forgotten her birthday by five days, so Julia hadn't been expecting him to walk through the door brandishing two wrapped packages in his arms.

The weather had been gray, and the skies had opened, the city pavements flooding with the hurried footsteps of people heading back home to dinners and musty hallways and rain pelting on the windows.

Henry placed his umbrella by the heavy door and took off his felt tweed fedora that he was almost never without. He shrugged off his overcoat, hooked it on the back of the door, and remembered to turn the three metal latches to lock it, as well as the one above that slid into the top of the frame. Sometimes he forgot how strange it was, to lock a door more than once, but this was New York, and he'd seen enough doors kicked in to remember.

Twenty years had passed since the steamship had docked in San Francisco. Twenty years since they boarded a train that seemed to take months, and where Slava had suffered with an upset stomach due to suspect food, and where their journey had finally ended as the train pulled into Pennsylvania Station, New York City.

Almost immediately, the smell in the air was of steel and exhaust fumes, along with the sounds of car horns, and the voices of crowds of people, and the calls of children sitting on stoops and playing games in the street.

The family found a small two-bedroom tenement apartment, on East 71st Street on the corner of First Avenue, in an area called Lenox Hill ("But there are no hills, Henry! Madness!"). It was on the street, which was odd—to them, anyway. There was no garden; there were only wide expanses of concrete surrounding doorsteps. The apartment was in the basement ("Henry, are we supposed to live underground? Who lives like this?") and they soon found out that their landlord, Jeffy, didn't like children. Jeffy was short and loud and had thick curly hair piled on top of his head, while his face was covered in small, round scars. He wore orange trousers that were wide at the bottom, and had a long index finger that he used to emphasize his words. "I. Don'. Wan'. Crazy. Chil'ren!" he would bellow in his thick Jamaican accent, and then laugh. It gave Slava nightmares. It was only over the course of many months that she would learn of Jeffy's own dark story, which he told her in quiet moments: Jeffy's grandmother and grandfather had been slaves, and he explained what slaves were, and then his mother had married a white man and when he'd been born, his father had rejected him and put out cigarettes on his face, as a result of which he spent his entire life feeling a specific kind of anger at the world, and felt lonely in a city that was teeming with bodies.

New York was full of colors and shapes and towers of concrete and brick, its streets scattering their capillaries of rubble and noise and life. There were rats, and sewers that steamed through the streets and subways that smelled faintly of urine and roasted peanuts, but it was beautiful in its own grotesque way. Julia had traveled from farmland and storms, open skies and animals, to a city that smelled like the color gray. It was wonderful and shocking and unnerving and incomprehensibly narrow.

She enrolled Slava in a small school down the road, on 69th and Second, and it wasn't an easy transition for her. Slava spoke very little English, and what little she had was tinged with an Australian lilt. As her long blonde hair fell down her back, she wore it in a plait wrapped in a circle on top of her head. She was indefinable and misplaced, which was seen as "weird" by most of her peers. Slava's name was purposefully mispronounced as "slave", or "saliva." These trials made her strong, but not without many tears.

Julia accepted a job at William H. Fisk Insurance Company, in a neo-gothic monster of a building with a facade that looked like an overuse of architectural styles on South William Street. As an assistant she enjoyed it, because it was the same, every day, and that monotony was comfortable to her. People found her likeable and hard-working, and she endeared herself to them—this small, dark-haired woman who had kind, sad eyes, and who always kept a small photograph of what looked to be her parents in her desk drawer. She arrived not a minute later than nine o'clock, and sometimes a minute before, and spoke very little, as her broken English was still an obstacle for her, though no one minded very much.

"Happy birthday." Henry handed her two boxes: one small one, wrapped neatly in gold paper, and one rectangular one, wrapped in red. His face was beautifully expectant.

She looked up from her sewing. "Bit late, no?" Slava was out with friends and had left an array of clothes on the fabric couch. Her tights had holes in them, and they weren't going to fix themselves, so she'd been sitting in her stockinged legs, Indian style, carefully mending them.

"I know, I know, but better than never." He sat down next to her.

"Well, thank you." She meant it. "That's sweet. But I didn't really ask for anything."

"Yes, but I always hear you when we walk down Fifth and you stop and stare through the windows." He took her needle and replaced it with the gifts. "Open them."

She looked at him with tenderness, a bit like a child, and gently undid the smaller parcel, her fingers weary from working all day.

He watched her cautiously, ever so slightly wary but connected. "I wasn't sure what you'd like, but I know you well enough that when I saw this, I thought it would suit you."

The gold paper revealed a navy-blue, rectangular box. In it was a bracelet: glittering strands of marcasite soldered into silver, strands as delicate as cobwebs, linked together and wrapped around oval pieces of flat, shining onyx. Black mirrors, six of them, surrounding her wrist as lightly as flower petals.

"Henry, my God. I love it. Where on earth did you find something like this?"

"There are a lot of little antique shops down by my building in Brooklyn, you know, by Prospect? The owner showed me this, said it was made in Poland. I'm glad you like it." His speech was unsentimental and somehow warm at the same time.

"I do, oh, I do." She started to open the second box, the larger of the two. "And... this? Can't think what this might be."

Before she even saw what was within, the paper seemed soaked with the smell of gardenia, lilacs, and lilies; comforting and familiar. It smelled of wet grass and wildflowers and summers spent without care. It smelled of childhood. The red paper revealed a box on the inside, pale pink, the profile of a woman's face etched on the front.

"What? You bought me perfume?"

"Yes. You love flowers, always moan that there aren't enough in the house, that you don't have a garden to grow them, and we don't have the money"—he paused, as if to say something else, but then continued—"and, well, I thought it would be a good memory for you, though I didn't do it *all* myself... the woman behind the counter had to help me, and oh, it was a *process*, let me tell you."

She laughed at the thought of Henry's height darkening a glass-underlit counter, opposite an immaculately groomed woman with shining hair and high heels, testing fragrances. Dark and light. "Well, the effort was worth it."

He remembered her this way, her hair falling forward, still long, but now with a dusting of silver strands underneath and by her forehead. "When I first saw you, in Lviv—I mean, I may be wrong here—but I think you were carrying a basket of flowers?"

"What? No, you're an idiot. It was a basket of washing, probably."

"Well, sorry! Either way, this is your gift." And he took his shoes off and walked to the kitchen to wash his hands and light the stove to make tea for them both. "When is Slava coming back?" he called over his shoulder.

"She's out with her friends, leave her alone. She is not a child anymore."

Henry walked back, rolling up his sleeves. "She's still a child in my mind's eye." He sighed, sitting down heavily on the chair opposite Julia.

By the time Slava was in her mid twenties, Julia and Henry had carved out a steady life for themselves in New York.

Using some money that he had saved from his time in Australia, and now in Manhattan, Henry bought his own rental building in Brooklyn. It was welfare housing and although it was going to be hard, he knew how to manage a piece of run-down real estate: phone calls in the middle of the night to fix persistent leaks, heating that had gone off, brownouts: this was his role. A doctor to a building. He would drive hours in a round trip, and still get up in the morning to bring Slava to her classes at Hunter. It was his, his own world of his own making; it all rested on his shoulders and not on the shoulders of a man in a high castle. His pride was put on a shelf whilst he kept his family safe and cared for. His life hadn't changed so much, he realized. He had gone from working until his back broke in the blistering sun and torrential rain, to working in basements at all hours of the night and day.

And, like the crumbling insides of these buildings, the couple spent this time repairing the damage that had almost been catastrophic to their marriage. The memories of Iliya had faded almost entirely, like a dream upon waking. The pain of separation from Lesia and Maksim ceased to wake Julia up nightly; had ceased to be the distraction and sadness it used to be, and had developed into more of a resigned sorrow. It lingered like a bruise, but it was manageable. They would be so different now, she thought many times to comfort herself, children no longer. The few letters that she had sent were returned, a red stamp declaring INCORRECT ADDRESS, so she slowly stopped writing them. Life had gotten too busy to worry about things she could not change.

Occasionally, she and Henry would drive out of the city and leave Slava at home, the two of them seeking an escape just with one another. The long drives ended on narrowing roads out east, on Long Island. The area that caught their eye was Glen Cove, a quiet community of houses and connected villages with gardens and parks, and a line of sand along the shore that looked out to Long Island Sound. It was an easy drive: a long, straight road, endless and quiet, the blue horizon and salty air encouraging them toward a simpler existence. They rarely spoke on the journey, but not out of any anger, now —it was only because they craved the stillness.

That night, Julia and Henry had drinks planned with friends at a bar in the East Village, and Julia realized that Henry had forgotten.

"You're sitting there like a lump, when we have to get ready." She picked up her sewing to tidy it away.

Henry unbuttoned his shirt and stroked his stubbled chin. "Oh, I forgot."

"Well, we have time." Julia stood up. "But this"—she gestured to his plaid shirt and trousers stained with bleach and confetti-like marks of paint—"is not acceptable at the Doma Ukraini."

Henry leaned his head back on the couch and sighed. "How do you have the energy?"

Julia held her hand out. "I learn from the best. Come now, let's make a drink. I can wear my birthday present." She smiled as he pushed himself up and walked to the bedroom, her hand prodding him as he went, laughing as she did.

* * *

Slava knocked softly at first, and then unlocked the door, her dress brushing the frame softly. "Mama? You here?" The apartment was quiet as she walked through the door, turned on the light, and threw her keys on the telephone table. She shut the door behind her and wondered if her parents had left already. "Mama? I need those earrings that you promised I could wear. Hello?" She shrugged her coat off and laid it on the sofa.

The apartment was silent: rooms quiet, neat as pins; the bookshelves messy with papers and stories and little trinkets that her parents had collected over the years. She walked through the kitchen in her green silk dress, the bias cut of the hem catching on her heel. Her blonde hair was up and twisted into a bun, and a thin gold necklace sunk into the hollow at the base of her neck, glittering in the light as she moved. Two glasses of wine were on the counter and a cigarette had been stubbed out. She walked through the small dining room with the embroidered tablecloth and the cracked sideboard heaving under stacks of china that they only used at Christmas and Easter, and then down the hallway toward the bedroom, the smell of lilies hinting at her mother's recent presence.

A few times a year Henry and Julia were invited to attend small social gatherings, through the Ukrainian diaspora in the city. There was a small but very close-knit community in the Village, and occasionally couples would meet in restaurants or bars and dress in grand nods to the era: jackets cut slim and lapels too wide, and drinks inevitably too strong. With Henry being overworked, it was a welcome escape. This particular evening, Slava was invited to join them, but had requested a pair of earrings, which Julia had left out for her.

Slava found what she had been looking for: the tiniest green emeralds given to her mother for Christmas from her father. They lay on the small table next to her side of the bed, and Slava placed them gently into her ears, fastening the back.

As she turned to leave, her heel pierced something that was sticking out from under the bed. She looked down and saw the corners of two pieces of paper, thin and old, like the leaves of an ancient book. She unpicked them from her heel and placed them on the bedside table. She looked at the thin watch on her wrist. She was late.

As she left the room, the fold undid slightly and the black lettering of QUEENSLAND, AUSTRALIA peeked out from the top. The room echoed with the sound of the door closing.

. . .

That evening, the Doma Ukraini glittered and gleamed, strains of music filtering through the air from the live band as people danced together and milled about in corners drinking and smoking. Laughter and conversations peppered the room, bouncing from wall to wall, with Ukrainian words and stories lacing together like an ornate tapestry.

Across a white-dressed table adorned with luxuriously thin dinnerware and wine bottles, Slava watched her mother. She watched as she leaned forward in conversations, smiling at a friend, gesturing to Henry, playing the role of wife and companion, hostess and lover. Her father had his arm around her mother, but she saw how rigid her body became sometimes, under his gaze. It fascinated her. Her mother's earrings were delicate gold hoops, her dress was a dark green, darker still in the folds of the silk that wrapped around her and embraced her shape. The small windows of the wine glasses and candle holders and vases altered her face as she moved, different perspectives and colors, the light playing it delicately, beautifully.

"Slava, you're miles away. Are you feeling alright?" Andrij, an older family friend who had known her for five years, leaned forward, the lapels on his suit jacket shining in opposition to the matte material of the body, his reddish hair matching his cheeks that had flushed with alcohol.

"Yes, fine. Just thinking."

"You think too much." Andrij winked at her. "About Emilian?"

Slava blushed violently. "Stop it!"

"So, where is he?"

"Working." She smiled. "I didn't want to subject him to the Ukrainian chaos and binge-drinking."

Andrij chuckled and slapped his thighs. "Well! Isn't that the truth! But that's part of our charm." He put a hand on her shoulder. "Speaking of. Need a drink?"

Slava played with the gold beading on her clutch absent-mindedly. It was her mother's that she'd also borrowed. Gold glass beading on cream-colored silk. "Actually, no. Just tonic water. With lemon."

Andrij's mouth fell open, mocking her. "What? Since when do you not have a drink in your hand?"

"Oh, stop it." Slava had nothing else she could offer. "Just not feeling myself, that's all."

"I'll drink your share, don't worry. Be right back."

When Andrij walked off, Slava saw her mother change seats, whispering confidences to an older woman as her father walked off.

"Mama..." Slava called across the table, reaching for the silver case of cigarettes at the center of the table and the lighter beside it, but then remembered herself, and left it there.

Julia turned to her. "Yes, what is it?"

Slava shook her head. "Nothing, nothing."

"Here you go." Andrij sat down next to her, and Slava took a sip. "Right. Care to dance with an old friend?" Andrij grinned, and took her by the hand, leading her to the dance floor.

Julia watched as Slava left the table and suspected that she had something on her mind. She thought better of pursuing it. Sometimes, it was better to let things work themselves out, in time.

Danka broke the silence. "Smile, Julia! Such a serious face!" Danka pointed the camera at the table, shouting at the others to lean in. Henry was standing to the side, and Julia leaned forward in her chair and laugh-smiled to the camera as she posed, her thoughts on an old ache that had stirred up inside her.

CHAPTER TWENTY-SIX

"Christ, that woman will always confuse me."

Slava threw her keys down on the only desk in their rented apartment: a small bookshelf that she and her boyfriend Emilian had found on 10th Street, in front of the charity shop that always smelled of cat piss.

"We should definitely take it," he'd told her. "We got our apartment cheap because we said *unfurnished.*" He'd seen the skepticism in her blue eyes and feared the worst; she wasn't the best at masking her true feelings. But she gave in, and there they were, in a dank basement with one window that looked out at feet hurrying along the sidewalk, and a piece of wood that they used for keys, eating their dinner on, and storage for old university textbooks.

She kicked the door closed with her heel and peeled off her running shoes. "Em? Are you here?"

Silence.

She pulled off the elastic band that had carried her hair on her run, and the thick blonde mess of it all tumbled out, half dry, half damp and dark underneath from sweat. She ran her fingers through it and opened the refrigerator as footsteps approached from the small room next to the bed.

"Hey—I thought I heard some rage and figured that was you, or maybe a highly neurotic burglar."

She laughed and turned to the familiar lilt of his voice. Emilian was carrying a few books in one hand, a pencil behind his ear, and he raised his eyebrows comically. "Emilian Morris at your service for all your emotional needs. I just came out of my cage. You need me?"

Their studio apartment had come with a strange, closet-type space that they couldn't even turn around in, but Emilian used as a makeshift office to study for his Series 7 exam to get into law school. "Series 7 sounds like a group of viral infections," Slava had said when they first met, and he had immediately wanted to know more about this girl with the strange name and the humorless voice. She was light, and he was dark, and yet their personalities were the opposite: she had a personality that held things close, almost coldly, while he had a voice that was perpetually at the end of a joke. It was the thing that she'd immediately liked about him when they'd met in—of all places—the public library, where his loud voice and tendency to easy laughter was entirely provocative.

He patted her on the small of her back as he moved around her to place his coffee cup in the sink and his books beside it. "Breakfast? I can make a mean fried egg and bacon."

Slava grimaced and closed the refrigerator. "Oh God, no, don't even... I don't feel well." She leaned over the sink, turned on the tap, and palmed some water into her mouth.

"What? You always rave about my poor-man breakfast."

"I can't." Her stomach lurched and she muffled a burp. "Besides, I'm meeting Alex in an hour."

Emilian feigned anger. "Who is this Alex, and do I have to kill him?"

"You're such a dummy. *Alexandra*. She's only been out to dinner with us about fifty times."

"Ahh, yes. The one who has a thing for true crime documentaries and good tequila."

"Yes, that's the one."

"I like her style." Emilian put a bagel in the toaster. "I thought you were off today."

Slava faltered. *That's right*, she thought. *I told him that.* "Well..."

"Research?"

Slava took the cue. "Yep. She has the latest labs for the Acute Phase Reactants..."

Emilian put up a hand. "Whoah. Stop. You had me at 'labs.' *No* idea what you're talking about, oh smart one."

Slava smiled. "Did you know that the amount of protein"—he leaned over and tried to kiss her. She moved—"means that there can be acute..."

"You're cute."

Slava grinned. "Stop it." Her voice was coy. "I'm very important."

"Yes. I have a damn smart girlfriend scientist. The best. I'm very proud of that fact." He reached around her and locked his arms behind her. "Fact is, I can't follow because all I know is Latin text in giant books that I probably will never understand."

"But you look good in a suit."

"Well, that's true."

She leaned her body toward him and placed her palms on his chest, sinking into his warmth. She saw the things she loved most as his face drew near: the green flecks in the hazel of his eyes, the freckles spattered across the bridge of his nose, and the reddish-brown mop of thick curls that were always gently unruly. "And if I ever get arrested, I'm almost positive I'd hire you."

"Nice." He kissed her and let go, walking back toward the

small room. "Listen, do me a favor. Don't try and be a burglar, because you'd be a pretty bad one, judging from your entrance earlier."

Slava rolled her eyes and took off her hoodie, revealing a sweaty T-shirt underneath. "Why would we have a burglar? We live in a place that has one piece of furniture." She looked around and pointed to the corner of the room. "Oh, and a bed."

"Beds are very valuable."

She took off her socks and then remembered that her mother had called earlier. "Argh. Totally forgot."

"What now?"

"Oh, forget it."

"Okay, okay, I'll bite." He came back into the kitchen area. "Let it out." He leaned back against the counter, careful not to break off the piece of yellow Formica that he'd superglued earlier. "What's got you annoyed?"

"My mother."

"Why am I not surprised? She's a tough one. A year in, and barely remembers my name and that we live together, but yeah, she's lovely." Emilian lifted a corner of his mouth.

"Yeah, well, she wants us to come for tea, and when she talks, it means she's planning something, or... I don't know. Who knows? She's a bit strange sometimes."

"When?"

She shrugged. "Eventually," she said. "Could be in a week, or a month. Time to her is immaterial, apparently. She exists in a bubble."

"My mother is like that. Maybe it's the Eastern European streak."

"Your mother is Hungarian, and your father is Irish. That's a *whole* other set of issues," Slava mocked.

"I know! Maybe she's pregnant?" Emilian offered, trying to lighten her mood. Slava was quick to anger, but she let go easily, and he knew the times that he could encourage her to. But in that moment, he saw Slava's face shift and the blue in her eyes darken. He came toward her. "Oh, c'mon. It was a joke. I didn't—"

And then suddenly, she came back to him. "Science even can't be *that* weird." She laughed. "You're such a loon."

Emilian softened. "But really, though, your dad is fine, she's perfectly healthy, what could it possibly be?"

"I don't know." She walked to the bed, exactly six steps from the kitchen, and sat down, facing him. "I'd like to say that it's a puppy, but I'm too tired to try out your jokes."

Emilian smiled at the effort, though he knew that something else was bothering her. There had been a simmering in her eyes recently, like the energy of a locked door. He knew better than to prod.

Slava pulled off her jogging bottoms. "Right. We have just under an hour before I have to leave." She looked up at Emilian. "What do you say we make the most of our second piece of furniture?" And then she took off her T-shirt, and leaned her face toward his, and they spoke of nothing else.

* * *

Slava walked through the door of the aptly named Coffee Pot on the corner of Seventh Avenue and 10th Street, satisfied that Emilian had believed her lie. The glass-muffled traffic surged outside as she scanned the room and then she saw her at a table in the corner, sitting straight, winding the thin watch on her wrist.

Her mother looked regal, in a camel dress coat, her hair tied back in a high bun, revealing sharp cheekbones and bright eyes. It was easy to forget who she was: a woman with a proud spine and a cool distance in the way she carried herself. It was beautiful, and Slava wished she'd observed it more when she was younger.

She slipped her shoulder bag off and sat down heavily, shrugging her jacket off onto the back of the chair. The coffee machines squealed and steamed in the far corner of the room and the air smelled of cinnamon and sugar.

"I'm late, Mama."

Julia didn't offer a reaction, and only checked her watch. "Yes, I am aware. Twenty-five minutes late." She motioned for a waiter to come over.

"No, more like a week."

There was a hint of a smile, and then Julia leaned forward, lacing her fingers together, eyes hopeful. "Are you sure?"

"I'm never late. But then again, this could be a false alarm. I just thought I'd tell you."

Julia waited a bit, and then nodded. "Well. Have you told Emilian?"

"No. I didn't want to start the ball rolling on that particular path."

The waiter came over with menus. Slava raised a hand. "Oh, I can't. Do you have any tea?" He nodded.

Julia smiled. "Two, please, thank you. With honey on the side."

When he walked off, she continued: "I am not sure of all these 'balls' and 'paths,' but you must think about this. Sometimes, it doesn't happen, but if it does, what a miracle."

"Oh, God, Mama." Slava snorted. "You're always so negative despite attempting optimism."

Julia nodded. "That may be so, but all I am saying is be prepared either way. Life is funny."

"You always strike me as so wary, nervous." Slava folded and unfolded the napkin in front of her. "It's like you're afraid to be bold, but you're also hard as nails."

Julia didn't respond. "You'd need to get your apartment ready."

"Hang on, slow down. You mean our closet space under the

ground? Yeah, well, our lease is up soon and who the hell knows where we'll move after that."

Julia reached for her daughter. "Don't you want children yet? Have you thought about it?"

Slava softened. "Well, not *really*. In an ideal world? No, not right now. I'd imagine that I'd be more ready than I am right now. Besides, there are options. I mean, an abortion wouldn't be ideal, but—"

Julia's face flushed and her voice rose. "Shhh! Don't ever say anything like that! That's disgraceful."

"Mama, calm down." Slava looked around, embarrassed for them. She was grateful the place was half empty. "Stop panicking. I never said I would *get* one, but hey, welcome to the seventies."

Slava watched as Julia became visibly agitated, and when the tea was brought there was silence for a good five minutes as the women sat in their own thoughts. Slava stirred honey into her cup, the spoon scraping the porcelain. "Mama—"

"Slava, don't. What you said is incredibly upsetting to me. You would be lucky to have a child. Incredibly blessed."

Julia had become almost possessive of Slava's news, as if it were her own.

"I know this, of course. But I also have a right to choose now."

"Choices are dangerous." Julia's eyes shone.

"Choices are good. It means you have freedom."

"No, Slava. You're wrong. One choice could change your entire life."

Slava had seen this before: her mother had a darkness to her that rarely came out, but when it did, it seeped slowly, as if it were an uncontrollable fire; smoke leaking out of a locked room. Today, it was more than she'd ever seen. She wanted to push her further, but instead, she reached across and gripped her mother's hand. "Mama, hear me out. I just wanted to tell you—"

"Why?" Julia interrupted. "Why would you tell me about something that you're not sure about?"

"Because you're my mother."

Julia took a napkin and dabbed the corners of her eyes. "I know, sertseh. I'm sorry. I never got to tell my own mother these things, that's probably why. There's no need for so much emotion."

Slava sensed the lie, but she left it. Julia composed herself and locked the darkness away again. "Thank you for telling me, no matter what happens."

The same waiter appeared carrying a pad and pencil and two menus. "Would you like anything else?"

"Milk, please," Julia replied, and smiled at her daughter, the pain dissipating. "For both of us."

Later that afternoon, Emilian was out and Slava walked through the empty apartment, slowly discarding one shoe, then the other, then her bag and finally her coat. She walked into the bathroom and stood in front of the small mirror, spotted with toothpaste flicks from morning routines.

She had a mere six months to finish her Master's, but had a steady job at Sloan Kettering, while Emilian had been promised a position at Smith Barney, working for his mentor from college. They had very little, but it was everything to them.

There was a large part of her childhood that Slava didn't remember, and things that her mother had never told her. "Such a long time ago, how could I remember?" she would say often. She'd been shown faded photographs of her smiling face in fields and farmhouses, tucked into the arms of her mother and father, but her own memories remained blank. And her mother never talked of the past, as if she'd moved on to another life when they'd arrived on the concrete paths of Manhattan. She'd lived a hard life, Slava assumed, and that was just the immigrant story. Keeping the past tucked away.

She walked out of the bathroom and over to the bed, where they had been, only hours before. She lay down and placed a hand on her stomach, slowly moving it across the thin material of her blouse and back again, her thoughts growing quiet as she fell asleep to the sound of the rain hitting the street just above her.

* * *

It would be a week later that her period would come, and she discarded the test that had given her false hope. As Slava stood in the shower and reinserted herself back into her life, she felt she'd accomplished something that she'd never done before: she had revealed a little bit of the woman that raised her.

CHAPTER TWENTY-SEVEN

"We are moving," Julia announced as she put her embroidery on her lap. The threads lay in a clump on her knees: black, cranberry-red and Kelly-green. It was going to be a bouquet of poppies. "Out of the city."

Two pairs of eyes were staring at her, and then Slava turned to Emilian and cocked her eyebrow. *See? I told you. Ridiculous.*

"What?" It was Saturday, the tea had been poured. Slava was sitting on the floor of her mother's apartment, arranging folders of lab results on the floor in front of her, the insignia of Sloan Kettering Hospital branded on the top of each. She had been inundated with work lately as labs never shut on the weekends and now she had been promoted to supervisor. Emilian sat behind her on the couch; his place was still as a spectator. Slava was looking at her mother in disbelief. "But why? You love the city."

Julia smiled. "Our life, Papa's and mine, it's always been so busy. Not once have we stopped working, but we're getting older now. He comes home like he used to: tired and covered in dirt. He never says 'No' to what anyone wants from him." She took a sip of hot tea and placed it back onto the coffee table.

"Well, you can't just move and... well, do you have a plan? Everyone needs a plan." Slava leaned back on Emilian's legs and folded her arms across her chest.

"Oh, Slava. Such focus. You remember how you used to shout at me '*Vava, do it!*' when you were five?"

Slava blushed in embarrassment. "Not really."

Julia continued. "Yes, there is a plan. You know the building that Papa bought on President Street a few years ago?"

"Yes, the one that was a dump."

"Well, over time, there have been a lot of buildings that have been bought on that street and done up really nicely: painted and renovated and the original brick restored."

"So, what does that have to do with Papa?"

"A few weeks ago, a couple of developers approached Papa when he was working and told him that they'd be interested in buying the rental off him."

"Holy God!"

The clinking of keys and the turning of the lock interrupted them. Henry was home. He lumbered in, his frame appearing in the door.

"Oh, Emilian. Slava." He took his hat off and hooked it on the back of the door. "What was that ungodly screeching? Was that you?"

"Yes, Papa. Mama just told me about the house in Brooklyn."

He peeled off his jacket and sat down heavily, nodding a hello to Emilian. "Well, they seem very interested, which is strange. But I guess the area will become popular, maybe? I don't know these kinds of things. But I'll take good money if it's offered. I've worked my bones raw in that building."

"What money, then?"

"They offered four times what Papa paid for it," Julia interrupted, proudly.

"She's talking to me, Julia," he admonished with a sigh.

"Yes, it was four times." He turned to Julia. "Always money with you."

Emilian and Slava shifted uncomfortably.

"Don't be argumentative just because you're exhausted, Henry. I'm glad it's a lot of money, and yes, it makes me happy to know that you're rewarded for hard work just like *every other* reasonably minded husband." She waved her hand toward him. "You can't just fix pipes and grow orchids your whole life and expect that to be okay, now, can you?" As soon as she said the words, she regretted them.

Henry stood up. "You're lucky I respect you that little bit not to dive into an argument. I don't have the energy for it."

Julia sighed. "Yes, yes, of course he'll take the money. We'll use it to find a place out in Long Island, where there's a nice little community."

"Ah. Where you and Papa disappear to sometimes?"

"Mmm. Glen Cove. It has a little main street with shops, a cinema, a beach, a lovely church, and plenty of space. It's what they call 'new development,' and it seems to have a lot of potential for us. Somewhere we can breathe a bit."

"What will happen to this place?" Slava looked at the embroidered cushions on the couch and smoothed the faded oriental rug where she sat. "There's so much history here."

"Well, it's good that you like it, as Papa and I decided that you can have it."

Slava's eyes widened and looked over at Emilian.

"Mrs. Rudnick, we couldn't possibly—"

"And what should we do with it then?" Julia interrupted. "Sell it to a stranger? We bought it from the owner of this building, years ago." Julia smiled. "We saved, and we bought it to have in the family."

Henry folded his arms across his chest and cocked an eyebrow. "Isn't your lease coming up soon?"

"Yes, sir," Emilian answered. "But with all due respect, we couldn't—"

"Too late," Julia interrupted, clapping her palms together to end the thought. "It's for you. It's history, as you said." She looked over at Slava. "And you can't rent if you have children."

Slava rolled her eyes and laughed. "Not again, Mama."

Emilian looked at her and winked and looked at Julia. "I keep *telling* her."

Julia frowned. "Marriage first. Do it properly."

"Oh, like everything you both have done is so proper." Slava snorted.

Julia blushed, and her face lost its smile. "Anyway, there you have it. That is our news."

"Thanks, Mama." Slava embraced her mother tightly. She always noticed how her body stiffened ever so slightly. She never understood it.

Slava kissed her father on his leathery cheeks and waited for Emilian at the door as she put her coat on—it was one that her mother had given her: brown suede with white, red, and green yarn woven in a flower pattern all along the edges of the sleeves and the bottom hem. It had been made in Ukraine by a friend of the family. It was history. Her parents, and now Emilian, and this apartment, all of it was now her home.

CHAPTER TWENTY-EIGHT

Despite having brought only a bookshelf, a bed, and a mirror, the apartment still hadn't been settled yet: there were cardboard boxes and packing tape lying around, and dishes that hadn't found a place to live yet. Her hands trailed over the dark wood of the hallway: her mother had left a few paintings—some wood etchings by Ukrainian artists that Slava knew nothing about. There were volumes of Shevchenko, old maps, encyclopedias that she used to use for school; dust had collected on their spines. She was home.

Her parents had left them a few pieces of furniture and taken the rest to Glen Cove in six separate trips, the process taking most of a weekend. Slava looked around, the lazy Sunday light flooding the windows of the living room, the shadow of the fire escape creating a pattern on the floor. The dark walls held so many old memories of their arrival in New York: the tenants who roamed the hallways and gathered on the stoop below, in the summer heat; the radiators spitting and popping during the winters that frosted the window panes; the blare of sirens that they got used to so quickly, and seemed comforted by over time.

"Do we want to keep these?" Emilian strode out of the kitchen with an armful of embroidered napkins.

"Yeah, let's just put them in a cupboard somewhere."

"We'll never use them, though."

"Did I ever tell you that my mother made some of those?"

He looked at the pile of material in his arms. "Um, no?" He cocked an eyebrow at Slava. "In her spare time? Sitting around and stitching red poppies?"

Slava smiled, sadly. "No. In the war."

Emilian flattened his lips. "Oh. Sorry."

"Don't worry."

"She doesn't talk much about any of that," Emilian responded, folding each napkin gently and placing it into a box. "Do you ever ask her?"

Slava shrugged, walking over to the small phone table by the door with a stack of letters on it. "I try to, but she shuts down. She once told me, 'No one will ever know the real me,' and I found that really sad."

"Yeah, that's weird."

Slava fingered each letter absentmindedly, her thoughts elsewhere. "Well, I don't know. I mean, it *was* a war." She stopped on one letter, addressed to *Julia Rudnick*. "Too many painful memories, I guess."

"Yeah, I get it." Emilian folded the flaps of the box over and pushed it aside. "What else you got for me?"

Slava stopped and stared at the envelope. "This is for my mother. From"—she turned it over in her hands—"Townsville State Department."

"There you go!" Emilian slapped his knee. "She's on the run from the government!" He laughed and stood up, walking past her into the living room, and opening a window. "I'm marrying into the Ukrainian mafia."

Slava looked up, blushing. "Excuse me now? What is this marriage you speak of?" She raised the hand that held the paper and pointed to her ring finger that now had a small band with a small round diamond on it. "I don't see a wedding ring on there!"

Emilian tapped his nose. "Working on it."

"Stop it, you're such an odd man." Slava rolled her eyes. and went to the phone to call her mother.

Her mother picked up on the second ring. "Slava?"

"Hi, Mama."

"Everything alright? How's the apartment?"

"Everything is fine, it's still a mess." Slava glanced at Emilian. "Partly due to my lazy fiancé in the corner over there..."

Emilian stretched his face into comedy shock and winked.

"What?"

"Never mind." Slava raised the envelope and looked at it. "Listen, someone sent something to this address, for you."

"Oh? Who?"

"Well, the envelope says it's from the 'Townsville Welfare Office.'"

Silence.

"Mama?"

"Sorry, go on, yes... and what was it?"

"Well, can I open it?"

There was a pause, and then, "Yes, sure."

Slava opened the envelope and unfolded the piece of paper. It was a news article, the headline read ANNOUNCE-MENTS OF BIRTHS, MARRIAGES, AND DEATHS, and then a handful of black and white squares with images and words.

Julia waited and then asked, "What is it?"

"Well, it's something about births, marriages, and deaths in an Australian newspaper."

"Nothing else?"

"No."

She looked over at Emilian as he sat on the windowsill; he was looking through an old photo album.

There was silence again, and Slava only heard her breathing. "Mama? Should I send it to you?"

"No, no. That's alright."

"You sure?"

"Yes, absolutely. Probably a case of mistaken identity or something. You can throw it away."

"Alright."

Slava was about to ask her mother something else, but Julia had already replaced the receiver.

"Hey, everything alright?" Emilian walked up to her, a pile of books in his hand.

"Sure," Slava responded, looking through him. "Yeah." She placed the clipping in the envelope, and then in a file, and placed it on the shelf.

She had always been good at listening to her instinct.

CHAPTER TWENTY-NINE

MELBOURNE

Ed had gotten the phone call before, and felt obliged to listen, though he knew what she was going to say before she said it. He also knew the inflections of her voice hinted at her state of mind. Siblings were strange that way, twins probably even more so; they read each other like books. He tucked the phone into his shoulder, trapping it to his ear, waiting patiently for her to continue.

"I don't know, maybe I'm being too sensitive, but I'm so..."—her voice hesitated on the other end of the line, and Ed knew why—"*nervous*, maybe, about it all. I mean, do you think any of this is a good idea? I mean, it's Mum and Dad's stuff. Won't it be really emotional? I don't think I can handle it." The tempo of her voice was halting, fractured, hinting at an invisible barrier to rational thought or reason in its staccato moments. "They'd only been sick for such a short time. This is just..." Her voice tapered off.

"I know, Roz. I know. But we can't start backtracking here. We agreed to sell the house, after all of this happened. And it won't happen overnight, either. Let's just take our time."

Roslyn had called him that afternoon, as she had done once

a week for the past six months after the funeral, to grieve, to talk, to tell him the details of her anxiety about it all, and share the shock of what had happened.

They'd both decided, soon after their parents' death, to start dividing up history—a life that their parents had kept protected for them—and now she would rather that they stick their heads in the sand and ignore it all. He understood it: it was painful for both of them. But there was no question in his mind that this was what they needed right now.

His neck ached from bracing to hold the phone, and it had grown hot at his ear. "Roz. I've already told you; you've got to relax with all this. I mean, you're the lawyer, for goodness' sake. Get your pragmatic brain on. It'll be fine—"

"Will it, though? I mean, seriously? I'm an estate lawyer for *other* people. Not for *my* family. What if—?"

"What if what? We find out our parents had really bad taste in furniture? We already knew that."

Helen opened the door just then, placing her keys on the table, a bag of shopping sagging in the crook of her elbow. Ed covered the receiver and mouthed, "Roz again," and she nodded and mouthed back, "Just let her get it out" in response and walked off.

"Listen," he continued, "just let me handle it and I'll let you know. It may not come to much, to be honest, so who knows, it may be something interesting at the least."

"Helen's there, isn't she?"

"Yeah, why?"

"You went quiet for a second. You think I'm being nuts. Your wife has much more time for me than you do these days."

"Well, that's a given." He laughed and ran his fingers across the keyboard distractedly and stared at the photo on his wall. It was a black and white photograph of the Kakadu National Park taken at a distance, with a little girl in the foreground, holding the hand of her parent, hair loose, the side of her face visible as she looked up, wonderingly. He'd taken this when he'd been on an assignment for the Parks Authority. He'd shot an entire series of landscape photos and had been about to leave when he saw two figures, in conversation: a parent and a child, wandering without purpose. And it struck him as if a remembered dream, and he'd immediately taken a few shots, grateful that he'd captured the moment for himself. "Anyway. I'll see you at the house in a few months, alright? The buyers are giving us time to go through and take what we need, and I have an assignment I need to finish up first. Do something to take your mind off it, because you're going to crack in half. I mean, I understand how you feel, but this is the right thing for us."

Roz was never good at being patient, even as a child. She'd always been willful and insistent, and Ed was the pragmatist. Where she was emotional and reactive, he was patient and thorough. They had always been opposites, but very close and protective of each other; their parents had always commented that they were the best kind of puzzle pieces: all angles and curves that fit together well, though occasionally a bit forced in their partnership with each other.

She laughed easily now, and he pictured her immediately, the husky, familiar voice perfectly congruous with her blonde hair and dark eyes that had always been so wild and wary. "Okay, fine. I'll talk to you soon, yeah?"

"Yep. No worries."

Ed hung up and placed the phone on the desk, quickly skimmed over the last of his edit, and then walked outside to sit alone on the porch. He'd built it himself, almost immediately after he and Helen first bought the property in St Kilda. The house was wide and open and easily lent itself to soft light, with windows on every side. It sat at the end of a road perched on a hill with views down to the small crescent beach—Ed had always craved, insisted on really, views of the sky and a bit of the sea—and the lush green trails of Foreshore, well-worn by a stream of constant hikers determined in their exploration.

The inside was representative of the plain outside: clean and modern, with pale wooden floors and old furniture, greens and blues and grays dominating the choice of paint colors and soft furnishings. At every turn, the walls around him displayed something new: contemporary aboriginal paintings done in black and red, with lines and circles and thousands of small dots scattered within and around; sunlit, undulating plains dehydrated in the blistering sun; black and white photographs taken by his parents from the family's travels to Fiji; the photos of Ed and Helen posing somewhere exotic, having accomplished an adventure; and the family photographs that were left to him and his sister after their mother—and then soon after, their father—had died.

Ed loved stories, and his parents had encouraged his appreciation of cultures and wonder, which was probably why he became a travel photographer. In recent years he had started consulting, as the plane journeys had become too much of a chore. He'd made a healthy career out of seeing worlds through a lens and meeting people that he'd never see again, though in the recesses of his memory he knew, and felt, that he had one more story to search for.

But how, he thought now, *will I ever find it?* And what would that mean for him and his wife, and would he regret seeking it?

He had never been able to answer that.

The rains hovered in the distance and the air felt luxuriously heavy; at any moment, a storm would begin. He would have to close the shutters in the bedrooms; the last time he hadn't, and the rain had coated the floor and ruined a thick stack of paper that he'd left on his desk: a year of documentation, paperwork, and filings about his parents' lives, any information that pertained to their work and their personal assets and information, correspondence with various banks and trusts and work colleagues—all of it had been soaked through and had taken a month to dry, while some papers that had been too badly soaked had needed to be fed into the shredder.

He stood up to go back inside when he saw a dust plume delicately dancing in the distance, and then heard a car pull up at the bottom of the drive. He heard the door squeak open, then heard it shut again, and waited for the car to retreat again before he walked down to the mailbox.

The rain started as he walked back to the house, gently at first then harder, soaking his hair just as he managed to get back inside. He sat down to look through the mail delivery: two catalogs advertising outdoor gear, a magazine about photography, and a white envelope with typed letters on the front, addressed to his parents, forwarded to him. The return address read: "Queensland Government, Department of Communities, Child Safety, and Disability Services."

"Ed?" Helen called out from upstairs.

"Yeah?" He held the envelope in his hand, poised to open it.

"Can you check the closet in the master bedroom? The hinges have come off again, sorry."

He groaned. "Yep, coming."

He placed the pieces of mail on the edge of the desk and walked off, not noticing as it all fell to the floor and into a pile slated for shredding.

CHAPTER THIRTY

GLEN COVE, 1979

On one of their trips to Glen Cove, Henry had seen a "For Sale" sign beside a small building: a yellow, one-level complex with ten rooms next to a long ribbon of beach. It had an old half-lit neon sign out the front that said "Treasure Cove." It didn't take long for both Henry and Julia to realize that this was the investment that they had been looking for, something to keep their minds occupied and their money and time working at their motel, away from a suffocating city and in a place that felt like a vision from Ukraine: green hills and clear skies. Within days, they'd put in an offer and became the new owners. It needed a lot of repair work, cosmetic mostly, the docks needed fixing and the units needed cleaning... but it was theirs.

In the very beginning, the couple decided that Henry would move upstate full time and Julia would continue with her job at Fisk. She had a stable job that treated her well, and she couldn't just leave it overnight. She needed time.

Every weekend, she and Slava would take the bus from Penn Station and travel the hour and a half across the city, over the bridge and into Glen Cove, with Henry picking them up at the station. It was something she looked forward to every week: it was their project that they shared. It brought them forward toward a goal. It was stabilizing.

* * *

An Indian summer had gently settled on Long Island. Green and gold speckled the trees and hinted of autumn, but the air still felt deliciously warm. It was the battle of seasons: the push of colder weather, and the pull of long days and nights where the sun didn't set too early. The heat, however, guaranteed business, and that pleased Henry. When he'd been a handyman at the old townhouses in Brooklyn, he was at the end of the phone at all hours of the night and day; he barely slept and ate in order to earn money for the family. He did it at a cost to his health and sanity, at times. But now, the days felt stretched out, calm, intentional. He looked over his shoulder less and less, he saw a bit of peace enter his life. This started feeling like home.

A few months prior, Julia had decided to give up her job and move upstate full-time. Slava had helped her pack, and Julia had moved to the motel to live full-time.

This particular Saturday felt quiet. Henry was laying down another coat of varnish on the docks to winterize them; the winters by the sea were occasionally sharp and insidious, despite the beauty they brought. The wood expanded and contracted like a beating heart, and cracks would form over time. It was best to protect it as much as possible.

The rhythm was comforting, the brush going forward and back, against the lapping of the water on the beach.

He heard footsteps and looked up; Julia was walking toward him with a cup of coffee.

"Is that for me?" He rubbed the sweat from his brow with his forearm.

"No. Did you want one?"

"Never mind." He put his brush down and reached for his cigarettes. "Well, hopefully, this will stay strong." He drew on his cigarette. "Not sure, but worth a try anyway." He exhaled.

"Yes, looks good, although the color is a bit off. Maybe a lighter color next time? A bit too dark."

"Okay, give me the instruction manual next time, then, eh?"

"Ach, sorry, should've just said it was fine."

"Yes."

"So, Slava called. She and Emilian are driving up later today. Maybe we can all have a nice dinner?"

"Sure, fine, we'll have a dinner. When she gets here, ask her to come out. She'll need to help with a few things." He stubbed out his cigarette and started varnishing again.

"Alright. Did you want coffee?"

"Yes. Cream and five sugars."

That evening, the oval wooden table was set with simple china, embroidered napkins and crystal tumblers. A few candles helped add to the light cast by two small table lamps in the corners of the room.

Julia was in the kitchen, her apron tied loosely around her, sipping a small glass of wine, navigating the steam emanating from the roast pork she had taken out just minutes before.

"Mama, do you need help?" Slava walked in, a fitted black turtleneck dress hugging her body, her blonde hair scraped back in one long braid that looped around itself at the top of her head. Emilian followed behind her to say hello, and then retreated to the other room to stand with Henry.

Julia swept her arm in front of Slava to direct her, deftly instructing her as her mother had done with her when she was young. The moment wasn't lost on Slava. She watched her mother—the salty streaks in her dark hair more prominent than ever—as she seasoned, and grabbed handfuls of ingredients, and mashed and chopped and stirred and kneaded.

"How do you remember all this, without a book?" She helpfully stirred, watching Julia season the vegetables.

"My mother taught me," Julia replied. "And I'm teaching you. Although I probably haven't taught you as much as I could."

"You're doing it now, though. That's what counts."

Henry asked Slava about work, Emilian asked Henry about the new house, and Julia spoke little: her preference was to observe often and engage and watch the people she loved as they moved and smiled and connected. When she did speak, she asked Slava and Emilian if they'd get married one day or had considered children at least.

Slava rolled her eyes. "No, Mama. Not now. Too busy."

Julia pushed a bit more. "Don't you want to have children one day?"

Emilian interrupted, forcing levity into the subject. "Hey, I hope I get a say in this?"

Henry laughed but said nothing, watching as the women bristled.

"Listen, Mama, I'm not lonely for children, and I don't, *we* don't, feel the need. What's the point?"

"Of course, yes, that's not what I meant, that you're lonely or bored, you know that." She looked over at Emilian and smiled and felt a pang of her own past. "You're just getting older now, so..."

"Come on, Em and I are both in our thirties. That's hardly *that* old."

"I'd already had *you* when I was in my twenties.

"Children aren't everything."

"Ah, but you're wrong. They are. Work isn't."

"Well." Slava leaned back from the table, her cheeks flushed from the interrogation and the wine and the gaze of her parents. "Maybe I don't want to have children."

"Don't. They're trouble," Henry interjected, and Emilian laughed, raising his glass to the comment.

Julia's tone became insistent. "Oh, please. Slava was fine. It was when the children were—" Henry looked at Julia and she caught his glance. She had forgotten herself—"if you decided to have more than one, that *would* be troublesome, I imagine." Henry looked away again.

"I'll figure it out, Mama." Slava had heard the change in her mother's voice, and she saw the pain in both their faces. It made her incredibly sad. "Besides, my life is too full."

"With what, exactly?" Henry challenged.

"Work, I *said*. Em is studying to be a lawyer. We both want to travel. I want to do things that you and Mama never did."

"Oh, we did more than you would ever do in one lifetime."

"Like keep running from country to country and argue with each other all the time? That's what you call 'enough?' And then you ask me if I want to get married and have children?"

"You know what"—Henry dug his fingers into the table and leaned forward—"you have absolutely *no* idea what we've been through."

"Henry, you're being a bit sensitive," Julia interrupted, protecting Slava from reaching a depth she wasn't prepared for.

Slava stood up. "Are you kidding? My whole life I've seen you both tear at each other because of some anger, or things that you don't want to say to each other." She felt Julia's hand on her arm, urging her to stop. "Don't you think I feel it, how you speak to Mama? How you both try so hard to ignore the things that make you so angry?"

Henry watched, immobile, as Slava pushed back her chair and stood.

"It's okay. We all have our ways. But please, please don't ask me about marriage or children because I don't think I've been shown the best example sometimes," she said, as her eyes welled for her mother, and for things that she had wanted to say for so long, but never dared.

Emilian stood up, addressing Julia first. "Very sorry. Thank you both"—he turned to Henry now—"for a great evening, but I'm going to go with Slava." They walked out together.

Slava walked, and then ran, out into the dark, toward the car, because she suddenly knew she couldn't stay: the things she said would leave lasting marks, fresh lashes of pain on all of them, and she knew too much as it was.

In the car, she wiped her eyes with her sleeve and rolled down the window, breathing the night in, and waited as Emilian opened the driver's door, got in and started the engine. He looked over at her, and all she could say was, "Just go. Please, let's just go."

And then the screen door to the motel opened, and a rectangle of light from inside the house illuminated the driveway.

"Slava, stop! Wait." Henry's footsteps lumbered forward in a slow, serious pace, his hands in his pockets. She watched him, not knowing what he would do. Would he shout at her? Would he disown her? Would he tell her that she had failed? Would he push her away? She couldn't bear any of the outcomes, she didn't have any energy left. She felt broken.

Emilian clutched the steering wheel and watched as Henry grabbed onto the passenger door and crouched down, his head framed in the open window. "Slava, I'm sorry. Sometimes I don't think I'm the father you needed," he whispered. "I love you."

Tears stained his cheeks: Slava knew this because it was a clear night, and the moon shone on his face.

She rested her hands on his. She stared at this man, her father, and realized it was the first time he'd told her he loved her.

She wondered if she would ever hear it again.

CHAPTER THIRTY-ONE

1984

Three years had passed, and it was now September, and the end of the tourist season. Henry and Slava had helped a few neighbors untie their boats from the dock that afternoon. Some pleasantries were shared—"Have a great autumn"—and then quiet, finally. The water lapped the shore, and Henry told his daughter that he was tired, and that he wanted a change.

"Well, no one can do the same thing forever, that's not realistic, is it? Maybe it's time to try something new." Slava stood up from where she had been sitting on the docks.

"Slava." Henry sat back in his chair and drew on his cigarette. "Not even something new can interest me now, I don't think. I have invested my money in property, and I feel that my body is aging, like those buildings."

He lazily watched the silhouettes of powerboats in the distance. The sky was turning pink, and the clouds reflected a pale sunset as they sailed across it. It was a nice luxury, watching the close of a day: he didn't remember seeing any sunsets when he was on the other side of the world, or with his father, or during his days smelling of sugar in the fields. Or maybe he had, he'd just forgotten.

Uncharacteristically for the family, they had created Slava, a child who was something of an optimist, something that initially had irritated Henry. He didn't understand how someone could be so naive, but he wanted to see what she had in mind.

"So, what do you think?"

"Not sure. I'm guessing the area is so popular that someone might want a piece of it?"

"Not a bad idea. But if I sell, I can't just sit around."

"True, but this place is just too big."

Henry sighed deeply. "I know. I just can't keep going. I've done the work on this place for years, mostly on my own. My life has been about maintenance and detail: long hours, little time for rest. Sweat and blood." He looked down at his shirt: pale gray plaid stained from varnish. His stomach softly protruded over his belt, and his breath was labored and contained a slight wheeze. "Maybe something smaller. I'd hate to completely stop."

"So, you're going to keep going in this property business?" She dragged over a white plastic chair from the beach and sat down.

"Probably. I like it. I like taking care of something and seeing the pleasure that people get out of something I've done. You know, I'm not the smartest man—"

"Ha!" Slava interrupted. "Who are you kidding? You may not show it off, but you're pretty solid company amongst idiots."

Henry nodded. "Not sure that's saying much, but good point." He winked. "I know how to work hard. My hands"—he lifted them up, weathered and worn, their square shape in stark contrast to the orange sky—"they've only known work. I can slow down, but I don't think I can stop yet. And, someday, once I feel that I can stop, then I will. I think I have my father's 'fight' in me. So do you." He elbowed his daughter gently. His affection for her had grown little by little since that explosion one night, and though it didn't change exponentially, they'd both noticed it, and were grateful for it.

"Yes, but there's something to be said for finding peace sometimes, though."

Henry stood up. "Right. Let's not get all soft. My whiskey is waiting, and let's pray your mother didn't burn the dinner— otherwise I'll have to go back to that bar again later... you know the one? Lone Bull? Just down the road by the Capri motel. They have the best pastrami sandwiches..." he mused, as they walked up the slope toward the house.

* * *

After he'd put the seaside motel on the market, Henry was surprised when the offer came so quickly, though he had been looking at new properties already. By then it was January 1984, and he'd had a buyer knock on his door, wondering if he'd be willing to sell.

"Twice the money, Julia." He piled sugar into his black coffee, reaching for the cream as he stirred. "It's a good offer." He coughed suddenly, slapping his chest to be rid of it.

"Really?" She sat down at the desk in the front office. "But it's January. Why now?"

He reached into his shirt pocket for a cigarette. "Well, think about it. Someone wants to get ready for the summer season, so they can probably buy it for less than they would if it was summer. Plus, it's still more money than we paid for it anyway." The smoke veiled his face temporarily and he waved it away. "Don't you want to have a smaller place to take care of? We're pushing seventy now, for God's sake. Do we want to break our backs making people's beds for the rest of our years?"

"A smaller place would be nice. Good idea."

"I know it is."

"You always manage to land on your feet, husband."

"It's a special talent."

"No, your arrogance is."

"Listen, why don't we go for a drive? I'll show you what I found."

"What? You already found something?"

He was putting on his coat. "Come on."

For Sale: 5 Units
Interested?
PLEASE CONTACT 212-668-7409

"What do you think?" Henry had turned the car off of Route 9N, the main road that cut straight through the village.

The sign was not one minute down Birch Avenue, painted crudely in white letters on a big piece of plywood, nailed to a post. They'd driven twenty minutes out of Glen Cove.

"Let's go have a look."

As they slowed down, Julia looked around: to the right and left there were meager, small clapboard houses with rickety-fenced borders. Their driveways had log piles in the corners, frosted with snow, and metal postboxes that needed paint. It was quiet, as if everyone had abandoned their houses in favor of somewhere better. Huge evergreens with thick snowy branches dominated the skyline. The heavy green and the smell of pine was almost oppressive.

He stopped the car. "It's over here—look." He pointed to his left. Two small gravelly paths, well-worn by cars, led about 100 feet in, separated by a small mound of grass trapped in snow, and a sickly tree.

On one side, there was what looked like a small gray one-bedroom bungalow unit, and on the other, a series of three gray connected units, each with their own set of wooden stairs.

There was a main "house" at the front, with long and flat concrete steps leading up to the wooden porch and screen door. Five separate metal postboxes guarded the front. There was no sign, and a small truck was parked toward the back of the property.

"Meh." Julia shrugged her shoulders. "Looks like beggars live here." She pointed at the units. "And the color! Gray? Like a dead mouse."

Henry rolled his eyes and reached his arm toward her, clasping her arm tenderly, resting it there. "Julia, see it for what it is: it's small and manageable, and can make us a bit of money in our old age."

She looked over at him. "Can't we simply sell and find a house to live in, find somewhere and just *live*?" Her head had become too crowded, it seemed. She hadn't been sleeping well and her hands ached often lately. She craved a home where time slowed down and the pace was less busy.

"And do what, exactly? Wait to die?" He leaned back and grabbed the wheel again. "No, thank you. God has given my body many more years, and I want to do something with what I've been given."

"Fine, let's have a look if you're going to be so stubborn about it."

Henry shifted gears and pulled the car over to park, telling Julia as he got out of the car to stay inside whilst he looked for the owner.

"Henry!" She called out of the open window. "I'm going for a walk, just down the road. I don't want to sit in here." She grabbed her purse, wrapped her coat around her and pulled her wool hat down, and watched as he waved her off. She knew he wouldn't be very long: once he made up his mind about something, it stuck.

Her boots sounded crisp on the snowy gravel, the heels giving off a muffled crackle as she walked. She'd left her hair loose today, the curlers from last night creating thick waves that hugged her neck and shoulders and peeped out of her hat in small collections of gray and brown. The road was straight and plain, and the houses on either side were few and far between. The ones that were there were simple family bungalows with unkempt gardens and broken fences out front. *I would change that,* she thought. *No need for fences. Everything needs space,* she mused. She passed someone walking their dog. She tried to glance through open windows as she progressed, tried to see what was happening behind the curtains, tried to hear voices. She wondered if she would walk this road often. She saw a rectangular brown and orange sign to her right: "Gage Rd.". Just as she started to turn back on her heel, she saw it directly across: "Evergreen Cemetery." It was surrounded by a heavy, dark gray steel fence: the kind of fencing that reminded her of Germany, during the war. It was imposing and formal, a strange contrast to the lushness and quiet within.

It made her think of her parents, whom she hadn't heard from in two years, and she wondered if something had happened, illness, or even worse. She looked up, the blue sky as crisp and cold as blue glass. She inhaled and closed her eyes. "Mama. Mama..." she whispered, as her eyes filled with tears. "Where have I ended up? What am I meant to do now? So much has changed."

As if in answer, she heard the sound of the car trundling up, crunching the road beside her. "Get in." Henry leaned over, opening her door. "We're about to have a new little project."

During the next few days, as they came to look at the property and start a list of things that needed working on, Henry and Julia saw a "For Sale" sign on a little gravel road that led to nowhere, called Cooper Street. The house for sale was positioned at the very end of the road and sat atop a small hill by the entrance to a bramble-covered path. It was a stone's throw from the very center of town. It was as if someone had placed it, patted it down, and left it for them to discover.

It had white clapboard siding, a black roof, and five concrete steps that led up to a yellow front door. It had a carpeted basement and an upper floor, three small bedrooms, two bathrooms, and a wide wooden porch that protruded in the back, over the half-acre garden that sloped down to an open field. The center of town had shop fronts and busy roads, and beaches that filled with children and families in the summer, but this small road afforded them a piece of the home that they had left behind so long ago—a footprint that stayed on the earth for a time.

Julia fell in love with it as soon as she saw it. Henry felt deeply happy that the two of them could see themselves living there, and with the money they'd made on Treasure Cove, they could afford to buy the Birch Avenue property to rent out, and buy this for themselves to live in.

Over the rest of that year, half of their days were spent at the larger property to develop it for rental: it was solid, built on a skeleton of hardy foundations, but there was a lot of work. There was paintwork to be done, the roofs needed completely new tiles, the bathrooms had accumulated a significant amount of mold in various corners and drains, and the drives needed paving.

Toward the spring, when the work was almost complete, Henry, Julia, and Slava together sawed, shaped and painted a large wooden sign out of heavy timber. They carved the silhouette of a pine tree on the front, with heavy coats of dark green, and brown letters underneath, spelling out SOSONKA.

The day they staked it into the ground, Henry smiled as he looked up. "Our little 'evergreen.' It fits."

. . .

Most of Julia's time was spent at the house on Cooper Street. She spent hours in the garden, though it was small comparative to the one from her childhood. It was potent, however, regardless of size; the tinny taste of soil on her tongue as she breathed, the hydrangeas huddled in the corner of the fence, by the peonies, overpowering everything with perfume. The gooseberries and currants ran rampant along the near side, competing for space, their thorny branches daring anyone to pick them. Sweet red tomatoes clung to vines in the middle, and there were yellow zucchini flowers and carrots peeking up on the left-hand side, while a useful compost heap had been created in the far corner.

The garden was at the bottom of a sloping green; the porch above it was where Julia would sit in front of sliding glass doors that led into the living room and dining room. She could walk nine paces in either direction to reach newly planted beds shaded by a pear tree, which was more than enough space for her to have a day's worth of work at her feet. And as she walked toward the end of the property, she could see through the metal fencing into an open field; she would lace her fingers through it, staring through the metal as she had done in Neumarkt, to a world beyond her reach—this time, her gaze landed on small houses dotted just beyond, with lush gardens of their own, bright flowers tucked into corners, freshly painted siding, new roofs, and a small school with a soccer field. Monotone versus color, fear versus safety, cold versus warmth.

The inside of the house was inviting and comfortable: the front room had pale green carpet and was surrounded by windows all the way around. The previous owners had left some furniture behind, which was useful, as they'd been spending money furnishing Sosonka. There was a long metal desk along the left wall, three drawers on each side with thin pull-handles. A rotary phone and a Yellow Pages sat on its surface. Above the desk were built-in shelves that had—even over such a short period of time—accumulated books that they'd brought with them from, and out of, various countries: Taras Shevchenko's poetry, *Zakhar Berkut*, *Kobzar*, *Haidamaky*, *Unordnung und frühes Leid*, and *The Magic Pudding*, among others.

The inner rooms were dark, with dark tiles and pale brown carpet: the kitchen, to the left, overlooked the street, while the living area, on the right, overlooked the garden. There was a stone fireplace with framed pictures of family, a crucifix hanging above overlooking it all. The dining room was further on, an oval wooden table in the center surrounded by eight chairs. On the right of the table, up against the wall, was a collection of china that had been painted with poppies and *vyshyvanka* patterns. These had been a gift from Jeffy when Julia and Henry had moved out of New York, and they thought of him often.

Down the hallway from the living area were four small bedrooms: two on the left overlooking the street, two on the right overlooking the garden, with a main bathroom at the end. Julia and Henry had decided to take the bedroom on the right: it had pale blue carpet, a dressing area and table with a mirror, and a sizeable closet. It also had a door that directly accessed the porch in back.

It was more than enough space for them, and it was perfect for guests and family to come and stay.

Julia walked in toward the living area and opened the door to the basement. There was a washing machine below, a wet bar, and a storage room that led to the garage. She walked downstairs, turning on the light. She immediately turned back and walked up, closing the door behind her. She didn't understand basements. It was a waste, and it made her feel uncomfortable in some way.

The doorbell rang, and voices called through the door

before Julia even opened it. "Hey! We're tired! Open it!" It was Slava and Henry.

Henry moved past her, smelling of sweat and paint. He dropped his various bags, brushes, and paint-splattered bandana on the green carpet as Slava moved in behind him. "We've been at Birch all day. I need a drink, both of us do, and not that fizzy cola nonsense."

"Alright, alright..." She moved past him and up the step into the kitchen. "Just leave any dirty clothes in the basement—I have enough to do than to worry about getting paint out of the carpet." She turned to Slava. "Are you staying the night? Should I start dinner?"

"No, Mama, I can't. I need to go back to the city tonight, as I have a meeting tomorrow morning."

"Lab technicians have meetings?" her father teased.

"Oh, God, not this again."

"Just get your drinks and sit down already," Julia scolded and walked back into the kitchen, stifling a smirk.

That evening, there was dinner, and wine for the parents and water for Slava, and conversations about politics. And then later Henry poured himself whiskey and explained his philosophy about how the government was corrupt, and Slava interjected her theories about how women in the workplace were under-valued and underpaid. Henry defended his position on how the government would never allow immigrants a fair stake in any country in which they resided, and Julia listened, and watched.

She watched her daughter, a daughter both of them hadn't given much time to understand, hold her own against a domi-nant personality like her own father. Henry labored to get his points across now, for he was too tired to be as clever as he once was and with many years of drinking and eating to excess, he'd become slower.

"Ay, come on with all the heavy!" Julia exclaimed. She

looked at Henry, his eyes growing sleepy. "Look at him." Julia gestured. "Slava, you need to get on the road, and we need to go to bed."

Slava stood up and came over to her father and put her hand on his broad, rounded shoulder. "Papa, I need to go in a minute. It's seven thirty, and I need to drive for a couple hours."

"I'll walk you out." Henry stood up, reaching into his shirt pocket for a cigarette as they both walked down the front steps and then toward the car parked in the driveway behind the house, to say their goodbyes.

The pair stood next to each other for a brief second: the five-and-a-half-foot girl next to the six-foot-three tall old man. She elbowed him gently on the arm. "Papa, you shouldn't smoke so much. It's bad for you."

He smiled. "Ahh, Slava. Don't worry about me. Get back to your important work." He winked at her.

Slava slipped into the car and looked back as Henry walked up the steps toward the porch. "Julia, leave the basement door open," she heard him say. "You know I like when doors are left open. Closed doors are bad omens." And then he turned back, smiled, and walked inside.

After Slava had left, Julia and Henry moved with a contentedness that could be described as monotony: she had washed and tidied the dinner plates away, one by one, and then dried the glasses, as he sat on his favorite chair outside on the porch, the cool night air on his face. The porch jutted out just enough that when he sat, he could only see sky. He watched as the smoke from his cigarette drew a silver line from his fingers, reaching for the navy summer night, dissipating peacefully.

Julia opened the door and leaned against the frame, drying her hands on her apron. "Need some company?"

He reached over and pulled an extra chair to him, the sound of wood on wood creating his invitation.

Julia walked over, untying the knot behind her back, dropping the apron over the back of her chair, and sitting down. She leaned her head back and looked up at the sky. "It's lovely and quiet here, in this spot." She pointed across. "Even at night, you can't see the garden, but it's there. Waiting. And then... the fields beyond."

Henry nodded. "Home." He meant it in ways that Julia didn't realize.

"Yes. Finally."

"I wonder, occasionally."

"About what?" It was unlike Henry to reminisce, or become nostalgic about the past, so Julia was curious.

"About the paths we've taken to arrive here." He raised his hand and passed it through the air in front of him. "Like stars, moving along the sky."

"They were all hard, in so many ways. But we wouldn't have arrived here without them."

Henry nodded. "Regrets?" He looked over at Julia, her face bathed in the half-light of a waning moon.

She smiled and looked at him. "Don't we all have them? But nothing that breaks my dreams." She saw that his eyes shone with tears, or maybe it was a trick of the moonlight. Julia locked her fingers together, as if clasped in lazy prayer. "You?"

He looked back at the night sky, and watched as the cigarette he held burnt out, the embers turning increasingly black. "Nothing that breaks granite." He exhaled a final plume of smoke. "Besides, if I had any, they are something that God and I will have to discuss one day."

His other hand reached for hers, and they both finished their evening in silence.

CHAPTER THIRTY-TWO

The night was still. Which was why, when Julia woke, she thought she was dreaming. It sounded like the beginning of a storm. Muffled. Troubled.

"What was that?" She didn't move her head off her pillow and sleepily waited for a response.

There was little wind that evening, and she could still see the moon as it hung in wait for the dawn: thin, silvery slices through the folds of the curtains. She'd heard a kind of thin, forced wheeze, then something heavier, more guttural, and it had woken her. She wasn't sure if it was the house creaking: it was always settling; and there were occasionally small animals in the garden.

The silence was more than that, though: she'd recall later that it carried with it absolutely no life. It was hollow. She opened her eyes again and listened. Nothing.

She closed her eyes, the relief of being half-asleep and hearing nothing, except for the wind shuddering through the trees. She'd never known Henry not to snore, so this felt wonderfully luxurious.

Five minutes later, she opened her eyes again as if she remembered something, for something had suddenly changed.

She turned over to face him, her hand reaching for his chest. No sound. She shook him a little. "Henry. Hey."

He was calm; the skin underneath his shirt felt different.

She listened to his breath. Nothing. "Henry. *Henry, answer me.*" She sat up then, and shook him with both hands, and she *knew.*

She slid off the bed, turning on the light as she ran out of her bedroom and down the small hallway, her nightgown flying behind her, the glut of material irritating her for some reason, her gray hair wild around her face.

She jerked open the door to the front room and reached the phone, dialing frantically. She knew her daughter's number by heart.

"Oh, Jesus. Oh, Jesus, help me," she repeated as she waited for an answer.

"Hello—?"

"Slava, Slava, help me..." She was gasping for air and hysterical. "Help me... it's Papa, he's... I can't... I heard a sound, I don't remember... I tried to wake him... Slava... what do I do...?" Her voice heaved and broke and sobbed and did the thing that voices do when no words come out, only sharp intakes of breath and heavy exhales.

Julia heard Emilian's concern in the background, and then Slava's. "Mama—is he breathing?"

"I can't wake him! What do I do? Oh, Slava!" She wailed on the line, her voice broken.

"Okay, call 911. Now. Do it. Call me when you've done it. Hang up. Dial 911. Do you understand? 9-1-1."

"Yes." The dial tone rang in her ear. She was alone. She didn't remember dialing the numbers, she didn't remember what Henry was wearing, she didn't remember how many men arrived at their house, the blue and red colors painting the sky like silent fireworks. She didn't remember how they got Henry onto a stretcher, she didn't remember if she cried, and how she looked, and if they'd had an argument the night before and what they'd said to each other before they went to bed. All she remembered was that his body had lost its spirit next to hers, and she'd felt it, and it made her feel a loneliness that crippled her.

The hospital on St. Andrews Lane, they'd said. She remembered that too. She didn't ask if she could go with them. She was in her nightgown. It wouldn't be appropriate, she thought, soberly and completely irrationally.

She remembered when they shut the door. She remembered watching the red lights fade down the road, winking feebly from a distance, and then disappear into blackness. She saw a neighbor's window light go off, as if they'd been watching the entire time.

She turned the house lights off, erasing her silhouette from anyone's view. She leaned against the closed door and felt her body slowly disintegrate. Her legs gave way until she sat on the floor, rocking forward, her head in her hands.

Henry.

Oh, God, Henry.

Slava.

Oh, she remembered. *Call Slava.*

"Mama?" It didn't even ring fully before she answered the phone. "Where is he, what's happening?"

"Slava, they took him"—her breath became labored again —"took him to the hospital. The one on St. Andrews. I can't drive, I don't know how to drive." Tears fell down her cheeks, the receiver wet as she spoke. "How have I never learned how to drive?"

"Mama, listen..."

"Shouldn't I go now? How do I get there?"

"Stop. Listen."

"Okay."

She sounded small. Slava listened patiently as Julia swallowed her sobs and tried to breathe. She was drowning.

"There's nothing you can do there right now, so we'll drive over, fast as we can, and we'll take you to the hospital. Is that alright? Just try and stay calm. It'll be okay."

"Okay."

"Mama. You'll be okay."

"Will I? Oh, Slava. Please hurry." And she put the phone down.

Julia was alone. The house felt like it would swallow her whole; her thin body felt invisible against the weight of his presence in this house. He was still here, and yet, he was gone.

She went into the kitchen and searched the cupboards blindly, found the tea, and set it next to the kettle. Then she withdrew the milk from the refrigerator. She took a teaspoon, dipped it into a pot of honey and watched it coat the bowl with a thin golden sheen and then slide slowly off it and back down into the pot. It was a ritual that her mother used to do with her. *Troshky, troshky davai. Bit by bit, let yourself feel.* Moments and memories lived in simple actions, but there was no one to witness it now, apart from her, in an empty house, sipping tea from a honeyed spoon like she'd done when she was a child.

It was the only memory she could recall then, and it brought her some comfort, as her tears fell.

* * *

The early morning sky was still a pale navy, and yet the entrance to the hospital was as bright as if it were already noon. There were paramedics standing to the side, surrounded by clouds of cigarette smoke.

Emilian and Slava were by Julia's side as they parked the car and led her to the entrance. There, Emilian and Slava exchanged a private look: *You go with her, I'll stay here,* and Julia was grateful that it would be only her and Slava walking in together.

"Mama, this way." Slava motioned, seeing that her mother was distracted.

"Ah, okay." She was blinded by what was ahead, not only by the lights but by what was happening. She had no idea what to expect: it was a childlike reaction to something serious; she was oblivious to the world around her, experiencing only the world that existed in her head. She was still in her nightgown and coat. Slava had brought a bag with some clothes for her to change into, but she didn't care.

They stopped at reception and Slava spoke. "Henry Rudnick? Which room?"

"Oh, sure, yeah, Rood-nick." The woman casually flipped through a chart. *Americans don't know how to trill their r's,* Slava thought. "Room 3F, on the intensive care floor. He was sent there from the neurodiagnostics department. You have to sign this and—"

"What did the scans say, then?" Slava interrupted, snatching the woman's pen and scribbling her name without looking down.

"You'll have to talk to Doctor Lee, ma'am. He'll be on the third floor."

"Thanks," Slava shot back. They had already started toward the elevator.

The intensive care unit was smooth, with sterile white floors as if no one had ever stepped on them before. The walls were the same color, with pale wooden paneling placed every five feet or so, to break up the monotone. Pictures of flowers and landscapes and happy, healthy people were framed, mocking anyone's pain with saccharine smiles.

Slava saw a doctor walking toward them, a clipboard under his arm. "I need to speak to Doctor Lee. Where's Doctor Lee?"

The man stopped, and placed a hand on her shoulder. "Doctor Lee will be right with you. I'll tell him you're looking for him. Who are you here to see?"

"Henry Rudnick. In 3F, they said."

"There"—he gestured down the hallway—"on your right, one of the last ones."

As they walked, they saw each room had small, wire-laced windows onto the corridor: thin, incompetent barriers that did nothing to obstruct the view of loved ones losing their battles.

3F
PATIENT: Henry RUDNIC

"Can't even spell his goddamn name right." Slava sighed.

She heard footsteps and saw Emilian walking down the hallway, his crisp jacket and worn jeans a comfort in the sterile, gray hallway.

Emilian touched her arm, and he felt her muscles suddenly slacken at the knowledge that he was there. He smiled softly as she looked at him. "I couldn't just leave you both here—I felt like I could be helpful, maybe. But you probably need to do this the way *you* need, so I'll be here"—he pointed at a molded plastic bench bolted to the wall in the hallway, with thin padding on each seat, magazines beside it—"in my very own, luxurious lounge chair."

They both laughed in the thin way that only happens when you grieve, and Slava was grateful for it.

"Do you want coffee? You haven't eaten anything. You need to look after yourself." He winked, stroking her arm.

"No, I'm fine." She smiled at his reference, kissed him, and turned back to face the door.

It was silent. And then, it was as if the ground softened under their feet.

Julia inhaled sharply when she saw Henry, whispering: "Bozshe miliy, moya lyubov." *Oh God, there is my love.*

"Henry..." She pressed her hands and forehead up against the glass, helpless, her tears wetting the window. "Slava, can I go in? I need to see him."

Slava backed away.

Julia opened the door quietly, as if not to wake him from a deep sleep or stir the plastic tubes from their metal hangers. He was covered in starched white sheets and gray felted blankets, his hands flat on the bed beside his body, eyes and mouth closed. His chest moved artificially, clear plastic snaking around his arms and his face and in his nose, all connected to constantly beeping machines. Numbers and lights flashed on two separate screens and an IV stand hovered, feeding him yellow-tinted fluid.

It was like the final act of a play. Serene. Sad. Final.

She saw a small metal chair, pulled it to his bedside and sat down, her two delicate hands covering his one wide one. Their wedding rings collided as their hands met. "Znova, do mene." *Come back to me,* she whispered.

She laid her head down next to his hand and felt warmth. He was still there. She waited for a response. She waited for his eyes to open and for him to say *my little Julia.*

She had waited for Maria this way, so long ago.

Only the machines spoke in clicks and flutters and metallic whines.

"Henry, I can't do this without you here, you know." Julia dried her eyes. "Look at the state of me, I'm in a damn night-gown." She laughed. "It would really embarrass you if you saw me right now." She stroked his hand and turned it over and saw that his calluses had softened. His hands had been so worn and toughened, the skin split and repaired so often, and now his energy and his stubbornness to prove that his life was worth something... had caught up to him. His body had stood in his way. *You never found peace*, she thought.

"None of this makes any sense. Here we are, finally at a place where we can stay. And have peace. No more turning back. Just like we wanted." She struggled to keep her voice even. "Please don't leave now. Not yet."

The sun broke through the window, followed swiftly by a cloud. She suddenly felt someone next to her. It was Slava.

"Mama, let's just be with him, that's what he needs right now. Talk to him, because he's still here. We don't know what will happen. Just pray. All we can do is pray." She pulled a chair over to sit down next to her.

The door opened, and a short balding man stood there, holding a clipboard. His tie was undone, as if he'd just finished a long shift. "Ma'am, are you the daughter?" Slava nodded and walked over to him as he stuck out his hand. "I'm Doctor Lee." He gestured to the door. "Let's speak in my office. I'd like to talk about your father."

Slava looked back at her mother. She was still holding Henry's hand, still in the same spot. "Mama?"

Julia nodded. "Yes. Go. I will be here."

Slava clenched her fists and felt like pacing the floor, but she remained seated, rooted to the spot. "I'm aware of what a brain aneurysm is. I worked in a hospital as a clinician."

Dr. Lee's office was decorated in the typical style: various certificates in frames on the wall, three shelves with thick medical textbooks, anatomy encyclopedias, leather-bound journals, a light box for x-rays, and a few awards. But there were things that said much more about who Dr. Lee was: a metal tray on the desk that held envelopes and forms and file folders with neon tabs stuck to the sides, a stress ball, three unfinished cups of coffee, and a few pictures with children in them, as well as colorful drawings stuck to the wall with scotch tape.

Dr. Lee's name was Mark, and that's what Slava called him now, for airs and graces disappeared in this kind of conversation. Mark was trying to explain to Slava that the veins in her father's brain had broken, flooded, fallen apart. He was using a metal pointer to describe the mass on the x-ray.

Slava had looked at a drawing of a cartoon mouse on the wall when he'd done that. She didn't need a diagram.

Mark was patient. He'd dealt with many versions of grief and pain before.

"Well, the aneurysm contributed to a subarachnoid hemorrhage. It was so severe that it makes me think it was happening over a long period of time, and that it just hadn't been diagnosed."

"Like a ticking—"

"Time bomb. Yes." Mark nodded and leaned back in his chair as if they were having the most natural of conversations, and not about a man who was dying in the other room. "What was his lifestyle like? Did he smoke?"

"Yes. All his life."

"Did he have a healthy diet?"

Slava offered a weary laugh. "If you can call inches of butter on his bread, and coffee white with heavy cream and plenty of sugar in it, and alcohol-fueled card games at midnight 'healthy.'" She wiped a tear off her cheek and cleared her throat. It felt like dry, broken glass. "What about his other scans, what did they show? Reception, or rather the nurse who was sitting at reception, told us that he'd been in the neurosciences unit."

Mark picked up a chart from the desk in front of him. "Well, it says here that when he was admitted, his blood pressure reading was 200 systolic over 105 diastolic..."

In essence, his veins had been expanding like a balloon, ready to pop. "Jesus Christ," she whispered.

"Yes. There was extensive bleeding on the brain, and the current scans show no activity at all." His face was sympathetic. "No change from before."

"So, the respirator is breathing for him, basically. But what about the rest of him?"

Mark put the charts down and leaned forward. "His brain shows no activity, but his heart is extraordinarily strong, considering what condition he was in when he got here. It could very easily keep going for days or weeks, or it could stop within hours. His brain, however, is... well..."

"Gone." Slava hung her head.

"Yes. There are no electrical impulses being sent from his brain. The machines are helping him breathe, which obviously circulates oxygenated blood through the body. The heart's intrinsic electrical system can keep the organ beating for a short while after a person becomes brain-dead, and some biological processes—including kidney and gastric functions—can continue for a week or so. Alternatively, the heart could just give up on its own."

"Okay, so what do I need to do?"

"I'd say give yourselves time with him, and then you can decide if you want to keep him on machines, or—"

"Let him die with dignity, and no artificial means," Slava interrupted.

"Yes, that's a way of putting it."

"Thank you."

Mark walked back around his desk and sat on the edge, folding his hands on his thighs. "I'm really so sorry." He stood up and walked toward the door. "If you need time in here, just take whatever you need. Or ask me anything. Do you need me to bring your mother in?"

"No." Slava shook her head. "I'll go back in a minute."

He nodded and walked off, Slava watching his white coat disappearing down the corridor.

She listened to the quiet of the room, and heard the noise of the hospital behind her, as if a thick fog had settled. Her father, the man who had seemed to be the strongest, most tenacious man she had ever met, had lost his fight; his mind had given up. And yet his heart refused to let go.

* * *

Glen Cove spread out in a spill of land connected by green spaces and winding roads that worked their way toward the Long Island Sound. It could all be seen on a clear day, standing at the perfect height, or seated on their favorite bench by the beach, watching the water lap the sand. Julia saw it all now, through the hospital window, and felt as if she were standing on the precipice of something unfamiliar. The feeling merged with a distant memory: of arriving at the western edge of Australia with Henry, looking out from the side of the ship and seeing nothing but water at their feet and the long coast of a country that she'd never set eyes on before. The difference now was that she was alone, and the cry of the seagulls had been replaced with the whine of machines.

Julia felt certain areas of her body light up, whilst the rest stayed disconnected: she was conscious of her breath, as if she had to focus to remember to breathe; her ankles hurt, but her feet and legs felt numb; her fingertips felt cold, and she'd been grinding her teeth apparently because her jaw now ached. She walked over to the chair that she'd just left, and moved it closer to Henry's bed, up at his head.

She leaned forward, her face a couple inches from his, and scanned his skin: it was pale and sunken, the dark circles under his eyes not as pronounced as they had once been, probably an effect of the machined oxygen coursing through his lungs. His hair was brushed back. When had it turned so silvery? *How have I missed that?* she thought. His lips were soft and flat, relaxed underneath the cannula under his nose that was taped to both cheeks. She couldn't remember the last time she'd looked at him so closely, so acutely aware of the texture of his face, the shadow of his eyelashes, the way his hair lay, the soft fuzz that had grown on the edges of his ears. It was the way a child would look at its parents: intently, face up close, digesting and imprinting it all.

She delicately followed the map of his face with her finger, creating a permanent mark on her memory. She spied a few freckles under his right eye, and saw the gray in his eyebrows, still as full and pronounced as they were when she'd met him. She followed the lines on his forehead, the shape of his hairline, his jaw, chin, and neck. She laid her palm on his head, as she remembered doing with Slava when she was ill.

"Henry," she whispered. "Henry, what's happened to you?" she asked, as she placed her hand in his limp one. She smiled at how big it still was, compared to her own. It felt heavy and lifeless and unnatural, and she hoped that by holding it she could warm it slightly.

She felt a hand on her shoulder. Slava pulled up a chair and sat next to her.

"You know"—she spoke without looking at Slava, tracing her finger around his wedding band—"I never thought he'd stop. I thought he'd live forever, or at least until he'd learn to slow down and spend time doing the things he loved."

"I know, Mama. I always thought the same." Slava leaned forward and rolled the IV drip to the side. The click and whirr of the ventilator responded. "It was too much for you both. Too much work, too much worry, maybe." She moved her hair off her shoulder, the blonde streaks bright against the blue of her sweater.

"He would be so disappointed with this." Julia gestured to the room. "'Dai bozshe! *For God's sake*, look at me now!' he'd say. 'Look at this useless body doing nothing but lying around!'" A laugh escaped as she blinked away tears. "So undignified, this end, for someone like him. And now what do we do?"

Slava rested her hand on Julia's arm. They let the silence in, the weight of the day. The minutes drifted as they sat with their own thoughts.

Julia turned to Slava. "Do you need a minute with him, Rabbit?"

Slava weakened at the childhood nickname that she hadn't heard in years. Her mother had carried a distance with her for so long, and this one little word revealed an incredible amount. "Yes, Mama."

She turned and saw that Emilian was still there, keeping quiet vigil, reading a book. "Emilian can help you get some coffee." She helped her mother up and led her to the door.

It was many minutes before Slava spoke. At first, she felt embarrassed that she had nothing to say, and no plan of how to say it. Her father had always called her a "planner." *You always need a reason for things. You probably get that from me.* She was in a room that felt like a vacuum. It could have been hours that she'd been sitting there, or it could have been seconds. Nothing mattered.

She leaned back in her chair. "Papa, can I tell you something?"

The machines whirred.

"I wish I knew more about you and Mama. I wish I knew more about what happened to her, to you, to your lives. I get a sense that I wasn't ever told much, just the things at the surface. It created distance; like I'd missed something important." She shifted in her chair at the admission. "Emilian always told me that it would get there. I would know more, just like everyone does when they get older. You know, parents ending up looking like regular people, doing their best." A sigh escaped. "But we never got there, you and I."

A beep from the machine prompted her to glance at the monitor, but it was nothing urgent.

"I haven't asked Mama about her life. Maybe I will, I don't know. I feel like with this happening, you here, I need to take that opportunity. Get to know her, I guess." Slava rested both hands in front of her stomach, fingers laced together. "Maybe that's something... that as a wife and a mother and a woman you just... you bury things, and solve them slowly on your own. Not letting people in. Maybe that's what you do for your children. For your husband. For your family. You lock things away so you can love each other the best way you can." Her throat caught. "Papa, you loved each other. I don't remember anything much about Australia, but I remember the love."

Please talk to me. Just one word.

Slava shifted her feet softly, like a child. "I remember anger too. Especially as I got older. But all you needed to say to each other was 'I love you.' It's not that hard."

She looked at him and pulled her hair down onto her shoulder, twirling it around her finger as she'd done when she was little. She was a daughter who was losing a father and telling him all the things that she'd never been able to. She'd just needed more time: more time to learn about who he was, more time to tell him who she was. So, she told him now, because she knew she would always do the same for the baby growing inside her—she would tell her everything.

"Papa, I love you," she whispered, and her chest crackled as she began to sob. "I'm so sorry for the things that I've never said to you and for the moments we never got a chance to share. I'm sorry for not being the daughter who listened and behaved, and for making you chase me around the house when I was naughty." She laughed through her tears. "I'm sorry I never took walks with you or asked you what your favorite season was, or your favorite piece of music." She pressed on her cheeks to dry the tears. "I'm sorry that we didn't hug, or kiss or show each other anything but expectation. I know it was always understood, but we could have said it more." The bedsheet was wet, her face swollen as she leaned on her hands on the metal rail beside his bed.

She turned her head to the side and her eyes became distant at the beginning of a memory. "Papa, do you remember that day that I walked into the greenhouse and you were angry at me because you were worried that I would break something, but then I watched you, and I listened? Mama told me that was the day you told me about the orchids. You told me how to care for them and how to raise them and how to protect them."

She stood up, the shadows of the afternoon filtering into the room, creating glittering shapes of the bits of dust in the air. She leaned over and kissed his forehead, like a mother to a child, lingering to imprint the feel of his skin on her memory. "Ya tebe lyublyu, Papa. I love you. Thank you for being my father."

She felt her stomach again. Only she and Emilian knew their secret, and now her father would. "I wish you could have met your grandchild."

The machines beeped and hummed.

When she left the room, she saw the name on the door again. RUDNIC. She reached over to his chart, withdrew a black pen and quickly wrote a "K" at the end. "There you go." She smirked and wiped a tear away. "You would've wanted me to do that."

That evening, as the streets grew dark and quiet and the bright lights of the hospital shone, Emilian, Julia, and Slava maintained a vigil in Henry's room. Slava had explained to Julia as plainly as possible that the man they had loved was dying. And Julia had known, despite the words breaking her heart. She had felt it in the air around him, in the room she had seen him in, even the night when she couldn't wake him up. Her strength was in knowing, and in the decision she knew she had to make soon.

Nurses drifted in and out at regular intervals, checking on vital signs. Sometimes the family were together, but oftentimes apart, one of them getting coffee or water or something to eat. Julia prayed at his side with a fist of rosary, and Slava paced, or watched her mother through the glass, wondering who the girl was that had lost the man she had loved.

"Hey, do you want to go home for a bit, for a little sleep, and then come back?"

Emilian looked as tired as Slava suspected she did, but she hadn't looked in a mirror all day. He was her mirror.

"Yeah, probably. We can stay at my mother's, if that's okay?"

Emilian nodded in response.

Slava looked through the glass. Her mother was still praying. "She'd be there all night if she could."

"She won't go willingly."

Slava shrugged and opened the door to the room. "Mama?" She walked over and saw her mother's face. She looked as if she was in a dream, her eyes staring and tired.

"Yes? Any news for Papa?"

Slava shook her head. "Listen, I think we should go home to rest a little, and then we can come back later, or tomorrow? You need to have some sleep."

"Can I stay here?"

"No, Mama. They'll take good care of him, don't worry."

Julia nodded trustingly. "Can you leave me? I'll be ready in a minute."

Slava nodded and walked out, softly closing the door behind her.

Julia stood up and went over to the window again. The sky

was the kind of blue that was lit from within, not the kind of night that was black as pitch and had no depth. She could see cottony white clouds, the scattered stars, and the red light of a plane, winking in the distance. Further still, she saw the faint warm lights of houses that lined the shore. And now, where would she be, without him? They had rarely been apart, and now they would be forever, and she could not imagine it, she could not imagine what that looked like, and how she would live. They had settled into their life together, piece by piece, and they had been happy. She would be surrounded by memories of him, and it would fill the space without him there. She grabbed her left hand, spinning her wedding ring round and round in a type of meditation. Forty years of seeing someone's life burn bright. And now, snuffed out.

She turned to look at him and the sight of his peaceful face made her lips tremble. Tears fell. "Henry, you know, you weren't the easiest person. But then, neither was I. We suffered greatly, you and I—so many broken pieces that we couldn't put back together." She tilted her head to the side. "But we had each other. And that was enough." There was forgiveness in her voice.

She walked over to him and sat down, taking his hand in hers, the touch of him still so comforting and safe. "I will miss you," she whispered, for "love" was too great a word to bear out loud. And as her lips touched his cheek, she watched his eyes, in the fleeting hope that he would respond with just a single movement.

* * *

The next morning, the sun dangled in the sky and a dark pink ribbon of cloud stretched across the horizon. Shops opened their doors and reversed their "Closed" signs. People carried their morning coffees to work, waves lapped the shore, and the sound of birdsong crept over the winds.

In the small house on Cooper Street, Slava slept in Emilian's arms, their secret safe and warm inside her.

Julia slept heavily in the other room, clutching Henry's pillow to her body.

The world was welcoming a new day with simmering activity. But in the room of Henry Rudnick, a man who had lived a life that had been vast and complicated and loud, the machines finally fell silent.

CHAPTER THIRTY-THREE

On the afternoon of the funeral, the gray stone church stood lonely against the sky, its stained glass muted. Cold rain ran in rivulets against the dark cars that collected on the road, the clouds an opaque gray. As they sat in the car in front of the church, at a distance behind the hearse, Julia rested her face on the window and looked out. They'd been there together, she and Henry, for an occasional Sunday morning mass. It was an easy walk from their house, a straight smooth gravel road and then a left past the cemetery.

They'd come there together even today, but she would leave alone.

"Mama, are you ready?" Slava undid the seatbelt that had nested itself under her belly and turned to Julia. She saw her mother gazing at the church, the car windows spattered with rain.

"My mother used to tell me that death is simple." Her voice broke. "It doesn't care for ceremony." Julia's face remained facing the church, recalling this memory in a trance.

Slava watched her mother as she grieved, and reached over

to Emilian in the driver's seat, finding his hand and squeezing it as Julia continued: "Death does not care about wind, or rain, or sun, for nothing matters when the time comes to meet with God." She wiped a tear from her cheek and looked down. "Yes, I'm ready."

Julia watched as people streamed into the church, the heavy, ornate wooden doors held open by two priests—one Ukrainian, one English. Some she recognized, many she didn't. Word had spread in the city, and then farther still to anyone who had known Henry, that a great spirit had dimmed. His obituary was a collective mourning for immigrants, for Ukrainians, for people who had survived the journey, and for those who hadn't. It was a celebration of his life, and a grieving for it.

People were huddled and whispering in groups: somber black suits and dresses adorned with red wooden beads and embroidered flowers, smells of hairspray and rose-tinged perfumes combining with heavy colognes. *Surely funerals should be private,* thought Julia. *People are only here to mourn their own loss, and eat the food carefully laid out for them.* Her anger was misplaced, but it was normal. Her husband had created a community of spirits, and his sudden absence in their lives unsettled them.

Julia and Slava walked, slowly, Emilian respectfully beside them, behind the heavy coffin as it was brought into the church and laid at the front. White flowers trailed from the corners of the altar and down the sides. Before the service the casket was opened, and lines of people solemnly walked up to it, pressing their palms on the shining mahogany and saying silent prayers.

Julia was last, and she watched slowly as his face appeared to her as she walked up. He was as she remembered him in the hospital, yet took comfort that there were no machines chained to his body. He was peaceful: there was no pain of the flesh, no presence in him now. He was gone. She turned where she stood and saw a sea of people sitting behind her, as far back as the door to the church, and even standing along the back walls. Young and old, people who had traveled distances to be there, people who lived around the corner and had never said but a few words.

The two priests began, one holding an overly ornate icon of a gold Jesus lamenting his fate on the cross, quietly reciting the hymns of St. John Damascene, both chanting in monotone Gregorian voices. The beatitudes followed while the three metal chains of the *kadylo*, the incense burner held by the priests, clanged and shook, releasing frankincense in heavy clouds, perfuming the body. It was intensely cathartic and heart-rending, the repetition and the smells creating a frenzy of melancholy worship. Then, the beginning of 'Vichnaya Pamy-at,' the hypnotic and dark funeral song, blessing the dead.

"In the name of the Father and Son and Holy Ghost, with God's almighty blessing..." one of the priests began, in a deep booming voice that cut through the silence, "shall this soul see his eternal reward." He held the notes, the walls reverberating with a sound that was almost otherworldly. "Peace will now be granted unto your soul, with Christ and the Holy Mother of God residing on their thrones beside you as you enter the gates of heaven." His voice rose within the minor notes of the song, the force almost withdrawing the blackness of the day and releasing a ghost.

The congregation began their response, the various harmonies richly filling the space: *In the name of the Father, Son, and Holy Ghost, may your memory live on, live on in our hearts, through our lives, may your memory be an eternal reminder to the souls you have left behind on this earth, a reminder that God will be waiting for us... may your memory live eternally, may you find the peace that your soul has longed for.*

The priest came forward again. "And now, Slava would like to sing 'Zhuravli.' Will everyone please rise." And Slava stood up and walked to the front of the church, her hand resting on her belly, her heels echoing in the space, and she saw her mother nodding at her in encouragement. She reached the front and turned around in her somber black dress that she had bought just for this occasion and would never wear again. She whispered, "Papa, I miss you," to herself, and through her tears she began to sing the opening notes of her father's favorite song:

> *Do you hear, my brother, my friend?*
> *The cranes departing, with silvery wings aloft*
> *Their voices calling out, as they cross the sea...*

Her voice lifted and echoed amongst the silent, cold walls of the church, and then a few voices joined her, slowly, and then more still—baritones and tenors and altos, men and women's voices joining together—as it was a song that they had all heard as children and felt deeply.

The far corners of Julia's life finally connected in their collective mourning, and their memories of Henry collided with their own realization: that death was the final freedom that he had spent his entire life searching for. It seemed that the sea of faces—not a single one dry—sang for the loss of a man who had lived a long life in too short a time.

At the end of the service, as people streamed out and black umbrellas unfurled against the sky and moved toward the cars, Julia sat on her own, a lonely figure in the front pew, thinking about what was left of her life. She looked around at the saints preserved in stained glass, and at the gold pots of incense in the corner, their chains hanging loosely on the floor. The only sound in the room was of her breath, long and steady, and the settling of the benches.

Julia placed her jacket around her shoulders and took up the bag next to her as she stood up. She walked to the casket, then kneeled in front of it and looked at Henry's face, and then down to his hands that were placed one on top of the other. She saw that the mortician had left his wedding ring on. "I will come back to you one day," she whispered, and clasped her hands in prayer. She felt her own ring on her finger—his promise to her. And she would never take it off.

When she stood up, she reached for the bag that she had placed by her feet, and from it she withdrew a fedora, the one he had always worn, and placed it delicately by his side.

* * *

The coming days blended into one another like watercolors. Once everyone had gone and the last bit of food had been covered and put away, once the bedrooms had been emptied of guests and the last light in the house had been turned off, Julia sat down in a house that was extraordinarily quiet. She was alone, and felt it like a sodden dress, or the pull of gravity.

She was still wearing her mourning dress: thin black silk that had long sleeves, a high neck, and a hem that delicately hugged her knees as she walked. She had barely slept: the phone had been ringing relentlessly, and well-wishers had been at her doorstep offering food and sentiment. For the first time in days, she'd finally captured a quiet minute.

She was sitting on the old, worn couch in the living area, arms at her sides, her bare feet sinking into the pile carpet. The wood-framed pictures above the stone fireplace smiled placidly at no one in particular. There was no dominant voice in the house. The moon-faced grandfather clock clicked its arm past midnight. Julia observed that, apart from the few extra plates and glasses from well-wishers, the house was exactly as she had left it when it happened; the day that Henry died. His flannel shirts still hung in the bedroom closet; his favorite slippers were by the door.

It was better that way, at least for the time being.

That night, Julia sat and closed her eyes, attempting to sleep somewhere that wasn't in a room where she still felt him. As she drifted off, she felt the hairs on her arms suddenly rise and the temperature drop, imperceptibly. She opened her eyes.

I probably left the door open, or a window, she thought, wondering where the draft was coming from. She looked toward the door to the front room. It was closed. To the right, the windows were shut; to her left, so was the door to the basement. *I'm just tired,* she resolved, leaning her head back and shutting her eyes again.

Shhh

One of the things that she'd learned to live with, when they moved to Cooper Street, was that the door to the basement was slightly too tight a fit for the height of the carpet pile beneath it, so as it closed, it always made a recognizable sound, like someone raising their finger to their lips and saying:

Shhh

She opened her eyes and stayed very still, as if in a dream not of her own making. As she slowly turned her head left, the door moved ever so gently open, as if a child was entering, or a breeze was finding its way through. She blinked hard, but it was still apparent that she wasn't dreaming. A ribbon of cold air traveled from her left shoulder, across her chest, then to her right shoulder, down her arm, and was gone. And then the warmth of the room embraced her, and she knew that she was now alone.

* * *

A month after the funeral, Slava moved back to the city for an indefinite period of time, waiting for their new arrival. She and Emilian's jobs had no leniency for time away, and they had both used all their compassionate leave. They said their goodbyes to

Julia and promised to come up on Saturdays to see her, and maybe occasionally during the week as well.

After their daughter was born, they helped Julia sell her share in the rental on Birch Avenue, the money from it a healthy sum that would sustain Julia comfortably for a while at least, before her social security afforded that little bit extra in the remaining years of her life.

CHAPTER THIRTY-FOUR

GLEN COVE, APRIL 2001

It could be said that loss lives within us and around us, comfortably. Like a scar, or a separation from a loved one, we don't "survive" it, or erase it but, rather, place it permanently in a part of our daily lives that learns to accept it, and be grateful for what it teaches us: it enriches us with an attachment to a memory of someone, or something, affecting us profoundly. Julia had lost her siblings, her parents had now died; she had given up two children and given three more to God, and she had now buried her husband. But loss cannot exist without love and so, with time, Julia discovered the beauty in the melancholy again.

* * *

"Why do you still wear it?" the young cashier asked, as she placed a handful of marigolds in the shallow box that Julia held. "I mean, after so long of him being gone, you know?"

Julia smiled. She had seen Alice every week for as long as she and Henry had lived there, which hadn't been that long, as he had gone. Alice was young and pale, with wide green eyes and a halo of red curls that were always gathered into a pony-tail. She had always been kind, always interested, if not a little naïve about the world. She had always said "Hello, Julia!" and waved, whenever she saw her walk down the path past the shop, toward the beach, heading home. She always asked questions.

It reminded Julia of herself of when she was that age.

Julia looked down at the worn gold of her wedding band. "Love persists, I think." She moved the flowers aside to make room for a few packets of seeds. "Within the things that force you to remember." She looked up. "Photographs, letters, jewelry. Little things can mean everything."

Alice pressed the keys of the cash register and took the money from Julia. "I think I'd be super messed up if my mom died. It's just her and me, you know. After my dad left." She rolled a piece of gum in her cheek and sighed. "Can't even think about it."

Julia retrieved her change and lifted the small box to leave. "You would be very surprised at what the heart can endure if it has to." And she walked home.

In the years after Henry's death, and after nearly an entire life of constant upheaval, Julia's life had finally settled, like the earth after a seismic shift. She knew her life would eventually end there, in the spot where Henry left her, and the only journey she was interested in was a small one: the daily visits to see the place where he was laid to rest.

The morning was similar to all the others before it: she dressed in trousers and a sweater for the invigorating weather, for it was bright sun but also brisk enough to redden her cheeks with an intense scarlet. She parted the thin curtains to reveal the view of the horizon beyond the garden; she smoothed the bedsheets, stacked the pillows, and shook out the throw. She arranged her perfumes in a line of various shaped atomizers on her dressing table and hung her robe in the closet and closed the door. She made her favorite tea, black with raw honey, and stood looking through the window above the sink that looked out onto the front of the house. As it steeped, she found the thick gloves and the small, rusted trowel that she'd always kept in the drawer by the door—the one that kept all the remnants and tools and odd bits of a house that had had a story once—and placed them in the oversized pocket of her thick parka that she'd left hanging on a chair by the hallway. *What's the use in keeping broken things?* Henry had often remarked to her as she would unearth strange metal clasps and knobs and old keys, and she would reply that nothing was ever fully broken; everything had a purpose.

She slipped on the pair of boots that she always wore, even in summer, and locked the front door, leaving instead through her bedroom and the sliding door that led to the porch and down the steps. She stayed for a few minutes to indulge in the view in front of her: the pines and oak trees standing in a line across the distance, with the small humps of mountains farther still behind them, their tops hidden by hovering clouds.

Past the pines that hovered at the stone gates of the church, past the small hotel that they used to own—it now had a new name—and then down the road toward the cemetery walled in by a plain iron fence and mounds of over-fertilized grass.

The contentedness in the solitary walks she took to see Henry was rivaled only by the joy of the hours she spent in her garden, or the time with Lyuba, watching how she spoke and moved and carried herself. This was a future that was slowly written in conjunction with the past, and it filled her heart, knowing that there were so many discoveries this child would make that would never be within a world of fear, never in a world that she had to always escape from.

Julia would spend most of her days wrist-deep in the dark earth of the tidy garden, wedding band winking, her now longer, whiter hair tied loosely by her neck and covered with a cotton scarf to shield her eyes from the sun, her knees resting by explosions of hydrangeas and marigolds. She didn't look over her shoulder anymore to see Henry walk through the wooden gate, though she had for the first few years after he'd gone. His presence diminished gradually, and now, twenty years later, Julia only spoke of him occasionally with Slava, or in her nightly prayers, sometimes leafing through pictures of him that she kept on her nightstand.

Before she walked in to the cemetery, she would look for the pale pink wildflowers that she'd seen once before and never again, vaguely remembering that they were called waxflowers. And anyway, there were usually many others hiding in the abandoned lot across the road, in the bramble overgrowth: blue-bells, dog violets, ground ivy, and foxgloves. She would pick them, and then, clutching the offerings in her hand, follow a wide footpath that curled around the perimeter and then toward the middle, leading her to a four-foot-tall rectangle of dark granite, engraved with a byzantine cross hovering over black letters:

Hironimus (Henry) Rudnick
Beloved father and husband
1916–1985

She knelt down and placed the flowers in front, noticing that a few weeds had grown at the base of the stone.

"Henry, today is going to be a good day." She took her wool hat off and brushed aside strands of tangled white hair hanging in front of her face. She spoke softly, as if to a friend. "Slava was here the other day, helping me organize some of your things. Lyuba says hello–did I tell you that she has a birthmark on her cheek like a star? Oh I probably have already. Slava is doing well at work, and told me that they would promote her to senior technician in the neonatal department, which has something to do with taking care of babies, she explained to me."

Julia's eyes creased; her smile flooded her face. "I wonder, sometimes, about my babies. I pray for them. I know you did too, when you were still here." She sifted some dead leaves from the side of the headstone and traced the letters of his name with an arthritic finger. "Slava is helping me sort out things that I have had cluttering the house for so long." She sighed. "I wonder if this is a way for her to keep me busy?" Her lips rose at the corners. "I wonder if, had you stayed, you would have started doing things differently? Smoking less? Working less? Would you have been happy?"

She paused, and answered for herself, the admission of love much easier when the dead had no answer. "We were happy, Henry. I know it. Despite it all. We tried our best." The uncertainty in her voice was met with her own confirmation of the past; the hindsight to her life was truthful, and it lent itself to a kind of peaceful acceptance.

Her knees ached, and she removed her gloves and placed her palms on the ground to shift her weight.

She moved to a soft spot in the earth where she knelt, left of the headstone, and her palm sunk into the loam slightly—it felt as if he had given her permission. From her right pocket, she withdrew the trowel and placed it in front of her; from her left pocket, she withdrew two pieces of paper, her hand closed around them.

She pierced the soil through the grass with the trowel until the handle almost disappeared, beginning to open up a bit of the earth beneath. She looked at the small, folded pieces of paper in her hand. Their birth certificates. *I will bury the past,* she thought. The soil waited for her decision, like an open wound, and she wondered if she could place them inside. But she realized that it would be letting them go a second time, so she placed them back in her pocket, and slowly her hands covered up the open earth again: dark, moist granules soft on her hands, spilling off, back to where they belonged.

Julia stood up, her gloves in one hand and trowel in the other, and walked away, leaving only the imprint of her knees on the ground in front of Henry's name, forever imprinted in granite.

She walked the long path out of the cemetery—past the fences that bordered small gardens, past the paths that disappeared into thick woods, past the stone church that lay in wait for another marriage or funeral, past the small grocery store that had only just opened its doors, and past the post office around the corner. Her patient steps took her along the familiar gravel road that narrowed gradually toward the small white house on the hill; the house with the yellow door, where hope still lived even though life had been unkind, and where a widow with a secret had lost so many things she'd loved.

* * *

This particular evening, after she'd had dinner at the long table that now only had one place setting, she ran a bath and indulged in it—her body so still and her thoughts so deep that the water looked as if made of glass. As the water cooled, she removed the plug and watched as the water cycloned toward the drain, and once the bath was empty, she stood up and retrieved a towel from the back of the door. She wrapped herself in a thin blue robe and looked in the mirror to survey her age. The heavy blue in her eyes that had once been described by Henry as "like the sea before a storm" had lightened, and there were dark spots on her forehead and cheeks, marking all the years the sun had chased her. Her nose, once sharp and Roman, had softened slightly, and the lines on her neck were deeply etched into her thin skin.

She walked out of the bathroom and toward the closet and stood on the very tips of her toes to retrieve a large, rectangular wooden box crudely engraved with sunflowers, which she brought back to the bed with her, her skin still slightly damp. It was light in weight, but the contents had sat heavy in it for years. She sat down on the bed, feet steady on the floor, and opened it and took the folded birth certificates from earlier and placed them inside. In the box was also a stack of unopened letters that had been returned to her, each with a stamp bearing the words RETURN TO SENDER—INCORRECT ADDRESS.

She had missed two entire lifetimes. She glanced at the letters and realized it would be pointless to search for answers now. She would stop wondering how their arms would feel around her. She would stop wondering if they'd ever asked for her, longed for her, if they'd craved for her to sing to them. For so long, her heart had filled with the unrelenting hope of seeing their faces again, and so she had held on to this withering evidence as proof: proof that they did, in fact, happen, and that they loved her once, and she them.

Julia took each sealed envelope and, without ceremony or emotion, slowly tore them in half, and then into quarters, one by one, until there was a pile of paper at her feet that resembled nothing but ink and empty words. She placed them all on the floor by her bed, and then she took the birth certificates and placed them on the nightstand, no longer hidden from view. Picking up the pale blue rosary that her mother had given her, and placing it in the pocket of her robe, she walked out of the bedroom. She proceeded down the narrow hallway, stopping in the kitchen briefly to shut off the small lamp by the window, and then past the grandfather clock, toward the door to the porch. She walked outside and down the ten wooden steps toward the garden, the bright moonlight stretching its silvery light across the perimeter of the garden and out into the fields, where it faded.

She stood, alone, her eyes reflecting what little light there was left, looking out across the dark fields, as she had done so many times in countries that she would no longer see again.

When she closed her eyes and felt her feet sink into the soft grass, she remembered again that it was Henry's birthday, and it was theirs too, and her only wish was that they knew how she'd loved them.

Therefore, I say to you, her sins, which are many, are forgiven, for she loved much.

—Luke 7:47–48

PART 5

2011–2015

CHAPTER THIRTY-FIVE

MELBOURNE

The spire of the stone church pierced the cornflower-blue of the sky, and the voices of the parishioners died down as the Sunday service ended. Slowly, the heavy, red-painted doors opened and a rainbow of silk skirts, pale shirts and ordinary trousers flooded the steps as everyone left, waving their hellos and goodbyes and shaking the hand of the priest as he stood, nodding. The inside of the church would be quiet soon, resting in the air that had been filled with incense and perfume just moments ago.

In one of the empty, dark pews sat a woman, her head bowed. Her neck was thin, her shoulders broad and delicate. Regal. Her body was tall, her gray-blonde hair scraped back and up, a single braid circling her head like a halo. She held a prayer book on her lap.

The echo of leather-soled shoes rang out crisply as the priest walked down to the woman, his form silhouetted by the light of the church's open door. He collected prayer books along the way and stopped as he reached her. He sat in the pew in front of her. She raised her head in greeting, her eyes wet as she smiled. "Hello, Father."

"Hello again." He nodded to the altar behind him, resplendent in white linens in front of the intricate stained glass. "Third time this week. How are you keeping?"

"Alright. As well as I can be, really."

The priest cocked his head sympathetically. "Death is never a stranger for long, in this life. How long has it been now?"

"Six months, just about."

"Still feels as if he could walk through the door, then?"

She smiled. "Yes."

"Do you have your daughter to help you manage for the time being?"

"Yes. She has been wonderful, really—she and her husband. And I have my friends to lean on; it's not that I need any help." She reached into her pocket and withdrew a handkerchief, dabbing her eyes. It had been her husband's, and still smelled of his cologne.

The priest leaned in, sensing something unspoken. "I know you well enough now to know that your church-going isn't entirely related to Walter's death. You have always been a pragmatic woman. Never wavering. There is something else."

She looked up. "Yes."

He nodded. "Is it something that we've discussed in the confessional?"

She looked back down.

The priest crossed his legs, placing his hands on his black robes. "The past can harm or heal, but the truth always heals a broken heart." He watched as the woman stayed silent. "Do you think it's time?"

The woman handed her prayer book to him and looked up, placing the handkerchief in her pocket. "I'm not sure I can."

"This has been a heaviness in your heart for as long as I have known you, and that's an easy twenty years." He sighed. "Did Walter know?"

"No," she replied, softly. "I never told him, and never told Irena. Only you."

"Do you think you can live with this any longer?"

"No. I don't think I can."

The priest stood up and placed his hand on her shoulder. "We teach our children never to run away from the truth. We teach them to face it."

The woman stood up, smoothing her skirt and straightening her trench coat. "I fear that I will not be forgiven for the years that I have waited." They both began walking toward the entrance, the light flooding the space around them. The priest stopped and turned to her.

"Elina, all you can do is hope. Forgiveness lives within hope."

After the service, Elina walked slowly along the sidewalk toward home, her mahogany cane helping her navigate the hard ground. Her linen trench coat swayed behind her and her cotton skirt peeked out from under it. A rosary glistened on her neck over her cream blouse as she walked, the sun hitting its facets proudly. She was grateful that the church had not been too crowded, for the small moments of peace that existed between the stone walls and the echoed hymns.

The sermon that morning had been about forgiveness, which was why she had lingered after everyone's footsteps had receded. As she had sat on the hard, wooden pew, her hands folded in prayer, she'd remembered a face from her past that she had thought about her entire life, but that featured more prominently in her thoughts, prayers, and dreams lately now that her husband was gone. He had never known of her past, and now it seemed the past had been catching up with her.

As she approached her house, Elina stepped onto the porch

and unlocked the heavy door, feeling the cool breeze from the front room spread across her face and her arms as she took off her coat. She hung it on the door, slipped off her shoes, and placed her cane against the wall, which was covered in photos. As she walked down the narrow hallway to the kitchen, she touched every single one of them: ones of her husband; of the two of them on their wedding day; and of his parents, long gone; and the photos of Irena as a child, and then as an adolescent, and then an adult. On the wall were also plates with red and black *vyshyvanka* patterns displayed on wire hooks, while wood carvings of sparrows and wheat fields perched on the high shelves. Time had passed considerably.

Elina walked into the warm and bright kitchen, past a small metal table with a chair and a telephone, set water to boil, and then walked through into the dining room and up the stairs to the bedroom, where she sat down on the bed, the lace-patterned white quilt sagging beneath her. She reached over and looked at a small picture in a silver frame, and it made her smile as she ran her fingers along the glass. The small face of the toddler grinned happily in her mother's embrace, people milling on the board-walk behind them on that summer's day. Elina remembered the day with her daughter as if it were yesterday.

She placed the picture in her lap as she slowly unbraided her hair and let it fall. Her eyes filled with tears, the weight of the past flooding her heart, the memories of so many moments that had gone terribly wrong. *And what now*, she thought. *What can I say now?*

She put the picture back in its place, and walked back downstairs to the kitchen, taking the kettle off the stove.

While the tea steeped and the water became darker, she sat down next to the telephone, pressing the numbers tentatively and lifting the receiver to her ear.

"Hello, my love... Yes, yes, I'm fine. You? ... Yes, yes... I was calling because, I was wondering... I will need you to use your computer for me. ... Yes... yes, I know I should learn, but I have you. Why—?"

Elina paused.

"I was wondering if you could help me find an old friend."

CHAPTER THIRTY-SIX

GLEN COVE

When the phone rang, Julia didn't hear it at first, as she had just slipped into a beautiful dream. She was standing in a field, barefoot, the crisp spines of wheat bending between her toes. The air was sweet and familiar, but she couldn't place the mild scent for certain. It reminded her of someone. The sky was wide and the lightest shade of pink she had ever seen, the yellow of the sun mixing to create a warmth that settled on her skin like dew. Her feet stayed still, and yet her eyes saw perfectly across the field as if she was walking across it, and then suddenly her vision changed and rose and she could see the field as if it rested beneath her, and then her hands reached out and skimmed across the tops of the trees, above and toward the dark, meandering river and then back down its length to then turn around and go back, as the crane flies.

Her hair was dark again, and long, and it had been taken out of its plaits, as she had used to do as a child before bed, the waves of it moving in the slight breeze like heavy silks. She looked down. Her dress was blue and soft cotton, and she recognized it only when she saw Henry in the distance, watching her; for it was her wedding dress. He was holding something on either side, his arms stretched down and slightly away from his sides, each hand clasping and attached to... what was it? She couldn't see yet—so she moved closer, curious, the square of his shoulders and the length of his body clearer at each step. And then she was there, looking at him, indulging in the heavy dark brown of his eyes, the way his cheeks protruded and rose as he smiled, the way his lips flattened beneath his moustache and his dark hair flopped lazily to the side, and the way the lines around his eyes proudly decorated the sides of his face. There was no smoke, no sugar, only the solid warmth of his body as he stood inside her gaze. Oh, she loved him still! Their lives had fallen together and apart and back together again, and that was the point of love—the falling together again.

She lowered her eyes, remembering that he was holding something in each hand, and it was then that she saw them: one small hand in each of his large square ones, their bodies shaped to his legs, giggling, as they looked up at her. He let go of them and she knelt down as they fell into her, slowly, burying their heads into her as she kissed their soft faces and smelled their warm skin. *My babies, my babies,* she repeated over and over again, her voice breaking, incapable of containing the flood of emotion that she had bottled up for so long and, *finally,* her heart untied and let love in, and she looked up at Henry and she saw his eyes, tears collecting in them.

She was grateful, and though forgiveness was never something he had asked for, she knew now that he had felt it there, in the locked place where grief resides with love and loss. For they were the same, their hearts. They had loved and lost and grieved in parallel, and it was only now that she understood.

The phone rang again. And again.

Julia opened her eyes and squinted at the clock by the bed, but being half asleep she couldn't read the numbers. She turned the knob on the light, and it flooded the room as she covered her eyes with one hand and placed the receiver to her ear. "Hello?"

There was an intake of breath on the other end. And then silence.

"Hello? Who's there? Slava?"

"Julia?" The woman's voice was thin. Reedy. It sounded like sand coated in honey. It was vaguely familiar. "Hello?" she said again. "Julia, is that you?"

"Who is this?"

"Please don't hang up when I tell you."

"What?" Julia frowned. "Who is this?"

"It's... it's Elina."

Julia felt her heart grow cold. Her hands began to shake. She squeezed the receiver as if it were the only thing that would keep her tethered to this world and it would soon melt in her grip. "Why are you calling me?" she hissed.

"Wait. Please listen."

"Just like you listened to me? How dare you!" With her other hand, Julia gripped the bedsheets and pulled them to her. "Why would I entertain anything that you say?"

"Because I need to tell you something. Something important. Please don't hang up."

She could so easily end the conversation. She could place the receiver down and never answer it again. But Elina's voice had ignited something inside her, and she wasn't entirely sure if it would be pain or joy, or both. So, she listened.

"I honestly don't know what to say to you, Elina."

"Then don't say anything. Hear me out."

"Fine."

Elina took a breath. "I'll start from the beginning. And I promise you, you will be glad you listened."

CHAPTER THIRTY-SEVEN

She repeated it over and over in her head, but it was as loud as if she were shouting.

They were mine. Henry's. Ours. They were ours. We could have kept them. It wasn't my fault. A son and a daughter. His. Her thoughts felt like knives, each new one stabbing her, forcing her to react.

"No. This is impossible." Julia's thoughts ran in circles in her head, her chest felt on fire, and her hands shook as she listened to Elina's voice, not wanting the truth to settle.

"They were yours, Julia. They were always yours." Elina spoke, her voice breaking with tears. "I am so sorry... I didn't realize it until I became pregnant with my second husband. I never told anyone this, but I had gone to the doctor to test myself for fear that I could not have children. And then, I was too scared to reveal any of it to anyone." She repeated this over and over again: it was a bomb detonating with the fresh smell of fire and metal.

Julia had been listening, her eyes wide, body as still as a statue. At points in the conversation she stood up and told Elina to stop and wait, because she needed to catch her breath. She

paced, she walked out of the room, shaking her head, tears falling, and then would come back to her voice, ask her to continue,
and then ask her to stop again. This went on for three hours,
until the entire story was revealed.

She had told Elina about the assault, and Elina had finally
told her the truth.

They had been Henry's. Her entire life had changed course
because of an assumption. An unknown. And now she had to
come to terms with it.

"Elina, I can't begin to explain to you the amount of life I
have lost," Julia whispered, tangling her fingers in the phone
cord over and over. "I'm not sure I needed to hear this now,
did I?"

"Of course you did. You have been wronged your entire life
because of a lie. And I was a part of it. I couldn't live a life
knowing that I had this secret."

"What good does it do me now, Elina? You are doing this to
ease your own guilt, maybe!" There was anger in her voice.

"I know you feel so much anger and sadness right now,
Julia, but you have to understand that I did this because I knew
that I might be able to help you. To give you something,
anything, after so many years."

"Elina, it's too much, I don't even know where to begin.
What do I do? Or say?" She sighed. "Why now?"

"Because we are mothers. And our children need to know
our stories." She paused. "Why don't I help you?"

"How?"

"I am in Australia still. Do you have anything that could
find them?"

"No. I only kept their birth certificates."

"Alright, well, that may help. Can you send them to me, if I
give you my address?"

Julia hesitated.

"Julia, you can trust me."

"Yes, but that's all I have. I have nothing else."

"Think. Are you certain?"

Julia looked around her room: nothing was out of place, and she knew the contents of every drawer, practically. "Hang on," she replied, and placed the receiver on her bed. She walked out of her bedroom into the dining room, and stood, looking at the pictures on the walls, the sideboard groaning with old china plates and heirlooms. She walked downstairs into the basement and switched on the light, and saw chairs stacked on top of one another, dress bags hanging on a clothing rail, boxes labeled "Henry" and "House things" and "Paperwork."

She turned to leave and then saw a box in the corner, next to an old dolls' house that had a layer of dust on its red-painted shutters. The box said "Slava" on it, and it reminded Julia of the time Slava had moved into the apartment on 71st street and Julia had moved to Glen Cove with some of Slava's things, prompting Henry to laugh that a mother and daughter always had a complicated connection.

Slava.

Upon reaching her bedroom again, she picked up the phone. "Elina." She was breathless. "Are you still there?"

"Yes, of course. Did you find anything?"

"No, but I know how to find it. Please can you give me your number and I will call you back tomorrow?"

Slava felt the mobile buzzing in her shoulder bag as she unlocked the door. She fished it out of her bag and saw it was her mother.

"Hello, Mama, hang on a minute." She walked in and placed the bag on the table and kicked off her shoes. Emilian walked into the room, taking his glasses off and placing a kiss on her cheek. He closed the door behind her. He had been working, and his fingers were stained with graphite. "It's my mother," Slava whispered, holding her hand over the mouthpiece.

Emilian moved her hand from it. "Hello, Julia, how're you?" he said loudly, smiling, taking Slava's jacket from her as she unzipped it. He asked Slava if she needed him, and she shook her head, continuing: "So, what's going on?"

"Hello, sweetheart, can I please ask you to do something for me? It's important."

"Sure."

"I need to ask you a strange question."

"I'm used to those, Mama."

Julia laughed. "Do you remember a long time ago, when you moved into the apartment with Emilian?"

"Of course."

"And you found a letter that was sent to me?"

"Wait, the one I called you about? The weird one?"

"Yes, yes. Did you keep it at all?" Julia's voice sounded apologetic suddenly. "Don't worry if not, it's fine, I just..."

Slava was already walking toward the study. "Funny. And here you've always told me that I'm too curious or sentimental." She stood on tiptoe and reached for a folder. "Hang on." She held the phone with her shoulder and opened the file. It was full of old drawings, pictures, ticket stubs, notes, and a torn, thin envelope with the newspaper clipping inside.

She returned the phone to her ear as she looked at it. "Yes, I still have it."

Julia sighed. "Alright, thank you. Can you please read out to me the return address on the front of the envelope?"

"Yes, sure, but why—?"

"Don't ask, I'll explain later."

After she hung up, Slava scanned the newspaper clipping and the envelope.

Emilian walked in. "Everything okay? What's the drama?"

"No drama. Just my mother being herself." She smiled, and

folded it all into her pocket, replacing the folder back on the shelf.

Julia walked over to her closet, slowly moving the hangers of clothes to the side, the sound of metal and soft cotton under her fingertips. On the last hanger, she stopped, lifting it up to her eyes, seeing how the blue and red material had faded to pale pink and gray. Small threads hung loose from the seams, and a button was missing.

She brought it to the bed and fanned it out, lifting up the lining, running her hands up along the inside until her fingers felt the extra stitches and small square lump. She turned the skirt inside out and with a fingernail gingerly unpicked the stitches, one by one, revealing the birth certificates inside. She lifted them out and held them to her heart briefly, pressing them to her chest, before walking downstairs and placing them in an envelope.

Before she sealed it, she took a framed picture off the shelf and removed it from the frame. Hidden beneath the back panel was a faded, silvery picture—Julia, with all three of her children. It was the only one she had.

She hoped Elina could find the twins; she couldn't bear losing them twice.

CHAPTER THIRTY-EIGHT

ONE MONTH LATER

The taxi left, dust and gravel scattering behind its wheels, and Elina stood at the door of the welfare office. She checked the contents of her purse, and she had the two weathered birth certificates in her hand, with the picture that had been sent with them. She smiled at the face looking out of it, with bright eyes and dark hair. She wondered what Julia looked like now and imagined that the hope in the face of her youth would come back to her, if she'd lost it long ago.

The room was quiet, with scratchy chairs that had metal legs, baskets with old magazines in them, and a plastic drinks dispenser in the corner. There was a young couple seated in the corner, waiting, looking through a magazine and whispering tenderly to each other. Behind the polished desk was a secretary, her straight brown hair curtained over her white shirt. She was checking her phone, tapping it lightly, leaning back in her chair.

"Hello, miss?" Elina leaned closer to the desk.

"Morning, how can I help you?"

"I'm here to see Mr. Bennett."

"Who?"

"The owner, or partner rather, of this place..." Elina's index finger made the shape of a circle in the air. "Is he still working here?"

"Oh, gosh, no. He retired a long time ago."

"Ah." Elina's face showed defeat.

"Can I help you with anything maybe?"

"Well, possibly. I am looking to find two people."

"Are they related to you?"

"No. But I knew their mother."

"I don't really have access to information like that, but maybe I can get someone else to help you." The woman picked up the phone and held it to her ear with her shoulder. "Hang on." She raised a finger.

Elina walked over to a chair and sat down, holding her purse in her lap, both hands clutching it. The wool of the seat padding felt hard under her skirt, and she pinched the silk of her shirt and fanned it delicately, grateful for the cool air on her skin. She looked out the window and saw the neon signs displayed above shops, bright yellows and reds and greens, and wondered when it had happened that the world had become so different.

"Excuse me, ma'am?" the young lady called out to Elina.

"Yes?"

"I found someone who can help, she'll be in shortly."

"Thank you." Elina folded her hands, her breath calm and shallow.

The click of heels on the floor grew louder as an older woman approached slowly, dressed in matching trousers and jacket, thin wire glasses perched on her nose, her wavy silver hair undone and hanging to her shoulders. She walked over to Elina. "Hello, I'm Katherine, and you are—?"

Elina stood up. "My name is Elina."

"Hello, Elina, why don't you come with me to my office, and we can chat about what you need, yes?"

. . .

Elina sat down in a leather chair opposite the desk while Katherine closed the door. She then walked behind her desk and took a seat. "I only work here part time now, but I'm happy to help you. So, what do you need?" She clasped her hands and leaned forward.

"I need your help finding two people."

"Yes, Andrea told me that much. I'll see what I can do."

Elina set her handbag next to her chair and undid her coat slightly. "Well, my friend has had a terrible thing happen to her, and only I can make this right."

Katherine held her hand up. "Wait, does this involve some kind of police investigation?"

"No, no. You see, she was forced to give up her children in the 1950s."

"Yes, there were a lot of adoptions at that time, sure."

"But she believed that they were the result of an assault. Which is why she was forced to give them up. Her husband thought they weren't his."

"Why didn't she report the assault?"

Elina raised her eyebrows. "It's only in recent years that women are starting to be believed. And she felt guilty that she had contributed to this assault somehow."

"How do you know all this?"

"Because it was my husband, at the time, who assaulted her." Elina looked across to the window at the blue sky over the Stratford skyline. "It was something that I had suspected, but never believed, because I had been envious of the fact that she could have children. And it was reason for me to assume that what he told me was true."

"What did he tell you?"

"That she had come on to him, and started an affair." Elina looked back at Katherine. "So, I told her husband."

Katherine moved her chair back to stand up. "I'm not really sure where I come into all of this, to be honest—"

Elina raised her hand. "Wait. Please."

Katherine sat back down.

"You see, when I told her husband, I can only assume that he calculated back to when the affair happened, and then he, and my friend, both realized that the twins that she had given birth were a result of this assault."

Katherine nodded, urging her to continue.

Elina shrugged. "She came to me, to ask me for help—she begged me to hear the truth of what happened, and I couldn't. I threw her out of my house." She stared at her hands. "She lost everything."

Katherine sighed. "I appreciate that you need me, but I don't really know what I'm supposed to do here."

Elina continued, ignoring the question. "I always thought it was me. I always thought I couldn't have children. I thought they *were* his children, don't you see?"

"I'm not following."

Elina reached down for her handbag and unsnapped it, reaching inside and retrieving two worn birth certificates, holding them in her hand as she spoke. "He had always blamed me for the fact that we were barren. We had never been able to have children. I just accepted that it was me, and when I saw those children and thought that they'd been a result of their 'affair,' it broke me. It broke my trust, and my friendship." She shook the papers in her hand. "But I was able to have a child. My daughter. I remarried, and then I knew." She placed the papers on the desk. "Then I knew that those children were, in fact, her own." Elina's eyes filled with tears and she reached for a tissue from a box on the desk. "She had to give up her own children. And I couldn't live with that knowledge anymore."

Katherine sat quietly, her mouth slightly open, then ran her palms over her eyes, shaking her head. "Elina. If you want me to release closed adoption records, I can't. What if the adoptive parents are unwilling? And even if they're not around anymore, I can't guarantee that these children are in Australia still." She looked sympathetically at Elina. "I understand your friend's tragedy, and it's heartbreaking, but I can't release this kind of information."

Elina leaned forward. "Katherine, please." She pushed the papers toward her.

Katherine sighed and looked down, unfolding the pages delicately.

BIRTH CERTIFICATE

Child

> Family name: Rudnick
> Christian or given name: Maksim
> Sex: Male
> Date of Birth: April 1950
> Place of Birth: Stratford, Cairns

Mother

> Family name: Rudnick
> Maiden family name: Mishik
> Christian or given name: Julia
> Occupation: Wife
> Age: 27
> Place of Birth: Lviv, Ukraine

Father

> Family name: Rudnick
> Christian or given name: Hironimus
> Occupation: Farmer
> Age: 29
> Place of Birth: Stryi, Ukraine

Marriage of Parents
    Date of Marriage: 1945
    Place of Marriage: Germany

She switched her gaze to the other, her hands turning cold, her eyes widening.

BIRTH CERTIFICATE

Child
    Family name: Rudnick
    Christian or given name: Lesia
    Sex: Female
    Date of Birth: April 1950
    Place of Birth: Stratford, Cairns

Mother
    Family name: Rudnick
    Maiden family name: Mishik
    Christian or given name: Julia
    Occupation: Wife
    Age: 27
    Place of Birth: Lviv, Ukraine

Father
    Family name: Rudnick
    Christian or given name: Hironimus
    Occupation: Farmer
    Age: 29
    Place of Birth: Stryi, Ukraine

Marriage of Parents
    Date of Marriage: 1945
    Place of Marriage: Germany

Katherine placed the papers back on her desk and folded her hands, smiling. Elina saw tears in her eyes.

"Elina."

"Yes?"

"Did Andrea tell you anything about me?"

Elina frowned. "No, why? She only told me that you would be in charge of something like this." Elina opened her handbag again and withdrew the photograph, handing it to Katherine. "That is my friend. Julia."

Katherine held it, wiping a tear from the corner of her eye. "Yes, I know." She nodded. "I remember. When I graduated high school in 1950, I came to work here. As a secretary." Katherine's voice was even, but expectant, the words hovering in her mouth. "I sent her a newspaper clipping from Australia years ago. I had always remembered her, and I managed to find her last known address in New York. The newspaper clipping was of one of the twins' marriage announcement." She shook her head in disbelief. "It's extraordinary, this story."

She gave the photo back to Elina. "Give me a week. Would it be alright for you to come back? I would hope to have what you need by then."

Elina let out a breath, knowing that she was now part of the story of her friend's life. This was forgiveness.

She nodded, gratefully. "Thank you."

CHAPTER THIRTY-NINE

The sky was a milky gray and snow had begun to fall as Slava fiddled with the knob on the car radio. The traffic was slow, and she wanted something to listen to that wasn't Christmas music. Another swipe of the wiper blade across the glass revealed the pink undertones of the sky. She loved this kind of weather in the late afternoon: the air sat heavy and comfortable on her skin and it smelled of sweet, humid cold.

The windshield wipers slowly and rhythmically swept the flecks of snow and she finally settled on an inoffensive radio station, with no talking and music that had no words.

Emilian wasn't with her, as he was at work, and their daughter Lyuba was at college after staying with Julia for a week during Thanksgiving. Lyuba was a sweetness that Julia had gotten used to over the years; she'd never imagined that her heart would open enough to be loved again, and yet here was this dark-haired girl with fiery green eyes and tall, narrow legs. Slava smiled at the memories they'd all shared over the years, and watched her mother soften so much, allowing herself to be unafraid and happy.

Emilian had encouraged Slava to do this trip alone, because

important things were always done alone, he'd said. So, she'd resolved to see her mother: the woman who may have held something back from everyone, yet had somehow never diminished any bit of her strength.

Come over, sweetheart, she had said. *I'd love to chat with you about something.*

Her mother never just "chatted."

Slava pulled the car up to the house just in time for the snow to finish settling, and walked into the house, shutting the faded yellow door behind her. The heat of the front room made her cold cheeks sting. "Mama?"

Julia heard her voice and walked out from the kitchen to meet her. She'd left the door unlocked that afternoon, expecting her. "Ey, don't get snow all over." She wiped her hands on her apron and undid the knot at the back. Her gray hair was dusted with flour from Christmas preparations, and she rolled up her sleeves, her thin fingers still graceful despite her age. She took Slava's coat as she peeled it off, and looked past her, expecting someone else. "Is Emilian not with you?"

"No, he has work."

"On a Saturday?"

"Money never sleeps, especially not in the city."

"I thought he was—"

"A secretary?" Slava laughed, her newly bobbed hair settling down as she took her hat off. "It's been so long, Mama. How do you not remember what he does?"

"Oh, Slava, look. You brought the snow in." Julia sighed and picked up fingerfuls of slush but shook them off, giving up.

"It's snow, Mama. It'll melt. I'm not five." She took off her gloves, her thin gold wedding band feeling too tight on her cold, swollen fingers.

"True. You were much worse, then." Julia chuckled and shook her head. "So much worse."

Slava placed her gloves on a wicker chair next to the door. "He's the secretary of a Wall Street firm, by the way."

"See?" Julia pointed at her. "I said. Secretary."

"Never mind. Anyway, listen, I—"

"Wine? Come, it's cold in here," Julia interrupted.

Slava saw her mother had a purpose. She followed her through the door and stepped into the warm, dark kitchen and then past the tall grandfather clock that stood opposite the dining room and sat down at the oval oak table where they had all once been together. The tablecloth was folded over on one side, and delicate china was set aside, along with napkins and sprigs of holly and poppies made into a *vinok* wreath that Slava used to wear on her head as a child in Christmases past.

The kitchen smelled of onions and oil and minced sauerkraut, and the kitchen counter was swollen with plates of *kutya,* and *pyrohy,* and stuffed cabbage leaves, *holubtsi.* She imagined her mother pinching the soft edges of the dough, and delicately spooning the molasses over the barley, the poppyseeds glittering underneath, black and sticky. It didn't seem to matter how much she had lost, or how distant she had been: there was a softness to her now, and a warmth, that was beautiful.

Julia moved past her and removed two glasses from the antique sideboard that held the *vyshyvanka*-patterned china and more black and red embroidered napkins. One of the glasses was chipped slightly. She took out a handful of napkins and added them to the already rising pile, reminding herself to press them later.

"How is my little Lyuba?" Julia said as she poured them both some wine. She loved saying her name. Short for *Lyubov.* Love.

Slava smiled. "Not so little anymore. So tall, such a whirlwind, stubborn, always wants her own way."

Julia wagged a finger. "Just like her mother"—Julia looked up to the ceiling—"and her grandfather," and looked back down. "It's good for you to have the child you need, not the child you want."

"Ahh, so you need me, do you?" Slava smiled.

"Ha!" Julia pinched the stem of the wine glass and rolled it between her fingers. "Both of you women. More than you probably know." It was an admission that lit the room for a second.

"Do you ever use any of that?" Slava asked, gesturing to the glass-filled cabinet. "I mean, it's not like there will be lots of people here for Christmas—just Em and me and you."

Julia looked at Slava. "Why do you call him that?"

"What. Em?"

"Yes. His name is Emilian. You should use it. It's beautiful."

"Well, it's affectionate, I guess. Didn't you call Papa by something short?"

Julia remembered that occasionally she'd use "Hirko" instead of Henry or even Hironimus, and it had bothered him each time she did, for in Ukrainian it meant *bitter*. She smiled at the memory but chose not to reveal it, for it was something that she didn't need anyone dissecting. It was her small thing to keep about her husband. "Yes, sure. You know, my parents had softer names for themselves."

"Oh? You never told me that."

"Yes." Julia smiled, remembering the sweet way they would call to each other. "My mother called my father 'Kolya,' and my father would call my mother 'Anushka.'"

"So, then you understand. I like 'Em.'"

"You know what is short for Emilian? Not Em."

"What is it?"

"Milo. Like my brother." Julia felt a sting in her eyes as she said it.

"Oh." For a second, Slava though it unwise to pick at old wounds this evening, but maybe her mother was ready.

She pointed to the cabinet again. "Why not sell most of it?"

"What, all these old things? Who would want them?

Besides, they have stories in them." Julia withdrew a small oval platter that displayed yellow bunches of wheat all gathered with red ribbon, painted against a pale blue sky. "This, for example. Papa had this made for me in New York. You know his friend, Roman, who worked at Bachinsky's deli on 9th Street?"

"God, that place. Everyone in there was Ukrainian. And also, the restaurant across the street, too—"

"Veselka."

"That's the one. Anyway, sorry. Roman. The one with the lazy eye?"

Julia laughed and remembered Slava as a child in the company of this man, confused as to which eye to speak to, so she'd developed a habit of looking at a spot in the middle of his forehead. "Yes, him."

"He painted?"

"Yes. He would do it to remember."

"Remember what?"

"Home."

She returned the platter and withdrew a teacup, small and thin enough to crack if placed on the table too energetically. It was white, thin as glass, with a sheer blue line across the top, and a rose engraved on the bottom. "And this, this I was given by Helen, the woman who let us live with her in Germany."

"I get it. Memories."

"I choose to think of them as stories. It's easier to say stories, because it's as if it happened to someone else."

Julia went into the kitchen and checked the stove and covered the resting dough with a thick tea towel. She returned to the table and picked up the wine bottle again. As she poured, a drop of red liquid caught on the chip at the top of her glass, like it had pierced soft skin.

Julia sat down and then took a sip, looking across at her daughter. "So."

"Yes, what?"

"I need to tell you something."

"Sure." Slava fingered the corner of an embroidered napkin; the stitches were blood-red.

"Not too long after Papa died, you and I were going through the paperwork with the lawyer and figuring out the will and the money and house, and, well, there was a lot of stuff to go through."

"I know." Slava sighed. "I didn't understand any of it. It was horrible to have to see Papa as if he'd existed only on paper."

"Yes, it was hard. But we got through it. And, anyway..." She paused.

Slava reached over and rested her hand on Julia's, because she thought it would help. Julia's eyes searched her daughter's. "I wanted to wait until after he died, one day, to tell you something about my life. And I honestly didn't think I'd have the courage to, but something happened the other day that made me realize how important the truth is."

"Okay. What about?"

"From when I was much younger. Something that we've never talked about."

Julia watched Slava's face change. "I know, Mama. You have always kept something inside, and I never could see what it was."

Julia's face flushed in embarrassment. "I'm sorry. It's just that life is complicated enough without adding so much more to it. Our plates have been full." She smiled sadly, her hands running across the smooth wood of the dining table.

Slava leaned in. "So, when, exactly? When we moved to the city?"

Julia ran her finger along the edge of the wine glass, and then down the stem. "No. Australia."

Julia cleared her throat and walked over to the kitchen. Slava watched her through the space between the cupboards and the center island. She saw as she rested her hands on the counter underneath the small window, her head hanging forward, her hair lit by the light above her, like a halo.

"Mama?"

Julia walked back toward the dining table and sat down. "Papa and I moved to Australia with nothing and built everything for ourselves. We had a farm, a life, and you. But that wasn't enough. We wanted more, and we tried for more children."

"Well, I am *more* than enough for one child." Slava smiled.

Julia laughed. "That may be true, but I came from a large family. And I had lost them all. It was lonely for me, the wife of a man who worked his hands raw. I wanted the noise of a large family, sitting around a table, like the memories of my childhood."

"Did you try?"

"We did. So many times. Each time my body refused it."

"Oh, Mama. I'm sorry."

"It's okay." Julia moved a lock of hair off her face. "And anyway, God had different plans for us. You see, there was a couple that we were friends with, that we lived not too far from, and the man in the couple worked with Henry." Julia couldn't bear to say his name out loud. "And the wife, her name was Elina, and she became my friend."

"At least you had someone there when Papa wasn't, right?"

"Well. Yes." Julia poured a splash of wine into her glass and stared at it. "It was a friendship that was lost, in the end."

"Why?"

Julia looked at Slava and searched her face. She was a sister. But what could she tell her? How could she reveal things about herself that had stayed dark for so long? A lie had been easier, but now the truth was bubbling underneath the surface, the layers had been skimmed from the top. "Because of the refusal to hear the truth."

CHAPTER FORTY

MELBOURNE

The cardboard boxes, filled with old books and papers, huddled in the dusty centers of the rooms. The furniture stood in corners exactly as it had done for fifty years, or maybe even more. There was a hint of gray ash in the fireplace that hadn't been used for years, the dining table had a sheet over it, and in the kitchen, the cupboards were bare and only bore the scratches from tin cans and the smells of a few old spice jars.

The windows were raised to let the air in, and Ed was on the second floor, in their old bedroom. Roz was downstairs, sitting on the floor, a glass of wine perched on a stack of books as she perused old files and photo albums. Their parents' lives were now in boxes labeled "Xmas," "Kids," "School," and "House."

"Ed, there is a lot of stuff to go through here, honestly." She took another sip and surveyed the room. "It's all interesting for sure, but why don't we just ask some guy to come over with a truck and put it all in a storage container?"

Ed's footsteps slowly navigated the stairs as he came back down, his arms full of a small desk clock, a table lamp, and an old leash. He set the pile down on the floor next to Roz. "Take it as a trip down Memory Lane, eh?" He picked up the bright red leash with a gold clasp, too small for a normal-sized dog. "Oh, God, speaking of Memory Lane, do you remember this? Remember old Barry?"

"Jesus." Roz let out a throaty giggle. "You were so hell-bent on Mum and Dad getting you a pet that you took your stuffed badger and dragged it around on this leash."

"I was four, right? Maybe five?" He turned the worn bit of leather in his hands. "Where did I even find it?"

"Think we were in a toy store and it was on the mannequin dog in the window." Roz pinched her eyes clear of the tears that her laughing had induced. "God, but you were a weirdo."

Ed threw the lead in an open box. "That may be, but I was creative, no one can argue with that."

Roslyn withdrew a wooden plaque with a gold statue of a man running attached to it. "Look at this! Ha!" She looked over at Ed with a crooked smile. "What a treasure!"

Ed rolled his eyes. "Right, you can stop that now, thanks."

"I'm your sister, that's what I do."

Roz walked up to him and waved the statue in front of his face. "I'm going to leave it on the mantel for the new owners, they'd be very pleased, I'm sure." She walked over and placed it on the shelf above the fireplace and smiled. "Remember cozy nights in front of this thing?" She pointed at the charcoal-stained stone surrounding the iron grate. "Probably why I've always liked winters."

Ed called out from the other room: "Hey, can you go look in the kitchen and see what in there needs organizing? You can be nostalgic another time." He reached into a toy bag and lifted out its contents and placed them in a box as she walked past him to the back of the house. "Hopeless romantic," he muttered, smiling.

· · ·

It was early afternoon when the glass on the door resonated with a series of delicate knocks.

"Roz, are you expecting one of the lawyers? Or the owner?" Ed called out as he stood up.

"No, why?"

"Don't worry," he replied, as he walked over to the door and opened it.

Standing in front of him was a tall woman, in her eighties, he guessed. She carried herself like a dancer, despite the cane she was delicately holding in one hand, eyes bright underneath silver hair in a braid circling her head.

"Hello there, how can I help you?" Ed smiled.

"Is this the Douglas residence?"

Ed detected a faint accent. "Yes, well, this was our parents' house, but my sister and I are here just going through some things. Did you know them?" He liked the look of her and smiled again. She seemed kind.

"No. I knew your mother."

"Oh, so you knew Irene."

"No. Your mother."

Ed laughed. Surely this old woman was a bit senile. "Listen, Mrs.—?"

"Kashiuk. Elina Kashiuk."

"Kashiuk. Right. I'm not sure whom you're referring to, but my mother, Irene, passed a while ago, not long after my father."

"I'm very sorry."

"Thank you."

Roslyn appeared at the door. "Hello." She smiled. "Who's this?"

Ed gestured with an open hand. "This is Mrs. Kashiuk. A friend of Mum's."

Roslyn extended a hand. "Nice to meet you. How did you two know each other?"

Elina realized she would have to play along. She leaned on

her cane a bit, her yellow skirts swaying delicately as she did. She gathered her jacket closer. "May I come in and sit, if that's alright? I can tell you how I knew her. It's a bit of a long story."

Ed looked at Roslyn, his eyebrows raised in a question. Roslyn shrugged in response, and Ed turned back to Elina. "Sure," he offered, pushing the door open wider and extending a hand to her. "I'm sure that'd be fine."

It was only an hour later, and an entire life had been upended, and secrets of the past had been revealed, the paternity, the rape, the adoption, the heartbreak. All like small explosions in the warm room of a house that had contained a happy family.

Now that life felt like a lie.

"This is ridiculous." Ed walked into the kitchen, shaking his head. "Roz, help me out here." A clattering of plates interrupted the silence as Ed busied his hands.

Elina sat stiffly, looking at Roz, who was staring at her like she'd just witnessed a death.

"You can imagine this is all a bit shocking." Roz laced her fingers together and undid them, and then laced them again. "How do we know you're not lying? How do we know you're not some"—she paused—"I don't know, *crazy* lady that walked in from the street and got her memories confused?"

"I am not senile, if that's what you mean." Elina's voice lilted delicately. "And I am not trying to disrespect your parents' memory, of course."

Ed walked back in, but didn't sit down, leaning against the mantle above the fireplace instead. "Well, it feels like an odd convergence of events, to be honest." He ran his hand over the wood, a layer of dust collecting on his fingertips. "Our parents aren't here to explain, and there's nothing in their paperwork"—he gestured to the boxes in the room—"that says otherwise." He looked at his sister. "Roz and I have literally no memory of being with anyone other than these two people, and now you're trying to tell us that we have another mum, and she had to give us up... I mean, it sounds like something you'd watch in a film." He shrugged. "I just can't see it."

Roz watched the woman in front of her: the way she sat, the calm, cool demeanor, the way she held herself so well, even seated in a chair, the way her clothes sat on her, beautifully still. Her eyes held a story. She was purposeful. She had intent, and energy, and Roz knew that there was something there. She wasn't trying to sell them on something, and she wasn't in a haze, or influenced by anything apart from the truth.

Ed continued. "Roz, I know I'm the practical one here, but you're the lawyer brain. Anything you want to say?"

Roz ran her hands through her hair and looked at Ed. "Well, we need some kind of proof." She turned back to Elina. "What you're saying is incredible, but we need something. Anything."

Elina nodded, and removed her jacket, placing it on the arm of the chair. She leaned forward, picking up her handbag and placing it on her lap. "I understand," she began. "Which is why..." She snapped open the metal ridge of the top, spreading the leather bag wide. She removed some papers and handed them to Roz. "I brought these."

Roz took them from her, and Ed walked up to stand next to her, removing a pair of silvery reading glasses from his top pocket and placing them on his nose.

"Oh, my God."

The siblings scanned the papers, handing the sheets back and forth between them, reading them again, pausing only to let out a steady stream of held breaths, and starting again. The sounds in the room were loud in their gravity: crisp paper, fingertips tracing the words.

Elina watched, her face showing neither a smile or a frown, but settled on the scene that was playing out in front of her.

Roz looked up, finally. "Our names. How...?"

"*Leh*-shya," Elina pronounced slowly. "It means, 'promised to God.'"

Ed looked up from his birth certificate. "And...?"

"Mahk-*sim*." Elina leaned back in her chair, as if someone had taken an invisible weight off her back. She looked at the man standing in front of her. "It means 'the greatest miracle.' It was your father's suggestion." Elina's eyes pricked with tears. "He had always wanted a son."

Ed walked over to the dining room, and came back with a chair, setting it down next to Roz. They formed a group of three, as if around a fire, listening to an old woman softly tell a tale.

"What was he like?"

"It would not be my place to tell you. But I can tell you that they both loved you."

"But why, then—?" Ed held the paper up. "Why?"

"It was complicated then, for women. The time was such that we were seen in certain roles, certain boxes, I guess. And any doubt sent ripples through our lives, our marriages." Elina paused, rubbing her hands together as if they ached. "We had to endure. We had to hide our—what is that word... *insecurity,* I guess—and sometimes survival meant sacrificing for the sake of the betterment of our lives. I realize that sounds very old-fashioned, now."

Roz sat back. "Well, it was common back then, I guess, but it's still hard to believe." She shook her head.

"We had no choice." Elina leaned forward. "And many of us now look back on our lives, and the paths we've had to take, and live with the decisions we made. We have to. Otherwise, it would drive us mad." She settled back in her chair.

Roz looked at the paper in her hands. "Wait a minute." She looked at Elina. "I never asked where you got this. And, to be honest, I don't even need to know how you found *this* address—

let's just focus on one thing at a time." She rubbed her temples. "So..."

"Julia sent it to me."

Ed clapped his hand on his forehead. "She's still alive."

"Yes. And she remembers. She has, all this time. It was when I realized—once I had my daughter with my second husband—that it was my husband at the time who could not have children, that I knew I had to tell her one day. The truth."

"So, you spoke to her," Roz interrupted, her eyes widening.

"Yes, and she sent me your birth certificates. She also sent me this." Elina reached into her handbag again and withdrew a photograph.

Julia's face peered out from the small black-and-white square. Her features were muted. Faded. But her dark hair fell in waves over a white cotton dress. She was standing in a field of tall grass, robust trees in the distance behind her, next to a small, dilapidated house. She held the hands of three small children. All of their faces were looking at the unknown photographer, smiling.

"She's beautiful." Roz inspected the photo closely, Ed leaning over her shoulder, waiting for his turn. She passed it to him, and she looked at Elina. "That was us. She was pregnant with us." The truth settled in her eyes as she realized the pain that that woman, her mother, had been keeping inside her in exactly that moment.

"Yes. It is the only picture she has of you all, and she hadn't told anyone she kept it."

Ed took his glasses off his nose and fed them into his shirt pocket, wiping his eyes. "Elina."

"Yes, Maks—" She caught herself and smiled. "Yes, Ed."

"You probably know what I'm going to ask you next." He looked over at Roz, and she nodded in response to his silent question.

Elina waited.

"Do you think I could call her? Do you think that would be alright with her?"

Elina closed her eyes and wept for the friend that she had abandoned long ago, then felt Roz clasp her hand with a kindness and warmth that was unexpected.

CHAPTER FORTY-ONE

"What do you mean?" Slava looked at the woman who had always been as true as rain. Despite her tendency to distance, she had always been quietly persistent, saying to her as a child, "Lies are more painful than the truth." And now Slava looked at her mother's face and saw a kind of pain that she didn't understand.

"I have been through so much, Slava," Julia said, with a sigh. "I have been unlucky."

Silence followed the word *unlucky*.

Slava wasn't sure what she was getting at, and all she could do was wait for more. More from the woman who had always said less was better. Safer.

Julia stood up and walked over to the hallway, and then stopped, and then turned back, as if she had lost her way, or her thoughts, or something had reminded her. She walked over to the porch window and moved the gossamer curtains to the side, revealing the sky settling after the snowfall.

The grandfather clock sounded a slow chime.

Julia walked back to the table, her hand on her chest, her wedding ring glinting. She sat down heavily.

Slava saw Julia's face change, a sculpture being more defined by its softening corners, its cracks and edges. She saw survival. She saw love.

"I don't know how to start—"

"Just try. Anything." Slava reached for her hand.

Julia smiled and heard Henry's voice. *All we can do is try.*

Slava shifted in her chair.

"It was so unfortunate. I"—Julia stopped and leaned her forehead into her open palm, her elbow on the table—"he was a friend. Or so I thought." She looked up at Slava, noticing that her face had grown pale, her eyes staring. "I didn't know what to do."

"Mama, were you—?"

Julia lifted her hand. "I don't want to hear that word." She hung her head. "I thought it was my fault. I thought I had welcomed the attention, I had enjoyed his company, and I didn't understand what went wrong that evening..."

Slava placed her other hand on her mother's, now covering it entirely. "Did you tell anyone?"

"I did, I went to Iliya eventually, I went to his house and his wife was there too, and I told them and asked them for help, but they refused."

"Then, what did you do?"

"I let it disappear. I left it as something that would go away. And yet"—Julia moved a lock of hair over her ear, revealing a silvery scar, no bigger than a thumbnail—"a mark remains."

"Oh, God, Mama." Slava shook her head in disbelief. "I can't believe you had to carry that with you all these years." She leaned back, letting out a breath. "But I'm confused about what that has to do with the friendship, with...?"

"Elina."

"Right. And she was—?"

"Ilya's wife."

Now Slava made the connection. "Jesus."

"She and I had become friends, of course, because Henry and I and she and that man, well, we had become friendly. She confided in me many things, and one thing was that she could not have children. That she suspected her body could not make any. I felt sad for her."

"Of course, but this... attack, happened—?"

"After we had become close," Julia clarified. "She didn't know until later on."

"So if she didn't know, how was the friendship cut off?"

Julia tented her fingertips above the table. "Well, that is part of what happened after. You see, another reason I could not tell anyone the truth was because I became pregnant."

Slava inhaled sharply. "What?"

Julia nodded, her face reddening. "I told no one, and had to pretend that everything was at it should be."

"What about Papa?"

"No one."

"So, Papa had no idea that this happened? None of it?"

"Not at the time."

"Oh, God, Mama." Slava stood up, rubbing her eyes and walking to the kitchen. "I can't believe this is you."

Julia looked over at her daughter, worried that she had said something wrong, her face contorted in panic. "In what way? Oh, no, Slava, I'm so sorry, this is all too mu—"

"No, that's not what I meant. The fact that you had to endure this, this..." Slava threw up her hands. "I don't even know what to call it."

"I know." Julia sighed. She patted the table, her clammy hands leaving a small imprint on the polished wood. "Come. Sit."

Slava came back, sat down, and leaned on her elbows, facing Julia. "Okay," she breathed. "Tell me."

"I had twins, Slava. A boy and a girl." Julia's eyes filled.

"Maksim and Lesia. They were beautiful. Maksim was dark, Lesia was light. They were mirrors of one another, but also so different. Maksim was sweet and patient, Lesia was impulsive and fiery." She wiped a tear from the corner of her eye. "I loved them."

Slava sat, staring in disbelief. *Twins. Dark and light.* It was as if someone was reading her a story about a life that she knew nothing about. And yet, it was a story from *her* life. "I'm almost afraid to ask, but..." She placed her fingertips on her temples and closed her eyes. "What happened to them?"

Julia nodded, her tears flowing more freely now. "Everything was alright, when they arrived. Papa was happy. He had his son, and he never thought he would have one. We had a loud little family, and it was all we wanted. Life became calm. After everything that we had lost in the war, we felt as if we had survived, finally; we had fixed what had been broken."

Slava opened her eyes. "Well, the obvious question, since I don't remember having siblings—"

"Is what happened to them." Julia nodded again. "Yes. Well, Elina's husband still lingered, and Elina had suspicions about me. And maybe it was the anger at him, or the fact that she could not have children, but our friendship faltered. And when she told Papa about what she suspected—"

"That the man attacked you?"

"No. That we were having an affair. Our friendship broke."

"And Papa believed her, and not you?"

"He was a proud man who feared many things. And he feared somehow that I was unhappy in my life with him. He never gave me a chance to explain. And the day that I tried to fight for the truth, he gave me a choice: he told me to choose him and you, or the twins."

Slava clapped a hand over her mouth. "And you chose us."

"Yes. I had no other option. I had to give them away." Julia's tears spilled now, dropping onto the table faster than she could wipe them off her cheeks. "It was the hardest thing I have ever had to do in my life; it was, and still is, a pain that has never fully disappeared."

"I can't imagine it." Slava thought of Emilian, and then of their own daughter, now a young adult, with dark hair past her shoulders like Julia had had as a girl, hazel eyes that were shadowed by long lashes. She imagined her face as a child, and her chest tightened at the thought of leaving her behind. The idea of that kind of pain was unbearable. "Where was I in all this?"

"You were young enough not to remember, or to understand. But old enough at the time to see a kind of sadness. But I want you to listen to something. The reason why I called you here."

"Surely there can't be more." Slava shook her head. "That's impossible."

"There is." Julia gave a tentative smile. "And this is something that life has given me—a gift, that I can share with you, after all of this."

"What is it?"

"I received a call from Elina a little while ago."

"What? Seriously? Why? She's still alive?" Slava's voice popped with energy, unable to contain her questions.

"She called to tell me something in her life that would affect mine. It might not be good news, I'm not sure. But she told me a truth. She wants to help me."

Slava frowned. "About what? With what?"

"Many years ago, after the twins were adopted and you and Papa and I moved to New York, she left her husband and remarried, and lived a happy life with her new husband and... daughter."

Slava pushed her chair back and squinted her eyes. "Wait. She adopted?"

Julia shook her head. "No. She gave birth to a daughter."

"But I thought she was..."

Julia looked up at the ceiling and closed her eyes. Fresh tears slid down her cheeks. "So did I."

Slava turned her head to the right, then to the left, as if trying to solve a riddle. She looked at her mother and drew in a breath. "Oh, my God."

Julia covered her face with her hands. The grandfather clock struck eleven, the metal face resonating after the muffled heaviness of the gong. "God will never forgive me."

Her voice sounded like a child behind her hands.

Slava wiped the tears from her cheeks and walked around to her, kneeling as she unpeeled her mother's hands from her wet face. "Mama, don't you see? You are loved. You have been found. He has already."

That night, as the clock struck midnight, and later still, with her head bowed, Julia began to tell her daughter the stories that she thought she'd forgotten, which had haunted her for so long. Through her tears, she told her daughter of the children she had wanted and had given to God, and the two children who had helped her heart heal after a crime that had broken it so badly, and the love that she'd had for all of them and then lost so painfully, so cruelly. She told her daughter that it wasn't her father's fault, and that she had forgiven him for the pain that he had contributed to, for he had also carried it in his heart to the end of his days.

She told her daughter how she felt about love: that it was a great and complicated tragedy of joy and pain, for hearts can be broken and fixed again through hope, and yet they still break.

They talked for hours, until their throats were dry and the tears had dried in tracks on their faces. Julia wrung her hands and clasped them over her daughter's, and presented an unflinching grief that she had never allowed herself to feel fully.

That evening, they both fell asleep under night skies that were dark and quieted by snow, felled by an incredible truth: that the lost can sometimes be found again.

CHAPTER FORTY-TWO

GLEN COVE

The bright green numbers on the clock flashed *1:30 a.m.* as the phone rang. It woke Julia immediately, as if she had waited every second of her sleep to be awake in that exact moment.

The phone stopped suddenly, and she thought that maybe she'd imagined it, so she waited, her body rigid.

It started ringing again, and she held her breath as she reached across for the receiver.

It stopped before she could pick it up, and she had a sense that whoever was on the line was either doubting they had the right number, or second-guessing themselves, or even that the line was faulty.

She reached for the lamp and switched it on, and lay back in bed, waiting. Curious.

It rang again and this time Julia grabbed the receiver. "Elina? Is it you?"

Static, and then a voice. "Hello? Is this Julia?"

"Yes?"

The line crackled and then a voice emerged. "Hello…" The voice sounded male, elderly, but clear.

"Yes…?" She was losing patience.

"I don't really know how to say this..." he began, still timid.

"Listen, it's late, whoever you are, and if you're trying to sell me something, I'm not interested, thank you." She was about to replace the receiver when he said, "Wait, please, Mama!"

And then she knew.

She placed the phone to her ear again. "Maksim?"

Timid laughter. "It's Maksim, this is Maksim." It was said in a rush, as if ripping the tape off a parcel and revealing its contents. *Maksim.* It sounded strange, this name that should be familiar to her, because it was said without the thick tongue of the Slavic *k* and *m,* and so her initial reaction was confusion, along with wondering if this was real. She looked around at the dark room, and reached for the rosary by the bed, her fingers lightly finding the facets and then pressing them into the pads of her fingers. It was real.

She mouthed his name to herself, silently. *Maksim.* Both her hands held the receiver to her ear now, as she leaned forward and closed her eyes. She felt his small body on her lap as she had done so long ago, his warm arms around her waist, his dark hair against her chest as he slept.

Her throat caught as she inhaled. "Oh, my God, I cannot believe it's you. Is it you?"

"Yes, it's me."

She saw the memories of her life like the pages of a book, fluttering to an end before it closed. She couldn't speak for fear of losing track of these memories that had been left cold for so long, now warming her entire body, and she wanted them, craved them, adjusted to them with fresh authority.

She covered her eyes with her other hand as if in a state of panic, not wanting his words to disappear into the crackle of a broken line, but also because she wanted to digest every soft tone of this voice, *his* voice, the voice that she had only ever known when he was a child; she heard it there still, faintly, despite the gravel of age changing it.

He was there. He had found her.

They spoke until they couldn't speak anymore, Julia listening to her son tell her so much about his life, or at least whatever he could fit into the next few hours. He would ask if she needed to sleep, and she would encourage him to continue. The minutes and hours passed swiftly, until the first hints of light spread across the morning sky.

As they ended the phone call, Ed promised that he would call with his sister on the line next time.

His sister.

My daughter, Julia thought. She replaced the receiver as if it were a piece of glass that would break.

In shock, Julia spent the rest of that morning walking at a slow and cautious pace, finally sitting outside on the porch that she had once shared with Henry. She sighed and leaned her head back, her face ruddy with tears, the sun drying them slowly.

The light, now. She felt the light come through, and smiled, a relief settling across her shoulders. She thought of her mother's words: *There is always hope left in a broken thing.*

CHAPTER FORTY-THREE

2012

Autumn had settled in green and gold on Glen Cove. After landing twenty-four hours earlier, Ed and Roslyn had taken a walk through the quiet streets of the sleepy town, just as it was coming alive in the crisp morning. The houses and shops on the streets had small porches and peaked roofs, with manicured gardens and mailboxes with painted numbers on them. The postal workers were clutching their coffees and delivery men were starting their trucks to begin their routes.

It was as if they'd taken a step back into someone else's life; an old memory that hinted at a sense of peace, a foothold in safety.

They walked out of town, on East Drive, past the pile of stone that represented an old monastery, past the park by the golf course, and found their way to Prybil Beach, a small spit of sand shaped like a crescent moon, with benches along the edge of the water.

Ed zipped his sports coat against the chill and sat down. "Wow. I can't believe we're here." He looked over at Roslyn, who was clutching a scarf around her neck, the orange strip of sky reflected in her bright eyes. "What're you thinking?"

"Honestly? I don't know." She let out a sigh. "This all seems a bit surreal." She looked at Ed. "If I was ever a smoker, maybe now would be the time to do it." The corner of her mouth lifted.

"What did you tell Martin?"

"Everything. And both girls, too. I told him that I needed to do this first, with you, and that if it goes well..."

"Of course it'll go well."

"You know what I mean. If it feels right, then we can all come and meet each other."

Ed nodded and folded his arms. "Fair point."

"What did you say to Helen?"

"Same. But, I mean... what could go wrong, here?"

"Do you think it erases our past? That's what it feels like."

"In what way?"

"Well, not entirely, but you know, our life with Mum and Dad."

"It made us who we were. And so will this."

"I don't follow." Roslyn looked at her brother.

"Well, isn't that the million-dollar question?" Ed chuckled. "It's a story about who we were, then. We're the same people, still, but our lives have gone in different directions. And we had more than one mother who loved us. That's something pretty great."

"What about our real father?" Roslyn clasped her hands in her lap tightly. "I mean—" She stopped, her voice apologetic.

"No, I know what you meant. I mean, we *had* a father." Ed shrugged. "And now we have two. Or, *had*, anyway."

"More than most."

"I wonder what he would have been like." Ed looked across at the Long Island Sound, the water lapping the shore. "We'll learn about him through Julia. And pictures, I guess."

"What do we call her?"

"What do you want to call her?"

Roslyn looked up at Ed and saw the brother who had been

kind to her, and patient, if not sometimes distant and pragmatic. She saw a lifetime that now had so many new memories to uncover and layer, like the pages of a book settling, gusting air as it closed.

"Mama, I think."

Ed nodded. The blue had overtaken the sky now, and the beach started to fill.

* * *

The room felt too small, suddenly. Maybe it was the curtains. Ed pressed his shirt down with his palm nervously and walked over to the window of the hotel room. He shifted the heavy curtains to the side, and stood with his hands in his pockets, scanning the parking lot's cars moving like silvery ants.

Roslyn knocked at the door, and he walked over to let her in.

"You look nice," she commented, as she walked into the room, setting her handbag down on the desk next to the phone. She looked at her reflection and ran a hand through her hair and closed her lips to even out her lipstick. "I look like shit."

Ed was back at the window and looked over at his sister. "You look fine, hon. You're just nervous."

Roslyn gathered her thick hair in a fist and placed it on one shoulder. "Maybe like this. Or a braid?" She pulled out a chair and sat down heavily, leaning back and clasping her hands together, her blouse billowing around her waist and her wrists. "This is weird." She looked over at Ed. "Ed?"

"Yeah."

"You okay?"

He pointed through the glass at a spot in the distance. "Did you know that Glen Cove is considered the Gold Coast of the North Shore? Funny."

"Oh, you mean that—"

"Yeah. Connections. Here we are, on the other side of the world from where we grew up, in a place that sounds so familiar."

"Where, if I can ask, did you come up with that one?"

Ed turned around. "Hotel pamphlets are great for that kind of stuff." He looked at his watch. "Ready?"

Roslyn shifted in her seat, the leatherette suddenly sticking to her bare legs. "Sure." It was a smile that was timid, and suddenly they both felt like children again.

Slava stepped out of the car and walked around to the other side to help Julia out, lacing her arm through hers and closing the door.

Julia straightened her back, a handbag hanging from her bent arm. Her trousers were a pale blue, and the pink of her silk shirt's collar peeked out from underneath her thin jacket. She touched her hair lightly, a wave of white now streaked with gray, still as thick as it had been when she was young. She placed her hand on Slava's, her wedding band catching the light. "Slava..."

"Yes, Mama?" Slava pushed her sunglasses off her face, nesting them in her blonde hair.

"I am not sure I can do this." Julia looked across at the familiar landscape of the town, that just then felt strangely unfamiliar.

"Yes, you can."

"How do you know?"

Slava squeezed her arm delicately, the fragile bone and soft skin underneath her fingers. "Because you taught me. You taught me what it is to be strong, no matter what you see in front of you." She scanned her mother's face. "And the proof of that strength is waiting for you right now."

Julia looked at her daughter, a relief spreading across her

face. She realized this wasn't her daughter anymore. She was a woman. A mother. A warrior for her family.

"Slava?"

"Yes, Mama."

"Did I tell you enough that I am proud of you?"

Slava frowned. "What?" Her mother was nervous, she knew that. But there was an openness in her words that felt different. Softer. "What do you mean? Of course I know you're proud of me."

"No, that is not what I mean." Julia leaned her face closer. "Did I ever *tell* you how proud I am? And that I love you? Was I enough? Or did I miss too many moments?"

Slava's eyes filled, and she quickly dabbed the corners. "Mama, I know. I know all of it. And it's never too late to say it out loud."

They began to walk slowly, across the lot, to the entrance of the hotel, and then to the bank of elevators. Slava pressed the "Up" button.

When the gold doors opened with a metal rattle and hiss, they revealed a wide mirror at the back of the elevator. Both women stood as the doors closed behind them, arms linked still, staring at their reflection. Julia, once dark, now light. Slava, still bright, her blue eyes against a strong face, her features sharpened by her age. Both women possessed strong shoulders and stood proudly, and Julia wondered how it was that her entire life had gone by without often acknowledging how beautiful Slava was, and how proud she was of her.

"Mama." Slava cocked her head to the doors as they opened. "This is us."

The hallway was long, the carpet soft and firm under their shoes, the pattern heavy with black and orange diamond shapes, echoing the orange-tinted sconces dotted on the walls.

Lilies sat in a glass vase on a telephone table halfway down the hall.

At the door, Slava looked at Julia. Her eyes were open, like a child's, simmering with energy and nervousness. She squeezed her arm. Julia nodded in response.

Slava rapped at the door and waited.

The door opened, and the first thing that Julia saw was light —the curtains were wide open, and a beautiful light flooded the room, hitting every corner. She squinted and walked through with Slava, the door closing behind them.

It was then that she saw them, standing side by side, by the window. At first, it was their silhouettes, the sun at their backs. Julia felt Slava's arm disconnect from her own, and she absent-mindedly handed her her handbag to hold.

Julia stepped closer, and they appeared. She saw Roslyn first, her wavy hair, with hints of red and gold, like strawberries, when she was a child. Her face creased in a smile as she saw the freckles that she used to count when she would put her to bed. She saw the proud nose and the wide shoulders. She was tall.

Julia looked across to Ed and inhaled sharply. The dark hair now with so much gray, the wide forehead, the flat lips and soft nose. The eyes that had shadows underneath them that hinted of sadness. It was Henry. She saw Henry's face, and she knew. She knew that he had lost his own son, so long ago.

Ed withdrew two pieces of paper from his pocket. They were thin and yellowed, and Julia recognized them immediately as he unfolded them. Her lips trembled as she heard him speak. "These are ours. Yours." Roslyn covered her mouth, her eyes creasing as the tears fell.

Her body shook as she walked to them, her head low. "Maksim. Lesia. My babies, oh my babies," she whispered over and over again, the words that she had said when they had left her side so long ago. She felt their arms around her, and suddenly the world felt incredibly small and simple and right; Julia felt as if her heart had landed, and settled, into a place that she never imagined she would feel. It was all she had hoped for, and her entire body unfolded into their arms.

She stepped back to look at her children again, hungrily taking in every detail of their faces, and patted the tears from her face. She turned, extending her arms to Slava, who was standing to the side, observing the reunion, her hands clasped in front of her, eyes staring and filling with tears.

"Sertseh." Julia gestured for her to come over, and looked back at Ed and Roslyn. "I never thought I would ever say this..." She placed her hand over her heart, her fingers splayed, wedding band glinting in the light, as if Henry was there in the room with her. Her eyes searched each of their faces as she realized all of her children were in one room. Together.

She turned to Slava and back to the twins. "I want you to meet your sister."

EPILOGUE

"Ready? Take my arm." I watch as her cotton shirt shifts and rearranges itself when she rises slowly, sitting delicately on her skin; both thin to the touch. The room is cold, but she is radiating heat. Her bones, still solid, feel warm under my hands as she leans on my arm. Her fingers squeeze my flesh and she looks up at me, searchingly. She is little, only as high as my shoulder now.

"When did you become so tall?" She smiles, her blue eyes wet, like a morning sea. "You used to be so little, Lyuba." She reaches over to my hair and pinches the ends as they lie carelessly on my jacket. "Your hair is dark, like chocolate. Mine used to be that dark." She winces. "It's so white now." Her knotted fingers pat her hair gently, as if remembering what was once there; as if trying to conjure something.

"Life happens in a blink, Babchya," I reply, and lean my head toward her. "It happens when you're busy with your exciting life."

She wags a finger at me, scolding me for my words. "Ha. My life didn't seem very exciting to me. Bez intrigi. *Without excitement.*" Her humility makes me smile.

She takes a step forward right alongside mine, and we walk in slow rhythm out of her room, down the airy gray corridor, past the nurses' desks with potted yellow flowers on them. One nurse smiles as she sees us pass; the plump, friendly one who sees me every afternoon, and comments that these visits are a gift.

She's had a hard life, she tells me.

I know, I always reply.

"This way," I direct her.

"In the garden?" She squints, as if she's never done this before. Memories always fade and return anew; they seem strange to her; she grasps at them with futile energy.

"Yes. The garden."

The green that surrounds our bench is robust and wide, not unlike her garden at Glen Cove, but the things that are missing are the marigolds, black-eyed Susans, peonies: color and fire. The tart smell of the gooseberries freshly plucked and ready for canning; the redcurrants in their ruby glory standing tall and spreading out across the perimeter fence. Blackberries, pears. Breezes that bring the *chernozem,* the black earth, across the fields through the farmhouse windows where she'd once slept peacefully. She remembered that most, the colors of her early life coming back to her in waves of memory before disappearing again. That farm didn't exist anymore and hadn't for years. We would always have the same conversations, dipping in and out of the quiet, her fingers circling the now dull gold of her wedding ring, that she'd never taken off.

Oh, Lyuba, she would whisper almost inaudibly. *I miss Hirko.*

I know you do, I'd reply.

He would be so proud of you, his little granddaughter.

And then she would drift to another memory. *I miss my brother.*

Tell me about him, I'd say. Though I knew it all, I would always ask her to tell it to me. And she would. Her eyes would darken, and a mist would fall as she remembered the fields, the cranes, and how she was taught to count the stars.

"Lyuba." She reaches over to set her hand on top of mine. Her skin seems as if it's submerged in milk, white and translucent.

"Yes, Babchya."

"I want to tell you a story."

I smile as I hear a sigh of contentment surround her voice. "Okay."

"It was night when Marioshka and I left home; night was the best time for us to escape. It was the last time I saw my parents, Lyuba."

Her blue eyes mist as she looks across at the horizon, the breeze sitting softly on us, around us, reminding us how to find the words; life waits for quiet moments for the words to come.

And then her voice, as if whispering under the weight of the world, softly says, "Mama," and I place my hand on hers, knowing how her voice sounds each time she tells the story.

And so, we begin again.

A LETTER FROM TETYANA

I'm honored that you chose to read *The Child of Ukraine*. If you enjoyed it, and want to keep up to date with all my latest releases, just sign up at the following link. Don't worry, your email address will never be shared and you can unsubscribe at any time.

www.bookouture.com/tetyana-denford

I hope *The Child of Ukraine* resonated with you, as it was a story that I felt compelled to write: not just for myself and my family, but for families all over the world. And if it did resonate, I would be so grateful if you could write a review. Knowing how you felt and what you thought makes such a difference helping new readers to discover one of my books for the first time. Not only that, it feels like a little "hello" from someone new!

I honestly love hearing from my readers—you can get in touch on my Instagram page, through Twitter, Goodreads or my website.

Thanks, Tetyana

www.tetyanadenford.com

twitter.com/tetyanawrites

instagram.com/tetyanawrites

ABOUT THIS BOOK

Julia and Henry's story was inspired by my grandparents, Yulia and Hironimus Rudnyckyj (I called them Babchya and Dido). They lived an incredibly epic and challenging life both separately and together, and as an only child, I knew that I had to write their story before it completely disappeared. Parts of the book had to be fictionalized in order to tie the big events together, so I was incredibly grateful to have so much war history and so many genealogy reports and accounts at my fingertips. But many of the events in the book actually happened: her escape from her home at seventeen, her survival in Germany, her meeting and loving my grandfather, their complicated life in Australia, and the assault that resulted in the forced adoption of her twins, and their life in New York... those events were all true, as well as the subsequent reunion where she finally saw the twins again.

The way this book came about was that a few years ago, my mother, Slava, received a phone call from Australia in the middle of the night from a man claiming to be her brother. This set into place a series of events, and a bit of research into adoption records and court filings, and emails from the twins to my mother that led to Babchya finally admitting what had happened to her. "God will never forgive me" were the first words she uttered to my mother upon admission of the forced adoption, which led me straight into the process of finding out more of her life, and about Ukraine (I travelled there in 2018). I felt that the act of asking for unnecessary forgiveness—regardless of the depths of love a mother has for her children—was an extraordinary act of humility.

Sadly, my grandfather Hironimus never saw them after he and my grandmother left for New York, and he died when I was five years old. I imagine that he would have been overjoyed to see them flourish into wonderful adults, and I hope I managed to convey his presence in this book as I knew him to be from memory: a complicated man with a heart that was always trying to do the right thing.

Soon after I published this book, and a week after her 96th birthday, Babchya quietly slipped away from us, on April 25, 2020. I remember a moment just before Yulia died, I told her that I had finished writing a book based on the story of her life, her response was, "Why on earth would you write about me? My life isn't that remarkable," which made me realize that hers was probably one of millions of similar, brave stories that have been forgotten over time. In my research of immigrant displacement and family stories of that time, she was one of thousands of women whose fate was forced and, as a result, they'd kept secrets from their families because of the fear of revealing their shame. I felt like it was my duty as a woman and as a mother to share how destructive that could be, but also that there is always resilience in the human spirit.

Her life, although unique to her, is still a universal story about love, loss, and motherhood, and about how important it is to learn about the path that someone takes to navigate their life; from the outside, it can look complicated and bleak, but despite it all, there is always hope.

ACKNOWLEDGMENTS

It always takes a village to write a book, and I'm so thankful to all the agents, fellow authors, and community of wonderful people (both strangers and friends) who gave me such support and feedback during the journey of this book in the very beginning. It would have been so much harder to persevere if it hadn't been for each of you, at different times, urging me to write this story and not to give up.

To Rhianna for being so kind and supportive, and to everyone on the team at Bookouture, you've been so empowering and fearless in realizing how important it is for Ukrainian stories to be heard.

To Nell, Elli, Helen, Beci, Cecilia, Angie, Marissa, and Victoria: strong, loyal, and loving women in my life who lend me their voices when I have trouble finding my own.

To my children: I wrote this for you. To know that I've added to your own family stories means everything to me. Babchya would be humbled to know that she inhabits these pages for you.

Mamo and Tato, thank you for being critics, cheerleaders, and for teaching me to be fearless.

And, never least, to Tom, the man who always tells me to "just keep writing." You challenge me to be patient, to be true to myself, and to fight for what I love. I'm so grateful I found you.